BLAMELESS

"SPINE-TINGLING SUSPENSE . . .
THIS BOOK IS A MUST.
MARY HIGGINS CLARK, WATCH OUT!"
Deborah Crombie, author of *Leave the Grave Green*

"A REAL THRILLER FROM THE GET-GO,
a classic page-turner full of twists and turns."
Steven Womack,
EDGAR Award-winning author of *Dead Folks Blues*

"BARBARA SHAPIRO HAS CRAFTED A WINNER!"
Katherine Hall Page,
AGATHA Award-winning author of *The Body in the Cast*

"EXPLOSIVE . . . ABSOLUTELY COMPELLING . . .
YOU WON'T WANT TO PUT IT DOWN."
Jacqueline Girdner, author of *Fat-Free and Fatal*

"A SPINE-TINGLER,
one of those compulsively readable books
that you want to finish
in two or three page-turning gulps . . .
Barbara Shapiro has proved her mastery
of the suspense thriller."
William Martin, author of *Cape Cod*

"ONE OF THE BEST
OF THE NEW BREED OF SUSPENSE WRITERS—
BARBARA SHAPIRO IS DEFINITELY
ONE TO WATCH!"
Lisa Scottoline, author of *Final Appeal*

Other Avon Books by
Barbara Shapiro

SHATTERED ECHOES

BLAMELESS

BARBARA SHAPIRO

AVON BOOKS ◆ NEW YORK

BLAMELESS is an original publication of Avon Books. This work has never before appeared in book form. This work is a novel. While inspired by a true event, neither the story nor the characters should be construed as real.

AVON BOOKS
A division of
The Hearst Corporation
1350 Avenue of the Americas
New York, New York 10019

First Avon Books Printing: March 1995

AVON TRADEMARK REG. U.S. PAT. OFF. AND IN OTHER COUNTRIES, MARCA REGISTRADA, HECHO EN U.S.A.

Printed in the U.S.A.

RA   10   9   8   7   6   5   4   3   2   1

To my parents,
who gave me my first typewriter and
the belief that anything is possible

ACKNOWLEDGMENTS

This book could never have been written without the support of my family, friends and colleagues. I owe each of you much: my writers' group, Diane Bonavist, Jan Brogan, Floyd Kemske, Rachel Plummer and Donna Baier Stein; my experts and reviewers, Michael Bogdanow, Laurie Bernstein, John Conklin, Dan Fleishman, Norman Shapiro, Kelly Tate, and especially Phyllis Kaplan-Silverman whose input was instrumental from initial story conception to final review; my agent, Nancy Yost; my children, Robin and Scott Fleishman whose interest in my work is a joy to me.

And finally, to my editor, Ellen Edwards, who drove me crazy on this project from day one, my deepest gratitude.

~1~

ANDERSON STREET WAS AS STEEP AS THEY CAME IN Boston, lined by narrow town houses with tin bays that had been tenements in the late nineteenth century. Diana Marcus was winded from both fear and exertion by the time she reached the edge of the crowd, which, despite the growing autumn chill and lengthening shadows, was large and buzzed with a hushed, ugly excitement.

"A shotgun?"

"Big mother shotgun."

Diana's stomach lurched, and she staggered into a tall man who smelled of gasoline. He gently righted her and asked if she was okay. She nodded and elbowed deeper into the crowd, trying not to listen to the ghoulish chatter, even as she strained to catch every word.

"One hell of a way to do yourself in. Me, I'd take a handful of pills. Use a handgun—a magnum—anything but a shotgun, for God's sake."

"Dude must've been crazy."

"Some yuppie stockbroker, I heard."

Diana's breathing became more labored as she worked her way along the sidewalk. She looked up at James's

1

house, and bile filled her mouth: The building was cordoned off with yellow tape.

"My sister-in-law's brother is the cop standing next to that cruiser," said a small woman in jeans as she juggled a toddler in her arms. "Told me it's a real gory mess in there—blood everywhere, bone even." The woman clucked her tongue and raised her voice. "On the walls."

Diana moved on quickly. She had to know what had happened. She had to know if James was still alive. But when she reached the front of the house, the young policeman on guard wouldn't let her through. "Can't do it," he told her, not unkindly. "The sarge'll have my head."

"I'm James Hutchins's doctor," she said, omitting that she was a psychologist, not a physician. "I just got a call."

The policeman lifted the tape, and Diana slipped under it. Standing on the cracked, steeply inclined sidewalk, she stared blankly at the scraggly geraniums flopping in the window box next door. The tumult disoriented her; for a moment she couldn't imagine what she was doing here or where to go next. It had been only a few hours since she had last stood on this very spot, only a few hours since James's incredible stubbornness had caused her to stomp from this house in frustration.

"It's okay," the policeman called. "You can go on in."

Diana nodded and walked resolutely up the granite steps and into the recessed doorway. She took a deep breath and pulled the scarred wooden door toward her. Then she marched into the dingy entryway and climbed the stairs to James's apartment.

This morning the building had been as silent and shadowy as a tomb. Now it bustled with voices and light and the unintelligible babble of two-way radios. A uniformed policewoman raced down the stairs, followed by a tall man in an ill-fitting suit who had the look of a cop. They glanced at Diana as she approached them; she put on her doctor face, and they let her pass. Three medics on the landing argued about the best way to maneuver a stretcher down the narrow stairs as blue lights from the street strobed through the dirty window above the stairway. There was a sharp, acrid bite to the air, but Diana also detected an animal-like smell that she didn't want to think about.

James's apartment was at the top of the stairs, and the door was wide open. As Diana reached the landing she could see down the narrow hallway and into the living room, although it was partly obstructed by swarms of people and medical equipment. Then the two policemen who had been talking in the living room doorway separated, and Diana gasped. There was a stretcher in the middle of the floor with a body on it. It had to be James. And he was covered with a sheet. She gagged and put her hand to her mouth.

"Hey, are you all right?" The young policeman from outside came up behind her.

Diana stared at the shiny badge on his chest. Number 247. Cameras flashed from inside the apartment, and for a moment she felt a flicker of relief: for herself and for James. Then she was overcome with a sadness so deep that it gouged at the center of her being. Sadness for James's loss, for his brilliance unfulfilled. Sadness for her own loss: never to see him, or talk to him, or hope to help him again. She was overwhelmed by guilt at her hand in it all. "What—what happened?"

"Can't tell for sure yet." The policeman shrugged. "But his head's pretty much gone and there are powder burns on his foot."

"His foot?"

"My guess is he pulled the trigger with his toe."

Diana gripped the stair railing, unable to push away the image of James calmly considering all the details of such a bizarre death scene.

The policeman nodded. "It's been done before."

Diana felt nausea push up through her body. She gagged again.

The policeman took a step closer, glancing nervously

at her slightly protruding stomach. "I thought you were a doctor." When she didn't say anything, he took her arm. "Better come with me, ma'am. Get some air."

She nodded but didn't move, her eyes riveted to the stretcher, to the two feet that dangled from below the edge of the sheet. The left foot was covered with one of the paint-splattered running shoes James always wore. The right one was bare.

She leaned into the policeman and groaned, seeing those sneakers pacing her office, tapping against the side of a chair. Seeing those feet, along with her own, leaving a wake of soft impressions in the tall grass of the Public Gardens on a long-ago summer day.

Diana watched one of the medics raise the stretcher while the other unfolded a black body bag. Before they could put James into that awful sack, before they could zip him into that airless cocoon, Diana turned and ran from the building.

~ 2 ~

$\mathcal{T}$HE DAYS FOLLOWING JAMES'S DEATH REMINDED DIANA of the time after her sister Nina's accident, when Nina lay pale and motionless, her tiny frame dwarfed by the adult-sized hospital bed. Every evening Diana and her older brother, Scott, went with their parents to Mount Sinai Hospital. They sang to Nina, held her hand, and told her the news of the day. And then, exactly one month after the accident, Nina just stopped breathing, dying without ever regaining consciousness. Diana was eight and Nina four.

Then, as now, it was as if Diana went through her days encapsulated in petroleum jelly, existing at 33 rpm while everyone else raced by at 45. The nights were even worse. For although she knew it was impossible, she felt as if she hadn't slept since the suicide. Suicide. It was such an ugly word. She stared up at the dark ceiling and watched the fuzzy arcs of dawn light seep around the top edge of the bedroom drapes. Now she could get up and stop pretending there was a chance she would fall back to sleep.

Waves of pain washed over her, and she closed her eyes again. How could she have made so many mistakes? She should never have terminated her therapy sessions with James last summer, despite the personal and professional

5

danger in which his bizarre actions put her, despite the advice of her colleagues, her friends, and her husband. She should never have referred him to Alan Martinson, allowing herself to believe that by furnishing him with another therapist, she had fulfilled her obligation, as if he were a dog left for a neighbor to feed and walk while she was on vacation. And she should have known better than to let herself fall so eagerly into the "great rescuer" role, allowing James's success to define her own, linking—and securing—their failures.

She had been his therapist for three years, three years of the hardest and best work she had ever done, three years in which she had made some of her biggest blunders. "Words are incapable of describing the density of my desolation when I am not with you," James had written to her when she and Craig had gone to Cape Cod for a week last June. And knowing that, feeling his neediness resonating within her, she had still let him go. She had abandoned him. Thrust him away. Just as they all had done before her: his mother, his father, his sister, Uncle Hank. But Diana, the great rescuer, had been the one whose abandonment had delivered James into his final hell.

It had seemed so easy in the beginning. In her mind's eye she could see James as he had been the first day he came to her office, leaning awkwardly against the doorjamb, tall and thin and gawky, his chiseled good looks capturing her complete attention. "Hi, Doc," he had said, shy and bumbling and slightly devilish all at the same time. "Big Sister tells me you're the one who can fix me up."

She hadn't been able to keep from smiling at the perfect pacing of his delivery, at the way his characterization of Jill so drolly captured both his sister's power and her absurdity. Diana had liked him immediately.

The failure, the guilt, and the loss twisted like spikes in her gut. She called out, and her eyes flew open. Craig stirred, and Diana gently pressed her hand to the thick muscles of her husband's upper arm, drawing strength from his closeness. Craig would never be called handsome; his nose had been broken one too many times during his high school football years, and his eyebrows were too bushy. But he was a sexy man: tall and big and kind. He smiled easily and always saw the glass as half-full. Children and animals loved him. As did Diana.

Craig turned and pulled her to him. Sweet with sleep, he nuzzled the back of her neck and snuggled her into the warm curve of his body. "Sleep any better?" he asked when they were molded together like a pair of nested spoons.

"A little," Diana said, not wanting to worry him.

He gently traced her jaw with his finger. "You were tossing around an awful lot."

She took his hand and rubbed it against her cheek. "I just have to get through feeling lousy," she said. "Eventually I'll get tired of all this guilt—and then it'll go away."

Craig chuckled low in his throat. "Letting go of guilt isn't one of your strong suits."

"I know, I know," Diana said. "And Nina wasn't my fault either." But inside her heart of hearts, Diana knew that James's death *had* been her fault. Just as her sister Nina's had been. She shivered, and Craig wound his arms around her more tightly.

"You can't blame yourself whenever something bad happens to someone close to you."

"But I feel so responsible—"

"Shush," he said, slipping his hand inside her nightgown and cupping her breast lightly. "You're a wonderful, caring therapist. You're sensitive"—he kissed the back of her neck—"responsive." He gently turned her toward him. "You've helped lots of people—and you'll help lots more."

Diana pulled her nightgown over her head and pressed herself closer to him, aching with pain and desire. She began to cry softly.

He kissed her eyes and her lips and her wet cheeks. "You can't rescue everybody," he murmured, rubbing the small of her back in deep, soothing circles. "Nobody can."

"I know." She buried her head in his chest. "I know." Then she was caught up in his hands and his mouth and his body. And, for a few luxurious moments, everything else disappeared.

Afterward Diana lay quietly, safely entwined in, and protected by, Craig's love. But all too quickly the world they had managed to hold momentarily at bay rushed back at her. James had killed himself. She touched Craig's cheek. "Mind if I take the first shower?" she asked.

He kissed her and then reached for the remote control on his night table. "Go ahead," he said, pointing the remote at the television. "I'll catch the news."

Diana went into the bathroom and threw cold water on her face. James was dead, and today she had to go to his funeral. No amount of love or sex or consoling words could change the facts. She pressed the cool washcloth to her eyes. Well, she didn't exactly *have* to go to the funeral. It wasn't as if she would know anybody there. Except for James's sister, Jill, and Diana was certain that Jill would be more than happy if she stayed away. She climbed into the shower.

Standing under the pounding water, Diana wished the shower could wash away her indecision along with the shampoo. Maybe she would just forget the whole thing. Twisting the faucet off, she stood for a moment in the silent, steamy tub. She had to go. She needed the formality of the funeral service. And she needed to say good-bye.

Diana dressed quickly, but instead of going down to the kitchen, she found herself in the nursery, thinking, not for the first time, that she had probably been the last person to see James alive. She shivered and rubbed her arms, looking around the room. Except for a solitary moving carton on the floor, the nursery was white and empty, a blank backdrop awaiting its character. The rising sun bounced slivers of light off the newly varnished floor, and an imperfection in one of the old windowpanes refracted a wavy rainbow over the closet. Diana suddenly realized that the last time she had been in this room, exulting in her own joy at the coming baby, James must have been pulling the trigger.

The day of the suicide had been wild even before she had received the phone call, a roller-coaster of highs and lows: her futile argument with James in the morning; the good news from the doctor; her colleague Adrian Arnold tearing her preliminary research results to shreds during their lunchtime peer supervisory meeting. After the meeting Diana had wandered around Copley Place, troubled by James's intractability, worried that perhaps Adrian was right, and overwhelmed with joy at Dr. Jasset's news that the amniocentesis results showed the baby was healthy and female.

She thought she would buy something special for the baby or the nursery—purchases they had been postponing until after the tests—but had found herself too agitated to make even the smallest decision. So she had gone home and tried to work on her research. But that too had proved futile, and after a couple of hours of twirling her pencil and staring blankly at computer printouts, she had climbed the stairs to the nursery.

Diana looked at the carton sitting in the middle of the empty room; it was just as she had left it that afternoon when the phone had rung. "You better come quick, *Dr. Marcus*," a gravelly voice had ordered. "To James's. He's tried to kill himself again. And this time it looks like he did the job right."

"Who is this?" she had demanded. "What's happened?" But the line clicked dead in her ear. For a long moment Diana had looked at the silent phone in her hand as if it were an alien being. When the dial tone began to buzz across the wire, she slammed the receiver down. James. She had to leave the nursery and the happiness it stood for. She had to go to James.

But the nursery was here now, silently urging her to reclaim her joy, to forget about James. Diana touched the slight curve of her stomach and looked up at the rainbow. The riot of strong colors confirmed Craig's decision to use primaries for the fantasy mural he was going to paint on the walls. And, Diana thought, the rainbow could be seen as a harbinger of their bright future.

Kneeling down, she reached for the carton of baby clothes her mother had sent the last time she had been pregnant. The carton she hadn't been able to look at—let alone open—for almost two years. Lifting the lid, Diana thought of the years of infertility, the ectopic pregnancy, the doctors' consensus that she would never be able to have children. Even with Craig's unerring support, she had used her career as a refuge during that painful time. Her success as a psychologist became an antidote to her sterility, as well as an outlet for her need to nurture. But now there was a healthy baby growing in her womb.

The scent of pressed cotton and baby powder and her own childhood wafted up to her. Gently, almost reverently, she lifted a layer of tissue paper. The paper was yellow and crackled under her fingers, but beneath it lay a baby-blue dress with pink and white smocking. The embroidery thread was satiny smooth to her touch, and her eyes filled with tears. She remembered Nina wearing this dress, but her mother had told her that she, Diana, had worn it also.

Pressing the dress to her cheek, drinking in its memories and its promise, Diana felt her career recede to its proper position in her life. Being a psychologist was no longer her only defining role. Suddenly she saw that Adrian's cutting critique of her research methodology was more likely due to his jealousy than to any errors she might have made. And James's death had been the inevitable result of his illness, not her own personal failure. Carefully returning the tiny dress to the carton, Diana promised herself that she would come back here after the funeral. She would go and say good-bye to James Hutchins. Then she would get on with the rest of her life.

Her step was lighter as she walked down the two flights

of stairs to the kitchen. They lived in a renovated nineteenth-century town house in a tiny neighborhood of Boston at the intersection of Back Bay, the South End, and the Fenway, and everything in the house creaked all the time: stairs, doors, windows, handrails—even the two of them, Craig said. As she turned a tight corner, a stair tread squeaked loudly. She pushed the tread hard with her foot; it gave more than it should, indicating that their repairs were far from finished. Making a mental note to tell Craig, she continued down the open narrow stairway that absorbed a quarter of every floor.

Diana loved living in the city. When life began to close in on her, when she got claustrophobic from the suffering her patients heaped on her head, from the calls to make and the exams to grade, she would burst through the front door and into the roaring, anonymous city. She walked for hours, down her narrow tree-lined street to the grand breadth of the Christian Science Center, across Boylston and down Fairfield to window-shop at the trendy stores of Newbury Street. She crisscrossed the Back Bay, wandering along the park-like mall of Commonwealth Avenue, gawking at the white marble and brick mansions, drinking in the bustle and excitement as a nature lover drinks in the scent of evergreen. Rejuvenating herself.

Diana looked out the dining room window at the silent, dawn-streaked sidewalk. All the houses on St. Stephen Street were small and narrow, their angles hard and no-nonsense; utilitarian homes well-suited to the sensible people who had built them, she liked to think. Although she and Craig admired the elegance and expanse of Commonwealth Avenue, they were more comfortable here. She turned and went into the kitchen, filling the coffee maker with the decaffeinated she had learned to tolerate over the past few months.

As the coffee dripped, permeating the room with its thick morning aroma, Diana looked out the oversized mullioned window into their "back city," as Craig called it—a couple of parking spots for themselves and Diana's patients, and a fenced area just waiting for a swing set. Dead leaves from their one tree swirled around the base of a fence post, in a forlorn, lonely dance. Watching the leaves, Diana felt her conviction waver and wondered if she might be better off skipping the funeral after all.

Feeling a light touch on her shoulder, she looked up as Craig wrapped his arms around her from behind. He rested his palms on her stomach. "Aren't you supposed to be bigger by now?" he asked.

She covered his hands with hers. "I just hope you learn to worry less after she's born—otherwise you're going to drive the child wild. I don't even want to think about what you're going to be like when she starts dating."

"Dating?" Craig cried in mock horror. "You think I'm going to let some pimply twerp paw at my daughter?"

They stood silently, watching the swirling leaves for a while. Then Diana said, "I thought I'd go to the funeral, but now I'm not so sure."

"Oh?" He let go of her and reached for his favorite chipped blue mug. "Want some?"

Diana nodded. "There's no point. And I'm sure Jill will appreciate it if I don't show."

He poured a cup and handed it to her. "So don't go."

She took the cup. "I canceled the therapy group."

"The one James was in before you kicked him out?" Craig asked, referring to her borderline personality disorder group.

"Terminated with him," Diana corrected.

Craig sipped his coffee and watched her closely.

"I canceled out of respect," she said. "But there aren't that many of them left anyway. Borderlines aren't exactly known for their stick-to-itiveness." Diana smiled sadly. "With James gone and Ethan pulling another one of his disappearing acts, well, there's just Terri, Bruce, and Sandy . . ."

"Is it even worth your effort?"

Diana sat down at the table and stared into her mug. "I

need to go to the funeral. If I don't go, I'll never really believe it's true." She took a sip. "I'll always think in the back of my mind that James is just playing one of his mischievous little games. That he isn't really dead."

"But you saw him . . ." Craig's voice trailed off. When Diana didn't lift her head, he popped some waffles into the toaster. "So go."

Diana watched him in silence for a moment. "But I don't want to."

Craig rolled his eyes dramatically at the ceiling. "So don't."

"This isn't a joke," Diana said. "I'm struggling here, and all you can say is 'go,' 'don't go,' 'go,' 'don't go.' "

Craig sat down next to her at the table. "Honey, I don't know what you want me to say. I'm just trying to help."

"Nothing," Diana mumbled into her coffee. "Just don't say anything."

Craig nodded and covered her hand with his for a moment. He gave it a quick squeeze, then stood up and walked through the dining room to get the newspaper off the front stoop.

When he came back, Diana held out her hands. "Sorry," she said.

He leaned over and kissed her. "It's okay." He handed her the front section of the paper and pulled out the sports for himself. They sat in silence for a while, Craig eating and reading, Diana motionless, staring, unseeing, at the *Boston Globe* headlines. Suddenly Craig put down his paper and turned to her. "Do me a favor?"

Diana just looked at him, saying nothing.

"Go."

She blinked.

"You need to go. To help you accept that James is really gone from your life." He leaned toward her. "That you aren't responsible for him anymore."

Diana looked at her husband, at his kind, earnest face, at his troubled eyes. She nodded. "I'll go."

~ 3 ~

$\mathscr{A}$s DIANA CLIMBED THE WIDE MARBLE STAIRS LEAD-
ing to the funeral home, she thought how perfect James
would have thought this day was for his funeral: dreary,
rainy, cold. It was even October, "the month of looming
death," he had once called it. James had loved it when
things matched, when everything was either black or white.
He had hated the incongruous, the grays. And there was
no incongruity here; everyone looked as miserable as the
weather felt.

They stood amid the oversized floral arrangements in
small whispering clusters of edgy gloom, somber organ
music pumping through speakers mounted on the walls.
Three diminutive older ladies, their creased faces display-
ing the resemblance of age as much as of blood, inspected
the card attached to a wicker basket. Nearby a circle of
uncomfortable young people squirmed; the men pulling at
their ties, the woman tugging at their skirts and fussing with
their hair. "The nerve," one of the older woman sputtered
as the other two nodded sagely. "Nora hasn't talked to the
family in twenty-five years."

These must be the aunts on the mother's side, Diana
thought. And the cousins. She knew James's mother was

dead, and that there were three aunts who had more or less continued their sister's negligible presence in James's life in the years since her death.

The father was long gone—dead or alive, no one knew for sure—but Diana guessed the fidgety bunch clinging to the wainscot in the corner must be his side of the family. They reminded her of James: tall, gawky, handsome, and nervous, playing with their rings, pursing their lips, looking from side to side. Obviously unused to being together, they avoided eye contact, while seemingly afraid to leave the security of one another. Could one of them be the infamous Uncle Hank? she wondered. He must have served out his prison term by now. Although she saw no sign of communication, suddenly, like a school of jittery lemmings, they moved in awkward unison toward the chapel.

Diana looked around furtively for James's sister, Jill, hoping she wouldn't find her. Jill and James's relationship had been tumultuous, to say the least, swinging from extravagant hurtful rages to claustrophobic binges of togetherness. Once they had lived six months almost literally not speaking to another soul besides each other; and another time—just recently—Jill had flushed all of the tropical fish in James's carefully tended aquarium down the toilet.

Jill and Diana's relationship was equally stormy. Three years ago James had called Jill in the middle of the night, high on cocaine and threatening suicide. Jill, well-aware of the childhood horrors James had repressed and terrified that he really might kill himself, decided that her brother would never be safe until he remembered the awful past and dealt with it. Leaving her husband and his two children in Des Moines, she had rushed to Boston to get James some help. It was ironic that it had been Diana whom Jill had so painstakingly chosen from a large field of highly qualified psychotherapists—including both Alan Martinson and Adrian Arnold. For over the course of James's therapy, as he had turned his devotion from Jill to Diana, Jill had decided that Diana was the personification of all that

was evil, the reason for everything that was wrong with
James.

Jill was a strange one. She was sharp, astute, extremely
competent—some might say as sane as they come. But she
was angry. And unpredictable. A year ago she had divorced her husband and suddenly moved to Boston, resum-
ing her role as James's overprotective parent as if she
hadn't been gone for almost six years. Without telling
James of her arrival, she cajoled his landlady into letting
her into his apartment, where she snooped around under
the guise of cleaning. A week later she charmed James's
boss into taking her to lunch and regaled him with fairy
tales of their happy childhood—for what possible reason,
neither James nor Diana could fathom.

Diana glanced quickly around the room again, thinking
about the last time she had seen Jill. It had been the previous spring. Jill was in a murderous rage, pacing in frenetic
circles around the office, waving her arms and screaming
at Diana. "I'd rather see him dead than see him the way he
is with you!" Jill had shrieked. And although Diana calmly
asked Jill to leave her office, informing her in a quiet and
unruffled voice of the inappropriateness of her behavior,
the crazed hatred in the woman's eyes had stayed with
Diana for weeks.

Who knew what state Jill might be in now? Consumed
with inconsolable grief? In a murderous rage? Diana was
tremendously relieved that Jill was nowhere in sight. Perhaps if she sat in the back row, she could get through the
service without having to confront the woman.

Diana's heels clicked loudly on the marble floor as she
headed across the foyer to sign the guest book, as much
from the desire to have a destination as to declare her presence. Even though she tried to walk softly, her footfalls
reverberated through the high-ceilinged room, and she felt
eyes turning to her. To quiet her shoes, she stepped onto
the carpet leading to the chapel. She glanced in the large
room. A shiny mahogany casket lay on a bed of flowers

in front of the pulpit. The lid was closed. Diana shut her eyes. James really was dead. It really was over.

"You okay, Dr. Marcus?"

Diana's lids flew open and she looked into Sandy Pierson's narrowed but still stunning gray eyes. "It's a tough blow for us all," Diana said, glad to hear that although her voice was soft, it was also calm.

"Looks like I'm the only one here," Sandy said proudly. She was tall and reed-thin, working out her eating disorder every day for two hours on a Stairmaster. She looked like a model, which was just what she aspired to be.

Diana glanced around the foyer. "Perhaps the others will get here before the service starts," she said, although she didn't believe a word she was saying. Sandy, along with James, Ethan, Terri, and Bruce, had comprised Diana's borderline personality disorder therapy group. Borderlines—as they were not so affectionately referred to in the field—were volatile and not known for their responsible behavior, so Diana hadn't expected any of them to show up for something as conventionally obligatory as a friend's funeral. Social contrariness was a classic borderline symptom.

"Ha!" Sandy snorted. "No way Terri or Bruce'll show." Although Terri and Bruce had the mildest cases of the five, they were also the most phobic; Terri's fear of being in public places manifested itself in a full body rash, and Bruce's blood-injury phobia, fear of illness or injury, caused him to faint if he was in the presence of any kind of sickness—let alone death. "Don't you think?" Sandy demanded, glaring at Diana's stomach and fingering the clasp of her omnipresent leather day-timer.

"You're probably right," Diana said, ignoring Sandy's glare, all too aware of the other woman's jealousy. "You have everything and I have nothing," Sandy had yelled when she discovered Diana was pregnant; Diana had stared at the gorgeous woman in wonderment, forever fascinated by the power of the mind to deceive. Now, as then, Diana knew her best tactic was mollification. "Sometimes I think you guys are more tuned in to each other than I could ever be," she said.

Sandy smiled. "Even though James and him hadn't been getting along so great lately, Ethan's the only other one besides me who might come." Sandy's tone was knowing and authoritative. "I haven't seen him since before James kill—uh, you know. But I called his apartment a bunch of times." She flipped open her day-timer and pointed to numerous days on which "Call Ethan" had been neatly lettered. "No answer." She shrugged.

"That's Ethan's style. He'll turn up soon," Diana said, glancing around the room, hoping that "soon" wouldn't be today. Just the thought of Ethan at James's funeral made her shudder. Yet another powerful and conflicted relationship in James's life. She didn't even want to think about what kind of scene Ethan might make.

Sandy stared into the chapel. "He really did it, huh?" she said with admiration in her voice. "I never thought he had the guts. Guess we borderlines are full of surprises—even to each other." She smiled broadly at Diana. "Never put anything past a borderline."

Diana nodded and turned. "See you inside," she said, walking back into the foyer, oblivious to the noise her shoes made. She picked up the gold pen chained to the leather guest book.

"How you doing, sweetie?"

Diana was enveloped in her friend Gail Galdetto's huge bear hug.

"We came to give you moral support," Gail added, pointing to Adrian Arnold.

"Thanks," Diana said, glad to see Gail and surprised to see Adrian. They were all in the same peer supervisory group—a half-dozen local psychologists who met every two months to discuss cases and give each other both professional and emotional support—and, although Diana and

Adrian had been quite close at one time, their present professional disagreement had opened a rift in their friendship. Diana's new research findings directly refuted Adrian's classic text, *Borderline States*, currently used in hundreds of universities; Adrian was unnerved by her results and had been making disparaging—downright nasty, Gail said— remarks about Diana during their last few meetings. On the day of James's death, Adrian had declared Diana's methodology "unprofessionally flawed," rendering her preliminary findings "unworthy of serious scientific consideration." Diana looked at him closely, wondering if he had come to gloat.

"Sorry about all this," Adrian said. "Difficult not to feel guilty." His eyes were full of sincerity—fake sincerity, Diana thought. But he had been a good supervisor during her post-doc, an extremely knowledgeable and busy man who had taken more time than necessary with a beginner.

"Thanks." Diana turned back to writing her name in the book.

"He insisted on coming," Gail whispered.

"Makes no difference to me." Diana shrugged. "As my niece Robin would say, it's a free country."

"And maybe now you'll be free too." Gail looked knowingly into Diana's eyes.

Diana shook her head. "Give it a rest," she said. Gail thought that Diana's involvement with James—and with the rest of her borderline patients—was a disastrous mistake, both personally and professionally. She had launched a one-woman crusade to "disconnect" Diana, convinced that Diana's "therapeutic talents" were wasted on borderlines, whose chances of recovery were slim. Gail pointed to the successes Diana had achieved early in her career with phobics, as well as her many well-received articles on agoraphobic avoidance, as proof positive that Diana should stick with patients whom she had a fighting chance of helping. "Those borderlines will eat you alive," Gail had cautioned. And in many ways—especially where James was concerned—Gail's warning had been all too prophetic.

"Think about cutting yourself loose from them," Gail was saying. "Now might be the perfect opportunity to disconnect."

"It's not all that easy to—"

"How nice to see you, Dr. Marcus," a soft voice interrupted. "So thoughtful and considerate." Jill Hutchins had come to stand next to them, her curly red hair even wilder than usual, her deep blue eyes—the exact same color as James's eyes—dilated with grief. Adrian was behind her.

Despite their turbulent past, Diana was touched by the raw pain on Jill's face. "I'm so sorry, Jill," she said, her voice breaking slightly.

Jill nodded. "Yes," she said, as if not exactly sure of what was expected of her. "Yes," she repeated again.

The four of them stood in awkward silence for a few moments and then Adrian walked away. Finally Diana cleared her throat. "We'll all miss him," she began. "It's so sad—"

"He was sick." Jill sounded more like a robot than a person: stiff, vague, unconnected.

Diana nodded.

"We came to you for help."

"And I only wish I could have done more," Diana said, growing uncomfortable with the conversation and the glazed look in Jill's eyes.

"And what did you do?" Jill continued quietly, almost conversationally. "You used him for your own perverse pleasures and then you threw him away."

Diana stared at the other woman in amazement.

"Get out," Jill said, her voice still slightly dazed, but becoming clearer and more vehement as it grew louder, as if her anger was blowing away her protective haze.

"Now wait just a minute—" Gail said, placing an arm around Diana's shoulders.

"Don't bother to deny it—James told me everything," Jill spat, never taking her eyes off Diana. "I even have proof."

"Proof of what?" Diana demanded.

"Proof that you used some psycho mumbo-jumbo on him. Proof that you two had a real sicko thing going." Jill burst into tears. "And then you got tired of him. You used him and dumped him and then, then . . ." She angrily swiped at her tears. "Then you just threw him away!"

"This is ridiculous," Gail snapped. "I know that you're upset—and rightly so—but you can't go around saying things like this. Making damaging accusations against a respected professional—"

"I told him he'd be better off dead." Jill continued speaking as if Gail didn't exist, tears running down her cheeks. "But I didn't mean it," she said, her voice dropping to a whisper. "I didn't mean it."

One of the aunts came up behind Jill and put her hand on her shoulder. "It's okay, Jilly, let's go on in now."

"This isn't your affair, Molly," Jill snapped, flicking her aunt's hand from her sleeve. "You haven't been around. You don't know the half of it." She stood back and pointed her finger at Diana. "My James is dead all because of you," she cried, her voice rising. "And you're going to pay!"

Diana backed away and probably would have bumped into the wall if Gail had not been holding her. She was speechless, unable to believe the words coming from Jill.

"Jilly," the aunt said softly, trying again. "Nobody killed James but James."

"That's where you're wrong," Jill said, her tear-streaked face reddening with anger. "That's where you're wrong." She turned to Diana. "I swear to you, you'll be sorry you ever laid eyes on my brother. Two days—three days at most—and then you'll know. Then you'll be sorry you were ever born!"

Regaining her composure as Jill's crumpled, Diana pulled a handkerchief from her purse and placed it in Jill's hand. "I know you're angry with me," she said softly, "but that's—"

Jill threw Diana's handkerchief on the floor. "I won't take anything from you," she ranted, stomping on the handkerchief as if it were a poisonous insect. "You've already done way too much!"

Stepping away from Jill, the aunt put her hand on Diana's sleeve. "Why don't you just go on home now, dear? It really would be better for everyone concerned if you left."

Diana looked from Jill to the aunt. Then, with Gail on her heels, she turned and, head held high, walked from the funeral home.

𝒟IANA AND CRAIG'S HOUSE WAS FOUR STORIES TALL
and only eighteen feet wide. They had scraped the bottom
of their bank accounts and borrowed from both sets of parents to buy it. And then, with no cash, but lots of sweat
and Craig's architectural brilliance, they had rearranged
the rooms to make the impossible floor plan a little more
livable.

The original kitchen—ground level in the back, but below
the street in front—was now Diana's office. The new kitch-
en, half of its cabinets still without doors, and the dining
room were on the first floor. Their "great room" filled the
entire second floor, and three small bedrooms comprised
the third.

It was the kind of house that turned the most impul-
sive person into a planner. After discovering a book or
set of keys forgotten in a bedroom, one quickly learned to
stop and think before leaving any floor. Despite the forced
planning, the depleting of their savings, and the fraternity
house two doors down, Diana loved it.

Diana came straight home after leaving James's funeral.
She walked into her office and dropped into her chair. It
swiveled under her weight and she was turned backward,

facing the window. She stared through the mullioned panes and naked tree branches to the fire escape crisscrossing the brick backside of the Chinese restaurant across the alley, trying to comprehend what had just happened.

Too agitated to sit, she jumped up and began to roam the room. *He was sick . . . We came to you for help . . . You threw him away . . .* Jill's words shook her, the hatred and vehemence with which they had been spoken, the truth they contained. *My James is dead . . . All because of you . . . Because of you . . . Because of you . . .*

Diana understood Jill's anger and pain. The woman had just lost her adored brother—perhaps the only person she had ever truly loved—in the most hurtful way possible. Diana knew Jill needed someone to blame for the guilt she carried within herself. On the other hand, grief-stricken or not, Jill had no right to speak to her that way. Not in public. Not in front of Gail. And Adrian.

Diana groaned and sat back down in the chair. She fumbled for the key hidden under one of the onyx bookends. Slowly she unlocked her bottom desk drawer and pulled out a thick fabric book covered with aqua and purple paisleys. She held it in her hand for a moment. Her journal. The place where she let everything flow, the place where she could be as foolish or as childish or as honest as she wanted. She pulled out a pen.

James is dead and Jill says I killed him. She shouted it in the middle of the funeral—although I'm sure no one there believed her. Most likely everyone just assumed she was addled by grief.

Her words echoed off the hard marble walls, and they will always echo in my heart. They will be with me forever. As will be my guilt.

It hurts. It hurts so much. It hurts because James is gone. And it hurts because Jill spoke the truth.

Diana put the pen down and absently fingered the water-marked pages. She had started her journal eight years ago on the advice of Adrian Arnold when he was supervising her post-doc. Adrian had suggested it as a way to deal with the powerful countertransference emotions she was experiencing from working with Kara, a young woman so agoraphobic that she had been unable to leave her apartment for two years.

Diana knew that in order for her patient to progress, Kara had to experience transference—imagining that, and acting as if, her therapist was the mother who had inspired her phobia. And although Diana had read all about countertransference, and understood on a theoretical level how a therapist might begin to respond as the person the patient believed her to be, she had been caught completely off-guard when she fell so deeply into the role of Kara's mother that she was overtaken by a powerful jolt of maternal fury in response to the young woman's stubbornness.

After a dream in which she had scooped a swaddled baby Kara from a grimy sidewalk, brought her home, and placed her in the crib that waited in her own bedroom, Diana went to see Adrian. "It's okay to have these feelings," he had told her. "It's better than okay, it's necessary if you're going to help her." Then Adrian had handed her a spiral notebook. "Don't act on the feelings," he had said. "Write them down."

Since then she had discovered that most of her colleagues had some vehicle for releasing the pressure: many wrote in a journal; Marc Silverman spoke into a Dictaphone; Alan Martinson talked with his wife. And almost everyone had some type of peer supervisory group where they could vent their inappropriate feelings in a place that was safe and confidential.

Diana had never kept a journal before Adrian had suggested it, and she had been amazed at its power to soothe.

She had filled half a dozen spiral notebooks her first couple years of practice, but had found that as her experience and confidence grew, her use of the journal tapered off. Three years ago Diana had been inspired to buy the aqua-and-purple book that now rested in her lap. She opened it and read the first entry.

A young man named James Hutchins came for his second session today. He's even brighter and better-looking than I remembered. And wonderfully perceptive. "I actually don't like cocaine all that much," he told me. "But it keeps my mind busy so I can't feel the pain." He's also full of denial. When I asked him to tell me what the pain was all about, he explained that his two lionfishes, the jewels of his tropical fish tank, had inexplicably stopped eating.

His sister, Jill, brought him to me, terrified that he was on the verge of suicide. Apparently Hutchins was horribly abused at roughly age eight (a disgusting, sordid story about an uncle and a child pornography ring) and has repressed the entire episode. He's also completely amnesiac about the year preceding the abuse (when the uncle moved in with them) and the two years following, in which the uncle and his partner were arrested, tried, and convicted.

Hutchins has been acting out since puberty: drugs, alcohol, truancy, petty theft, suicidal threats—the whole bit. Sister thinks his only chance of seeing thirty is for him to remember and confront the abuse. I agree with her.

There is something about this James Hutchins. About his quick mind, his sense of humor, his self-deprecation, that is immensely appealing. I want desperately to help him.

Diana looked at her next notation; it too was about James. "Zestful energy. Witty. Charming," she had scribbled. "Sad in his core." The words brought back the session as clear as a photograph. James, some of his thick dark hair falling sideways as he tilted his head, was joking about Jill. "The admiral," he said, referring to his sister, "runs a tight ship named James. It's been her favorite occupation since we were kids." He sat back in his chair, crossed his arms, and flashed Diana a dimple. "Unfortunately, I don't maneuver as well as she would like."

It was during the same session, with the same flashing dimple and deep velvety voice, that James had calmly described an incident that had taken place five years earlier. He and Jill had moved up to Cambridge together when he had started at MIT, both glad to be out of Norwich, Connecticut, and to begin a new life. But James found the complexities of his freshman year overwhelming and had decided to drop out of college. When he told Jill, she had pulled a knife on him, threatening to kill him if he didn't start going to class.

Despite Jill's warning, James had quit school anyway. Believing that Jill might really hurt him, he hid out with his drug-dealing pal Dominic for a couple of months. When James finally returned to the apartment, Jill was gone. He found out a year later that she was married and living in Des Moines.

It was during the knife story that Diana first saw through James's cheerful nonchalance. When she was first touched by the deep sorrow he couldn't quite keep from his eyes. She had yearned to help him.

Diana turned her chair so she was facing the window; she stared into the gray alley. How long ago that day seemed. How young and naive she had been: fascinated by Jill's engulfing obsession with her brother; drawn into James's world by his powerful charisma; ensnared by her own egotistical belief that she could help them.

Flipping through the book, she read an entry she had written about a year and a half later.

> *James's progress is amazing. His job is going well, his cocaine use has stopped, and, for the first time, he actually talked positively about the future. "Perhaps there really is a world out there for me," he said today.*
>
> *I wonder if "cure" is a completely wild concept?*
>
> *With his intelligence and charisma—and with the right kind of help—the man can be anything. Maybe not today or tomorrow certainly, but perhaps not too far in the future . . .*
>
> *As his therapist, I must walk a fine line: allowing him enough support so he doesn't feel abandoned, while giving him enough autonomy so he doesn't feel closed in. Sticking close, but remaining distant. Can I do this? I think I can.*

Diana shook her head. She had been so foolishly secure in her ability to walk that impossible line. Now she knew that sticking close and remaining distant were mutually exclusive.

Diana jerked her head up and sat completely still. She swiveled in her chair and stared at the bookshelves that lined two walls of the office. *Perverse pleasures . . . psycho mumbo-jumbo . . . sicko thing going . . .* She broke into a sweat, and her skin began to prickle. *I even have proof,* Jill had declared. What proof? There could be no proof. *Two days—three days at most—and then you'll know . . .*

Diana threw her journal into the drawer, locked it, and wandered upstairs. When she reached the front door she froze. The hallway reeked of James—or, more accurately, of his cologne. Eternity, he had said it was called the day she had complimented him on the scent. "I'll wear it for all eternity—as a symbol of my eternal love for you." And he had. Until he got angry with her for going to Cape Cod. Then he adopted a policy of wearing the cologne, far too much for her taste, on the days he was pleased with her and made a point of flaunting its absence when she wasn't meeting his criteria for perfect therapist.

The scent seemed to surround her, to be stronger than it could possibly be. Feeling foolish, but unable to stop herself, she cautiously ventured to the middle of the entryway and stuck her head in the dining room, looking through to the kitchen. Nothing. The house was silent. There was nobody here but her.

She ran her fingers through her hair. "Blue-black like Snow White's," James had once said of her hair. "Unbearably shiny and erotic." Dinner, Diana thought, pushing away thoughts of James. She would make dinner. Change into jeans. Check the mail. She bent down and scooped up the envelopes that lay scattered on the floor in front of the mail slot. Once again she was overwhelmed by the smell of James. Still holding the mail, she opened the front door and slipped outside, letting the door close behind her.

Feeling better for being out of the house, she took a deep breath and leaned against the wrought-iron railing, watching the narrow, busy street: a man with a ponytail pushing a double stroller; three street people arguing over a shopping cart; two college students, hand in hand, with silly lovesick smiles on their faces; a couple of businesswomen in designer suits. Everyone was hurrying, walking briskly under the gray and threatening autumn sky. "Safety in numbers" kept running through her head. "Safety in numbers."

Safety from what? she wondered, shaking her head at her own ridiculousness. Safety from ghosts? Could numbers save a person from ghosts? Perhaps numbers could save you from real ghosts, but not ghosts of the mind. Olfactory hallucinations were not an unheard-of psychological phenomenon.

Diana began to sift through the mail. But, strangely, this only seemed to make the odor stronger. Suddenly she stopped. In her hand was an envelope that smelled as if it had been soaked in Eternity. An envelope addressed to her. The return address was Anderson Street.

She ripped it open and pulled out a single sheet of paper. The rest of the mail slipped from her fingers and fluttered to the stoop as she read.

My darling doctor,

I am sorry for any unhappiness I may have inadvertently caused you. I hope you can forgive me, as I have forgiven you for forcing upon me no other option than to take this drastic step.

Perhaps I should also thank you for my final freedom.

I cannot live without you and have no desire to do so. As promised, I shall love you and be with you for all of eternity.

In death, as in life, I am,

Eternally yours,
J

~ 5 ~

*D*IANA WAS SWIMMING NAKED. SWIMMING IN A SEA of Eternity. It held her buoyantly aloft, flowed through her hair, and slid smoothly behind her cupped palms as she stroked a leisurely crawl. She breathed it in and breathed it out, as if it were gas rather than liquid, air rather than perfume. It tasted delicious. It felt velvety and sensual and all-enveloping.

She flipped smoothly onto her back, arching her body, stretching her toes, and lifting her hands high above her head. The cologne sustained her, caressed her, tickled between her legs.

She giggled, and suddenly she felt iron fingers grip her ankles. She tried to kick free, but her legs would not heed; they did not kick, they did not move. Two hands were pulling at her. Pulling her down to a place where she couldn't breathe, to a place where the sweet perfume that had been her support was now her enemy.

And she was powerless.

Powerless to fight the fingers that yanked on her. Powerless to free herself as they tugged harder and harder. As they dragged her, forcing her into a swirling black vortex,

31

into a ghastly, loathsome, and airless place from which she knew she could never return.

Diana jerked her leg hard and, gasping for breath, opened her eyes. Light was forming around the edges of the drapes and shooting cheerfully onto the ceiling; it was going to be a sunny day. She needed a sunny day, she thought, watching the brightening room and trying to shake the lingering foreboding of the dream.

It was only a dream. And an uninspired, almost embarrassingly predictable one at that—given what she had been through in the past week. But it was over. It was time to put it all behind her. Time to think of the baby and Craig and their future. Time to move on.

Craig turned and threw a sleepy arm around her. He pulled her to him, and gradually her ragged breathing became more normal. Her heartbeat began to slow, and the nightmare receded into the welcome fog of lost dreams. It was over. She put her hand on her stomach, hoping to feel the gentle kick of their child, yet knowing it was probably still too early.

Craig's hand closed over hers. "Feel anything?" he asked.

She shook her head, the last fragments of her dream retreating beyond her reach, leaving just a shadowy touch of unease.

"Good thing," Craig mumbled.

Diana craned her neck toward him. "What are you talking about?"

Craig looked at her with a serious expression on his face. "It means she doesn't have your feet," he said, breaking into a smile. "If she had your size tens, she'd have been pummeling you months ago."

Diana jabbed her elbow lightly into his stomach; the size—and, she had to admit it, the ugliness—of her feet was a long-standing joke between them. "Yours ain't so tiny either, buster," she said, then snuggled more closely into him, nesting her long lean body into his long bulky one. Craig was a wonderful man, and he was going to be a great father. She had dated a lot before she met him at a party toward the tail end of graduate school, but after that, there had been no one else. It had taken her about six months to convince him that he felt the same way about her. A year later they were married.

Despite their two demanding careers, the tight money, and the fertility problems that were supposed to drive couples apart, Craig was her best friend. She loved him passionately, but also loved him in a richer, more profound way. She pressed his palm to her stomach, knowing that despite all the craziness of the past week, she was still the luckiest of woman. "How come you're sleeping in so late?" she asked him.

"Hard to get up when you're sleeping with such a beautiful woman."

"Bet you say that to all the girls."

He gave her a quick hug, then swung away. "True," he said, standing and stretching. "But it's easier than admitting I'm just a lazy bastard."

"Yeah, right," Diana said. The last thing Craig Frey was was a lazy bastard. A senior project architect at one of the most prestigious firms in Boston, Craig also had his own business on the side. His dream was to open his own firm: Frey and Associates it was to be called—even if there were no associates for a while.

Craig's dream of Frey and Associates kept him sketching family room additions and small office buildings on weekends and in the early mornings. He had a drafting table set up in the far corner of the great room and spent as many of his at-home hours there as he did asleep. Diana wished he wouldn't work so hard, that he would get more rest and they would get more time together, but, knowing how much it meant to him, she also wished for his success.

Diana watched him as he shrugged into his bathrobe, thinking how nice it would be to pull him back into bed, but knowing that they both had to get to work: Mr. Frey and Dr. Marcus, the disciplined professionals. Diana had not changed her name when they married because she had already published a few articles and achieved a certain level of recognition in the field as Diana Marcus. Whenever anyone commented on this fact, Craig would pronounce that "he had decided to keep his own name." She wondered how anyone could *not* love a man with a line like that.

Diana reluctantly sat up and grabbed her own robe from the narrow slice of floor between the bed and the wall. As she was tying the belt, the telephone rang.

"You get it," Craig said, sticking his head back into the bedroom from the hallway. "I've got to get into the shower—big presentation this morning on the new mall above the Central Artery."

Diana hesitated before reaching for the phone that sat on Craig's night table. It was far too early in the morning for casual chitchat. But the phone's warble demanded attention. She lifted the receiver.

"Dr. Diana Marcus, please," a wide-awake, no-nonsense voice requested.

"Who's calling?" Diana asked, a shadowy image from her dream creeping through the back of her mind.

"Is this Dr. Marcus?" the clipped voice persisted.

"Yes it is," Diana said, giving up the game. Who else could she be at this hour? "And to whom am *I* speaking?"

"Risa Getty. *Boston Globe*."

"What can I do for you?" Diana asked, relieved. Probably just a request for a story on suicide, or borderlines, or perhaps even a comment on James. She glanced at the clock. At seven-thirty in the morning?

"Dr. Marcus, I'm sorry to bother you at this ungodly hour, but I'm the medical reporter for the *Globe* and—"

"It's okay," Diana said, her relief returning: a medical reporter. "No problem. I've been up for a while."

"Great. Because I was hoping you'd be able to help me with something." Risa's words came more slowly. "Yesterday afternoon the city desk passed on a tip—and I've been checking it out."

"Tip?"

"About a complaint to be filed in court first thing this morning and, well, frankly, I just don't know what to make of it."

"Complaint?" Diana's heart sank.

"I'm real sorry to have to be the one to tell you, but"—Risa's voice was kind—"according to this, you're being charged with malpractice."

Diana sat down hard on the bed, afraid she already knew the answer to the question she had to ask. "By whom?"

"James Hutchins's family," Risa said. "Or to be more precise, his sister."

"Jill?"

The sound of flipping paper seemed to reverberate across the phone lines. "Jill Hutchins is the complainant."

Diana stared at the black-and-white abstract pattern on the closed drapes and said nothing. It happens to almost everyone, she reminded herself. It had happened to Gail and to Alan Martinson. It had even happened to Adrian. Twice. In the litigious nineties, malpractice suits were becoming a standard occupational hazard for psychologists.

"Dr. Marcus?"

"I'm here."

"I'm sorry, but it gets worse."

"Yes?" Diana's voice came out as a hoarse whisper.

"They're also accusing you of wrongful death."

"Wrongful death?" Diana repeated, unable to believe what she was hearing. "You mean they're saying that it's *my* fault James killed himself?" she demanded, feeling the blood draining from her face. "They're charging *me* with a crime? In court?"

"It's civil court—not criminal court." Risa paused. "But in essence, that's the gist of it."

"That's absurd," Diana said, her fear sparking anger. "Therapists can't be held responsible for their patients' suicides. No one would be able to practice."

"That's why I'm calling," Risa said quickly. "I wanted to hear your side of the story."

"I don't have a side." Diana shook her head to clear it. "Except to say that sometimes people kill themselves."

"People like James Hutchins?"

Diana hesitated; she had to be careful. This woman was a reporter, after all. "I'm not really at liberty to say."

"Let's be frank here, Dr. Marcus. You know James Hutchins committed suicide and so do I—what's the big deal about saying he was at risk?"

"All kinds of people are suicide risks," Diana said slowly. "Depressives, alcoholics, schizophrenics. That normal-looking, middle-aged guy who sat next to you in the Mexican restaurant last night."

"Did James fall into one of those groups?"

Again Diana hesitated.

"I could look it up in any number of reference books," Risa pressed. "But I'm sure you can give me a more accurate picture."

"James was one of the normal-looking ones. Most of the time he was highly functional—charming, bright, terrific sense of humor. Exceptionally kind . . ." Diana swallowed a lump in her throat, remembering James giving Ethan his favorite leather jacket because Ethan had no winter coat, remembering James driving Sandy to Worcester in the middle of a snowstorm because she had finally decided it was time to confront her grandmother.

"And?" Risa prompted.

Diana took a deep breath. "Hardly anyone would have guessed there was anything wrong with him." But James had known. He had a recurrent nightmare of being curled up, fetal and naked, inside a transparent eggshell. Of watching helplessly as huge fingers wrapped around his shell and cracked him into a hot frying pan.

"But there was?" Risa persisted. "Something wrong?"

Diana grabbed a pillow and hugged it to her. "Whatever was 'wrong' with James Hutchins was caused by what others did to him."

"Dr. Marcus, did he have a borderline personality disorder?"

"Borderline personality disorder isn't easy to diagnosis," Diana answered quickly. "Nor is there even a strong consensus in the field on exactly what it is."

"It would really help me a lot if you could be more specific. The more I know, the better I can cover the story. And," Risa added pointedly, "the fairer I can be."

Diana was silent for a moment, then in her best professor voice she said, "Borderline personality disorder is actually just a name given to a cluster of symptoms: instability of self-image and mood; chronic feelings of emptiness; inability to sustain long-term career goals or relationships; lack of control over anger . . ." Diana tapped the corner of her mouth with her finger, her conviction growing that Jill was clearly barking up the wrong tree: Holding a therapist responsible for the suicide of a borderline was an impossible contention to support—in or out of court.

"Are they dangerous?"

"More often to themselves than to others," Diana said. "They walk a kind of tightrope between sanity and insanity: They can function, appear perfectly normal—and they rarely have hallucinations or lose touch with reality."

"Doesn't sound too serious to me."

"We're beginning to think that they're just normal people who have been damaged by some horrible childhood trauma. And, unfortunately, that can be very serious indeed. These people are often desperately unhappy. Threats and attempts of suicide—and other kinds of self-mutilating gestures—are all too common in the more severe forms of the disorder."

"Which James Hutchins had?" Risa pressed.

"It's a fuzzy line," Diana hedged. "Specific diagnostic criteria for levels of severity have never been definitely established by—"

"But he *had* tried to kill himself before?" Risa interrupted.

Diana didn't answer.

"It'd be real easy for me to find out," Risa said quickly. "And if he actually had tried before, telling me will only help your case. All I have to do is check with a few of his friends. Call in a few favors at the hospitals closest to his apartment . . ."

"Twice," Diana said slowly. "But only once for real." The first time almost didn't count: It had been such a blatant plea-for-help gesture. That frantic call New Year's morning almost two years ago. James's roommate hadn't come home as he had planned, and James was afraid the tranquilizers he had taken might really kill him. "You're the only one who can save me," James had pleaded. "Please come."

And she, the great rescuer, had gone to his aid, dragging him into the bathroom, making him vomit, forcing him into a cold shower, and finally, after determining that he hadn't taken nearly enough pills to really hurt himself, stripping off his wet clothes and putting him to bed. She had held his hand, fingers pressed to his pulse, until he had fallen asleep. Then she had lightly brushed his damp hair from his high forehead, pressed her finger to the deep cleft in his chin. So handsome. So sad.

"Look," Risa said. "Not to worry. This sounds like it'll all come to nothing. People are filing complaints against each other all the time. Hoping to get money. Trying to get someone in trouble. My editor was just interested in the suicide-wrongful death angle—and I've got to admit, it's an unusual take."

"Thanks for the encouragement," Diana said, letting her breath out in a long sigh. "This stuff can get pretty hairy." Craig stuck his head in the room and raised his eyebrows.

Not wanting to worry him, Diana waved him away; she heard him going down the stairs.

"But what I don't get," Risa was saying, "is why the sister's bothering at all." She paused. "Any bills in dispute?"

"No," Diana answered. "James had money. A trust fund. Apparently quite large."

"Oh?" The pitch of Risa's voice raised. "The sister too?"

"No," Diana said. "Just James." When Hank Hutchins's pornography ring had been broken, almost a million dollars in cash had been found along with tins of 8mm movies and cartons of photographs. The four boys who had been victimized had been awarded a quarter-million each. It would be worth twice that much now—if not more—after almost twenty years of careful investment by a bank in Connecticut.

Risa was silent for a few moments. "Got any idea who's the beneficiary of the will?"

"Jill, I suppose," Diana said, although the vague stirring of an elusive memory caused her to shift uncomfortably on the bed.

"Have you ever met the sister?"

Diana once again heard Jill's words at the funeral. "A couple of times."

"What's she like?"

"Bright. Capable. A little hotheaded, perhaps."

"Oh?" Risa's voice registered high interest again. "Did you fight with her? Do you think she's out to get you?"

Again Diana warned herself to choose her words well. "These things are very complicated, Ms.—?"

"Risa. Risa Getty."

"Family members often don't understand, Risa. Sometimes they can't face the suicide of a loved one and need someone to blame. Sometimes the patient says things that aren't true—makes things up to hurt the people he feels have wronged him. And it isn't unusual for the therapist to be perceived as one of these people."

"So you *did* have some kind of argument with Jill Hutchins?"

"I suppose you might call it that," Diana said carefully. "But nothing that explains the complaint. And definitely nothing that makes her absurd accusations any less absurd."

"Let me do a little more digging," Risa said. "I'll sit on this for a while, and, if it all checks out and the sister's substantiation remains weak, well, there's really not much here to run with. You wouldn't believe the number of ridiculous jacked-up court cases that are just Cousin Bill's petty personal vendetta against Aunt Elma—or how many crackpots there are out there."

"Given my business," Diana said with a laugh that sounded forced even to her ears, "I would believe."

"Guess you would, at that." Risa chuckled. "Listen, figure the sister's just one of those crackpots, and don't spend a lot of time stewing over this. I'll give you a call if I need any more information—or if I get my hands on anything that might help you figure out what's going on. But my bet is, as long as TV doesn't get wind of the story, I'll have nothing to run."

"TV?" Diana croaked.

"Yeah," Risa said. "Once it's on the local news, we've got to cover it—they make it news."

"Local news?"

"Not to worry. With all the craziness going on in the world—and only half an hour of airtime—my bet is that they'll never even bother." Risa's voice was confident and cheerful. "Thanks for your cooperation. I'll be in touch."

Diana put the receiver in its cradle and stared at the telephone, at its innocent buttons and numbers. The black foreboding prescience of her nightmare slowly returned. *You'll be sorry*, Jill had said at the funeral. *You'll be sorry . . .*

～ 6 ～

𝒟IANA TAUGHT AT TICKNOR UNIVERSITY, HER GRADU-
uate school alma mater, on Tuesdays and Thursdays. She
wasn't an official member of the psychology department—senior Lecturer was her title—and she liked it
that way. Diana had never wanted to be a professor.
From the moment she took her first abnormal psychology course, she knew she was going to be a
therapist.

As a nineteen-year-old sophomore, sitting in a huge lecture hall not all that different from the room she taught in
now, listening to Dr. Kaplan describe the infinite variations
in human behavior, Diana had been hooked: fascinated by
the intricacies of the mind; enthralled with theories of cau-
sation; captivated by the idea that she might actually learn
to help those struggling with their mental demons. Then,
as now, she just couldn't imagine doing anything else with
her life. During graduate school, when all her classmates
were teaching assistants, she had volunteered at a halfway
house in Roxbury.

She had always been curious about other people's lives,
peering into windows, eavesdropping in small restaurants,
wondering what the woman on the park bench was *really*

41

thinking. Here was the perfect profession for a nosy person like herself, a way to connect without getting too close. A way to do something worthwhile. And perhaps, a way to make amends for her sister Nina's death. Although Diana had been only eight at the time, she had known Nina's accident—and her own culpability in the tragedy—would be with her forever.

Diana and Nina had been playing in the front yard while Beth Yaffo, the fifteen-year-old who lived down the block, baby-sat. Diana could remember everything about that late summer day: her brother, Scott, arguing with their mother that he didn't need any new clothes for school as they climbed into the station wagon; the languid, sticky heat; the low buzzing of the somnolent bees as they moved listlessly from one droopy flower to another; the yellowed grass and dusty bushes thirsty from the long drought; Beth's boyfriend driving up in his father's new cream-colored Oldsmobile Cutlass; Beth's admonition that Diana watch Nina for "just a sec" while she took a spin around the block with Mitchell.

Nina was laughing and turning in circles to make herself dizzy and then suddenly, inexplicably, she darted into the street. Diana would never forget the sound of her own scream as she watched the red-and-white appliance truck moving slowly, inexorably, toward Nina. She had shouted and started to run, but before she had crossed half the front lawn, she heard the surprisingly solid thunk of the little body as it was hit by the truck—and the deadly crack that it made when Nina came down hard on the macadam. Frozen with terror and overwhelming guilt, Diana had stood motionless, watching the stocky truck driver standing over the tiny, still form, crying and punching his fist in the air, beseeching his God.

Sometimes she still dreamed of that truck driver, tears running along the wrinkles engraved in his weathered face, and of the little girl who had been herself, shivering uncontrollably in the hot summer sun. Whenever she dreamed of those long-ago people, Diana was glad for the profession she had chosen.

She had gone to Ticknor right from Brown University and completed her Ph.D. in psychology in five years. After a clinical post-doc at Beth Israel Hospital, she had gone into private practice, continuing her affiliation with BI as a research fellow. So she had never thought about the university, and her foray into teaching had been completely serendipitous.

Two years ago she had unexpectedly run into Bradley Harris, her mentor and head of her dissertation committee, at an American Psychological Association conference. Over lunch he told her he was now chair of the psychology department at Ticknor and in desperate need of a last-minute replacement to teach an abnormal psych course. Would she be willing to save his neck?

It had worked out surprisingly well. Not only was she far better at teaching than she would have expected, but she really enjoyed it. Diana had also picked up some clinical hours at the student mental health center and been placed on the university referral lists. She now taught the course every semester and had so many referrals she was forced to wait-list patients. She also knew that the university connection had added bonus points toward the award of her latest research grant.

After the phone call she had just received from the *Globe*, Diana was glad she had a class today. She stood up and dressed hurriedly; her class was at ten and she still had to review her notes. Teaching would get her out of the house and keep her occupied, too occupied to waste any time worrying about what effect Jill Hutchins's words might have on her life. No effect, she thought as she headed downstairs toward the kitchen. No effect at all.

As Diana poured herself a cup of coffee, she briefly described Risa's phone call to Craig, downplaying the conversation, hoping not to worry him before his big presentation.

"Do you think we should call a lawyer?" he asked as he stood up and put his mug in the dishwasher, worry creasing his face despite her best efforts. "I don't want you upset by this."

"I'm not upset," she assured him, wishing she could also assure herself. "And it's just not worth the time—it's all too stupid to be believable."

"But what's the harm of calling? Of getting some information?" he pressed. "It'd be covered by your malpractice insurance, wouldn't it?"

"That's not the point," Diana said, standing and giving him a hug. "You're the one who's always telling me not to worry—so let's take your advice and wait to worry until there's something to worry about."

Craig let her change the subject to the party they were invited to that weekend. But Diana could feel his eyes on her as she ate her breakfast. And he gave her an extra-long hug before he went out the door.

After Craig left, she bustled around the house, throwing in a load of laundry, making the bed, reviewing her lecture notes. But no matter how busy she kept herself, every once in a while a voice would call from the back of her mind: *You'll be sorry . . . You'll be sorry . . .* Diana pushed it away, reminding herself that there was no way she could be held legally responsible for James's suicide. That Risa was right—as unprofessional as it might be for Diana to agree. Jill *was* a crackpot. A crackpot with no case.

But the haunting voice wouldn't stay away, and the same thing kept happening at Ticknor. She would be busy, happy, going through her professor motions: gossiping with the department secretaries; giving an amusing and informative lecture on the difference between narcissistic and antisocial personality disorders; meeting with her teaching assistants to plan this week's discussion sections; explaining to a student why his excuse of an "unexpected wedding"—on a Thursday, no less—would not change the F he'd received on the exam. And then it would be there, striking her like a slap in the face: the voice. *You'll be sorry . . . You'll be sorry . . .*

For about the fifth time she told the voice to shut up and raced home for her two o'clock appointment: another extra session with Sandy Pierson. Diana had been worried about Sandy before James's death, but now, after yet another abandonment in her life—no matter how unplanned—Sandy's precarious grip on reality could easily slip. Diana knew that Gail would reprimand her for giving Sandy so many free appointments, that Gail would say she was too "enmeshed" for her own, or for Sandy's, good. But Diana also knew that Sandy needed her, and, despite being a bit over their heads on the house, it wasn't as if she and Craig were desperate for money.

As she pulled into the alley, it occurred to her that there might be a message from Risa waiting for her. A message telling her it was all a mistake—or a message verifying the worst. When she walked through the small waiting room and pushed open the door to her office, she didn't know whether to be relieved or disappointed: The red light on her answering machine was still. There had been no calls.

But as she sat, trying to focus Sandy away from James and toward her father—the real source of her abandonment—the machine began to click, indicating an incoming call. Two more times it clicked. Three calls. Blink. Blink. Blink. Diana glanced at the clock mounted discreetly on the shelf behind Sandy's head. Fifteen more minutes.

"There's not much there, Dr. Marcus," Sandy was saying softly. "It's mostly a big blank. A curtain."

Diana leaned forward, putting her elbows on her knees. "Can you see anything nudging the curtain?" Blink. Blink. Blink. The red light burst into her line of vision as she bent toward Sandy; Diana leaned back in her chair. "Anything trying to come out from behind it?"

"No," Sandy said, opening and closing the latch on her day-timer.

"Any shadows you can discern through the curtain?"

Sandy stared out the window behind Diana, her eyes focused much farther away than the perpendicular shadows cast by the fire escape on the brick wall across the alley. "Red Sox," she croaked.

Diana thought she misheard. "Red Sox?"

Sandy burst into tears. "He took me to a Red Sox game," she said between sobs.

"It's okay," Diana said softly, handing Sandy a tissue. "It's hard to remember hurtful things. It's okay to feel sad." Blink. Blink. Blink. Diana squared her shoulders and sat straight in her chair, furious with herself for her lack of concentration. "It's okay," she repeated, forcing all her attention on the sobbing woman. "It's often the things you're afraid to feel that keep you from getting well."

Sandy shook her head, tears sprinkling her blue jeans. "We . . ." she started, then took a deep breath. "We had a wonderful time."

"Pleasant times lost can be hard to remember too." Diana flashed on the day she and James had sat barefoot and cross-legged at the Public Gardens, eating turkey sandwiches and laughing over a "Saturday Night Live" sketch they had both seen the previous weekend. She and James had met unexpectedly at the Boston Public Library and, although she knew some of her colleagues might think it inappropriate, she had impulsively acquiesced to his suggestion that they share lunch and the summer day. The jab of grief that the memory evoked emphasized the truth in the words she had spoken to Sandy. Diana looked down at her hands for a moment, then looked up, allowing Sandy to see her pain. "Things are very rarely all good or all bad."

Sandy's sorrowful eyes locked onto Diana's, then they lightened with understanding. "People either," she said, her voice barely a whisper.

Diana smiled sadly. "It's a thin line." When she glanced away, she caught sight of the clock: The hour had passed. Slowly she closed her notebook.

Sandy blew her nose and stood. "Next week, same time?" She flipped open her day-timer and raised her pen expectantly.

"Let's see how you're doing before we schedule another individual appointment," Diana said gently, congratulating herself on her cautiousness and thinking of how Gail would approve. "You'll be here on Monday for group."

Sandy's face paled and the pen in her hand trembled slightly. "But I know I'll need to see you—"

"If you need to see me before Monday," Diana interrupted, "you will." As Diana rose, the blinking light caught her eye. She turned her back on the machine and walked the troubled woman through the waiting room and down the hallway to the back door.

Sandy closed her book and slipped it into her oversized shoulder bag, an expression of gratitude crossing her beautiful face. "Thanks," she whispered as she stepped out into the alley.

Diana walked back into her office and punched the button on the answering machine. Three messages. As the tape rewound, she watched Sandy climb into the battered sports car that was parked next to their equally battered jeep. Sandy angrily wiped her eyes with the sleeve of her coat as she turned the key in the ignition. Then she threw the car in reverse and sped out of the alley.

The machine set itself to replay, and Diana turned her attention to the messages. She didn't realize she had been holding her breath until the recording played itself out and the air escaped from her lungs in a rush. Risa hadn't called. There was only a cancellation, a referral, and a staticky message from her missing patient, Ethan, telling her that he was holed up in Provincetown.

Diana dropped into her chair and swiveled it so she was looking out the window. A blanket-clad figure was huddled on the fire escape across the alley. For a moment it seemed to Diana as if he or she was staring at her, watching her, waiting to do her harm. As Diana snapped the blinds closed, she decided that they were just going to have to find the money to fix the alarm system. She shivered and briskly rubbed her arms, futilely trying to depress the goose bumps the sight of the shrouded figure had raised.

Craig was a rock. During every crisis of their eight-year marriage, he had remained resolute and unshakable in his contention that until the worst is verified, there is no point in assuming it will occur. His calm optimism had gotten Diana through her father's heart surgery, her ectopic pregnancy, and their years of infertility. In every case, Craig had been right: The worst had never materialized.

Despite the fact that she hadn't heard from Risa—or maybe because of it—by the time Craig got home, Diana was feeling pretty jittery. As they sat over a dinner of cheese omelets and salad, they rehashed her conversation with Risa Getty.

His unflappability was soothing. "This whole wrongful death thing is nuts," he said. "Malpractice is one thing—and she doesn't even have a case there—but wrongful death." He shook his head. "Don't even bother worrying about it."

Diana played with the salad on her plate. "We've got to face it," she said. "There *is* a death involved."

"This isn't just 'a death'—this is a suicide," Craig disagreed. "When therapists start being held responsible for their patients' suicides, no one's going to be able to practice. It can't happen."

"That's just what I told the reporter," Diana said. "But isn't that what malpractice is all about? That a doctor is responsible for the health and safety of his or her patients? For providing quality care?"

"Fine," Craig said. "Let's go from that premise." He put his fork down and crossed his arms in imitation of a television lawyer. "Would you say, Dr. Marcus, that you used standard procedures in treating James Hutchins?"

Diana smiled at him and then sobered, thinking of how poorly she had navigated the line between sticking close and remaining distant. "I don't know, Craig. There really are no 'standard procedures,' per se. There are . . ." She paused, looking at him, begging him to make her feel better. "There are theories, acceptable practices . . ."

"And did you follow these 'acceptable practices,' Dr. Marcus?" Craig boomed, waving his finger in her face. "Do you have notes? Professionals who can verify that your therapy was appropriate?"

Diana thought of her incredibly complete files, the ones Gail and Marc always laughed at, calling her a perfectionist-obsessive; she must have hundreds of pages on James alone. "Yes, Mr. Prosecutor." She grabbed his finger and stuck her tongue out at him. "And I'll be glad to give the court copies of every note I ever took on James Hutchins—if you've all got a spare month or two."

"See?" he said, coming over and kneeling next to Diana's chair. "She's fishing. There's no substance." He wrapped his arms around her. "There's nothing there."

Diana snuggled into him, feeling better for his words, for his arms, for his love. "I just worry because Jill isn't your usual person. She's quirky. Volatile." Diana played with the top button of his shirt. "She runs hot and cold. She did to James. She did to me." Diana shook her head. "I just don't think we can count on her to see things as they really are—or to do the reasonable thing . . ."

"Honey," Craig said, raising her chin. "Don't you see, it doesn't matter. She doesn't have anything to go on— reasonable or unreasonable. This is a matter of law. There *is* no case."

Diana nodded and dropped her head onto his shoulder. He was right. Of course he was right. She took one of his hands and placed it on her stomach. They sat in quiet contact. The voice was finally still.

Through their silence, Diana heard the street suddenly come alive: brakes squealed; car doors slammed; voices were raised in excitement. Another frat party. Didn't those guys ever study? Diana wondered, listening to the intensifying street noises as the dining room windows glowed from the approaching headlights. "Thanks," she said.

"I love you." He rubbed her stomach. "Both of—" Craig was cut off by the chime of the bell. He looked questioningly at Diana; she shrugged. They both stood and, their arms still around each other, walked to the entryway. Diana stepped to the side as Craig pulled the heavy oak door toward him.

The door swung open, and they were hit by a blaze of lights so bright that it might have been noon. Diana stood frozen, like a rabbit caught on the highway, the sinking feeling in her stomach registering the catastrophic significance of what she saw before her befuddled brain could fully assess the scene.

"Ned Holt. Channel 5 News," declared a short man with the manufactured look of a doll, his face painted the color of Mercurochrome. He stuck a microphone under Diana's nose. "Is it true that James Hutchins's family is holding you responsible for his death, Dr. Marcus? Do you have any comment on the family's allegations?" he added before she could even comprehend his first question.

Dr. Marcus. Dr. Marcus. Her mind was whirling. How did they even know it was she? "I, ah, I—" She blinked into the intense light, trying to discern what was out there, trying to find a place to run. "I don't really know," she finally said, groping for Craig.

"But this isn't the first you've heard of it?" Holt was demanding, waving his hand for a squat heavyset boy with a camera on his shoulder to climb the steps. "You were aware that a suit was filed? Charging you with malpractice and wrongful death?"

Before she could answer, another reporter came from behind a van with "Channel 7 News" lettered on its side in diagonal black graphic. "You did know that you were the beneficiary of James Hutchins's will?" asked a vaguely familiar woman.

Diana gripped the wrought iron railing. Once again she was at 33 rpm, separated from these frenetic plastic-looking people, not of the same world as everyone else. She was only peripherally aware of Craig's hands gripping her shoulders as the memory that had eluded her that morning came flooding back. "Without you I'd be nothing—you've saved my life," James had told her after his promotion at Fidelity. "And to show you my gratitude, I'm going to change my will so that you're my sole beneficiary. When I die, you'll be a rich woman." She had dismissed the whole thing as another one of his meaningless grandiose gestures, forgetting the incident completely. Until now.

"We deny everything," Craig boomed in a strong, angry voice, coming around to stand in front of Diana, blocking her from view. "This is completely trumped up and ridiculous."

"Do you deny that your wife is the beneficiary of James Hutchins's considerable estate? We have information from a source in Hutchins's lawyer's office . . ."

"No one has contacted us." Craig hesitated, his voice not nearly as confident as before. "We have seen no documents." He turned and propelled Diana toward the open door. "We have nothing else to say."

As they slipped into the foyer the woman called out. "What about the sexual abuse charge?"

Diana and Craig stopped and turned as if one. "What?!"

"Jill Hutchins charges that Dr. Marcus was having sexual relations with her brother," Holt said. "She claims he told her the whole story. Told another psychiatrist too." The microphone once again rose up in front of Diana's face. "Do you have any comment, Dr. Marcus?"

"That's completely insane," sputtered Craig, shoving the microphone away from Diana and pulling it toward himself. "It's a complete and total lie!"

"If you knew anything about people suffering from borderline personality disorder," Diana said, "you would know that—"

"Don't say anything else," Craig hissed at Diana, just about pushing her into the house. "We'll countersue," he said into the microphone. "For defamation of character," he called over his shoulder before he shut the door.

Diana leaned back against the cold plaster wall, her eyes locked onto Craig's; he appeared as shaken as she. Jill's words reverberated through her brain. *You used him for your own perverse pleasures . . . James told me everything . . . You two had a real sicko thing going . . . I even have proof . . .* Diana reached out for Craig's hand. He pulled her to him and held her tight.

~ 7 ~

*D*IANA TOOK HER LECTURE NOTES FROM THE FILE AND spread them before her on the desk. Although she was quite familiar with the material, she liked to spend at least half an hour reviewing her notes before each class. This allowed her to speak without consulting the pages, giving her lectures a more extemporaneous feel and, as she told Craig, bamboozling the students into thinking she knew what she was talking about.

Bipolar disorder with psychotic features, she read, although the words might have been engineering jargon rather than psychological nomenclature for all the sense they made to her at the moment. Schizoaffective schizophrenia. Mania.

How was she going to pull this off? she wondered as her eyes skidded down the paper. By just doing it. She started at the top of the page again, forcing herself to concentrate. Bipolar disorder with psychotic features.

Yesterday she had hid in the house, studying her picture in the *Boston Globe*. She was unable to grasp that the stunned, obviously pregnant woman standing on the stoop, her hair blown backward off her high forehead, was really she—that Diana Marcus was the center of this media

53

circus. No one could possibly believe this nonsense. Not her friends. Not her colleagues. Not those who knew her. But what of all the others? They would believe it; it was in the newspaper, ergo, it must be true. What else could they think? As she stared at the picture, her horror grew. They could think she was pregnant with James's baby.

TICKNOR PSYCHOLOGIST CHARGED WITH WRONGFUL DEATH IN PATIENT SUICIDE, read the front-page headline. The subtitle of the article noted the malpractice and sexual abuse charges in thick black letters. Ned Holt's eleven o'clock news story had been tame compared to the *Globe*.

The paper had focused almost entirely on Jill's allegations: James's tales that Diana had shared her erotic fantasies with him; a postcard Diana had sent him from vacation on the Cape; Jill's contention that, prior to his contact with Diana, James had been completely normal. Craig called to tell her that the *Inquirer* was even worse. SEX DOC SAYS SHE'S NO MURDERER, the tabloid headline screamed.

She had stood staring out the front window, careful to stay behind the curtains so that curious eyes could not see her from the street, watching for reporters, watching those blessed with anonymity go about their wonderfully normal lives. She had been just like them only last week: worried about whether Craig's firm would win the Central Artery project; worried about firing one of her teaching assistants; worried about whether hobbits were too scary to include in the baby's fantasy mural. She would give anything to have those worries again, to go back to when it was safe.

Today she had to go out.

Yesterday she had canceled all her appointments and talked only to Craig and her mother and Valerie Goldman, the lawyer her insurance company had retained. "Best malpractice lawyer in the Commonwealth," the woman at Joint Underwriters of America had assured her. Diana had met Valerie Goldman once when she spoke at a New England

American Psychological Association breakfast last winter. Her topic was "Protecting Yourself From Malpractice Suits," and the room had been completely full.

Valerie was tall and carried an extra twenty pounds, but her perfectly tailored suit turned what would have been heft in another woman into a look of substance and competence. Her speech had been coherent and informative, and she had answered questions from the audience—half of whom had been involved in malpractice suits—with an ease that showed the depth of her knowledge. But she had also struck Diana as humorless; she never smiled, and she looked puzzled at Marc Silverman's joke about the lawyer, the psychologist, and the rabbi that had cracked everyone else up.

In Valerie's defense, Diana did remember that halfway through her speech, she had ripped off her Italian leather heels. "Men designed these shoes to make sure that woman couldn't run as fast as they," Valerie had said without a smile as she placed them on the chair next to the podium. And Gail swore by her: Joint Underwriters had hired Valerie to handle Gail's malpractice case also. This morning, after a quick phone conversation with the woman, Diana was even more convinced of both Valerie's competence and her humorlessness.

Yesterday Diana had prowled her office, listening to the endless stream of messages on the answering machine. Channel 7. The *Globe*. The *Inquirer*. Gail. She hadn't even talked to her brother, Scott; Craig had called him back in the evening. The *Worcester Telegram*. Channel 4. The *Providence Journal*. She hadn't bothered to pick up the phone when Valerie called to say that, after trying Diana's house, the sheriff had served the complaint at her office. Valerie had agreed to accept service. They had twenty days to file an answer in court.

Today she had a class to teach.

Yesterday she had indulged her anger and sorrow. She had slammed doors and yelled into the empty house. Then she had called her mother and sobbed out her humiliation, just barely finding the strength to resist her parents' offer that they come East immediately. As much as she needed the support, they were better off in California, geographically spared the brunt of her shame. She hollered out her fury at the media. "Would you be doing this if I were a man and James was a woman?" she had yelled out loud. "Would this be front-page news if our sexes were reversed?"

And although she knew that it was Jill and the media and society's sexist values that were really at fault, most of her anger was focused on James. She pictured him as he had been last July, right after she had terminated with him. He was waiting for her outside the dry cleaner's, leaning against the plate-glass window, his arms crossed and his blue eyes flashing defiance. "I'll just kill myself and save you the trouble of doing it slowly!" he had screamed at her. And when she had ignored him and walked calmly down the street, he had gone home and swallowed a bottle of Seconal, coming extremely close to making good on his threat.

Diana didn't care that James was now dead, that his threat had been fulfilled and her worst nightmare realized. She didn't care that she was being immature and unprofessional. She wanted to hurt him. To punish him as he was punishing her. So she brought back every detail of him, until James Hutchins loomed large and three-dimensional in her mind. She breathed life into him and then mentally threw darts into his chest.

Valerie had called a third time to say that Diana had to go out, that if she didn't continue on her normal schedule, her behavior could be construed as an admission of guilt. "It's like falling off a horse," Valerie had told Craig. "Make her get up and go to work tomorrow."

So she had. She had gotten up, showered, and put on a new purple maternity dress, hoping the feel of the soft wool against her skin would raise her spirits. After checking the sidewalk for reporters and finding none, she had even eaten some breakfast. The *Globe* sat on the front stoop, unretrieved by anyone; Diana was afraid if she saw the paper she would lose her nerve. Craig wanted to go into work late and drive her to Ticknor, but Diana assured him that she was fine and shooed him out the door. After he left, she had walked down to her office, her steps heavy but resolute, the purple dress doing little for her spirits.

Bipolar disorder with psychotic features, she read yet one more time. Schizoaffective schizophrenia. Mania. She snapped the folder closed and stuffed the notes in her brief-case. It was no use. She glanced at the clock and stood up. It was time anyway.

Then she sat down again, relief flooding her body. There was really no reason that she had to go into the psychology department offices today. If she waited another ten min-utes, she could go directly to class and then leave right after the lecture. Perhaps not exactly her normal sched-ule, but normal enough. She could go to work, as Valerie had ordered, while still avoiding her colleagues. Diana knew she couldn't do this forever, but for today, she felt it would be acceptable. She would take a lesson from Scarlett O'Hara and not worry about tomorrow until tomorrow.

The lecture hall was filled to capacity. Diana had not seen it this crowded since the first exam. She roughly calculated the number of occupied seats. She knew there were one hundred and fifty-three students enrolled in the class. There had to be well over two hundred people in the room.

She swallowed hard, keeping her eyes focused direct-ly in front of her, and walked to the lectern and began. The room quieted, and Diana was quickly caught up in the concentration necessary to convey complicated infor-mation in a clear and interesting way. She became lost in the material, safe for the moment. For the first time since Ned Holt's orange face had blazed up at her, she almost forgot.

The fifty minutes flew by all too quickly, and as her voice faded away, reality returned. Stuffing her notes into her briefcase, Diana pictured her jeep in the parking lot. All she had to do was put on her coat and walk out of the building. The lot was right at the bottom of the hill. She could be home in twenty minutes. Safe behind the curtains.

Diana slipped on her coat and watched the rapidly emptying hall. No questions today, she thought wryly. No students worried about missed lectures or confusing explanations in the text. They were all too afraid to face her. Or too anxious to run off and gossip.

Stop it, she warned herself. Just stop it. Twenty minutes and she would be home. But then she saw Bradley Harris standing at the rear door. Department heads did not normally attend their faculty's classes.

He smiled sadly and motioned her to join him. Climbing down the steps toward him, Diana noticed he had the same look on his face that her grandfather had had the day that Lori and Bev told her she was not invited to their fifth-grade sleep-over party. And she thought, not for the first time, that Brad reminded her of Grandpa Jack.

"I'm so sorry, Diana." He reached out to hug her. "I'm sure it'll all blow over quickly."

"It's too ridiculous to take seriously," Diana said, stepping back, afraid that if he touched her, his sympathy might crack her thin veneer of control.

"Would you rather talk here, or in my office?" he asked kindly.

"I'd really rather not talk at all, if you don't mind." She tossed her hair back and looked him straight in the eye, trying to prove to him, and to herself, that she really was doing just fine. "Maybe I'll stop by next week."

Brad shook his head. "There's something I need to tell you today."

Diana dropped into one of the seats. "Shoot."

"There's going to be a meeting," he said, coming over and touching her shoulder. "The dean called it."

"About me?"

"To decide if you should be allowed to continue teaching."

"I see," she said, both surprised and not surprised. It hadn't occurred to her that they would do this, but now that they had, it seemed all too predictable.

"You know that I don't believe a word of this media garbage." He sat down in the chair across the aisle from her and rested his head on the back of the seat. "I told them their behavior was despicable," he said to the ceiling. "I told them I would vouch for you personally." They sat in silence for a moment, then he turned to her. "I tried. I really did try . . ."

Diana leaned across the aisle and touched his knee. "I'm sure you did." She was also sure that sensational headlines with "Ticknor Psychologist" in them didn't go over well with the rich alumni who were financing the new "world-class" art building of which the university was so proud.

Brad shook his head, worry etching deep lines in his face. "I might as well tell you that they're also talking about taking your name off the referral lists—temporarily," he added. "Until this blows over."

She nodded. "Of course."

"Do you want to be alone?" Brad asked. "Or would you rather I stayed?"

"I'm fine, Brad. Really I am," Diana said, standing and busying herself with her briefcase and purse. "I think I'll go home now."

Brad pushed himself slowly up from his seat with the stiff motions of an old man. Awkwardly he tried to hug her again; this time Diana let him. "I feel so terrible," he said, his eyes bright with compassion. "I'll do everything I can."

She gave him a quick squeeze and then stepped away. "But you don't think it'll make any difference," she said matter-of-factly.

"Of course it'll make a difference." He shook his head emphatically. "There are a lot of fair-minded people in this university. A lot of people who'll be on your side." Then he was silent for a moment, looking at his feet. "Would it help if I talked to the press?"

Diana shrugged and lifted her purse to her shoulder.

"What if I told them all the good things about you? About your commitment to helping. Your status in the field. How your cutting-edge research is sure to lead to new treatment options?" Excited by the idea, he grabbed her arms. "What if I told them I'm convinced that this Hutchins character was destined to kill himself no matter what his therapist did?" He shook her slightly. "How about it, Diana? Wouldn't that help?"

"Don't make any offers you're not willing to follow through on," she warned.

"Just tell me who to talk to."

"Let me think about it."

"Call me," he said, giving her another quick hug. "I really want to help."

"I know you do." She touched his cheek. "And I may need all the help I can get."

When Diana pulled in behind her house, she was so relieved to be home, and to find the alley empty of reporters, that she jumped too quickly from the jeep. She tripped over her scarf and fell to the asphalt. Swearing, she rubbed gravel from her ripped stockings and skinned knee. Then she flipped the scarf over her shoulder, grabbed her purse and briefcase, and rushed for the safety of her back door.

But when she got to the door, she stopped in confusion. The door was swung inward, open and unlocked. The place where the deadbolt had been was a mess of splintered wood and twisted metal. Slowly the reality of what her eyes were seeing filtered through to her brain: They had been robbed.

She stared at the damaged door, furious at the thief, and even more furious at the reporters, at the excited babble that would arrive on the heels of the police cars. Without considering the possibility that the thief might still be inside, she stalked into the house and stomped through the small waiting room and into her office. Then she froze. The room was in total disarray. It had been ransacked.

File cabinets had been pushed over, shelves had been emptied. Files, books, and papers lay ankle-deep on the floor. Her desk looked as if a child had thrown a temper tantrum and waved angry arms across it. It had been swept clean, its contents strewn atop the papers and books. The desk drawers had been pulled from their housings and flung, by the same enraged and powerful child, to every corner of the room.

Diana knelt down and picked up one of her onyx bookends; it was broken. She turned the pieces around and around in her hand, letting the sharp edges press deeply into her palm. She and Craig had splurged on the bookends while in Mexico on their honeymoon. Now they were broken. Broken in two.

Heat pulsed through her body as the extent of the violation began to dawn on her. She dropped the bookend and grabbed a desk drawer. Then she grabbed another, and another, and another. She turned them over. She shook them. She flung one to the floor. "Shit!" she yelled into the devastated room. "Shit! Shit! Shit!" But no matter what she threw, or how loud she swore, the reality remained the same: The drawers had been emptied. All of them. Even the one she kept locked.

She began combing through the debris. Frantically she pushed through the books and the files and the papers. It wasn't there. She knew it wasn't. It would be easy to spot with its deep aqua-and-purple cover. Her journal was gone.

Her private journal. The place where she kept her innermost self. The place where she confided the things she suffered in the darkest furrows of her soul. The things she could never tell another human being. Not Gail. Not her mother. Not even Craig.

She fell to the floor and wrapped her arms around herself. Her private journal. Filled with her secret thoughts.

Filled with wild and erotic fantasies. Fantasies meant to be forever her own exclusive possession.

Some were about Craig. Some were about faceless men. Some were even about women. She rocked, gripping her calves tighter and tighter, pressing her chin into her knees.

Some were about James.

~ 8 ~

*A*FTER REGAINING A MODICUM OF COMPOSURE, DIANA called Craig, Valerie, and then the police. But before she checked her files, before she climbed the stairs, even before the swelling sirens could be heard racing toward her, she already knew: The only thing missing was her journal. This was no random burglary. This was a premeditated, personal attack.

Valerie was in court and Craig was at a building site on the North Shore, but the police came quickly enough—as did what appeared to Diana to be the entire Boston press corps. And then some. Did they have some kind of disaster telepathy? Diana wondered as she followed Detective Levine through the house. Diana guessed Levine to be about ten years her senior. He was very tall and had a full head of curly salt-and-pepper hair that must have been a rich black in his youth. His eyes were an incredible icy blue, and although they regarded Diana with sympathy, there was a cold edge to his gaze that made her slightly uncomfortable.

The two patrolmen who had come with him raced ahead, sliding against walls and jerking open closet doors. Diana nodded and answered Levine's questions, once again in automaton mode.

Yes, this was her house.

Yes, this was her office.

Yes, they did have a security system, but it was broken. They were going to have it fixed, but the contractor wanted too much money.

Yes, this was the kitchen.

As ridiculous as the whole process seemed, Diana was actually relieved to be going through it. At least she was occupied. Listening to the inane questions and producing the self-evident answers gave her a chance to focus on something besides who would want to do this to her. Something beside her missing journal.

Her journal. Don't think about it, she warned herself. Don't think about what was in it. Or who might have taken it. Or what he or she—most likely she—planned to do with it. Diana placed her hand on her stomach.

Herb Levine's eyes followed her motion. "Dr. Marcus," he said, turning abruptly and leading her back to her office, "I understand you're currently involved in a pretty big malpractice suit?"

Diana righted her desk chair and sat down, waving the gangly detective into one of the others. She nodded.

He looked around at the disarray, swiveling in his chair to carefully scrutinize every corner of the room. He crossed his long legs and pulled out a small notebook. Diana assumed he was taking some kind of inventory, compiling clues, determining potential suspects. Instead he looked at her and asked, "Where's the couch?"

"I don't do that kind of therapy."

"I thought you all used couches."

"And I thought all Boston cops were Irish and that anyone named Herb Levine had to be an accountant."

His smile crinkled his face into a mass of appealing wrinkles. "Got me there," he said, chuckling.

"No fingerprint dusters?" she continued, wondering how she could possibly be so glib when the shavings of her life were curling around her on the floor. "No photographers and fancy forensics?" This must be shock, she decided. Her hands were ice-cold but steady, her heart beating normally, her voice composed, her emotions in some kind of numb, frozen limbo. And if it wasn't shock, whatever it was was more than welcome to stick around for a while. It was far superior to what she was going to feel when the ice started to melt.

"If we did that for every burglary in town, we'd bankrupt the department in a month," Levine was saying, chuckling again. "It's just a fluke you got me. I only came because of your other case. Someone recognized the name and address when you called in. I'm homicide—and fortunately having a slow week."

Homicide. The word caught Diana off-guard, and she startled. She felt the heat rising to her cheeks and noticed that Levine had stopped smiling. "Homicide," she repeated, groping for something to say that would distract her from her growing unease. Then she realized she had far less to fear from a homicide detective than from the fact that she was a household name to every police dispatcher in the city of Boston.

"So," he said, finally pulling his eyes from her face and flipping his pad open. "Now that you've uncovered my true identity as a Jewish homicide detective, do you have any idea who might have done this? Or why?" He looked up and stared at her in a searing way that made Diana glad he wasn't here in his usual capacity. "Do you think there's a connection between this and your other thing?" he asked.

Diana nodded, then hesitated. She saw Jill's face at the funeral, florid with anger. She remembered a story James had told her about a girl who had danced too many dances with Jill's date at the junior prom; the following Monday, Jill had sat down behind the girl in math class and calmly cut off her ponytail. Diana shook her head. "I think I really need to talk to my lawyer before saying anything . . ."

Levine raised his eyebrows. "Oh?"

"It's not that I have anything to hide—or that I don't want you to find out who did this." Diana felt sweat prickling under her arms. "It's just that it's, well, it's just very complicated."

"In that case," he said, snapping his notebook closed and standing, "this is just another burglary—obvious forced entry, but nothing of value stolen—one of hundreds logged every week."

She jumped from her chair and followed him to the office door. "Does that mean you won't even try to find out who did it?" She waved her hand. "Or to get my journal back?"

"Look," he said, his eyes grazing her stomach again, "you seem to have enough trouble here already, so I'm not going to bullshit you." He glanced around the room and shook his head. "This kind of break-in almost never gets solved. Once in a while we catch a guy with stolen goods and someone lucks out and gets their stuff back." He shook his head again. "You and I know that's not going to happen here."

"So you're saying there's nothing you can do?" Diana asked, anger lapping at her protective numbness, melting it a bit. "What are you going to tell the reporters?"

"I've had lots of experience with those sniffers," Levine said as they climbed the stairs to the front door. "Don't worry about me. I can handle them just fine."

The two patrolmen were coming down from the second floor. "Clean as a whistle," one of them said.

Levine handed Diana his card. "You get your lawyer to call me and, if he gives me something to go on, then maybe I'll be able to check out a few things for you. But as it stands now, not much can be done." He held out his hand, looking honestly sorry.

Diana shook his hand and thanked him, then opened the door just wide enough for the three policemen to slip out.

As she closed the door against the hubbub Levine's appearance had created among the sniffers, the telephone began to ring. Figuring it must be Craig, and not knowing if her answering machine was still in one piece, Diana picked up the kitchen phone. It was Valerie.

Valerie was pleased with Diana's refusal to talk to Herb Levine, but horrified at the theft of the journal. "Now let me get this straight," Valerie said. "You write down all the erotic feelings you have about your patients and that makes the feelings go away?"

"It's not just erotic," Diana said. "Sometimes you might feel anger or frustration or overprotectiveness."

"And this works?"

"It's called countertransference," Diana tried again, all too aware of the difficulty a layperson would have with the concept. "It's part of the therapeutic process. The patient relates to you as if you were someone in his or her past— and you can't help taking on some of the feelings that accompany the role he projects on you. A therapist can't act on the feelings—but you need some way to deal with them."

There was silence for a moment before Valerie finally said, "Sounds weird to me." Then she demanded that Diana reconstruct some of the more damaging passages.

Diana searched her memory, her mind flipping back through the entries she had written in her journal over the past three years. Many of them were quite benign: a description of how infuriated she was at Sandy's grandmother for her relentless fault-finding; a sheepish admission that she really couldn't stand Ethan; notes on a dream she had in which she protected Bruce from his brother by waving a huge gun in the brother's face.

A flush crept up her neck as she remembered the entries about James; many were sexual—and those that were were uniformly wild. A hot, unrestrained fantasy of ripping each other's clothes off in a utility room at the Boston Common garage, the thrill of possible discovery sending her into a flurry of multiple orgasms. A slow, steamy fantasy of making love to James on the stage of a large lecture hall, in front of two hundred mesmerized, note-taking students.

"Diana," Valerie said, interrupting her rumination, "it's imperative I know everything you can remember."

Diana took a long, faltering breath. "Most of it's pretty dull. But, uh, some of it . . ." She paused and tried again. "Well, some of the entries are sexual—but they're nothing really unusual. They're the kind of fantasies everyone has." Diana knew that although her words were true, in the current context, the journal entries would be construed as anything but usual. "You know, sex in strange places . . ."

"Such as?"

Diana thought of the entry she had written one afternoon this past June. It had been a hot, sweltering day and James had been dressed in a pair of cut-off jeans and a red tank top. He was tan and lean and his biceps gleamed with a thin layer of sweat; when he moved, his muscles rippled with the grace and strength of a stalking lion, and when he laughed, his eyes flashed blue and luminous against his tanned skin.

After he left, Diana had poured her unabashed desire into her journal. She had described how, throughout the entire session, all she could think of was ripping off James's shirt. Of their eyes locking and the aching pain of the passion she would feel as he slowly unhooked his shorts. Of his beautiful body, naked and sweat-covered and wanting her as much as she wanted him. She had written, in excruciating detail, how she and James had made love on the floor of her office, the old creaky air conditioner drying the sweat from their bodies. She groaned softly. "A closet, a classroom," she whispered. "My office."

"You and Hutchins?"

"Yes."

Valerie was silent for a long moment, then she said, "This is bad." Although her voice was calm, Diana detected a note of amazement in it.

"It was only for me," Diana tried to explain. "No one was ever supposed to see it."

"If the journal surfaces—and I think we have to assume that it will," Valerie said as if Diana hadn't spoken, "we'll immediately file a motion in limine to stop—"

"A motion in what?" Diana interrupted.

"A motion in limine. It's a request to prevent something from being introduced as evidence. From what you've told me, the last thing we want with this sexual abuse charge is for your journal to be a part of the court record."

"My journal can't be evidence," Diana cried in a horrified whisper. "It's my journal. It's private. It's confidential—and it was stolen."

"All that's true enough, but the confidentiality argument has traditionally been weak," Valerie said. "Once the journal's existence and contents are accepted as fact, Hutchins's attorney will undoubtedly file a motion for court ruling on admissibility, citing its direct relevance to your guilt or innocence—stolen or not."

"But someone broke in here. They busted through my locks and ransacked my office. A crime was committed!" Diana's voice grew louder as her fury completely thawed the numbness. "Doesn't that make a difference? It *has* to make a difference!"

"If this were a criminal case, you'd have a point," Valerie said slowly. "Civil law's not so defense-oriented. Seems to me, I remember a Missouri case where stolen records were admitted into evidence . . ." She paused and Diana could hear her typing into a computer. "Nothing on first query," she said. "But either way, it's a long shot—we may be better off with privilege against self-incrimination . . ." Her voice trailed off and the tapping began again. "Think it was Jill Hutchins?"

"Who else could it be? Who else would care about my journal?"

"Lots of people. The press. Some loco patient." Valerie paused. "Know anyone who would benefit from you being smeared? A colleague whose promotion might be assured if you were out of the picture?"

"My business doesn't work like that," Diana said. "I'm pretty much on my own."

"You and your husband having any marital problems?" Valerie asked.

"Yeah, right—Craig broke in here and ransacked his own house. You and I both know that Jill Hutchins either did it or arranged for it to be done. She's the only one who would benefit—"

"Did she know about the journal?" Valerie interrupted.

Diana was silent for a moment. James had known about the journal; he could have told Jill. "It's possible."

"How many other people knew about it? Where you kept it? What was in it?"

Diana paused again, mentally running down the list: her peer supervisory group; Craig; her borderline therapy group. Telling her peer group and Craig was fine, but why had she told her borderline group? Her heart hit her stomach. How could she have been so stupid? She remembered the day she had discussed it with them. It was about two years ago; Ethan wasn't in the group yet and it had been just James, Sandy, Bruce and Terri. Diana had suggested that they each begin keeping a diary to track their emotional states, and had used her own journal as an example of what a powerful and helpful tool it could be. What had ever possessed her to listen to Adrian's advice about "being real," about the importance of the therapist's personal revelations to the borderline patient's identification process? What a crock of shit. "A few," she said slowly.

"Look," Valerie said, "you make a complete listing for me of everyone who knew about it—"

"No one really knew what was in it."

"—and exactly how much they knew," Valerie continued. "Then I want you to keep quiet and sit tight. Let me check this out with a couple of my partners—we're moving beyond the parameters of your usual malpractice suit, here. This kind of thing just doesn't come up that often."

"Sit tight?" Diana asked, her voice rising again. "I'm just supposed to sit around and wait for the next disaster to strike?"

"And what do you propose as an alternative?"

"Something. Anything," Diana said. "Why can't you tell the police we suspect Jill? Have them search her apartment. Maybe they'll find the journal—or at least get her to admit that she stole it."

"If you think Boston's finest are going to waste their time tracking down suspected diary thieves"—Valerie made a strange noise that must have been a chuckle—"you've been seeing too many movies."

Diana said nothing. She wasn't going to let Valerie or Levine—or anybody—stop her. There were private detectives. Or she would confront Jill herself.

"Look," Valerie continued, "there's no reason for you to get involved in this. Just go on with your normal routine and let me handle it from my end."

Diana was silent, trying to remember what James had said about Jill's schedule. Something about her losing her job as a graphic artist for Marshall's and free-lancing at home.

"Okay?" Valerie asked. "I'm your attorney, and your insurance premiums are paying a lot of money for my advice—so take it."

Diana was so distracted that she nodded.

"Well?" Valerie demanded.

"Okay," Diana said quickly. "Okay. Sure."

"And before I forget," Valerie added, "I'm supposed to pass on the message that you've got an appointment Monday morning."

"Appointment?"

"Jill's attorney, Ron Engdahl, called to tell me that James Hutchins's will is being read at his office at nine o'clock Monday. As you know, you're on the list of beneficiaries."

"Do I have to go?" Diana asked.

"You don't have to, but you probably should—especially if you really are getting a big chunk of money."

"I don't want the money."

"Find out what you have before you decide you don't want it—and if Jill is going to fight you for it." Valerie snapped. She paused for a second, then offered, "Do you want me to come with you?"

"Let me talk to Craig about it." After copying down the necessary details, Diana hung up. She dropped into a chair at the kitchen table and stared out into the shadowy alley. Idly she watched a gust of wind playing with what appeared to be a clump of used napkins. The wind tossed them up and down, twirled them in a jerky two-step, hurled them hard into the brick wall. And then the wind died, allowing the whole mess to drop unceremoniously into a puddle of muddy water.

She had finally caught a break, Diana thought wryly a few minutes later when she returned to her office and found the answering machine still connected to the telephone, all the attendant numbers and lights lit in their proper places. Now she would be able to screen for Craig's call. Craig. What was he going to say about the journal? How was he going to feel if the contents were revealed in court? Diana thought again of the graphic detail of some of the entries, and despair rolled through her. How would Craig be able to hold his head up in the office? How could he look his clients in the eye? She had to get the journal from Jill before the courts, or Craig, or anyone, saw what was in it.

Diana jumped as the phone at her elbow rang. She let the machine intercept the call. The *Globe*. Apparently the reporters hadn't been satisfied with Levine's statement. They must have sniffed out that there was more to the story than what he had told them. She didn't pick up the phone.

Instead she stood in the middle of the ravaged room, her anger growing. She would go to Jill's right now. She would get her journal back before it did any damage. She reached for her coat. No, she had left an urgent message for Craig; she had to wait. He would be wild with worry if he called and got no answer. He would be sure there was something wrong with the baby.

Before she even realized what she was doing, Diana began to straighten up the mess. She pushed the file cabinets back against the wall and gathered books from the floor. She kept herself busy organizing and rearranging as the calls kept coming in. The *Boston Inquirer*. A patient canceling an appointment. She shelved her social psych books next to the few sociology books that she had. She stood back and admired her work, then picked up a couple of anthropology texts and placed them next to the sociology section.

An hour went by, and Craig still hadn't called. The office looked much better, but Diana was feeling worse. The longer it took him to call back, the more worried she became. If she had been able to reach him when it had first happened, she would have just blurted out the whole story. But now, now that she had had time to reflect and remember, she was growing obsessed with how best to present it to him, how much to tell him, how to soften the blow so that it would hurt the least.

She had tried to explain countertransference to Craig, but knew he didn't really understand—although he had listened carefully and nodded in the appropriate places. Diana realized that for a person who had never experienced the transference-countertransference of therapy, it was an almost impossible concept to comprehend.

In James's case, he had needed to face the childhood abuse he had repressed. Transference was what had happened when James had projected his feelings about his uncle to Diana: his need for Hank Hutchins's approval; his awe of his idol, the only adult who had ever shown him any attention or affection; his need to explore his budding sexuality. Countertransference was what Diana felt in response to James's feelings. She had handled James's awe and his demand for her unconditional approval, but his sexuality had been so strong—and he had been so damn good-looking—that she had responded to him with a full-blown case of lust. Her feelings had gotten out of control, and she had turned to her journal.

She shoved the books back onto the shelves. Things had been bad enough for Craig before this. How does a man feel when his wife's name is besmirched? When her picture is on the front page of the newspaper? When he knows that everyone is wondering about them, about their marriage, wondering if indeed Diana had had an affair behind his back? However Craig felt, he had responded with unflinching support—public and private. But this new twist might demand too much of him. And as much as she knew he would deny it, she was afraid the journal might make him wonder if there was any truth to the allegations.

She reorganized her library so that her alcoholism and substance abuse books were in the same area as those on addiction, a far better method than before. The calls kept coming, sometimes so fast that the machine couldn't answer them all, getting stuck resetting itself while new calls were coming in. The *Providence Journal*. Gail. Ned Holt. Brad Harris. Scott. But no Craig.

The reporters all wanted to know if the burglary was related to the malpractice suit. Gail and Scott sent their love and support. Brad left a message saying that the dean's meeting was scheduled for Wednesday afternoon, but for her not to worry. He had been lobbying on her behalf, and the vote was sure to come down in her favor. She arranged an entire corner devoted to personality disorders, but still Craig hadn't called.

He must have had his own problems at work, she thought, labeling folders to hold the research papers that had been thrown from the shelves and scattered on the floor; she had been meaning to file these papers for months. He probably hadn't gotten back to the office yet. Her hand froze above the half-written label. Maybe he wouldn't go back to his office at all. She stared at the words she had written. If he didn't call, then she would have to tell him in person.

Diana began working more quickly, as if putting things back the way they had been could somehow erase what had occurred. Craig knew she kept a journal, but not what was in it. He knew every inch of her body, but had no clue of the wild things she often imagined while they were making love, the somewhat perverse fantasies she entertained. Although they professed to tell each other everything—and almost did—this was a piece of herself Diana had kept from him. Maybe she was afraid he would be hurt. Or maybe she was just embarrassed.

Suddenly overwhelmed by exhaustion, Diana dropped into her chair. It spun around and she was facing the window, staring into the dark alley. Once again she saw the huddled figure on the fire escape. As she stood to close the blinds, she heard the front door open. Craig was home.

9

$\mathcal{A}$T THE SOUND OF CRAIG'S GREETING, DIANA FROZE, her hand on the drawstring to the venetian blinds. What was she going to tell him? How was he going to react?

"Diana?"

This was Craig, she reminded herself as she let go of the string. He was her husband, her best friend, her staunchest supporter. He would understand. "Down here," she called, slowly climbing the stairs. Craig was hanging his coat on the rack when she reached the entryway. Stay calm, she ordered herself. Stay in control. She started to give him a quick hug, but found herself burying her face in his suit jacket; her head ached from the strain of holding back the tears.

Craig kissed the top of her head lightly. Then he stiffened and pushed her from him so that he could see her face. "What happened?" he asked sharply. "Is something wrong with the baby?"

"No, no," she managed to assure him. "The baby's fine." Then she led him downstairs and, as calmly as she could, told him about the break-in.

They walked along the narrow hallway to the back door

and Craig silently inspected the shattered wood and broken deadbolt. "Jesus," he muttered. "Are you sure nothing else is missing?"

"The police figure the thief never even made it upstairs," Diana told him as they headed toward her office.

"But that doesn't make any—" Craig stopped in the office doorway and stared at her. "There was sexual stuff about Hutchins in that journal, wasn't there?"

Diana nodded miserably. "Remember when I told you about countertransference?" She walked into the office, and Craig followed. "Well, James was a real struggle for me. He was so needy, so demanding . . ." She sat on the edge of her desk and looked at Craig, her eyes begging him to understand. "So good-looking."

Craig dropped into a chair and stared at her. "Let me see if I've got this straight: Hutchins transferred his sexual attraction to you—and you countertransferred it back?"

Diana smiled weakly; Craig had understood more of their conversation than she had thought. "That's about it."

"So . . ." Craig hesitated, his expression bewildered. "You wrote in your journal about being attracted to him." He ran his fingers through his hair. "And that made you feel better?"

"It's like talking a problem over with a friend," she said, overwhelmed with guilt at what her blunders were putting him through. "You get it off your chest, and it doesn't seem so bad anymore."

"Did it make you stop being attracted to him?" Craig asked, his voice hoarse with hurt.

Diana knelt down next to Craig and wrapped her arms around him. "It's not like that," she said. "It's like being attracted to a movie star. Like James was Tom Cruise." She looked up at Craig, who sat with his arms held rigidly by his side. Despite her best efforts, her eyes filled with tears. "It never meant anything. Nothing. I promise."

He looked at her for a long moment, but didn't move to touch her. "I know it didn't," he said slowly. "Of course it didn't." He stared over her head into the dark alley. "So what exactly did you write?"

Diana stood and walked to the window. Turning her back to Craig, she rubbed her hands together, suddenly cold. What should she tell him? He needed to know enough so that he would understand the impact of the theft. But, since there was a chance he would be spared actually reading the journal, there was no point in giving him too many details. Diana snapped the blinds shut and turned. "Most of the entries are pretty benign," she began slowly, "but some could be bad for us." She looked down at her hands. "The things about James are the worst."

"Like what?"

"Well, there are some dreams—weird, mixed-up images . . . And there are fantasies . . ." When Craig didn't say anything, she took a deep breath and plunged ahead. "About how handsome he was." She raised her head and looked Craig straight in the eye. "About how I wanted to have sex with him."

Craig flinched at her words, and his face paled. "Oh," he said, his knuckles white on the arms of the chair.

Nausea coursed through Diana; she gripped the edge of the desk for support. "I'm so sorry."

Craig stood up. He didn't say anything and he didn't look at her, he just paced the small room. Then he stopped pacing as abruptly as he had started. Standing in front of Diana, his arms crossed, he said, "We're not going to let James Hutchins tear apart everything we've built."

Diana dropped her head in relief. She wanted to rush into his arms, but she had to know if he really understood. "What if the journal ends up in court?" she asked softly, raising her eyes. "It would be so humiliating. It could destroy us. You. Professionally, personally . . ."

"People get bored easily," Craig said. "If the worst happens, we'll just tough it out until they do. But," he added, motioning her to sit down in the chair next to him, "we're not going to let the worst happen. We're going to figure out a way to get that journal back."

Diana sat and they began to analyze the situation from all sides. She told him the details of her conversations with both Detective Levine and Valerie. Craig suggested a private detective, but Diana dismissed the idea as far too expensive. Craig was silent for a moment, then he asked, "Have you thought about what you want to do with James's money?"

Diana stood up and played with the sociology-anthropology shelf, rearranging it so that the sociology books were directly beneath the social psychology on the shelf above. "We don't even know for sure that there *is* any money. Or if Jill is going to contest the will."

"You wouldn't be asked to the reading of his will if there weren't money—and if it was done legally, the money's probably going to be yours."

Diana stopped fussing with the books and dropped back into her chair. "Is it really important to you?"

He rested his elbows on his knees. "Is it important to you?"

"It's like being rewarded for my screw-ups . . ." Diana looked him directly in the eye. "I can't take it. It's blood money . . ."

"You mean you want to tell them to keep it?" His voice was both resigned and disappointed.

"We could give it to charity."

He searched her face. "This is your call," he said slowly. "I'll go along with whatever you decide."

"Then I want to give the money to AIDS research or the homeless or maybe some halfway house for borderlines."

He nodded and smiled sadly. "I've got to admit I had a few thoughts about all the things we could do. As much as I'd love to be rich and get Frey and Associates off the ground," he said, reaching over and touching her cheek, "I know this is the right decision. And to tell you the truth—I'm proud of you for it."

Diana dropped her head to her hands and finally allowed herself to cry, overwhelmed with love for Craig and with fear for them both, overwhelmed with guilt for everything she had done. Craig rubbed her back, murmuring consoling words. When she regained her composure, they returned their attention to the theft.

Craig proposed that the thief had been a crack junkie or some overzealous reporter. But Diana knew enough about drug users to be quite certain a junkie would go straight for the easy-to-carry, easy-to-fence items: jewelry and silver, perhaps the answering machine and a few CDs. It just didn't make any sense for a junkie to break into a house and steal a diary. They then came to the reluctant conclusion that although the story was hot, it was equally unlikely that a reporter would risk arrest just for a front-page byline. No matter how they tried to dodge it, the only possible culprit was Jill: There just wasn't anyone else with enough motive.

After a heated discussion of both the personal and legal implications of the journal becoming public, Craig was reluctantly forced to agree with Diana. She had to try to talk Jill into giving it back—and the sooner the better. "I know when you get that expression on your face that I'm not going to be able to stop you," he said. "Just promise me you'll be careful and that you'll call me as soon as you get home."

She must be in the anger and irritability stage of the grieving process, Diana decided the next morning as she hurtled across the Mass Ave. bridge, raising her fist at a weaving bicyclist, jabbing the horn when the traffic came to a dead stop in front of her. Of course, all her gestures were futile. Nothing moved but the man in the pickup truck in front of her with a Red Sox hat jammed low on his forehead. He raised his third finger in a gesture more resigned than angry.

Or perhaps this was bargaining. She shook her head. Or better yet, just plain insanity. According to the psychological literature on grief, successfully managing the loss of a loved one involved going through a particular sequence of emotions; she had certainly experienced loss and was, equally as certainly, fighting her way through a maddening swarm of feelings. The grief experts said that shock and denial came first, followed by anger and irritability, bargaining, depression and finally, acceptance. "You can't do that!" Diana yelled to the car triple-parked at the light in Central Square. "Move!" Yes, she thought, this was definitely anger and irritability.

Fury was boiling within her—a fury at herself, at James, at Jill, and at the unlucky fates. A fury she would have considered both predictable and healthy if she were one of her patients. "It's okay to be angry," she would have counseled the irate client. "As long as you use it the right way. As long as you don't let it motivate your behavior."

Diana laughed out loud, a harsh laugh reflecting no humor. As long as you don't let it motivate your behavior. That was a joke. For here she was, on her way to Jill's.

Diana usually dealt with her anger by swallowing it, by trying to avoid confrontation. But there had been times in her life—such as when Scott was wrongfully accused of selling marijuana during college, or when her father's heart specialist wouldn't return her mother's calls, or when Mary Lessing, a clinic patient from her Beth Israel days, had been mistreated at a homeless shelter—when Diana had felt it was necessary to stand up and demand both an explanation and an immediate remedy. Even Craig had been forced to agree that this was one of those times.

Diana swung the jeep neatly around a gaggle of hesitant pedestrians nervously making their way across the busy street. She could handle Jill. She would have the element of surprise in her favor, as well as the fact that she knew much more about Jill than Jill thought. James had spent a lot of time discussing the bizarre relationship he had with his sister.

When James was growing up, he considered Jill his mother; their real mother wallowed in a lifelong depression

that rendered her a ghostlike figure who floated powerless-
ly in the background of her children's lives. Although Jill
had been only thirteen at the time Hank Hutchins's pornography ring was exposed—and had known nothing of
its existence—she had taken it upon herself to ensure that
nothing untoward ever happened to James again.

Jill loved her brother passionately and unconditionally:
encouraging him with his schoolwork; coaching him to
first place in the Connecticut Elementary Student Math
Challenge; scrimping to save money for his tropical fish;
monitoring his friends; restricting his hours of television.
And although James loved her and needed her desperately,
her overprotectiveness enraged him. They fought a lot and
they played a lot and they worked together a lot. For the
five years following the trial, James began to grow into the
man he might have been.

But Jill was just a child herself, and in the engulfment-
abandonment pattern so common to borderlines, she had
left her brother when he needed her most. James was just
turning thirteen when Jill took off for Omaha with her boyfriend. As enraged by his sister's desertion as he had been
by her overprotection, James began hanging around with
the "bad crowd": doing drugs, skipping school, commit-
ting petty crimes. When Jill suddenly returned two years
later—minus the boyfriend—she clamped down on James
as if she had never been gone. James graduated from high
school with a 3.9 average and 1550 on his SATs; he was
accepted early admission at MIT. James and Jill acted out
their engulfment-abandonment roles many times over the
years; they had been in the middle of another episode when
James had killed himself.

Diana didn't blame Jill for any of it: James's illness, his
fury and acting out each time Jill left, his death. From what
James had told her, he wouldn't have survived as long as
he had without his sister's support. But she knew Jill must
blame herself. Diana also knew how passionately Jill loved
James. And how lethal that kind of passion could be.

But Diana was confident she could handle Jill. She was a licensed psychologist, after all, trained to deal with the troubled. She would convince Jill to give the journal back. Two could play the manipulation game.

As the light ahead changed to yellow, Diana accelerated and turned hard to the left. What made her think Jill would give her the journal? Why did she even expect Jill to be home at eleven o'clock on a Friday morning? Desperation, Diana thought. Pure, unadulterated desperation. Maybe she had just discovered a new emotion in the grieving process.

But Jill was home. She buzzed Diana through the door without any of the anger or questions Diana expected, and then graciously waved her into the narrow "railroad car" apartment, the same apartment to which Diana had come that first New Year's Day to make James vomit the tranquilizers he had swallowed in his plea-for-help suicide attempt. James had never really liked Cambridge, so when Jill left her husband and came back to Boston a year ago, he turned the rent-controlled apartment over to her and moved to Anderson Street.

Dressed in a thigh-length sweatshirt and leggings, her mass of red curls even wilder than usual, Jill leaned against the living room doorway calmly scrutinizing Diana. She was tall and lean and languorous—and she reminded Diana so much of James that Diana felt a shiver run up her back. Guilty, Diana thought, watching a slight smile flicker across Jill's face. Guilty as charged.

"Please come in and sit down," Jill said cordially, pointing to the couch. "Can I get you a cup of coffee?"

"Please," Diana answered in equally sweet tones. This must be the Jill who had charmed James's boss and landlady, she thought as she watched Jill walk gracefully down the long hallway to the kitchen. Not a bad act. Then she remembered that Jill had started out soft-spoken and gracious at James's funeral too. Another cold chill ran up her spine.

Sitting gingerly on the edge of the couch, Diana rubbed her damp palms on her pants and thought of the story James had told her about Jill slicing the tires of her boss's car after he had fired her. How might a woman like that react to the person she thought had killed her brother?

Before Diana could answer her own question, Jill was back with two mugs of black coffee. Diana accepted the offered mug and, although she preferred cream and wasn't supposed to be drinking caffeine, took a sip.

Jill sat down in the chair across from Diana and smiled. "I've been expecting you."

Diana nodded. So much for the element of surprise.

"You want me to drop the charges," Jill said, as if she were commenting on the colorful fall foliage outside the window. "That's why you're here."

Startled, Diana put her cup on the table. "I would love you to drop the charges," she said slowly. "But that's not why I'm here."

"I'm not dropping the charges." Jill's tone was friendly and chatty. "People must be accountable for their own behavior. It's my strong feeling that this lack of personal responsibility underlies many of the problems in our society today. I hate all this suing of bartenders and hosts—don't you?" She looked over at Diana expectantly, seemingly anxious to hear Diana's opinion on the liability of drunk drivers.

"Isn't that just what you're doing?" Diana asked. "Making me responsible for James's behavior?"

Jill raised one eyebrow, an amused smile on her lips. "Oh no, you don't understand, do you?" She shook her head. "You see, you *are* responsible for James's death."

Diana took another sip of coffee before she answered. "I'm confident that the facts will completely exonerate me in court," she said with a calmness she didn't feel. "I came here for my journal."

"You are not only responsible in the passive sense—as I had at first believed," Jill continued as if she had not heard

Diana. "But now that I see you manipulated James into changing his will to favor you . . ." Her language became more formal and precise, but her tone remained cool and conversational, almost detached. "Cutting out my three dear aunts, as well as myself. Well . . ." She paused, sighed, and then stared sadly at her steepled fingers. "It now appears that I must congratulate you on a brilliant, carefully crafted, and almost perfectly executed murder."

Diana watched Jill carefully. This woman was as dangerous as she was unpredictable. But, Diana reminded herself in an effort to keep her fear in check, she understood dangerous, unpredictable people. She knew how to handle them—or hoped she did. "I'm sorry you feel that way," she said softly. "I know you cared deeply for James and feel his loss keenly."

Again, it was as if Diana had never spoken. "What I don't understand—truly don't understand," Jill said, her voice full of sincerity, "is why you need the money. You and Craig must make more than enough to cover the mortgage on that cute little town house. It *is* on the edge of Roxbury and it *does* back up to that gamy alley behind the Chinese restaurant, after all—so how much could it cost?" She looked at Diana's stomach and smiled her best garden-party smile. "Perhaps it's the coming expense? Little girls can put quite a dent in their parents' pocketbooks—but I'm sure you'll find her worth every penny."

"I've come for my journal," Diana said, fear hammerlocking on her soul at the familiarity with which Jill discussed her home and her family life, at the flippant reference to the baby's sex. How could Jill know it was a girl? No one knew but their parents and a couple of close friends—and her peer supervisory group. Diana hadn't meant to tell her peer group; the doctor had called right before the meeting and she was so excited that she had just rushed in and blurted out the news. But she knew she had never told James. She remembered all too vividly that James had killed himself only hours after she discovered she was carrying

a healthy girl. Pushing the thoughts from her mind, Diana
leaned forward, forcing her voice to be calm and authoritative. "Please get the journal for me. Now."

For the first time Jill looked directly at Diana, shrewdness splintering her polite act. "You think I have some kind
of journal?" she asked, sitting back in her chair and smiling, a smile that reached her eyes, a smile revealing true
elation. "How interesting. Must be something very important in that journal to get you over here"—she looked at
Diana and grinned—"begging."

"Just go get it," Diana said softly.

"Beg for it," Jill said.

"I'm not begging for anything. The journal belongs to
me and—"

"Beg!" Jill leaped from her chair and grabbed a poker
from next to the fireplace. She waved it in the air, then
stabbed it into the carpet. "Get down on your knees and
beg."

"Don't be ridiculous," Diana began.

"I said beg!" Jill ordered. When Diana didn't move, Jill
smiled slightly and slowly lifted the poker until it pointed
directly at Diana's stomach. Then, with painstaking delib-
erateness, she took a small step forward, bringing the poker
infinitesimally, but ominously, closer to Diana's slightly
swelling abdomen.

Diana looked from the poker to Jill. She knew she could
not show weakness, but she also knew that she had to dif-
fuse Jill's anger and get the hell out of her apartment.

Diana pushed the poker aside calmly and slid to her
knees. "Please give me my journal," she said, her voice
composed and authoritative.

Jill burst out laughing. "I don't have your stupid journal,"
she said. "I don't even know what you're talking about."
Then her laughter stopped as abruptly as it had started, and
her eyes narrowed. "Now get off the floor and get out of
here!"

Diana did.

~ 10 ~

$\mathcal{V}$ALERIE'S LAW FIRM, BOGDANOW, FEDERGREEN, STARR, and Calahane, was located on Beacon Street, just a few doors down from the State House. Diana had planned to stop by on her way home from Jill's to drop off the photocopies of the treatment notes Valerie had requested. "The Hutchins Files," Valerie called them, as if they were a made-for-television movie. As she slammed the jeep door behind her, Diana looked down at the mound of papers sitting on the passenger seat. The stack was well over three inches thick and held together by two large elastic bands. Diana winced; the last person she wanted to see right now was Valerie. Valerie, who had had the foresight to warn her away from confronting Jill. Valerie, who had made her promise to mind her own business.

All the emotions Diana had kept hidden in Jill's narrow Cambridge apartment now deluged her; she felt raw and exposed and incredibly stupid. Blood hammered in her ears, and her hands began to tremble on the steering wheel. How could she have been such an idiot? She pounded her door lock down and then reached across to lock the passenger side. Furtively she looked through the rear window to see if Jill was coming out of her building.

Go, she told herself. Just start the car and get the hell out of here.

Her hands did her mind's bidding, and before she was really aware of it, she was speeding out of Jill's neighborhood, crossing the Charles River and swinging onto Storrow Drive. She was driving herself to Valerie's office—even if it wasn't where she really wanted to go. Within minutes the spires of the Longfellow Bridge rose thick and squat over the river, dwarfing the brilliant death hues of the trees along the Esplanade. Diana glanced to her right at the brick Victorian townhouses marching seamlessly down Pinckney Street, gazing into the flats of Beacon Hill, an area containing some of the most expensive real estate in the city of Boston, an area that had once been primarily used for the stabling of horses. Who ever knew how things would turn out? she wondered. Who ever knew how things, or people, would shift or change or even reverse themselves? But she should have known about Jill. She had heard all the stories. About what Jill had done to James's tropical fish and her boss's tires and the girl at the prom. Jill might actually have hurt her. Or the baby.

As she stopped at the rotary off Charles Street, the rusty-green elevated T tracks towering over her, Diana dropped her head to her hands. The worst part of the whole episode was that it had all been for nothing. She lifted her head and stared at the cars and trucks surrounding her, at the swarming crowds of pedestrians, at the concrete and glass of Mass General looming over her. She had taken a huge risk for nothing: Jill didn't have her journal, Diana was sure of it.

Against all the odds, she found a legal parking spot on Charles Street. An omen, she told herself as she dropped a quarter into the meter. Sure, she had made a mistake going to Jill's and had come back empty-handed, but it was over and done with. There were other ways to protect herself from the journal. There was Valerie's motion in limine. She and Craig would come up with an alternate plan. Or perhaps it really had been some crack junkie.

Placing the bulky stack of paper under one arm, Diana headed down Charles Street toward Beacon. As she approached the Coffee Connection, she noticed two young mothers chatting on the sidewalk, their babies strapped into matching red-and-blue strollers. Soon, she thought. Soon she would be standing with a stroller discussing colic and diapers and the best time to start solid food. Soon all of this ridiculousness would be over and she and Craig and their daughter would be able to get on with their lives.

Diana smiled as she got closer and noticed that both babies were waving their pudgy little fists; the one on the right seemed to think he was carrying on a conversation with the sky. Diana couldn't help reaching down to touch the baby's cheek. But when she raised her eyes from the stroller and straightened up, Diana saw that the mothers had stopped chatting. Both women were staring at her—and the expressions on their faces were not friendly. Diana took a step backward, but the women didn't avert their gazes. If anything, they seemed to intensify their scrutiny. Diana shrugged and continued on. Boston was apparently going the way of New York when young mothers were suspicious of a pregnant woman. Then she glanced down at her long coat and realized that they probably couldn't tell she was going to have a baby.

The smell of fresh apples wafted up at her as she passed the open bins of fruit in front of DeMatteo's. Unable to resist the display of native tomatoes, Diana reached out and squeezed one. It was perfect, so she popped it into a paper bag and reached for another. But as she was squeezing a few more, she felt that creepy, tingly sensation that told her someone was watching her. Putting down the tomatoes and shifting her stack of paper so it fit more securely under her arm, Diana slowly turned around. To her relief, she saw only the usual Charles Street traffic, two men buying yogurt, and an elderly lady completely focused on choosing between Delicious and MacIntosh apples. Reaching back for the tomatoes, she suddenly had the dismaying thought that perhaps the mothers in front of Coffee Connection weren't being routinely suspicious at all. Maybe they were just suspicious of her, Diana Marcus, "Sex Doc."

She forced herself to pick up some milk and orange juice, reprimanding herself for her paranoia. Those women didn't know her. Most people didn't even read the newspaper, let alone remember what they had read three days earlier. And yet Diana was unnerved. She suddenly recalled the briefcase-toting businessman who had stared at her as she entered Jill's building; at the time she had been vaguely flattered, but now that she thought about it, he had been far too young and good-looking to be attracted to her. And she had had that same creepy watched feeling when she had run out to get her dry cleaning that morning. Although she knew she was being ridiculous, Diana quickly paid for her purchases and made no more stops on her way to Valerie's office.

Still shaken from her experience at Jill's and the eyes at DeMatteo's, Diana wanted only to drop the papers off with Valerie's secretary and go home. But as soon she entered the conservatively subdued law suite, the young woman behind the glass partition jumped up to greet her. "Dr. Marcus?" she asked, although it was obvious she recognized Diana. "Ms. Goldman was hoping you'd come by before she left for court. She's very anxious to see what you've brought and asked me to have you come right down to her office. You've got a moment?" Again, it was clear her question wasn't really a question.

Diana nodded and followed the striking woman in her designer suit. How did a receptionist afford such an expensive outfit? she wondered glumly as she walked through the hushed, wainscoted hallway. Diana was beginning to wonder if perhaps she hadn't picked the wrong profession.

When they got to Valerie's office it was much smaller and more modern than Diana expected, given the rest of the suite. But the office was the whirlwind of papers and activity that Diana could easily have predicted. Valerie waved her into a chair while she talked into the phone, ate a sandwich, and stuffed her briefcase with files. As usual, she was barefoot. Hanging up the phone, Valerie held out her hand. "Looks pretty hefty," she said, waving her manicured fingers in the direction of the papers on Diana's lap. "The Hutchins Files."

Diana handed them to her. "I've been accused of being a bit compulsive when it comes to record keeping."

"Good thing," Valerie said between bites of her lunch. She carefully but efficiently ripped off the elastic bands and quickly flipped through the pages. "Proof positive," she said, patting the stack, "of your professional competence. Let Engdahl try and prove substandard care now."

"Substandard care," Diana echoed. The whole situation was too impossible to believe. She had never provided substandard care to any patient. And definitely not to James Hutchins. But that was just what Jill was contending: that Diana had failed to do everything, from devising an appropriate treatment plan to properly terminating with James—and that she had mismanaged everything in between.

Valerie swallowed the rest of her sandwich in a large gulp and grabbed her suit jacket from a hanger on the back of the door. "If they're admissible," she muttered almost to herself.

"If what's admissible?" Diana asked, catching something in Valerie's tone that she didn't like.

"The treatment notes," Valerie said as she shrugged into her jacket.

"You mean my treatment notes might not be admissible in court?" Diana stared at Valerie. "What are you talking about?"

Valerie sighed and pulled a pair of gray leather heels from the bookshelf over her computer. She came around and sat on the edge of her desk. "It's that damn doctor-patient privilege," she said, wincing as she pushed her plump feet into the narrow pumps. "It's often sacrosanct."

Diana couldn't believe what she was hearing. "Are you saying that my personal, *stolen* journal is admissible—but my professional notes aren't?" she demanded.

"Now don't get all excited," Valerie warned. "You just caught me talking to myself. First of all, I've already drafted the motion in limine to keep the journal out—so forget about that. And I'll find some way around this confidentiality issue too." She forced her other foot into its shoe and stood up. Frowning at Diana, she picked up her briefcase and tapped the stack of treatment notes again. "I'm trusting that you're good at your job," she said. "You're just going to have to trust that I'm good at mine."

By the time Diana got home she was completely exhausted by the emotion of the morning. Warily, she pushed the button on her answering machine. There were three messages. The first was from Craig. Her stomach squeezed as she listened to his deep, soothing voice. "We've gotten through tough times before, Di. We'll get through this too. Hang in there, hon. Call me as soon as you get home."

While she waited for the next beep, Diana rested her hands on the curve of her stomach. She really was quite small for five months, and she still hadn't felt the baby kick. Although she knew from the amniocentesis—could only eight days have passed since she had received the results?—that everything was fine, she was still a bit worried. And even though Craig was still cracking bad jokes about her shoe size, she knew he was worried too. The little one had probably been kicking away for a week, Diana consoled herself. She had just been too distracted to notice.

Distracted was definitely the word, for the second message was from her obstetrician's office, reminding her of her appointment later that afternoon. Diana had forgotten until this moment that she had one. She usually looked forward to her appointments with Gerri Jasset for days, writing down questions, reading up on fetal development, anxious to hear the rapid pump of the baby's heart through the stethoscope Gerri placed on her stomach. And today she had almost forgotten.

Listening to the message, Diana stared at her blotter, following the deep red threads of the pad as they wove in and out, in and out, crossing over and under each other until they formed a solid mass. She thought of the empty whitewashed nursery three floors above her, just waiting for curtains and a crib and maybe some of those cloth primary-colored balloons she had seen in a window on Newbury Street. But instead of joy, these thoughts filled her with unease.

Diana was startled from her self-reflection by the third message. It was from her wandering patient Ethan Kruse—and it was very strange. His words were hard to understand because his voice was so shaky. It got louder and softer, and at one point he burst into hysterical laughter. There was no doubt in her mind that Ethan was in some kind of trouble. But, of course, this was nothing new. She rewound the tape and played it again.

"Dr. Marcus, it's me, Ethan," the message began. "I heard about James—I read it in the paper. I'm fine but you need to check out James's records . . ." His voice dropped to a whisper, and it sounded as if he had turned away from the phone. She heard him giggle. "Something's weird," Ethan said quickly, as if his dime were running out. "Something no one knows but you need to find out to . . ." Here he hesitated once again, and Diana heard a loud burst of laughter in the background. "To understand," Ethan finally said. "I'll be in touch." Then the phone was slammed down with a loud bang.

Diana stared at the machine as it clicked and blinked, resetting itself for the next call. What the hell was that all about? She replayed the tape and wrote down the message word for word. Then she played it back again to make sure her transcription was correct.

Everything was about as fine with Ethan as it was with her. Not that anything had *ever* been fine with Ethan. She had clearly made a mistake putting him in the borderline group, for he was far more unmanageable than the others. He had no ability to empathize, rendering him virtually useless as a group member, and his blatant drug use and violent outbursts had had an unsettling influence on them all—especially on James.

It was Ethan's horrendous childhood trauma that had fooled her. He had fit so neatly into her theory that borderline personality disorders were really a protracted form of post-traumatic stress syndrome—that it wasn't bad mothers, but some kind of horrible childhood abuse, that made her patients the way they were. Diana had allowed herself to be duped by Ethan because she desperately needed more subjects to increase her sample size, to complete her research, and to topple Adrian Arnold from his throne as the national expert on borderline personality disorders. How absurd and misguided her ambitions seemed now.

Suddenly she cared little about the scientific upheaval her results might cause among a tiny group of borderline experts. Diana realized that besting Adrian Arnold and becoming the new rising star had little appeal. She froze and stared at the silent answering machine. Adrian? Could Adrian have stolen her journal?

She laughed out loud. While he might have the biggest ego she had ever encountered, there was no way her little research project was going to turn one of the most eminent psychologists in the country into a cat burglar. Adrian Arnold, the next president of the American Psychological Association, arrested for breaking and entering. She really was losing her grip.

After leaving a message with Craig's secretary that she was home from Jill's, Diana flipped through her Rolodex and found Ethan's telephone number. As she listened to the hollow ringing, she once again berated herself for letting Ethan into the group. She had exposed her other patients to his disruptive influence and had potentially retarded their improvement just because she needed more data to prove her precious theory. And it hadn't worked anyway.

For it turned out that witnessing his mother's murder was only one of a long line of horrors Ethan had suffered as a child. And right before James's death he had confessed that he had excluded arson, aggravated assult, and two arrests for a scam on elderly homeowners from the "minor problems with authority" he had described to her at their first meeting. Based on everything she had learned and observed about Ethan since that first interview, Diana had finally come to the conclusion that he didn't have a borderline personality disorder at all. Now it appeared that he suffered from an antisocial personality disorder. Ethan was what they used to call a psychopath.

Diana had planned to present Ethan's case at peer review last week and ask for a recommendation. But after Adrian's criticism of her research, she had decided to skip it. Now Diana wished that she had discussed Ethan; she had been seriously considering suspending him from the group when he returned. But after what had happened to James, she was gun-shy about making another mistake.

She looked back down at her notes. "Check out James's records." What records? James's school records? Psychiatric records? Medical records? Phonograph records? "Something no one knows but you need to find out to understand." To understand what? Her journal? James's death? Suddenly Diana's stomach squeezed in a new kind of fear. What exactly *did* Ethan know about James's death? What *could* he know?

She pushed herself from her chair and began pacing the room. Stopping at the window and staring into the autumnal dreariness, Diana rubbed her arms to fend off both the inner and outer chill. Then she went to the file cabinet and grabbed the stack of manila files that sat on top of it: James's records. Although she had just had the whole batch photocopied for Valerie, she hadn't read through most of the material in ages.

Clearing her research materials from the desk, Diana placed the pile of files on her blotter. She flipped through them: treatment plans, histories, individual session notes by year, group session notes, and a fat miscellaneous file. She opened the miscellaneous file and sifted through the odd assortment of materials: a copy of the signed release from Mass General giving her access to James's hospital records after his suicide attempt; postcards he had sent her last summer; a letter of reference she had written to Fidelity. These records were all that she had left of him.

He had had such a strong need to survive, such a powerful urgency to help himself and others. He was always running errands for Mr. Berger, the parapalegic who lived in the apartment below him on Anderson Street, and he was always bringing home strays—both animals and people. He took yoga and oil painting and stress-reduction classes. He sweated through hours of excruciatingly painful therapy. But despite the courses and the therapy sessions, despite his generosity with both his money and his time, James had always sensed that his future was foreshortened. "When I think of all the things I'm not going to achieve," he had told her last spring, "I already feel as if I don't exist."

Diana closed the miscellaneous file and opened the one containing her notes on his individual sessions. James would be pleased with the bulk of his legacy. There must be at least one hundred and fifty pages from last year alone. Substandard care. It was ludicrous. Ridiculous. For, despite her ultimate failure, she had brought James so close to success.

When he first came to her, he had been completely blocked, unable to remember a large chunk of his childhood, unable to see the events that haunted and controlled his life. For the first two years she had worked to help him unlock the chains, to guide him safely toward—and through—the wall he had built to protect himself from the horrors. The wall that kept him from being who he really was.

Diana would never forget the day she and James had finally broken down the wall. That dark afternoon in early November, when for the first time James had allowed himself to remember what had happened to that little boy, had held so much pain and so much promise for them both.

For months James had described dreams of being surrounded by bright lights, of clowns playing with his toes, of being suffocated by the smell of horse manure. "I keep seeing these weird images," he said, "but I know they can't be real." He smiled his arresting self-deprecating smile. "Maybe I'm more nuts than I think."

Diana watched him closely, knowing what he was trying to remember—and trying not to remember. Jill had told her the whole depraved tale: the dilapidated old barn Hank Hutchins had used for his filming; the clown costumes he and the other men had worn to gain the boys' trust; what they had done to James and the others after their trust had been attained. "Or maybe you're not nuts at all," Diana had told James gently. "If you keep thinking and feeling these things, keep seeing them, then maybe there's something to them." She paused, gripping her hands tightly under her desk, her eyes locked on to James's. "Maybe they're some kind of body memory trying to tell you something."

James immediately started to deny her suggestions, then he stopped in mid-sentence and turned deathly pale. "Oh my God," he whispered, staring over her shoulder and into the past. "Oh my God," he repeated. He shifted his eyes and looked directly into hers, his face such a mask of pain that she could barely stand to hold his gaze.

"What is it, James?" Diana asked softly, all too cognizant from Jill's tearful description of James's years of sodomy and violation what he must be seeing. Her heart ached so for that little boy—and for the man he had become. She was simultaneously nauseated by the fact that she had forced him to look into the pit and exhilarated by her knowledge that what he saw might ultimately set him free.

"He—he—" James stuttered, covering his face with his hands as if to stop the flood of memories. "In a barn. A cold barn. Uncle Hank. He held me down while the clown—the clown—" He began to sob, huge wrenching sobs that shook his whole body.

Diana had truly understood for the first time in her life what murderous rage actually meant: For if Hank Hutchins had walked through the door at that moment, she would have killed him. Instead, she stood up and walked around her desk to where James was sitting, huddled and hurt and as wounded as if he had been physically attacked. She knelt and wrapped her arms around him. "He can't hurt you any-more," she murmured, caressing his hair and holding him as if he were a small child. "It's over and you're safe here," she had repeated rhythmically, rocking him as she spoke. "It's over and you're safe."

Tears rolling down her cheeks, Diana stared unseeing at the thick stack of files on her desk. It was after that day that James had started his slow march toward health. The ghosts from his past began to recede, and the James Hutchins who should have been—who would have been, had Uncle Hank never entered his life—began to emerge. He was kind and bright and full of wry humor. After a few months James's drug use ended and he landed a good job as a stockbroker for Fidelity Investments.

He had been so happy and proud of himself—and thank-ful to her. When she refused his extra payments and the jewelry and fur coat he had bought her, he sent ten thou-sand dollars in her name to the AIDS Action Committee, her favorite charity.

Diana pounded her fist on the folders. She may have gone over the line at the end, but her treatment strategy had been faultless. Jill was wrong, and she, Diana, was going to prove it. She would call every psychologist and psychiatrist in the city and get statements attesting to her competence and standing in the community. She and Valerie would go through every record she had on James until they had amassed a paper trail of proof so thick that no one would be able to question the fact that she had delivered only the highest quality care.

She would prove how absurd the allegations were. She would make her journal moot. She would free herself and her family from this horror named Jill Hutchins.

~ 11 ~

GERRI JASSET'S OFFICE WAS ON THE CORNER OF COM-
monwealth Avenue and Dartmouth Street, about a mile
across town. Sometimes Diana walked, strolling past the
reflecting pool at the Christian Science Center mall, stopping for ice cream in the Prudential Center, peering into
store and apartment windows in the Back Bay. But today
she decided to drive.

It was too cold to walk, she told herself. It would be
almost dark by the time she returned home. She had spent
so long mulling over James's records and talking with Craig
about Jill that she just didn't have time. But Diana knew
none of these was the real reason. The real reason was the
eyes.

She reminded herself that Boston was a large anonymous city where people didn't recognize their next-door
neighbors, let alone a nameless woman who had been in
the news a few times. People were more concerned with
paying their next MasterCard bill than with some minor
court case. Nevertheless, she couldn't forget the two young
mothers or the businessman in front of Jill's. She had felt
eyes at DeMatteo's and in the alley yesterday afternoon.
She threw on her coat and climbed into the jeep.

But when she got to Gerri's office, there was no place to park. After circling around the block a few times, Diana made a larger circle and finally found a spot down on Beacon Street near Mass Ave. She might as well have walked; she was more than six blocks away. Swinging her purse to her shoulder and holding her head high, she turned toward the doctor's office, searching for people uninterested in her presence.

There were many. She didn't even merit a glance from the three teenage boys walking toward her; she was clearly too old and too conservatively dressed for their taste. The bag lady sitting on the curb just nodded when Diana gave her a dollar, not bothering to look twice at her face. The guys working on the street just kept pounding their jack-hammers. The cop directing traffic just kept waving his arms. And the cars just kept whizzing by.

By the time Diana got to the medical building, she was feeling much better, sure she was worrying too much, seeing signposts that weren't there, and looking forward to hearing the baby's heartbeat.

The receptionist informed her that Gerri was running almost an hour late. Diana nodded, thinking that this was just another indication of her level of distraction. She always called first to check on Gerri's schedule; today it hadn't even occurred to her. She settled into one of the deep couches— too deep for pregnant women, a detail someone should have picked up on by now—and reached for a three-week-old *Time*.

"Dr. Marcus?" The matronly nurse-practitioner who worked with Gerri stood at the desk with a clipboard in her hand—Annie, Diana thought her name was. Annie smiled and motioned for Diana to follow her into the inner offices.

"Quickest hour I've ever sat through," Diana remarked as she rolled up her sleeve to have her blood pressure taken.

"Oh, we decided to squeeze you in, dear," Annie said, patting her hand before she pumped up the cuff. "We thought it would be best."

Diana smiled. "Well, that was awfully nice of you. Tell Gerri thanks. I appreciate it."

"Under the circumstances we thought you'd prefer not to sit out in the waiting room," Annie said, watching the fluid rise in the meter. "You know, all those people."

Diana just stared at the older woman.

Annie ripped off the blood pressure cuff and scribbled on the chart. "Good, good," she said. "Almost as low as before." Then she turned and looked at Diana, her eyes full of sympathy. "We're rooting for you, dear." She patted Diana's hand again.

Stunned, Diana nodded. "Thanks," she said.

Annie told Diana to take off all her clothes and handed her a thin blue-and-white checked johnny. She patted Diana's hand yet one more time. "Doctor will be with you in a moment." Then she left the room.

Diana slowly began to remove her clothes. Did this mean that she hadn't been imagining it? That all those people really had been staring at her, whispering about her? That the eyes were real? She wrapped the thin belt of the johnny around her middle, but it wouldn't close completely. When she pushed herself up onto the examination table, her back was exposed.

The cold air on her bare skin made her shiver.

On her walk back to the car, Diana tried to concentrate on the healthy double-time of the baby's heartbeat pounding through Gerri's stethoscope. But all she could feel were the eyes. And her own vulnerability. She watched her step carefully, telling herself she was avoiding the broken pieces of sidewalk. But she was all too aware that she was really avoiding the eyes.

By the time she reached the jeep, an ache in Diana's neck was beginning to develop, as was her annoyance with her skittish paranoia. She couldn't—and wouldn't—live like this. She jerked the door of the jeep open and slammed the key in the ignition. Heading down Mass Ave., she vowed to fight Jill until she won. Until her family's future was safe and she could walk down the street and hold her head up without fear.

Diana was so intent on her thoughts that she almost missed the turn onto St. Stephen Street. She hit the brakes hard, and her tires squealed as she careened around the corner. She yanked the wheel and pulled into her spot behind the house, stopping the jeep with a jolt.

When she turned off the headlights, she realized that it was completely dark in the alley. Night comes so quickly in October, she thought. It had taken her by surprise, and she hadn't left a light on for herself. She started to get out, then stopped. She felt them again. The eyes.

Diana peered through the front window into the shadowy darkness. She looked left and right, then turned and scanned the back window. Nothing. There was nothing there. Nevertheless, she didn't move. She couldn't shake the creepy feeling running up and down her back. She couldn't shake the eyes. She pulled out a small can of Mace.

Holding the Mace out in front of her, Diana opened the jeep door with one hand, jumped out, and slammed it with her hip. Her eyes darted everywhere. Nothing to see. But something to feel.

Her key missed twice as she tried to put it in and pull it out of the two new heavy-duty deadbolts. One lock open. One more to go. Nothing to see. Something to feel.

Finally the last bolt twisted back and the door swung inward. But before she could step into the safety of the house, two powerful hands gripped her shoulders.

An electric current of fear pulsed through Diana's body. For an instant she felt the inside of every bone, as if her marrow were on fire, her skeleton outlined in neon. Adrenaline poured through her. Wrenching herself from the iron grasp on her shoulders, she raised the Mace can and turned to face her assailant.

But when she saw the anxious face before her, her arms dropped to her sides and weakness filled her bones. "Sandy!"

she cried, her voice reflecting both terror and relief. "What is it? What's the matter?" Diana grabbed the taller woman, her fingers trembling slightly. "What are you doing here—you almost gave me a heart attack!"

"I—I just had to see you," Sandy said, her hair falling in her face. "I just had to."

Her heart still pounding, Diana pulled her distraught patient into the house, flicking on lights as she went. She looked at Sandy's white face and the fierce set of her mouth, well-aware of the turbulence storming beneath the surface. Diana propelled Sandy toward her office. "Go in and sit down," she ordered. "I'll be back in a minute." Then she turned and hurried upstairs.

Diana hung up her coat and took a series of deep breaths. She went into the kitchen and poured herself a glass of water. Looking out at the back alley, she placed her hand on her stomach. "It's okay, little one," she said softly. "It's okay." When she finished the water, she put the empty glass on the counter, took a few more deep breaths, and headed back downstairs.

Sandy, unaware that Diana had returned, was pacing the office. Diana stood silently in the doorway, watching Sandy march back and forth in front of the desk. Sandy picked up the stapler, the Rolodex, a picture of Craig, and then dropped each one unceremoniously back into place. She reached down and gently ran her finger around the lopsided edge of Diana's clay paper-clip holder; it was crooked and erratically glazed with blotches of green and brown enamel, clearly the work of a child's hand. It had been a birthday present from her favorite niece, Robin, and Diana loved it. It was all she could do to keep herself from crying out when Sandy raised the small piece and pressed it tightly to her chest.

Still holding Robin's gift, Sandy walked over to the window and stared out into the alley, craning her neck as if trying to see something on the fire escape across the way. Diana thought she caught the glimpse of a smile on the corner of Sandy's mouth, but doubted her perception, given the slump of Sandy's shoulders and the misery that had made her beautiful face appear haggard and plain under the glare of the hallway light.

Without taking her eyes from the window, Sandy opened her oversized purse and raised the paper-clip holder as if she were about to drop it into one of the large compartments.

"Hi." Diana strode into the room and took Robin's gift from Sandy's hand.

"I was just admiring this," Sandy said, as if she had not been caught in the act of stealing it. "Who made it for you?"

"Please sit." Diana waved Sandy to the chair in front of her desk and then sat down. She folded her hands across the blotter and looked at the other woman. "What's going on for you?" she asked.

Sandy didn't sit. Instead she continued to prowl the room, flipping her long blond hair behind her shoulders every few seconds. She was agitated and jumpy, her every movement an exclamation point to her resentment and anger. She began to walk in wider and wider circles, taking larger steps and running her fingers along the furniture and book spines—even across a framed poster that hung on the wall. "Looks different in here," she said.

Again Diana thought she caught a slight smile, but this time she felt a stab of hope. "Why do you think you noticed that?" she asked quickly.

Sandy turned her back to Diana and shrugged, flipping her hair. "Don't know." She shrugged again. "The colors are changed or something."

"Sandy," Diana said in her best velvet-covered-iron voice, "come over here and sit down."

This time Sandy obeyed, turning and dropping gracefully into the chair across from Diana. She studied her professionally manicured nails, then looked up. "I got the modeling job for Filene's."

"That's great," Diana said, honestly pleased despite her annoyance. "Maybe this'll be your big break."

Sandy beamed, her beauty shining through despite her disheveled hair and tear-streaked cheeks. "My agent says that even though I'm kind of old, I still might be able to really make it. He says the nineties is the decade of the older woman."

Diana had to smile. At twenty-six, Sandy hardly classified as an older woman—especially with a body that looked as if it belonged to an eighteen-year-old. "I'm happy for you," Diana said, leaning forward. "But somehow I don't think you waited in a dark alley just to tell me about the Filene's assignment."

Sandy stretched out her square fingernails. Some new nail style from France, she had told Diana proudly. Diana had been forced to control her face so that Sandy wouldn't see how ridiculous she thought they looked. Sandy carefully inspected the nails on her right hand for imperfections in their squareness. Then she checked her left. Apparently finding none, she dropped both hands to her lap and finally said, "I missed you."

Diana sat back in her chair. Sandy's neediness again. "We're having group on Monday," she said softly. "That's only a few days away."

"I know," Sandy whimpered. "But—but we didn't meet this week. And—and it was just real long for me. You know how I get. How I need to make sure that you're okay?"

"It *has* felt like a long time since we've seen each other," Diana said. "But it's actually been just three days. Remember you had that extra appointment the day after James's funeral?" It didn't seem possible so little time had passed.

Sandy looked down at her hands again. "I saw you since then," she mumbled.

"What do you mean?"

Sandy sighed and looked up. "I kind of followed you around a couple of times."

"Oh?" Diana dropped her hands into her lap so Sandy couldn't see her clenched fists. Just what she needed right now: an obsessed fan. Then her hands relaxed. Obsessed fans often broke into the homes of those they admired. Stole their possessions . . . "You followed me around?" she prompted.

"I, ah, I kind of went to your class yesterday. And—and . . ."

"And?" Diana looked at the large purse hanging on the back of Sandy's chair. An obsessed fan might steal a personal object. And, even more important, an obsessed fan might keep that personal object in her possession. Diana couldn't take her eyes from the purse. Perhaps her journal was sitting right across from her.

"And I saw you on Charles Street this morning." Sandy hung her head like a guilty child. "I followed you to DeMatteo's."

"Did you do anything else? Follow me anywhere else? Or do something . . ." Diana paused, searching for the right words. "Something that was maybe—maybe a little more wrong?"

Sandy shook her head, swinging her long hair back and forth, but she didn't raise her eyes.

"Are you sure?" Diana asked, hoping against hope that Sandy was lying. "It's easier to just spill it all now."

Sandy checked her nails for squareness again.

She *is* lying, Diana thought jubilantly, her eyes once again drawn to Sandy's purse. She *does* have the journal. "You can't do this, Sandy," Diana said gently. "You frightened me. I understand what you're feeling, I understand that you worry about me, but that doesn't make it okay."

"You don't understand anything!" Sandy stood up and began stomping around the office. "How can you?" She marched over to the desk, grabbed Robin's gift, and waved it under Diana's nose. "How can you understand what I feel when you have someone who makes something like this for you?" she demanded. Then she seized Craig's picture with her other hand. "When you have him?"

Diana silently watched the angry woman, her jubilation dying. That was the thing with borderlines: They adored you, and then they hated you, and there was not much sense to be made of what turned them one way or the other.

Sandy slammed Craig's picture to the desk and began raving again. "Even with all this stuff in the paper, with all the things going on that you probably think are so terrible, you—you still have everything. This." She waved the paper-clip holder in the air, then pointed to Diana's stomach. "The baby, that nice husband." She dropped into the chair and burst into tears. "And—and if you stop the group, I won't be able to afford individual sessions and then I'll have nothing!"

Diana nodded. So that was it. "We're not going to stop the group."

Sandy looked up, her huge gray eyes shiny with tears. "But James and Ethan are gone."

"James hasn't been a member of the group for months," Diana reminded Sandy. Despite her misgivings about Ethan, she added, "Ethan's called twice in the last few days, so I'm going to assume he'll show up soon. Bruce and Terri and you are still in. Four's enough for now. Maybe, after we've dealt with the effect of James's death on us all, we can discuss whether we want to add a new member or two at some later date."

Sandy's face was suddenly radiant. "I know I did the wrong thing when I followed you—and I'm sorry, truly I am. But, but I was so afraid of losing you. Now that Sam and me have broken up, I've only got you—my doctor." She tilted her head and smiled up at Diana. "My good doctor."

Diana stood. "We'll meet on Monday afternoon, as usual," she said. "We can talk about all of this then."

"Sure." Sandy jumped from her seat and placed the paper-clip holder carefully back on the desk. "Sure, that'll be great!" She swung her purse over her shoulder and just about danced out of the office.

Diana pressed her fingertips to the desk, as if to balance herself against the barrage of relief that was flooding through her. Sandy had the journal; it had to be. There was no other explanation. It wasn't Jill. It wasn't Adrian. And it obviously wasn't some junkie. So it had to be Sandy. There was no one else.

She dropped into her chair and smiled. Valerie was going to exonerate her in court, and the journal was going to stay safely hidden in the bowels of Sandy's purse. Diana touched her stomach lightly. It's going to be all right, she silently reassured her daughter. It looks like it actually might be all right.

~ 12 ~

DIANA SAT IN BED, IDLY WATCHING A BAD SKIT ON "Saturday Night Live." She was waiting for Craig to come out of the bathroom so they could finish the party postmortem. Once a month Diana and Craig got together for dinner with six other couples; one member of each couple had gone to graduate school with Craig, and the fourteen of them had been close for almost ten years. They rotated houses, made lavish dinners, and usually drank a bit too much—with the exception of whoever was pregnant at the moment. That night Krista had put on a gourmet Mexican feast, and Diana and Linda had abstained from the margaritas. "Why do I always think this show is going to be better than it is?" Diana asked Craig when he finally walked into the bedroom.

He took off his pants and shirt and climbed into bed next to her. "So you started to tell me what Ann said about Bill losing his job."

"I can't believe Bill didn't tell you himself," Diana said. "What were you guys talking about at your end of the table?"

"The Celtics. Rock and roll." Craig grinned. "Barry was doing his little old Jewish man bit."

Diana shook her head in feigned annoyance, but she smiled.

"All Bill said was that he'd wanted to get out of Digital for years. That this was the best thing that could happen to him." Craig propped up his pillow so he could lean against it. "Is Ann worried?"

"You know Ann." Diana shrugged. "She worries about everything."

Craig nodded. "She's worried about you."

"Seems I'm a hot topic of worry in that group." Diana moved closer to Craig and rested her cheek against his chest; he put his arm around her. "Everyone seemed so up on the details." Although she had tried not to show it, Diana had been both surprised and unnerved by how much her friends had known. Even though everyone had been supportive—and careful not to discuss the case too much— the whole thing had made her feel uncomfortably exposed, like the dream she frequently had of glancing down during a lecture and discovering she was wearing only underwear. Except tonight it had felt as if her underwear was dirty.

Craig gave her an encouraging squeeze. "Tim and Mark both missed the burglary write-up in the paper."

"Steve and Carol too," Diana said, raising her head. "I guess we should be glad for those drive-by shootings Thursday night—they must've kept our break-in off the front page."

Craig played with a lock of her hair. "Thank God for urban violence."

"Our resident feminists were outraged."

"Kathleen and Lisa?"

Diana nodded. "They went off on a tirade about how the media would be ignoring this whole thing if I were a man and James had been a woman."

"Even Kevin said something like that."

"I suppose I should take that as a good sign," Diana said dryly. "No one's ever accused Kevin of being a feminist."

"Don't worry." Craig pulled her closer and kissed the top of her head. "Your reputation's going to be just fine—Sandy's got your journal and Valerie's going to put Jill in her place with your treatment notes." He placed his hand over the curve of her stomach, and Diana covered it with her own. "And we're going to be a family."

"I told Valerie I'm not going to the reading of the will," Diana said.

"Was she upset?"

"She seemed more resigned than angry. She's going to go as my 'legal representative.' "

"Good. The farther you stay from Jill Hutchins the better." Craig raised the television remote. "Mind?" he asked. When Diana shook her head, he clicked off the television, and they snuggled down into the bed.

"I think I'm starting to believe this really is going to blow over. That it's—" Diana stopped mid-sentence and held her breath. She felt something. A movement. A fluttery butterfly of a movement in her stomach. "She kicked," Diana cried, tears welling in her eyes. "She actually kicked! Feel," Diana ordered, pressing Craig's palm to her stomach. They waited in complete silence for a moment and then it came again: a faint, gentle pressure from inside her womb.

"Yes," he said softly, almost reverently. Then he burst out laughing. "Damn," he said. "Do you think this means she *is* going to have your feet?"

The following morning the Sunday papers were wonderfully devoid of any mention of the case, and Diana's optimism continued to grow over the week. The media lost interest in her story as a rash of gang murders hit the city. Sandy was edgy and jittery in therapy group Monday afternoon, refusing to meet Diana's eyes and reinforcing Diana's belief that she did indeed have the journal. Even the news that Diana was the sole beneficiary of James's estate—estimated at five hundred thousand dollars—was less upsetting than Diana would have expected. "We'll set up a charitable trust," she told Craig and Valerie. "Invest the principle and give away the income." Craig nodded— a little glumly, Diana thought—and Valerie warned her not to do anything rash and at least wait to see what, if anything, Jill did about contesting the will. But Diana felt good about the decision.

"These past couple of weeks have made me realize how lucky we are—and how easily it can all be lost," Craig said over dinner Tuesday evening. "Let's get away and revel in what we've got." So Diana booked them the front room with the fireplace at the Echo Lake Lodge for the coming weekend.

On Wednesday Ticknor voted to allow Diana to keep her teaching position, and even permitted Brad Harris to issue a memorandum of support on university letterhead. And her colleagues all rallied around her. By the end of the week, everyone in her peer supervisory group—with the exception of Adrian Arnold—had given her written statements of support to release at her discretion, as had Brad Harris and three psychiatrists she had worked with at Beth Israel.

Now that it appeared Sandy planned to keep the journal to herself, the other good news was that Valerie and Ron Engdahl, Jill's attorney, had petitioned the court for a speedy trial and won. Judge Hershey had been more than happy to set an early trial date as this would give him points with the governor, who was pushing to streamline the court system. And Hershey's known sympathy for the defense gave Valerie additional confidence about winning the motion to admit Diana's treatment notes.

Diana quit working early on Friday afternoon so she could pack for the weekend; Craig was due home at five and their plan was to leave for Vermont by six. Straightening her desk, Diana picked up the file that held the statements of support from her colleagues, increasingly confident that the letters would clear her—as would the mass of notes and articles she was slowly organizing into an unshakable defense. Valerie had explained her four-pronged attack against the

substandard treatment charge: Diana's detailed treatment
plan for James's therapy, substantiated by regular progress reports; Diana's professional competence and credentials, including degrees, published articles, and professional
associations; the seriousness of James's illness and his pro-
pensity for self-mutilation and suicide; and the extreme
difficulty of treating people who suffered from borderline
personality disorders.

Valerie had instructed Diana to talk to her colleagues
and get their input—in writing—supporting each of the
"prongs." She was then to go through her treatment notes,
the psychological literature, and her personal files to find
information bolstering Valerie's positions. Everything from
James's past suicide attempts, to Diana's prestigious post-
doc, to research showing a low cure rate for borderlines was
relevant. And everything had to be copied, corroborated,
and organized under the correct prong. "While you're at
it," Valerie had added, "might as well see if you can find
whatever it was your weird patient was talking about."
Although Diana knew this to be a tremendous amount of
work—and was doubtful she would find what Ethan was
talking about—she was confident that she could produce
the material Valerie needed.

Diana dropped the statements into a file drawer and
pushed it closed with her hip. It really was going to be
okay, she thought as she flicked off the lights. The baby
was healthy, the trial would come soon, and her exoneration
would be swift. Then she would be able to reclaim her life.

The doorbell rang. With the sound of the chimes, Diana
was filled with a sudden foreboding. Despite her previous
optimism, she somehow knew that the news on the other
side of the door wasn't good. She ran up the stairs and
peered through the peephole. Valerie was standing on the
stoop. Her face was grim.

"I didn't want to tell you over the phone," Valerie said,
as soon as Diana pulled the door open. "Your journal has
surfaced—and it couldn't be in worse hands."

*   *   *

Diana led Valerie up to the great room. She sat on the edge of the couch and listened with a sinking heart as her lawyer told her that twenty-five photocopied pages of her journal had been delivered to Jill's lawyer's office that morning. Valerie explained that Ron Engdahl was planning to submit the pages in court as evidence that Diana had indeed had an affair with James Hutchins.

Diana stared out the front bay window, watching the shadows shift on the translucent window shade across the street, as all her hopes died. The shadows turned one way and then the other. Two shadows, three shadows, seemingly without purpose, crossing and melting into one another, only to emerge as separate entities once again. Diana turned toward Valerie. She ached with disappointment. She was nauseated with fear.

"Engdahl is a smug bastard in the best of situations—and on the phone this morning he was positively strutting. He told me that the excerpts were 'very juicy' and that there was no way any jury would believe you after they had read them," Valerie said as she kicked off her pumps. "Mind?" she asked Diana, nodding toward her feet.

Diana shrugged her indifference, and Valerie droned on about admissibility and motions in limine. Although Diana knew she needed to be concerned, that she needed to understand, all she could think of was Craig. Of how hurt he would be. "Motion in limine." She repeated Valerie's words in robotic tones. "To keep the journal out of evidence."

"That's right," Valerie said patiently and then continued. "Turns out my secretary, Katie, has a friend who works in Engdahl's office. So I had her scout down some info for me."

Diana shook her head as if to clear it. "Will it get in the newspapers?"

Valerie didn't appear to hear the question as she pulled a legal pad from her briefcase; she flipped through it with the back of a pencil. "Katie found out that the journal came without a note, and that it had been sent—and paid for in cash—from the Government Center Federal Express office."

"Federal Express from Boston to Boston?" Diana asked, feeling more disoriented by the moment.

"More importantly, with a fake return address." Valerie dropped the pad to the coffee table with a loud thump.

"So much for detective work."

"I'm a lawyer, not a detective," Valerie snapped. "My job is to prevent that journal from being introduced in court. And don't you worry: I'm going to do just that." She leaned toward Diana. "I'm going to hit Engdahl with a motion in limine that's going to wipe that cocky smile right off his alligator-preppy face."

"What about the newspapers?" Diana asked again.

Valerie frowned and tapped her pencil on the table. "What about them?"

"Do they know about it?" It took all of Diana's strength to keep from screaming at the woman. She swallowed hard. "Will they print it?" she asked softly.

"Even if the person sent them copies," Valerie said, "I doubt any newspaper would risk it."

"What's the risk?" Diana asked, although the blood was pounding so hard in her ears that she knew she would have trouble hearing Valerie's answer.

"We don't have a lot of law on this in Massachusetts," Valerie said slowly. "And although it wouldn't be libelous—it *is* your diary, after all—printing it in a newspaper would be a pretty clear invasion of privacy." She paused and looked up at the ceiling. "Chapter 214. Right of privacy. If I remember correctly, it protects against something like 'unreasonable, substantial, or serious' interference with a person's privacy . . ." She shook her head. "A legitimate newspaper printing an unauthorized personal diary sounds pretty unreasonable, substantial, *and* serious to me." She shook her head. "I just don't think they'd pull it."

"We could sue them?"

Valerie nodded emphatically. "In a flash."

Diana sighed in relief and leaned back into the couch. Then she bolted up as another thought came to mind. "What about the press if you lose the motion in limine?"

Valerie hesitated, playing with her pencil and avoiding Diana's eye. "If we lose the motion in limine," she finally said, "it becomes admissible in court."

Diana felt sweat prickling under her arms. "And then the sniffers can print it?"

"I'm sorry, Diana, but once it's public record then the . . ." Valerie paused and looked questioningly at Diana. "What was it you called them?"

"Sniffers."

Valerie nodded. "Then the sniffers will be all over it."

Nausea boiled up toward Diana's throat. She pressed her hand to her stomach. "We can't let that happen."

"I'm not going to. I'll win the motion—both motions," Valerie said, putting her pad and pencil back into her briefcase. "I got this hearing combined with the hearing on the admissibility of your therapy session notes."

Diana realized she was biting the cuticle on her thumb and yanked her finger from her mouth. "We still have the good judge?"

Valerie nodded again. "Hershey's cool—and he doesn't like clutter—so my guess is that he'll rule on both motions Tuesday," she said, slipping her shoes back on. Then she turned and stared out the window. "The thing that worries me is that he might construe both motions as hinging on the same issue: confidentiality versus direct relevance . . ."

Diana felt her stomach plummet to her knees. "What does that mean?"

"According to that logic," Valerie said slowly, "one would assume that *both* the therapy notes and the journal would fall into the same category."

"And?"

"And that both motions will be either granted or denied. From our point of view, we'd get a split decision."

Speechless, Diana stared at the lawyer. If the journal was allowed into evidence, Craig would be devastated. If her therapy notes were not allowed into evidence, her career would be devastated. "Is there anything I can do to help?"

Valerie stood up and reached for her coat. "Not unless you want to spend the weekend boning up on privilege against self-incrimination." She looked at Diana, and for a moment her face softened. "You just need to sit tight until Tuesday and have some faith."

"I'm not a religious person," Diana mumbled.

Valerie burst out laughing, the first real laughter Diana had ever heard from the woman. "I didn't mean in God—I meant in me." Chuckling, she walked down the stairs and let herself out of the house.

Great, Diana thought as she heard the front door slam. Now the woman develops a sense of humor.

~ 13 ~

DIANA CANCELED THEIR RESERVATIONS AT THE ECHO
Lake Lodge. When Craig came home and she told him what
had happened, he went to the video store and rented a half-
dozen classic movies. The two of them spent the weekend
holed up with Humphrey Bogart, Lauren Bacall, Clark
Gable, and Marilyn Monroe. They didn't talk much, just
sat close together on the couch and ate lots of popcorn.

Diana didn't tell Craig about the worst of the entries, still
holding to the hope that Valerie's motion on Tuesday might
spare him from reading them. But there was ice around her
heart as she worried about direct relevance and Valerie's
skill and whether whoever sent the pages to Engdahl might
not also send them to the *Inquirer*.

But she kept these worries to herself as she held Craig's
hand and watched Bogie in *Casablanca*. Sometimes she got
up and roamed around the house. Often she found herself in
the empty nursery, her mind wandering to images of driving
up to Albany to visit Craig's parents, she and Craig laughing as the baby gurgled from her car seat in the back of
the jeep. Of the house on the Cape they had talked about
renting in August with their friends Larry and Sheryl and
their one-year-old son. Of what it would be like if Craig

was so hurt and angry after he read her journal entries that none of these things ever happened.

On Monday morning Craig went to the office and Diana saw a few patients. After her borderline group left, she tried to analyze some of her research data. But she didn't get much accomplished. She was just too scared to concentrate.

By Tuesday she was exhausted from both stress and lack of sleep; she was having difficulty concentrating on anything but the hearing scheduled for that afternoon. The journal had to be ruled inadmissible. It had to stay out of the papers. And out of Craig's hands. Diana tried to focus on the lecture notes for her morning class, but her worries kept intruding. The fact that the lecture, which she called "Who's Really Crazy Here, Anyway?", was one of her favorites didn't seem to bolster her ability to focus on it.

Social expectations, social stigma, negative sanctions, she read, Every word, every concept, seemed to relate to her own plight, seemed to be speaking directly to her. She was violating social expectations. And that was why she wasn't sleeping, why her stomach was squeezing and turning and leaving her in a constant state of nausea. She was scared. Scared of the negative sanctions. Terrified of the social stigma. And, just as her lecture notes said, it was making her crazy.

"It's in the bag," Valerie had told her last night. "I'll call you as soon as it's over." Diana had nodded and hung up the phone. Then she turned to Craig, "It's in the bag," she repeated. Craig had hugged her and said that he was sure that it was, his trusting eyes full of compassion and a slight puzzlement over the fact that she didn't seem to be comforted by Valerie's optimism.

Was Valerie's optimism just a front? Part of her tough-lady personality? Or could they really win both of the motions? Diana forced her eyes and her mind back to the page. Mental illness as a social phenomenon. Sanity and insanity as socially defined states.

Diana loved throwing the sociological perspective on mental illness at her students. The sociological arguments turned the theories she had been discussing all semester on their heads and got even those slumbering in the back row to sit up and think. Perhaps R. D. Laing was right after all, she would suggest to the class. Perhaps insanity *was* just a form of "supersanity"; perhaps psychosis was just the sane response to an insane world.

She sure could relate to that, for she was struggling to respond to a world that no longer made any sense. She, a psychologist with no interest in the legal profession, was obsessed with motions in limine and with the intricacies of confidentiality versus direct evidence. She, a pregnant woman with a devoted husband and a promising career, was obsessed with the fear that her entire life was falling to pieces around her. It *was* truly an insane world. And it was definitely making her nuts.

Could the judge really be convinced to interpret the two motions as different issues? Valerie said that she had come up with an unimpeachable argument for separating the two—something even Engdahl wouldn't be able to counter. "You'll be getting your money's worth on this one," she had assured Diana.

But Diana was far from assured. Valerie hadn't seen the love and support in Craig's eyes last night—nor had she seen the fury that filled them just a few weeks ago, just before James's suicide, when Diana had told Craig that James was following her. That she had seen James sliding through the corridors at Ticknor, ducking into classrooms when she turned around. That James had hidden behind the garbage cans and jumped out at her as she walked to the back door, hurling insults and wild nonsense. Her gentle Craig, rocklike and stoic, could become a different man if he thought someone he loved had been wronged.

Diana rested her hand on her stomach, searching for a butterfly flutter. She closed her eyes for a moment. If it had to be one or the other, she prayed to a God she didn't really believe could hear her, please err on the side of confidentiality. Please don't let Craig read the journal.

Diana opened her eyes and focused on the words in front of her. Residual rule breaking. Exceeding the limits of eccentricity. Defective coping strategies. It was no use. Nothing was computing. She threw her pen down on the desk, grabbed her hat and coat, and walked out the door.

She crossed the busy intersection at Symphony Hall and headed toward the reflecting pool at the Christian Science Center. Well, at least her coping strategies weren't all that defective, Diana thought as she strolled among the soaring columns, breathing in the fresh air. She felt much better already. Sitting on a bench in the open plaza, she watched the pool spilling over itself, marveling at the serenity of the water flowing perpetually over the brown-speckled marble. She had always wondered how a religion so seemingly closed-minded could have such a vast vision of architecture.

Nothing made any sense. Not the Christian Scientists. Not the obviously impoverished kids running through the plaza in their hundred-dollar sneakers. And certainly not her present situation. Diana shook her head and watched the water rolling over the pool's rounded rim as if it were a living creature. A soft breeze played across one end of the basin, rippling the water, changing its form, separating it into a myriad of tiny waves. But when the water fell, it resumed its smooth totality and disappeared as a complete entity over the edge. Everything was strange, Diana thought, pulling her coat more tightly around her and shifting to the other side of the bench to remain under the anemic touch of the autumnal sun.

The plaza grew more crowded, filling with scurrying figures trying to beat the threatening clouds to their destination. Some clutched briefcases, others children's hands, and still others held brown paper bags close to their chests. Most, being city-wise, looked neither left nor right. But here and there, a few adventurous souls cast their gaze on Diana.

She stiffened as a tall man in work clothes, the head of a hammer sticking from his back pocket, slowed his steps to get a closer look at her. He pushed his face close to hers, and his eyes lit up as if with recognition. "Howdy," he said, but when Diana didn't respond, he shrugged and sauntered away.

Diana pulled her hat farther down on her forehead to avoid the probing, beady eyes of an elderly lady carrying a plastic shopping bag. But Diana's attempts were futile; the woman stopped right in front of her and dropped her bag on the ground. Lifting a pair of glasses from her ample bosom, the lady perched them on the end of her nose. Then she sighed, clearly disappointed, picked up her bag, and continued on her way.

Diana shook her head. Her growing paranoia was straight out of her lecture: Once she labeled herself as being watched, the signs were everywhere. Self-fulfilling prophecies. The looking-glass self. If she wasn't careful, she would soon be falling down Lemert's slippery slope to madness.

The sociologists were right: The stress, the fear, and the labels were all making her crazy. The tall man had just been trying to pick her up. The elderly woman's myopic eyes had momentarily mistaken Diana for a long-lost granddaughter. Diana took a series of deep breaths and forced herself to focus on the rolling smoothness of the water. Both her paranoia and her fears were unfounded. And self-defeating.

A young man in a wheelchair, a briefcase across his legs and a Red Sox hat on his head, rolled himself across the plaza toward the elevators. Diana watched him smile and wave away another man who tried to help him. Then he raised himself on one arm and pushed the button. The man in the baseball cap didn't give up, Diana thought as she watched him wheel himself into the elevator. He must have problems far more serious than hers, and here she was giving up, declaring defeat, before defeat had even occurred. This was all wrong. Valerie was still fighting. She would keep fighting too.

Okay, Diana thought, her eyes trained on the water as it curled around the edge of the pool. Think positive. Act positive. Valerie said it was in the bag; ergo, it was in the bag. She had a class to teach, James's records to finish compiling—perhaps even Ethan's "something" to find within them.

Chin high, she headed home, choosing a route that took her along her favorite street in Boston: St. Germain. As she stepped onto the narrow lane, European and appealing with its flower boxes and rounded recessed doorways, she decided to put her fears out of her mind. She would trust Valerie and let Valerie take care of her business while she, Diana, took care of her own.

She stepped briskly, taking in the beautiful wrought-iron grillwork along the street-level windows, feeling the quiet harmony of the tiny enclave. She would go teach her class and then come back and hit James's files. Gail always contended she was a control freak. Well, now was the time to focus on things she could control.

Diana's stroll had made her late. She grabbed her notes and rushed from the house, ignoring the blinking answering machine. Feeling better than she had in days, she practiced her lecture on the way to Ticknor. Halfway across Cambridge, she decided that she knew her stuff. She turned on the radio and sang along with an oldies station until she reached Medford.

When she got to campus, the swarms of students that filled the quad between classes were gone, presumably already settled in their seats, notebooks open and pens poised. Diana hurried toward Eaton Hall, huffing from the climb up the steep stairs. She glanced at her watch. Not so late that the students would have left. Twenty minutes was the rule. And it was only ten minutes past ten. Still, her steps lengthened. She hated to keep anyone waiting. Especially one hundred anyones. Especially when she had such a strong lecture to give.

As soon as she opened the door to the building, some-where, on some lower level of consciousness, Diana felt that something was wrong. Dismissing the premonition as another bout of unfounded paranoia, she bounded up the half-flight of stairs toward her room. But when she reached the landing, she *knew* something was wrong. The hall was too quiet. That many students waiting for a tardy professor would be making an uproar. And there was none.

Moving even more quickly, Diana entered the lecture hall. She stood in the door, frozen with bewilderment. The room was empty. Was it the wrong day? No, she thought, remembering the hearing, today was definitely Tuesday. The wrong time? She checked her watch once again. Then she looked up at the podium. On the black-board behind the lectern was a large message: "Psych 112 Canceled Today."

Canceled? She hadn't canceled class. Diana raced down-stairs to the psychology department offices. She ran past a few open doors without taking the time to talk to anyone and headed straight for the secretary's office. Peg, who knew everything that went on in the university, would surely know what was going on with her class. But Peg wasn't there. The office was empty.

As Diana turned toward the Xerox room—Peg's second home—she noticed a copy of the *Boston Inquirer* on top of a file cabinet. She stopped, her stomach squeezing so hard she had to grab the wall for support. SEX DOC'S DIA-RY VERIFIES ALL, screamed a headline so big and so thick that it took the entire top half of the tabloid's first page. She flipped the paper over so she could read what was written beneath the fold. She stared in stunned disbelief; her own face was staring back at her. The kicker along the bottom of the page said: "Excerpts Inside."

~ 14 ~

WITHOUT CONSCIOUS AWARENESS OF WHAT SHE WAS doing, Diana grabbed the newspaper and shoved it into her briefcase. Then she turned from the office and ran. When she got to the jeep, she punched the locks and sat staring out the windshield at the rows of cars in front of her, her breath coming in labored gasps.

With trembling fingers, she pulled the *Inquirer* open and turned to the page listed under the headline. When her eyes fell on the first excerpt, she was filled with relief: It was not only relatively mild, it also brought out the whole issue of countertransference.

I know it's countertransference. I know that I need to feel these feelings to do my job well. That it's normal, even desirable. But it's scary. The man is just too sexy—and too crazy about me.

I look into his eyes and I think thoughts I should never think. I brush his arm and dream dreams I can't dream. And yet, I long for the thoughts and yearn for the dreams. When I wake from a James-dream, I close my eyes and try to find the thread that will

126

*lead me back to him again. I am being drawn to the
forbidden—and I am afraid it is where I want to go.*

But when she turned the page and read the next, her
heart plummeted. They had used the first entry as a teas-
er, a scene-setter, and now they were coming in for the
kill.

*It is hot. Steamy. But not unpleasantly so. The old air
conditioner creaks and labors in the window, rattling
the narrow blinds closed above it to hold back the
midday sun. We are alone in the dim, hot-coolness
of the cavelike room. Sweat beads along James's
collarbone and I ache to touch it. To taste it with my
tongue. He speaks, but I can barely hear his words,
so focused am I on my need to feel the smooth ripple
of the muscles in his arm.*

*Then he grows silent and still and his eyes lock onto
mine; a bad-boy smile plays along the edges of lips
that already appear bruised from love-making. Slowly
James holds out his hands. I stand and walk toward
him, pulled by an invisible magnet that I know I must
resist, that I know I must fight. But I keep walking.
Walking forever across the short distance that sepa-
rates us, the pain growing outward from the center
of my being until it consumes and becomes every
nerve of my body. The horrible, glorious pain of the
forbidden.*

*And then I am upon him. And he upon me. The
pain both sharpens and abates as we crush together, tasting and touching each other in a ferocity that
obliterates all else. It is heaven. And it is hell.*

There were more: the one describing the two of them
making love in the parking garage; the one in the lecture

hall; one she had forgotten about where she related how she and James had performed gymnastic feats in the hot tub at her friend Susan's trailside ski condo as skiers rode the chairlift over their heads. As Diana read, panic roared through her. Sweat broke out on her forehead and on her upper lip and on her chest. The back of her blouse was wet. She saw Jill rubbing her hands with glee. She heard Kathleen and Lisa yelling about gender equity and sexism in the media. And she saw Craig, hurt and bewildered, his gentle eyes filled with pain.

As if coming out of a deep slumber, Diana slowly became aware of the frigid chill of the air. She adjusted her coat snugly around her, but the icy cold that emanated from within and her damp clothes made her begin to shiver uncontrollably. A small moan escaped her lips; she bowed her head on the steering wheel and cried.

When Diana pulled onto St. Stephen Street, a man and a woman were lounging against the streetlamp in front of her house. Despite their superficial nonchalance, the couple was alert, scanning the sidewalk, whispering and pointing at something written on a pad the woman held. Sniffers. Through some incredible stroke of luck, neither noticed Diana as she swung her jeep into the alley.

How had this happened? she asked herself for about the hundredth time since seeing the *Inquirer* headline. Valerie had said it couldn't. Valerie had said until the journal was part of the court record, no newspaper would risk it. It was against the law. But the *Inquirer* had obviously chosen not to abide by the law; they had weighed the cost of a possible suit against the gain of a juicy story and an expanded readership, and had—just as obviously—decided the risk was worth taking.

Driving slowly down the alley, Diana looked right and left, peering around the trash cans and the cars and the sagging planks of wood that roughly demarcated property lines. She even checked the deep sinkhole behind the house next to theirs. No sniffers. No neighbors. No street people rifling the Dumpster behind the Chinese restaurant. Either the reporters hadn't figured out that there was a back entrance, or, more likely, they were far too mindful of the realities of urban life to risk hanging around in a dim alley—no matter how hot the story.

But despite the stillness, Diana felt the eyes. She felt them on the back of her neck as she pulled into her spot. She felt them watching her from above as she scampered to the house. She felt them poring over her, surrounding her, swallowing her, even as she slipped inside the door.

Her breath coming fast, Diana leaned against the cool plaster of the hallway, pressing her cheek to the wall. Unfounded paranoia, she had called it just a mere hour ago. Founded paranoia was what it was. The mothers on Charles Street and the businessman in front of Jill's. The elderly woman and the man with the hammer at the Christian Science mall. It was like the old joke: Just because you're paranoid, that doesn't mean they aren't following you.

Diana wrapped her coat around her—whether to warm or protect herself, she did not know—and walked slowly toward her office. Craig. She had to call Craig. And Valerie. She looked at her watch. Valerie might already be on her way to the hearing. The hearing. Diana barked a harsh laugh containing no humor. The judgment she had looked upon as defining her life had been completely voided of its power.

She stood in the doorway to her small waiting room and looked through to her office. She could see the red light blinking on the answering machine. Perhaps Craig had called already. He must have seen the paper by now. She pressed her palm to her stomach. Someone would have showed it to him.

Despite Craig's unflinching support since James's death, Diana knew he had never been comfortable with her relationship with James. Even during the first year, before there was any indication of the problems to come, Craig had questioned her involvement. "It seems as if you're always talking about this Hutchins character," Craig had said right before James had his memory breakthrough. "Don't you think you should give your other patients—not to mention your husband—a bit of your time?" he had teased.

But after she had terminated with James, after James had begun to harass them both, Craig had stopped teasing and become angry. About a week before his death, James had sneaked into the backseat of the jeep, jumping up from his hiding place while Diana was driving to Ticknor. She had been so startled, she had slammed on her brakes and skidded into a parked car. She did little damage to either the jeep or the other car, but she was quite shaken—as was Craig. "Either you get rid of that loser, or I'm calling the police and getting a restraining order," Craig had told her. "You talk to him or I will." But before she or Craig could do anything, James had gotten rid of himself.

Diana was startled from her reverie by the slight kick of a tiny foot beneath her palm. What was Craig going to think of her relationship with James now? Talking about James was one thing; writing about having sex with him was another. "Oh, little one," she whispered, "let's hope your daddy understands."

She turned and headed up the stairs. On some level, she could appreciate that she was nauseated and terrified and furious. But really, what she felt most was calm. A strange, detached composure, almost as if she were once again acting in a high school play, as if she were both mentally and physically unable to believe that this was really her life.

She climbed up to the great room and, swinging wide toward the back of the house, approached the front window from the side. She pulled the edge of the drape. The sniffers were still there. Straightening a pillow on the sofa, she wondered how long they would stay and then wandered out of the room. Leaning over the stairwell, she looked through the narrow opening between the balustrades and the landings to the floor two stories below. "I'll be with you always,"

James had told her the day she had terminated with him. "Even when you think I'm finally gone."

Diana twisted her head and looked up at the clouded, dirty skylight one story above. James's prescience was definitely spooky. She climbed one more set of stairs, drawn to the small room at the front of the house. To the empty, freshly whitewashed room with three windows at the treetops and a shiny new hardwood floor.

But when she entered the nursery, Diana was jolted from her cool reverie. She raised one hand to her mouth as a small gasp escaped her lips. For there, standing in the corner of the room, his arms hanging limp at his sides, was Craig.

"Craig—" Diana started, and then her voice cracked. She wanted to run to him, to bury her head in his chest, but something about the stiff, uncomfortable way he was holding himself stopped her. "I'm so sorry," she whispered, looking at her hands, unable to confront the hurt on his face. A shiver of apprehension ran down her back: The cold eyes she had felt on her in the alley had been Craig's. "So sorry."

"Lionel dropped the paper on my desk as soon as he got in this morning," Craig said softly. "Then he suggested I take the rest of the day off." Lionel Lunt was Craig's boss. He was one of the most powerful architects in the country, and his opinion regularly made—and unmade—people's reputations.

The full impact of the situation hit Diana like a punch in the gut. "This whole disaster is all my fault," she said, taking a step toward Craig.

"Don't." Craig held his hands up, whether to stop her from coming any closer or to stop her from speaking, Diana wasn't sure. "Don't blame yourself," he said, but he didn't move toward her.

"They canceled my class without telling me."

Craig nodded, his back pressed to the wall. "When did you see the paper?"

"It—it was in the department office. I went down to find out why the class—why my class was—why it—" She couldn't speak; she couldn't get the words past the huge lump in her throat.

"I know you didn't do the things you wrote about," Craig said, still not moving toward her. "But it just seems so—so *real*, to read it in the paper like that . . ."

Diana stood alone and defenseless in the middle of the barren room. She hung her head, thinking of the thousands of people who would read the *Inquirer*: their friends, their family, her colleagues, a sea of opinionated strangers ready to think the worst. "Everyone's going to believe it," she whispered.

Craig dropped his arms. "No, they won't," he said, shaking his head. "It's too wild to believe. The stuff at Ticknor. In the parking garage. Susan's ski house . . ." Then the images seemed to be too much for him; his tenuous control collapsed and his voice rose. "Why did you have to write it?" He lurched forward and grabbed her by the shoulders. "Why did you have to be so graphic?"

Unable to speak, Diana just stood there.

"Why, Diana?" he demanded, his fingers digging into her coat. "Why?" His angry words ricocheted harshly off the bare floor and walls. Then as quickly as he had seized her, Craig suddenly let her go.

Diana staggered backward and then righted herself.

Craig was staring at his hands in horror. "This can't be happening," he said, shaking his head as if to shake himself out of a trance. "This can't be us." He pressed his hands under his armpits and walked to the window, turning his back to her.

"It was *my* journal." Diana crossed over to Craig and took his arms, forcing him to turn and face her. "Now it may seem stupid—but when I wrote in it I never expected anyone to read it. It was my private journal. And it was stolen," she added. "I kept the damn thing locked up in my desk, for God's sake!"

Craig nodded slowly, but his fists remained stuffed under his arms.

"I couldn't help what I thought, the feelings my job caused me to feel," she tried again.

"I know that," he said, letting his arms drop to his sides, but not meeting her eye. "I understand your work. You don't have to ex—"

"But I do," Diana interrupted, terrified that Craig would be so hurt or so angry or so disgusted with her that they would never pick out a crib with bright-colored bumpers and a quilt to match. "I don't want to lose you. I don't want our daughter to grow up without a family. I want us to be together . . ."

"This is nuts." Craig threw his arms up in the air and began to pace the perimeter of the room. "Completely nuts."

"It may be nuts," Diana said, "but it's also the truth. This countertransference stuff is for real. Don't you remember what happened with Sandy? How I was mothering and overprotecting her? How I had to talk to my peer group and work it out in my journal? She was responding to me as her mother—and that was a good and necessary part of her therapy—but I needed to learn not to respond back from that role."

Craig stopped his pacing. He crossed his arms and stood at the far end of the small room.

"It was the same thing with James," Diana said softly. "I needed to let him relate to me as someone I wasn't. I had to be Hank Hutchins for him. He had to make me into a sex object to work through the pain. Don't you see? Then I needed to work it through on my end—to learn how not to be the sexualized person he made me into."

Craig took a step closer and searched her eyes. "So this countertransference thing is pretty powerful . . ."

"That's what I've been trying to tell you." She looked up at him. "You have to believe me. You have to."

Although his brow was still slightly furrowed, Craig stepped forward and touched her cheek. Diana dropped her head, her hot tears fell onto his hand, soaking into the gray wool of her coat. They stood like that for a long time in the center of the empty room. "I guess a person has a right to put anything they want in a private journal," Craig finally said. "I guess you just did what you thought you had to do." Then he pulled her toward him and held her close.

When Valerie called to report on the results of the hearing, the irony of the situation was not lost on either Diana or Craig: confidentiality had prevailed over direct relevance. Neither the journal nor Diana's treatment notes would be admissible in court.

"But what about your 'unimpeachable argument'?" Diana demanded. "What about all that 'in the bag' business you were handing me last night?"

"I'm sorry, Diana," Valerie said, her voice softer than Diana had ever heard it. "Truly I am. The truth is, you never know what's going to happen in court—with a judge or a jury. I was wrong to be so confident. Wrong to get your hopes up." The rapid tapping of fingers on a computer keyboard came over the phone lines and then Valerie cleared her throat. "I'm, ah, I'm also real sorry about the *Inquirer*. You two doing okay?" she asked awkwardly.

Diana had to swallow the lump in her throat that Valerie's sympathy had elicited before she could answer the question. "Craig's being great," she finally said, turning to smile sadly at him. "A real trouper. I think I'm still numb."

"I guess there must've been a leak at Engdahl's."

"Or whoever sent it to Engdahl sent it to the *Inquirer* too." Diana chuckled without humor and then added, "I just can't imagine who it might have been."

Valerie was silent for a long moment. "If it makes you feel any better," she finally said, "after reading the paper this morning, we're lucky that journal isn't going to be allowed—tough as the loss of the treatment notes is."

She paused again. "Those entries would have crucified us, despite the fact that its obvious most of them aren't true and there's no corroboration."

"Corroboration?"

"The only person—besides yourself—who knows if your entries are fact or fantasy is dead."

Now it was Diana's turn to sit in silence. "So what do we do now?" she finally asked.

"Well," Valerie said, her voice perking up, "I figure we continue with our four-pronged attack to build up your credibility and tear down James's. Ultimately proving that no one—not even a top-notch therapist such as yourself—could have stopped a true loony like Hutchins from killing himself."

"Can we do that without the treatment notes?"

"It won't be as easy, but it can be done," Valerie assured her. "We put you on the witness stand and have you start to describe what was in the notes, Engdahl objects and, although his objection is sustained, I get the judge to instruct the jury that extensive notes were taken—even if their content is privileged."

"That doesn't sound like enough."

"It isn't," Valerie agreed. "But we've still got your credentials, James's history, and all those articles you told me about proving that borderlines are impossible to treat. And if a number of your colleagues testify to the existence of your notes—and I can elicit a few pieces of specific information from them before Engdahl objects—we'll be able to portray you as thorough and competent and always maintaining the highest of professional standards."

"I've got support letters from almost a dozen professionals in the field."

"Fax them to me as soon as we hang up," Valerie ordered. "We may have to make some changes so that the language emphasizes the right things."

"But the stuff in the paper may—"

"Diana, I know that having your journal in the *Inquirer* is a terrible personal blow," Valerie interrupted. "But you've got to remember that it's irrelevant to this suit. All that matters right now is what's in court." She then went on to direct Diana to put together a resume as complete and impressive "as if she were going up for tenure at Harvard" and set up a meeting to review Diana's list of potential witnesses. "I want you to keep organizing your treatment notes as if we were still going to use them—that way I'll have full knowledge and be able to work what I can into evidence. Oh," she added, "I also need you to come down to my office to review some hospital records I got from Engdahl—you'll probably need three or four hours."

"Hospital records?" Diana asked.

"Mass General. Looks like Hutchins was admitted there for a suicide attempt this past summer. You knew that, right?"

"All too well."

"That's what I thought. Anyway, Engdahl seems to think the records contain proof positive of your incompetence, but I figure we can use them to show how sick Hutchins really was."

Diana agreed to check her schedule and hung up the phone. Then she sat back down at the kitchen table where she and Craig had been pretending to eat a late lunch, but had, in actuality, been moving mounds of reheated linguine marinara in circles on their plates. Diana repeated Valerie's words, although Craig had caught the gist from listening to her side of the conversation.

"So she's still optimistic?" Craig asked.

Diana picked up her fork and twisted some pasta around it, carefully soaking up as much sauce as she could. Then she just as carefully pushed it all from her fork and to the other side of her plate. "I guess."

"If she's still optimistic," Craig said, "then we should be too." He put a large scoop of linguine in his mouth and looked at her thoughtfully as he chewed. "Figure it this way, if you can convince the supposed 'wronged husband,' you can convince anybody."

Diana went ice-cold. She knew Craig meant for her to be consoled, but the words "wronged husband" and the calmness of his tone terrified her more than any angry outburst could have.

"If I stand by you," he said, "everyone will know that it can't possibly be true—and then they'll all go away and leave us alone."

Diana played with her linguine. If only it was as simple as Craig made it sound. If only he believed what he was saying. If only she believed it. As she lifted the fork to her mouth, the telephone rang. She looked at Craig and shook her head; he jumped up to get it.

It was their friend Lisa. "Yeah," Craig said, "the lawyer's pretty sure we've got a good case. Invasion of privacy." He smiled at Diana and rolled his eyes. "I don't know about sexual harassment. It seems like a long shot when there's no proof the *Inquirer* wouldn't have done the same thing to a male psychologist. But Valerie Goldman's the—" He listened for a moment. "She's doing okay, but she's not really up to talking to anyone now." He nodded. "I'll tell her," he said and hung up the phone.

Craig told Diana that Lisa sent her love and resumed eating his lunch.

"Do you think I should call that reporter at the *Globe*?" Diana asked after a while. "To get out my side of the story?"

Craig shook his head. "Forget about the press—let them have their little fun. Then let it die down."

"But—"

"No," Craig interrupted. "You start trying to refute your own words and you're just begging for trouble. It'll prolong the whole thing and turn this into a citywide *Globe-Inquirer* battle—blow it up into an even bigger circus than it already is." He took another bite of pasta. "Better to concentrate on the things you can do that'll help. Like getting all those

papers on your desk in order for Valerie. Like getting people to testify for you."

The telephone rang again and Craig sighed. "Your turn,"
he said.

"Let the machine get it."

But Craig had never been one to let a ringing phone go
unanswered. After a few rings, he stood up and grabbed it.
This time it was his brother Paul's wife. "We're hanging
in, Martha," he said, looking over at Diana and raising his
eyebrows. "It's nice of you to call." Martha was not the
person they would have expected to come through for them
in a crisis.

Diana shrugged and mouthed the words, "Maybe she's
not as selfish as we think."

"I took the afternoon off to be with Diana," Craig
explained. "We're just having lunch." As he listened to
Martha, his eyes hardened and his chin jutted forward.
"No," he said, "I don't think that at all. My last name
isn't Marcus, and neither is Paul's—I doubt either one of
us has anything to be concerned about. Now I've got to
go. Tell Paul I'll talk to him later." He hung up the phone
without saying good-bye and sat back down at the table.

"She's worried about the effect of this on Paul's reputation?" Diana asked, surprised, but not surprised, at her
sister-in-law's self-centeredness.

Craig nodded as he twisted a huge wad of linguine around
his fork.

"See?" Diana said. "I have to call the *Globe*. I have to
try to clear myself—for all of our sakes."

"You don't have to do anything because of that idiot
Martha," Craig snapped.

"But if I don't explain about the journal, if I just let it
stand the way it is in the *Inquirer*, it's as if I'm admitting that what I wrote really happened." Diana stood and
dropped her full plate in the sink. Then she walked over to
the window and looked out at the shadowed alley. The gathering clouds of the morning had fulfilled their promise. It

was raining. When the phone rang for the third time, Diana didn't turn around. "I'm not here."

"Oh, hi Lionel," Craig said with false joviality in his voice. "We're doing pretty well, thanks. Just having a little lunch."

Diana closed her eyes as Craig listened to his boss, her stomach squeezing. How could she have been so stupid? What had she done to them all?

"That's really thoughtful of you—but it's not necessary. Diana's got a great lawyer and we're sure this whole thing'll blow over in a day or two." Craig paused. "No, no, really I'm sure. I'll be in in the morning." He paused again. "Okay, right, I'll call. But expect me at the usual time."

Diana turned as Craig dropped into his chair. This time he didn't bother to feign interest in his linguine. "He offered me the rest of the week off. 'Take a few personal days,' he said. 'We'll cover it out of overhead.'" Craig shook his head. "That'd be four days counting today. Lionel Lunt's never covered four personal *hours* out of overhead without someone holding a gun to his head." Craig looked up at Diana and smiled ruefully. "Sorry," he said. "Bad choice of words."

She shrugged. "I guess that clinches it. I'm calling Risa Getty."

"Face the facts here, Diana," Craig said, pulling at his ear and staring over her shoulder. "It's going to be tough to refute that journal. You have to admit that you wrote those things, and once you do . . ."

Diana didn't say anything. She watched Craig, hoping that she was imagining the anger she heard building under his words.

"Damn it!" he yelled, pounding his fist on the table.

Diana jumped at the sound. "Craig, don't—"

"Damn that Hutchins!" he exploded. Then, in a single forceful motion, he stood, picked up his plate, and threw it hard against the wall. To Diana's surprise, it didn't break. It clattered to the floor, turned a few revolutions, and then came to rest facedown in a puddle of red sauce and linguine noodles. "Damn him!"

"Stop it, Craig," Diana cried, rushing to him and trying to wrap her arms around him. "Stop it."

He pushed her away and began to pace the room. "The guy's dead! The fucking guy's dead and he's ruining our lives!" He grabbed Diana by the shoulders. "When will it end? When we're broke and divorced and the stress has made you lose this baby too?"

Diana shook her head. "Don't," she whispered. "Don't even say those things."

Craig dropped his arms and glared at her. "I'm suffocating," he said. "I've got to get out of here."

"Craig," she began, reaching out toward him.

He held up his hands. "I'm not mad at you—I've just got to get some fresh air." He turned before she could say any more and slammed out the door.

Diana stared past the place where Craig had been, through the window, into the murky grayness of the alley. Sheets of rain cut diagonally into the brick wall and bounced off the railings of the fire escape. She closed the blinds.

~ 15 ~

ON WEDNESDAY DIANA OBEDIENTLY FOLLOWED VAL-
erie and Craig's advice. From the time she awoke at five
A.M., to the time she fell into a dead sleep at eleven P.M.,
she ignored the media, marshaled her colleagues, started
compiling her "Harvard tenure" resume, and searched the
psychological literature for research supporting Valerie's
contention that borderlines were untreatable. She even had
a telephone appointment with the one patient who hadn't
canceled that week: a man so agoraphobic that not only
was he unable to leave his apartment, but he couldn't read
newspapers or watch television either.

But on Thursday morning, when Gail's voice, furious and
righteous, boomed over the phone lines ordering Diana to
sue the bastards at the *Inquirer* for defamation of character,
Diana knew that one day of obedience was all there was
going to be. Pulling the brim of her hat low on her forehead,
she slipped into the 7-Eleven, dropped her money on the
counter, and hurried from the store with both the *Inquirer*
and the *Globe* under her arm.

When she got home, there was a message on her machine
from her friend Alan Martinson, the psychologist to whom
she had referred James after she had terminated with him.

141

"I'm on my way out for the day," Alan's message said, "but after seeing the *Inquirer*, I had to call and apologize to you. The damn reporter twisted everything I told her. She left things out and she purposely used my words out of context—I'm writing a letter of complaint first thing tomorrow." There was a long pause on the tape, and Diana opened the *Inquirer* with trembling fingers. TWO SHRINKS CONFIRM SEX DOC'S ABUSE, the headline asserted. She closed her eyes against the pain of the words, but the thick letters blazed red against her eyelids. Would this never end?

"She bamboozled me, Diana," Alan's voice continued. "I'm sorry. She got me to tell her—I'm still not exactly sure how—that Hutchins said he was having sex with you. But as soon as I realized what I said, I explained how I didn't believe him—that borderlines make up things like that all the time. I also told her that when I asked Hutchins if he'd give me permission to file a sexual abuse complaint against you, he refused." Alan's sigh was audible on the tape. "Unfortunately the bitch chose not to print that part. I can't tell you how sorry I am, Di. Hang in there, kid. I'll call you this evening."

Diana quickly flipped through her Rolodex and dialed Alan's number; when his answering machine clicked on, she hung up the phone and began reading the paper. "Who the hell is this Pumphrey?" she called into the empty room as her eyes scanned the story. Then she remembered: John Pumphrey was the young resident on call at Mass General in July when James was admitted for his Seconal overdose. Diana vaguely recalled serious dark eyes surrounded by smooth, sallow skin. "He's just a kid!" she yelled as she read. "He doesn't know anything!" But kid or no kid, Pumphrey had informed the *Inquirer* that James had told him he wanted to die because his therapist was breaking off their affair; the *Inquirer* had printed Pumphrey's words as if they were fact, and Alan Martinson was quoted as the second "confirming shrink."

When she finished reading the article in the *Inquirer*, Diana snapped the paper closed and turned to the *Globe*; the only mention of her was a small piece in the Metro/Region section noting Judge Hershey's decision not to allow the journal into evidence at the trial. She threw the *Inquirer* into the trash. Trash. It was irresponsible, unsubstantiated trash. Anyone reading it would know that.

She began pacing the small office. Then she stopped, staring at the newspaper sticking out of the wastebasket. How would they know it was trash? If anything, this corroborated the journal entries that had been printed on Tuesday. The only thing people reading the *Inquirer* would think was that she *had* had sex with James Hutchins. She reached for the telephone and dialed Craig's office.

"I know we decided I should stay away from the press," she said as soon as he answered, "but now I can't." After describing the contents of the article, Diana told him that talking with Risa Getty was the only way she could see to prove her innocence. "Not responding is tantamount to a declaration of guilt."

Craig was silent for a moment. "I thought Valerie said you should concentrate on getting the trial materials together."

"This won't take that long," Diana said.

His silence lasted even longer this time.

"I can't just sit here and let my name be dragged through the mud," she finally said.

"If you start fighting the *Inquirer* you're going to see a whole lot more mud." Craig's voice was flat, as if he was too deflated to care.

"But what do you think?" Diana persisted. "Should I contact her?"

"It's your call, Diana. Frankly, I don't know what to tell you," Craig said, then he sighed.

There was something in his wording, maybe in his sigh—Craig never sighed—that made Diana's blood turn to ice. "Is something wrong?" she asked.

"No," he answered quickly, then sighed again.

"What?" Diana demanded.

"Lionel took me off the Central Artery project."

For a moment Diana forgot her own concerns. "But that's been your project from day one," she protested. "You made all the contacts. The whole concept was your idea."

"Lionel said he was sorry, but it was an 'upper management call.' " Craig's voice was bitter. "Told me the competition is so tight that he didn't want the slightest hint of wrongdoing."

"Wrongdoing?" Diana repeated.

"He's giving me the Nashville project."

Diana closed her eyes for a moment, the pain gouging deep through her gut. "Out of town."

"You might say Tennessee's out of town."

Diana ran her fingers through her hair. "Jesus, we don't even have the same last name."

Craig didn't say anything.

"What about Keith or Will?" Diana demanded, her pain turning to fury. "Can't you get them to talk to Lionel? You've worked with them forever—they're your friends."

"Can't even get them to talk to me. Whenever I walk into a room the conversation stops."

"Oh," she whispered. "I'm so sorry."

"I'm sorry too, hon. I know you don't need this." He paused for a moment, then added, "Now that I think about it, you might as well call that woman at the *Globe*. At this point, what've we got to lose?"

"It's a pack of lies and I need you to help me prove it," Diana told Risa Getty when she reached her at the paper. "My husband and I can't live like this—and I won't."

Not having seen the *Inquirer*, Risa asked Diana to slow down and explain. "It seems odd this Dr. Pumphrey would disclose that kind of information," she said after Diana had described the article. "Doesn't doctor-patient privilege still hold after death?"

Diana hesitated, surprised that she hadn't thought of Risa's point. "I think my lawyer said all of James's hospital records were subpoenaed—would that make it okay for Pumphrey to talk?"

"Maybe," Risa said. "But I would still think he'd need permission from the family."

"Jill," Diana muttered. Jill was behind the whole thing; Diana was sure of it. She saw Jill sitting comfortably in her living room, her voice chatting and friendly. *Oh no, you don't understand, do you?* Jill had said with an amused smile on her face. *You see, you* are *responsible for James's death.*

"Even so," Risa was saying, "I thought there was more of a brotherhood between doctors. You know, that you folks protected each other."

"There was some comment in the article about how he had once had a patient 'ruined by psychologists like her,'" Diana said, her voice coated with disgust. "He's a psychiatrist."

"And psychologists and psychiatrists aren't in the same brotherhood?"

"Alan Martinson called to apologize," Diana said, leaving Risa's question unanswered. "He said the *Inquirer* reporter twisted everything he told her. That what she wrote was misleading and that she had quoted him out of context."

"And you want me to talk to him?" Risa asked slowly.

"To him. To me. To a whole bunch of other people who'll tell it from my side." Diana paused, her anger boiling as she thought of the things the *Inquirer* had printed—and not printed. Of what this was doing to Craig. And to her. "According to Alan, the reporter bamboozled him into admitting James said he was having sex with me."

Risa whistled. "Pretty slick."

" 'Bitch' is the word Alan used. He's going to complain. He said she omitted his clarifying remarks."

"Like what?"

"Like how he tested James by asking him if he'd give his permission for a sexual abuse complaint to be filed—and James refused. How borderlines—"

"I don't understand," Risa interrupted. "What do you mean 'tested' him? Does a patient have to give permission before a complaint can be filed against a doctor?"

"If the complaint comes from him, he does," Diana said. "And I wouldn't doubt, if we checked with Pumphrey, we'd find Pumphrey asked James the same question—and that James refused to let him file too." Diana wanted to slam her fist into the desk and scream. Instead she swallowed her fury. "I need your help."

"I'd be one hell of an idiot if I didn't jump at this interview," Risa said, still speaking slowly. "But I've got to let you know up front, I can't just play it from your side. I'll be more than happy to give you an opportunity to tell your story. But my job's to be objective—not to vindicate you."

"Objectivity is all I ask."

Risa was good to her word, and the next few days were a whirlwind of dueling experts in the media. Diana and Craig rode the peaks and the troughs of the resultant elation and disappointment as well as they could. He went to work and pretended that everything was fine while she maintained the facade of in-control righteousness: giving interviews; coaching allies; working with Valerie.

Diana had trouble sleeping and was exhausted all the time. Craig was irritable. He complained that there were no English muffins in the freezer. He stared at a spot behind her shoulder when he spoke to her. And he turned from her in bed, claiming that he "just wasn't feeling affectionate."

Although Diana was worried about Craig, she had to focus her energy on John Pumphrey and the *Inquirer* and some idiot the reporters kept quoting—someone calling himself Benjamin J. Talcott, M.D., borderline personality disorder expert—although neither Diana nor any of her colleagues had ever heard of the man. Valerie said that, although she had initially advised against it, the media fight was actually helping her prepare for court. She claimed the reporters were doing half of her job for her: highlighting the strong and weak witnesses; finding holes in each side of the case.

But whether they were helping Valerie or not, it was clear the journalists were having a field day—and that a lot of papers were being sold. Risa quoted Brad Harris in the *Globe* as explaining that borderline patients were more likely than those with other mental illnesses to falsely accuse their therapists of abuse. Then she added that Benjamin J. Talcott, M.D., borderline personality disorder expert, had countered by claiming false accusations of sexual abuse were actually quite rare.

Marc Silverman, one of the members of Diana's peer group, stated that a therapist who was having an affair with a patient was unlikely to present that patient's case at supervision, as Diana had done. And he declared it even more unlikely that an abusive doctor would solicit advice from a Harvard expert on a sticky countertransference issue with said patient, as Diana had also done. But then Benjamin J. Talcott, M.D., borderline personality disorder expert, suggested that Diana discussed James's case with her colleagues just to cover herself in the event that James made their affair public.

Risa did determine that John Pumphrey had indeed received permission from Jill to make James's medical records public. The man was interviewed ad nauseam—and his remarks were invariably in opposition to Diana's. He said he had found James exceedingly normal, even likable, noting that James had a strong self-image, had denied ever using drugs, and had a long history of goal-oriented behavior. He stated that James's clinical picture clearly indicated that he was suffering from a "reactive depression, perhaps complicated by a mild affective instability"—not the severe personality disorder Diana had diagnosed.

Never did Pumphrey mention that he had spent a total of three days with James—versus Diana's three years.

Although Diana was unable to get Adrian Arnold to speak to the press, she was able to get more than half a dozen other experts to refute Pumphrey. Gail was a particularly effective spokeswoman, asking why the last three cases of sexual abuse against therapists filed in Middlesex District Court had been almost completely ignored by the Boston media. Could it be because the therapists in those cases had been male and their patients female? she demanded.

The battle raged, filling the front pages of both Boston newspapers, as well as receiving national attention and debate. But no matter how hard Diana worked, no matter how many authorities she found or studies she cited, someone always came forward to refute her experts or data— and to erase her advantage. At the end of every day, after all the words had been read and written and spoken, it was invariably a stalemate.

A co-worker at Fidelity stated that James was charming, hardworking and dependable.

A childhood friend reported that as teenagers, he and James drank heavily, smoked marijuana, and used cocaine.

The *Inquirer* reported that Diana was not really a faculty member at Ticknor, only an adjunct, implying that she had misrepresented her credentials.

When pressed by Risa, Pumphrey admitted that James had refused him permission to file a sexual abuse complaint against Diana.

A minister in James's hometown of Norwich, Connecticut, said the Hutchins family had always been well-respected churchgoers, and that James had been a happy child, particularly close to his sister, Jill.

When Adrian Arnold claimed prior commitments, Brad Harris went on the Channel 5 News to discuss borderline personality disorder. He reported that many therapists refused to work with these patients out of fear of just such a situation as Diana was facing. And he managed to squeeze in a couple of statements about Diana's uncompromising dedication to her patients and the promising preliminary findings of her research.

And in a journalistic coup, the *Providence Journal* discovered that when Diana had been an undergraduate at Brown, she had amassed five unpaid parking tickets—one more than the number the university automatically excused—and the bursar's office had had to threaten to withhold her diploma to get her to pay up.

By Sunday the story had slipped from the headlines to the inner pages, the repetitive arguments and lack of clear villain or victor obviously boring the public. Diana's disappointment with the ineffectiveness of her campaign was somewhat mitigated by her relief at finally becoming a bore.

"Waste of time," Craig muttered as he turned the pages of the *Sunday Globe*, breaking the silence of their glum brunch. "Just stirred everything up."

"I had to do something," Diana said, hearing the whine in her voice.

Craig raised his eyes from his bagel and looked at her directly for the first time in days. He didn't say anything, but his thoughts were clear. *Haven't you done enough?* Diana read in his eyes.

Pouring herself another cup of coffee, Diana left Craig with the newspaper and went down to her office. Craig was right: She had been wasting valuable time—three days to be exact—in a vain attempt to maintain some idiotic status in the minds of people she didn't know. Wasting her time battling Jill in the media—instead of in court where it mattered. Although Valerie was increasingly optimistic about the trial, she kept reminding Diana she needed her resume, the support statements, the literature review, and her treatment notes organized as soon as possible.

As the resume and support statements had practically generated themselves out of the media battle of the last few days, Diana's priorities were to search the psychological literature for research supporting Valerie's "impossible borderline" prong and to organize James's records under the "self-mutilation" and "treatment plan" prongs. Picking up the thick pile of manila folders containing her notes on James, Diana paused a moment to mourn their loss as evidence. Then, reminding herself to keep an eye out for Ethan's elusive "something," she turned to the task at hand. She had skimmed through the notes last week and marked segments that might be useful to Valerie. Now it was time to carefully scrutinize every word. And there were many.

She had seen James for almost three years, on an average of twice a week, resulting in over three hundred pages of individual session notes. He had also been part of her borderline disorder group for almost as long; her group notes were not as detailed, but they were voluminous, and references to James would be more difficult to ferret from her general comments. Roughly another three hundred pages.

Intakes. Histories. Treatment and discharge summaries. Consult reports. Copies of hospital forms from his suicide attempt. Lab slips for blood work monitoring his medication. A couple of pictures James had given her: one of him clowning at the beach with friends and the other of him and Ethan standing in front of Ken's Pub in Cambridge, arms thrown over each other's shoulders, grinning their bad-boy smiles for the camera. Postcards. Letters. The crushed black orchid he sent after she had terminated with him.

This was going to be both long and painful. Pulling the individual session files from the stack, Diana ordered herself to focus. But from the very first page, she found herself distracted, unable to keep from getting lost in James. Every sentence she read, every word, brought him back. James, lost and confused and hiding behind his repressed memories the first year. James, gaining strength and confidence during the second year. James, losing it completely at the end.

She forced herself to jot down notes and make piles for Valerie. But before long, her mind strayed once again. It hadn't just been James's good looks or winsome charm that had won her over, as Gail often teased. Diana had known enough to see through the perfect manners and flattery. "I know this is how you've charmed your way through life," she told him in response to his comment that she was the best therapist he had ever had, that she was "right on target," that she saw things about him no one else had ever even glimpsed. "You don't need to do that here," she had said.

It wasn't what showed on the outside that had gripped her, it was what was inside: James's potential, his spirit, his energy, his health, hiding beneath the shell he had built to protect himself. It was his love of literature, the voracious way he devoured Homer and Tolstoy as well as Anne Tyler and Agatha Christie. It was how he had painted his downstairs neighbor's living room because Mr. Berger was in a wheelchair and the landlord refused to pay for it. It was the software program he designed at Fidelity that had a better performance record predicting stock prices than Magellan, Fidelity's own superstar fund. It was that perfectly sane, perhaps even brilliant, James who had haunted Diana, who kept her awake at night, who roamed her dreams. It was that bruised, beautiful boy she had longed to unearth, to bring back to life. "I feel like I'm floating alone in space," he told her early in his treatment. "Lost in ghostly solitude."

Diana squeezed her eyes closed to hold back both the tears and the raging guilt. She had brought him so far, only to fail him. He had been doing so well after he remembered what Hank Hutchins had done to him. But about six months after his breakthrough, she had suffered an ectopic pregnancy. And nothing between them was ever the same after that.

Guilt twisted through Diana and she dropped all pretense of reading her notes. She swiveled her chair and looked out the window. It had been a cold, bright day, not all that different from this day. But it had been mid-winter; it would be two years this coming February. The twelfth of February, to be exact.

James had been edgy and excited, alternately wringing his hands and laughing as he told her about his fantasies of killing Uncle Hank. "I dreamed last night I was in a castle. A dark, brooding castle. In a room with a pointed ceiling so tall I couldn't see to the top. I had him on a rack—a metal rack like ones you see in those old horror movies. I had strapped down his wrists and his ankles with thick leather thongs and he kept begging me to release him.

"But I just laughed in his ugly face," James said, his eyes shining with both fear and excitement. "Then I yanked on a huge lever mounted in the cement wall behind me and the rack began to pull apart. It pulled his arms one way and his legs another. He screamed and screamed and then he exploded into a million bloody pieces." James looked up at her with a guilty smile. "Am I a terrible person?" he asked.

When Diana assured him that he was not, that his anger was a normal—and positive—response, he began talking about how thrilled his boss was with the performance of his software program. "I feel like a great albatross has been lifted. I'm going to be able to do it now. I really am." James grinned at her, his deep blue—almost purple—eyes locked on hers. "Because of you," he said softly. "All because of you."

The intensity of James's stare sent small ripples of desire through Diana. She looked down at her desk. The guy was just too damn good looking. More than good-looking. He was steeped in sex appeal—he reeked of it. Only an ice woman could withstand this kind of idolatry from that kind of face. She twisted her wedding ring and looked at a spot above James's head, hoping the flush that she felt rising to her face was not visible. "I'm glad if you think I've been of some benefit," she said stiffly.

James grinned at her. "The only reason I have this job is because of you. Because of the help you gave me."

"It's because of *you*," she corrected. But before she could continue, a pain cut through her belly and jackknifed her forward in her chair. A moan escaped her lips as she looked down and saw blood spreading across her lap.

James was beside her in seconds. She looked up at him, the agony in her eyes and the growing circle of blood on the chair communicating everything he needed to know. Before she could say a word, he grabbed her coat from the hook outside the door and wrapped it around her. He lifted her in his arms as easily and as gently as if she were a child. "Don't worry, everything's under control," he said as he carried her outside, kicking the door closed with his foot. "Beth Israel's the closest."

The pain was so great that Diana couldn't speak. Tears squeezed from her eyes as she hunched into a fetal position in the front seat of his new Porsche, blood spreading over the leather upholstery. Her baby. Her baby was flowing from her and there was nothing she could do to stop it.

James kept up a soothing prattle as he sped to the hospital. "You're going to be fine," he said. "You're going to be fine. I'd never let anything happen to you." Steering with one hand, he gently pressed her lower back with the other, as if he had some instinctual sense of the source of her pain. "Fine, fine," he kept repeating. "You're going to be fine."

"Sorry," she managed to whisper. "Blood. Car." Something was very wrong. This hurt far too much to be a normal miscarriage. Something else was happening. Something very bad.

"We're going to one of the finest hospitals in the world," he said as if reading her thoughts. He applied more pressure to her back, rubbing in a soothing circular motion. "In the world," he repeated.

He swerved into the emergency entrance and jumped from the car almost before it stopped. "Quick! Quick!" he yelled as he ran toward the door, carrying her in his arms. "She's bleeding. She's bleeding badly!"

The rest had always been pretty much of a blur to Diana. Even at the time, her daze of pain and fear had kept her in a fuguelike state, dissociated from the orderlies and the stretchers and the lights and the noise, until finally some kind of rubbery mask turned the world into sweet blackness. But through her fog, she had been keenly aware of two warm, protective hands cupping hers. And she could still hear that velvety voice. "They're going to take good care of you here," James kept repeating. "You're going to be just fine."

~ 16 ~

ᗞIANA SPENT THE NEXT THREE DAYS READING AND organizing and rereading every word she had on James Charles Hutchins. The whole process was even longer and more painful than she had anticipated, an emotional roller-coaster that threw her from the depths of sorrow to the heights of rage, and just about every feeling in between. But finally, she was finished. She called Valerie to tell her that she had everything she needed—including a number of recent studies concluding that recovery from borderline personality disorder was a long shot, at best. They agreed that Diana would bring the documents over the next morn-ing and go through the Mass General records from James's July suicide attempt at the same time.

Diana was happy to have the job behind her and relieved that she could finally get out of her house and on to some-thing beyond her own files. But the next moring when she stopped into her office to pick up the materials for Valerie, she noticed the light blinking on her answering machine. And when she heard the voice on the tape, she knew that her hours with James's files weren't over yet.

It was Ethan Kruse, and he had left two messages. The first was an unintelligible jumble, something about not being at the Cape anymore, followed by some gibberish about his feet. But the second message was distinct and straightforward. "It's in the records," he said clearly, although he giggled between sentences. "The records."

Still standing at the side of her desk, Diana shook her head as she replayed the messages for the third time. There was no "it" in the records. She had been through every one at least twice—many of them three or four times. There was nothing in them. And there were no more records to search. For about the tenth time in the past couple of weeks, she dialed Ethan's number.

As she listened to its empty, endless ringing, Diana stared at the bookshelves across from her, waves of exhaustion and anger washing over her. It was as if Ethan's message had been some kind of catalyst, releasing the hostility that she had been trying to suppress. For suddenly she was mad at everything: at the world, at the media, at James, at Jill, at Craig's boss Lionel, even at her mother, who kept calling with homilies about being glad she had her health. She was mad at her sister-in-law Martha, who had telephoned Craig at work to complain of the embarrassment this was causing his brother Paul. She was mad at the sickos who left obscene messages on her machine, and she was mad at the strangers who wrote her touching letters of support. And right now, she was especially mad at Ethan. She slammed the phone down.

Diana had to admit to herself that she had never liked Ethan: his lack of remorse after his drunk-driving accident, his cruelty to anyone weaker than he, his uncanny ability to hone in on that weakness, his powerful—and negative— influence on James.

And now this. If Ethan was so hell-bent on helping her out of this mess, then why didn't he just tell her what she should be looking for? Why didn't he call when she was home? Or better yet, why didn't he just show up with the proof? Because Ethan was amusing himself with some kind of sick joke, Diana thought, not for the first time. Toying with her, punishing her for some slight of which she was unaware—or had never committed. James had once told her he was afraid of Ethan. Mortally afraid.

Diana sat down at her desk and tapped her pen on the pile of papers she had compiled for Valerie. Maybe the ectopic pregnancy hadn't been the beginning of James's slide, she thought. Maybe it had been Ethan. She had lost the baby in February, and it really wasn't until that summer that James had started to slip. She opened a file and quickly found the notation she was looking for: James had met Ethan in May.

About a year and a half before his death, James went to a party where there was far too much high-quality cocaine and, as he told Diana, he had had far too little willpower. He and Ethan met around the coke mirror and stayed up all night doing lines and "relating." Diana checked her notes again. It was subtle but clear, now that she knew what she was looking for. After becoming friends with Ethan, James had started to deteriorate. Before Ethan, James had stopped using drugs completely; after Ethan, his drug use quickly escalated to dangerous levels. And as James and Ethan spent more days at White Horse Beach and more evenings partying, James's attitude toward work became more laissez faire; he complained that his boss was "leaning on him" too hard, and in July he confessed to Diana that he had been calling in sick a lot. "I never sleep at night," he told her. "Ethan says you draw strength from being awake while the world rests." When Diana pointed out that he didn't seem to be getting the strength he needed, James had just hung his head. "I'm sorry," he whispered. "I just don't know any other way to be." Not long after that, James had been picked up by the police, dazed and wandering along the Harvard Bridge at three o'clock in the morning.

Although James and Ethan's relationship was obviously destructive, neither seemed able to stay away from the other. Diana immediately saw what Ethan got from James— money—but she had always been confused as to James's payoff. One thing she knew for certain: James, or any-one suffering from a borderline personality disorder, would never get into a relationship without some clear advantage accruing to him. Maybe it *was* just for companionship, she thought. But she doubted it.

They fought all the time. Violent fights. One even land-ed them both in the emergency room. Diana would never forget that winter afternoon when Ethan had shown up for group wearing James's favorite leather jacket, mimicking James's accent and gestures. When James objected, Ethan punched him in the stomach and they had both been bloody and bruised, and her office in complete disarray, before they finally fought themselves out. It had been horrible, brutal, full of hate. Bruce had fainted.

Diana told both James and Ethan they would not be allowed back until they were willing to contract with the group that there would be no more violent outbursts. James agreed but Ethan stormed from her office and disappeared for a couple of months. James had improved after that— until Ethan returned.

Diana flipped through the folders, looking for her notes from that period to verify her memories. "Don't coddle James so much," she had written to herself. "Let him feel some of the consequences. Don't allow your narcissism to maintain his pathology: Watch it." Diana smiled sheepish-ly. Even then she had known that James's idolatry had made her feel too powerful for her own good. That it wasn't healthy for either of them. That it had the poten-tial to lead her over the line.

She frowned as she reread her words. Here she was doing it all over again: acting like a mother who was blind to the guilt of her child, who always blamed "that wild crowd he runs with." Ethan might be jerking her around with his messages, but what had happened to James wasn't Ethan's fault. And it wasn't her fault either. It was James's fault. James had done it. James was responsible for his own behavior.

Diana jumped from her chair and began to pace back and forth between the bookshelves, thinking about one of the last times she had seen James alive. It had been this past August, a few weeks after she had terminated with him—just after he had been released from the hospital for his Seconal suicide attempt. Coming home from a peer supervisory meeting, she had actually been worrying about whether James felt he had been abandoned yet again, and wishing she could help him through the difficult transition. She had been distracted as she pulled the jeep into the alley and was halfway to the door when he jumped out from behind the garbage cans.

"You're still my doctor!" he had screamed at her, waving his arms. Then he had grabbed her shoulders, almost lifting her off the ground, shaking her. "You know you love me. You know it's my baby you're carrying! Mine!"

Somehow, although she never remembered quite how, Diana had managed to free herself. Terrified, she had rushed into the house and called the police.

But James was long gone by the time they arrived.

The view from the conference room of Bogdanow, Federgreen was spectacular. It was on the second floor of a Back Bay town house, a small slice of a once-grand ballroom belonging to a once-grand Boston family. Floor-to-ceiling bay windows overlooked the Public Gardens. Even at this time of year, the strollers crisscrossing the park and walking along the edge of the lagoon were an entrancing sight. Diana's eyes lingered on a large oak; its once emerald leaves, now a rusty brown, clung tenaciously to its limbs. She and James had shared a sandwich sheltered from the summer sun by that oak's spreading green canopy.

But Diana had no time for irrelevant memories or entrancing sights. She turned her back to the windows and reached for the files Valerie had given her, Valerie's words still in her ears. "I'm feeling pretty confident about our side of the case, but these medical records look bad to me," Valerie had said as she led Diana to the conference room. "They're just what Engdahl ordered: They read like Hutchins wasn't that crazy. This doctor makes the suicide attempt sound like some minor mental aberration—like being depressed after a divorce. Or having insomnia. Is that possible?"

"It's not possible." Diana shook her head. "But it appears to be *Dr.* Pumphrey's conclusion."

"Look, the guy tried to commit suicide—a couple of times—and he had been in therapy for years." Valerie handed Diana the medical records. "And this attempt was only last July, right? So he succeeded in killing himself less than three months later—that doesn't sound too healthy to me."

Diana nodded and glanced down at the file.

"See what you can find in there to buttress our contention that he was one sick cookie: errors, omissions, ways we can undermine the credibility of the other doctors—anything and everything. I can't believe it'll be all that difficult."

"It's so amazing to see this here," Diana said, flipping through the pages. "Hospitals treat medical records like gold locked in Fort Knox."

"Limited discovery." When Valerie noticed Diana's confused expression, she tapped the top file with the tip of her manicured finger. "Production of documents because of the speedy trial. Judge Hershey ruled that in order to proceed in such a short time frame, both Engdahl and I had to get copies of all evidentiary documents to each other immediately. Pumphrey's notes and Hutchins's medical records are part of Engdahl's case—I have to give him copies of everything you just gave me."

"You mean one side gets to see everything the other side's going to use in court?" Diana was amazed.

"That's the law," Valerie said as she walked to the door. "I'll check back with you later."

Flipping through the hospital files, Diana was overwhelmed with remorse. She had terminated with James on July 25; he had swallowed an entire bottle of Seconal on July 31. Pushing away her guilt, she focused on the records. They were even more dense and complicated than she had expected. Considering that James had been in the hospital for only three days, it didn't seem possible that so much could have been written about him. She quickly began sorting the papers into piles: intake interview, medical evaluations and tests, a neurological assessment, psychiatric consults, psychological test results, lab reports, daily rotation notes. She shook her head. Incredible.

She decided to start with the psychological information, figuring that held the most promise. Glancing quickly at the grandfather clock standing at the far corner of the room, Diana bent to her task.

She was familiar with most of the test results—she had copies of the same pages in her personal files—although a few were new to her. She was not surprised to discover that James had achieved an extremely high score on the WAIS, an intelligence test, or that his mode of aggression, measured by the Rosenzweig Picture Frustration Study, was extrapunitive—that he projected his anger outward, toward other people. Disappointed, she skimmed through the rest of the tests; but whether she was searching for proof of James's illness, a discrediting bit of evidence, or Ethan's "something," there didn't appear to be much of anything there.

The grandfather clock chimed, and Diana jumped in her chair. She squinted at the clock as it chimed nine more times, guessing that it was going to go off at least every half-hour, perhaps every fifteen minutes. She turned to the psychiatric assessment done after James had been stabilized in the medical unit. Pumphrey had administered the interview and, although he had recommended ten days of psychiatric evaluation, Diana now understood Pumphrey's diagnosis: James had lied to him. The problem was proving it.

Diana was all too aware of how easily, and how well, James could lie. She knew for a fact that Ethan was capable of reciting complete fiction and passing a lie detector test, for his lack of a conscience—and therefore any physical manifestations of guilt—easily fooled the machine. And although she didn't like to acknowledge too much similarity between James and Ethan, Diana had often wondered whether James would be an equally successful subject. Even though James had thoroughly fooled Pumphrey, that didn't make him a psychopath. In his defense, Pumphrey was a new resident, completely unfamiliar with James. And probably equally unfamiliar with the deceptive nature of borderlines.

According to Pumphrey's notes, James had been "lucid" and "charmingly forthcoming." Diana had to smile at the description: James at his best—and most manipulative. James had denied any drug use, any past suicide attempts, said he was never troubled by insomnia, had no problems concentrating, and had just recently left a job he had held for almost two years. She nodded as she read Pumphrey's diagnosis: moderate reactive depression, single episode. Unfortunately for their case, it was a reasonable diagnosis, given the information he had.

The clock chimed again, and again Diana jumped. She was relieved to see that it was ten-thirty—at least the damn thing wasn't going to go off every fifteen minutes. She turned back to the records and then laughed out loud. Pumphrey had done a suicidality evaluation to determine James's chance of attempting suicide again; on the basis of the test, he had concluded that James was low-risk. She pulled the test sheet from the pile: Finally she had something they could use to show an error in Pumphrey's judgment.

She pushed away the psychiatric and psychological piles and skimmed through the rest of the reports. Her stomach churned with frustration. Valerie was right: These reports made James look good. She supposed they could use the suicidality evaluation to show how tests—and doctors—could be wrong. But she knew it was weak at best.

Diana stood up and walked into the bay. As had happened earlier, she was overcome with both exhaustion and a surprisingly strong anger. She clenched her fists and actually raised one, as if to punch it through the mullioned panes of the window. Stop it, she warned herself, pulling her arm down and opening her fingers. Now was not the time to lose it. Perhaps she could find something that would help their case—and there was always the remote possibility that Ethan actually *was* trying to help her.

Diana sat back down at the table and reached for the intake interview. James had overdosed on barbiturates and alcohol—Seconal and Scotch, to be exact. He had been brought in by ambulance, barely conscious, with a laceration to his head, apparently from a fall down the front steps of his building. His blood had been analyzed, assessed for toxicity, lethal levels established, and then his stomach had been pumped. After he was stabilized, they had run him through a battery of neurological tests.

Just as Diana was reaching for the neurological reports, Valerie walked into the room and asked if she had found anything. When Diana shook her head, Valerie sat down across from her. "What can I help you with?" she asked. "I've got about an hour."

"See if anything jumps out at you," Diana said as she pushed the intake and medical piles across the table, figuring they would be easier for Valerie to understand than the neurological. "You know your four prongs as well as I do." Valerie began to read.

When the clock chimed eleven times, Diana stiffened but didn't look up. Although she couldn't imagine finding anything helpful in the neurological reports, nonetheless she flipped through the poor-quality copies; the originals had been on flimsy yellow or pink paper, and the contrast was very bad. She squinted at the words: a CAT scan, an MRI, an EEG. All showing normal brain activity. The neurological tests had been run because James had been admitted with a head injury; there had never been any real expectation that something was wrong. Just covering their butts, she thought. Something with which she should have been a little more concerned.

Alertness assessment: normal. Orientation to time, space and person: normal. Reflex assessment: normal both knees; normal left Babinski; no Babinski contraction of all five digits of right foot, no plantar reflex. See recommendation. Diana drew in her breath and read the reflex assessment results again. *No Babinski contraction of all five digits of right foot.*

"What?" Valerie asked. "What is it? Did you find something?"

Diana didn't say anything. Her eyes flew to the bottom of the page where the recommendation was recorded. "Patient reports paralysis of five toes on right foot due to nerve damage suffered in motorcycle accident, 8/90," she read. "Seek medical records to explore history and extent of previous injury."

"What?" Valerie demanded. "What?"

Stunned, Diana simply handed the paper over to Valerie. Valerie quickly scanned the report. "I don't get it."

Diana pointed to the recommendation, her finger shaking slightly. "James couldn't have killed himself," she said, unable to believe she was actually speaking the words she heard coming from her mouth. "Or at least not the way that we thought," she added.

"He couldn't have?" Valerie frowned and read the paragraph again.

The clock ticked in the corner, horns honked from the street, voices called to one another in the corridor on the other side of the door, and Valerie held the poor copy up to the light. But Diana was alone. She was separate, apart. It was as if the noises and movements of the living were happening on another plane while she existed within this unearthly fog of incredulity. A fog that muted sound, light, time. A fog that buffered her from this overwhelming new reality.

"His right big toe was paralyzed," Valerie said, her voice slow and incredulous, as if hearing the words spoken out loud would lend them meaning.

Diana was back on the landing of James's apartment building on Anderson Street, looking down the narrow hallway at the still form that lay on the stretcher, at the two feet that dangled from the edge of the sheet. The left foot was covered with James's paint-splattered sneaker. The right one was bare. *There's powder burns on his foot,* the policeman had said. *My guess is he pulled the trigger with his toe.*

"His right toe was paralyzed," Valerie said again. Then a huge grin split her face, and she actually let out a whoop. "You're off the hook—he couldn't have committed suicide!"

Diana listened to the high whine of an approaching police siren drop as it raced passed the building, rushing to its emergency. She said nothing.

Valerie's smile disappeared into her more customary severe expression. Her eyes locked onto Diana's. "But if Hutchins didn't commit suicide . . ."

Diana nodded grimly.

"Then," Valerie said slowly, "he must have been murdered."

~ 17 ~

*T*HEN HE MUST HAVE BEEN MURDERED. VALERIE'S words seared like a neon stamp into Diana's brain. *Then he must have been murdered.* Through her protective haze, Diana could feel a fragment of dread in the center of her soul, an apprehension that she feared would soon grow and overpower her.

Valerie leaned forward in her chair. She raised her eyebrows slightly, but she said nothing.

Neither did Diana. *Then he must have been murdered.*

Finally, Valerie placed her hands on the table, fingers splayed, and began to push herself from her chair. "I'll go call Engdahl," she said.

Diana's hand flashed forward. She grabbed Valerie's wrist before she could stand. "Do you have to?"

Without taking her eyes from Diana's, Valerie sat back down in her chair. "Why shouldn't I?"

Diana released Valerie's hand and looked down at her own. She shook her head. Valerie said nothing, and Diana could almost feel the force of the challenge in Valerie's reticence. Although Diana didn't raise her head, she mumbled, "They're going to say that I did it."

Valerie was silent for yet another moment. When she

finally spoke, her words were slow and deliberate. "Why do you think that?"

"For all the reasons I was responsible for his suicide," Diana said, still looking at her hands. "But now it's even more compelling." She slowly raised her eyes and looked at Valerie. "I've got plenty of motive: five hundred thousand dollars' worth of it. And . . ." she paused as the potential horror of the situation struck her. "And I don't think I've got an alibi for that afternoon."

"Don't you think you're jumping to conclusions here?"

"But what about my journal?" Diana asked. "What if the police decide I did it to get rid of a difficult patient— or because James and I were having some kind of lovers' quarrel?"

"You're really stretching, Diana," Valerie said, smiling and shaking her head. "And if it came to it—which it won't—the rules of evidence are different in criminal law."

"What does that mean?"

"It means that although your journal might have been admissible in a civil suit, it would never be allowed in evidence in a criminal proceeding. Criminal law is much more advantageous to the defendant. And anyway—"

"But don't you see how this looks?" Diana interrupted. "I've got motive and opportunity."

"I can't believe this." Valerie threw her hands in the air in mock despair. "You've just gotten the best news you could ever get and you're talking like some character from 'Murder, She Wrote'." She shook her head. "You remind me of my Grandma Rae—always looking for the cloud in the silver lining."

"But—"

"But nothing." Valerie stabbed a fingernail at the neurological report. "This completely exonerates you in James Hutchins's death, and Engdahl will be forced to drop all the charges." She chortled happily. "There's no basis for either wrongful death or malpractice—and this undermines the hell out of the sexual abuse aspect."

"What does this have to do with sexual abuse?" Diana asked, although she felt hopeful for the first time. "Why should Jill let that go?"

"I'd guess she'd be too embarrassed not to."

"You think the press will drop it too?"

Valerie looked thoughtful for a moment. "You know what I think?"

Diana shook her head.

"I think that the same media that has had such fun crucifying you is now going to do a one-eighty." She nodded as if heartily agreeing with her own words. "Yes, I wouldn't doubt it at all. Not at all." Valerie began to chuckle. "Don't you see—the sniffers are going to feel *guilty*. They've backed the wrong side, and we'll make sure that it's thrown in their faces!"

Diana leaned forward. "We will?"

"I have a few friends in the press," Valerie said slyly. "And we've got a hell of a defamation of character suit against the *Inquirer* to add to the right-to-privacy violation."

Diana's smile was half-bitter, half-amused. "Spoken like a true lawyer."

Valerie stood. "The truth is, no matter what you might want, as an officer of the court, I'm under a legal obligation to report this information." She lifted the neurological report and let it drift slowly back to the table. "Not to mention that it's part of the official court record."

"But its importance would probably be overlooked."

Ignoring Diana's comment, Valerie picked the report up again. "I'd just love to take this over to Engdahl myself," she said, waving it in the air. Then she looked at the clock. "No time—I've got to be in court in an hour. I'll have to be satisfied hearing his voice and imagining what splattered ego looks like all over his face." She pulled open the heavy door and left the room.

Diana remained at the large table, papers scattered all

over its marble surface, listening to the happy clicking of Valerie's heels on the hardwood floor.

The weekend following Diana's discovery passed in a whirlwind of chaotic emotion. One moment she soared from her public vindication, and the next she plummeted from the suspicion and innuendo. She was buffeted and bloodied by the storm of media conjecture. SEX DOC INNOCENT, the *Inquirer* headline screamed in a double-edged exoneration the morning after the suit was dismissed. HUTCHINS MURDER INVESTIGATION OPENED, declared the *Globe*.

Valerie had been right in her prediction that Jill would drop all the charges. With the evidence that James couldn't have committed suicide, it was clear that the wrongful death and malpractice suits were moot, and apparently Engdahl felt that without Diana's journal, even his sexual abuse case was too weak to prosecute.

Unfortunately, Valerie's prophecy of the press's one-eighty wasn't quite so accurate. Although the *Globe* ran an editorial exploring the role of the media in her persecution, comparing it to the media's mishandling of the Carol Dimaiti Stuart fiasco—when Boston police had harassed and arrested a black man for the murder of a white pregnant woman, only to discover that her husband was guilty—much of the coverage was negative. With the lurid fascination of a bypasser at a highway accident scene, Diana followed the talk shows and tabloids as they debated the various possibilities of who might be charged with murder—she, Jill, or even Ethan, who became a suspect when the press got hold of two police reports of Ethan and James fighting in a Cambridge bar. Still, most people seemed to think it would be Diana who would be charged. Diana had wished for an end to the agony of the civil suit; now she understood the full meaning of the old saying: "Be careful what you wish for."

Despite the suspicion about her, which Diana felt like a binding cocoon, friends and colleagues called to congratulate her, and Ticknor asked her to complete the semester. Her sister-in-law Martha actually apologized for worrying about Paul instead of Diana, and her mother was exuberant, claiming to have never doubted for a moment that Diana would be cleared. On Sunday afternoon, when she stopped for gas, the attendant told her he had known all along that it wasn't her fault. Although Craig didn't get his Central Artery project back, his colleagues restored him to full-member status in their water-cooler conversations. And he began singing in the shower again.

Diana nodded and smiled and graciously accepted everyone's good wishes, as well as Ticknor's offer. But despite what looked from the outside to be a change in fortune, Diana was wary of too much celebration. For until she knew she wasn't a murder suspect, it all meant nothing.

The police came first thing Monday morning, when she fortunately had no patients scheduled. And when the bell rang, Diana knew from the insistent pressure who would be waiting on the other side of the door. Her feet were heavy on the stairs.

Two unsmiling men dressed in street clothes stood on the stoop. They flashed their badges simultaneously, almost as if they had been choreographed, and asked to come in. She ushered them up to the great room, offered them coffee and went down to the kitchen to call Valerie.

Although Valerie didn't do criminal work, she had promised Diana that she would sit with her through this first interview to determine if a criminal lawyer was necessary. Valerie said she would be there within the hour. "Don't say a word," she directed Diana. "Not a single word." Diana was stunned by Valerie's final instruction: "If they want to take you down to the station, call me back and I'll meet you there."

After canceling her ten and eleven o'clock patients, Diana dragged herself back upstairs, straining to appear as normal and calm as she could, trying to assure herself that there was little chance they would arrest her.

"My lawyer says she can't be here for at least an hour. Would you prefer to wait, or to come back later?"

They preferred to wait, and Diana spent what turned into an extremely uncomfortable hour and a half, repeating that she did not want to say anything without her attorney present. Neither man ever smiled, or registered any emotion whatsoever, as they patiently asked question after unanswered question. Although this was clearly getting them nowhere, neither appeared the least bit perturbed.

When Valerie finally arrived, the police obtained little more information than they had gleaned from Diana's nonanswers. "My client often works alone," Valerie said in response to their request for verification of Diana's whereabouts on the afternoon of the murder. "It's the nature of her profession," she added, her voice haughty and more than a little condescending. "She often sets her machine to screen her calls so that she can pursue her scientific investigations without interruption." Valerie smiled and looked over at Diana for confirmation.

Diana nodded, unable to speak. She was sure Valerie was going to anger the detectives with her arrogance, and that the two men would soon jump up, snap handcuffs on her wrists, and drag her off to jail.

But they did no such thing. Instead they wrote down everything Valerie said. Finally, once again in unison, they flipped their notebooks shut and stood up. One even smiled as he told Diana to call and leave a number where she could be reached if she was going to be away from home for more than a day.

"Nothing," Valerie said as she flew out the door, already late for her next meeting. "Jack-shit," she called over her shoulder cheerfully. "They've got jack-shit." She promised to phone Diana later in the afternoon.

Diana spent the remainder of the morning trying to work on her research project, but ended up spending most of her time pacing through the house. Murder. She was a suspect in a murder investigation. She could really be arrested. She could go to prison. For life. It was small consolation that Massachusetts had no death penalty.

She had been to prison once, during a field trip for a criminology course she had taken in graduate school. A "correctional facility," they had called it. But no matter what name they used, it was still a prison: a haphazard arrangement of concrete and cinderblock buildings completely encircled by a double row of tall barricades topped by spiral loops of barbed wire. Lookout towers stood like castle turrets at the four corners. A large German shepherd had come up and nuzzled her hand while they were waiting for the group to assemble. As she bent to pet the animal, its trainer told her the dog had once ripped a man's leg to the bone.

But the inside of the prison was the worst. Claustrophobic, windowless cells originally planned for one inmate were crammed with two or three, sometimes four, cots. The mattresses were thin and worn and a single toilet stood along the back wall of each cell—most often, the toilet had no seat. Two stories of cells lined a large open "rec room" where a few picnic tables and pieces of broken exercise equipment sat amid a wide expanse of green linoleum. It smelled of Lysol.

From the one-way window of the guardpost high above the rec room, they had watched the prisoners loitering around the tables in their ill-fitting uniforms. Their shirts and pants were of a coarse, scratchy-looking fabric dyed white, gray, orange, or red. "Middlesex Correctional Facility" was stenciled in large black letters on their backs. The sheriff giving the tour explained that the brighter the color, the more serious the crime. "Murderers and rapists wear red."

When the horn blew its wrenching minor-chord blast, all the inmates slowly rose from their places at the tables, or on the floor, or leaning against the walls, and trudged to their cells. The horn blew again, and the cell doors all clanged shut.

Diana shook her head and forced herself to sit down at her desk. She opened the thick stack of computer printouts that had been gathering dust while she concentrated on her case for Valerie, hoping to lose herself in the statistics she had run before James had died. But the numbers all swam before her eyes, and her brain refused to function. *Murder. Suspect. Prison.*

Forcing herself to concentrate on the data, Diana flipped quickly through the pages. Then she slowed down to scrutinize the individual numbers, caught by the results despite her concerns. It really was unbelievable how well her theory was holding. At least half of the ANOVAs were statistically significant and her discriminant function model was looking very promising; three variables were well over 1.0 and significantly contributed to the amount of change in lambda.

Her data was clearly contradicting the traditional wisdom, established by Adrian Arnold, that borderline personality disorders were caused by a disturbed early maternal relationship. Diana tapped the printouts with her pencil. None of her maternal variables were showing any statistical significance at all. It was amazing how powerfully linked childhood trauma was to a person's chances of developing a borderline disorder. Regardless of age, sex, or race. And the more chronic and horrific the traumas, the stronger the relationship. That sure explained Sandy. James too. *Murder. Suspect. Prison.* She pushed herself up from the chair and resumed her pacing.

When her borderline group arrived for their weekly session, Diana put aside her statistics, happy for the distraction. But she soon found that neither Sandy's loneliness, nor Terri's inability to get herself to ride the subway, nor Bruce's nightmare of being lost in a hospital with no exit doors, could keep her from her own worries. *Murder. Suspect. Prison.* She forced herself to focus on Sandy's face, to look Bruce directly in the eye, to listen to Terri with her entire body. But the concentration just wasn't there.

Finally the hour was over and they left. Soon after, Valerie called. She told Diana that her partner Mitch Calahane, the criminal lawyer to whom she wanted to refer Diana, had gotten the "courthouse gab" on the Hutchins case. "They have even less than I thought," she said. "Less than jackshit. Three suspects—but nothing on any of you."

"So why did the police act like they knew I was guilty?"

"Because it's their job to make people nervous," Valerie said. "But what's really interesting here is that it seems your old nemesis—and co-suspect—Jill Hutchins is saving your skin."

"Jill is saving *my* skin?"

"Well, not on purpose," Valerie said. "And she's saving her own as well as that other guy's—but, either way, it seems that she destroyed all the evidence. And without evidence, it's just about impossible for the prosecution to sustain its burden in a criminal suit—where burden of proof already favors the defendant."

Valerie went on to tell Diana that after the funeral, Jill had had James's body cremated and scattered his ashes off the coast of Provincetown. Jill also sold the shotgun—now the murder weapon—and had the apartment thoroughly cleaned. Then she subleased it to a couple of college students, omitting the grisly details of what had happened to its last occupant.

Valerie explained that at the time of the murder, no hair, no fibers, no blood or fingerprints had been collected. No witnesses had been questioned or crime lab photos taken. Although technically every death was supposed to be considered a homicide—and every crime scene treated as such—Jill's positive identification of the body, combined with James's history of suicide attempts, had been more than enough for an overworked police force to step out of the case. "And now the trail's stone cold," Valerie chortled. "Or, more accurately, there's no trail at all."

Diana exhaled the breath she wasn't aware she had been holding. "So I'm in the clear?"

"Well," Valerie said slowly. "Circumstantial cases have been built and successfully prosecuted with less physical evidence, and I would recommend retaining Mitch. But if pushed, I'd have to say that you're in pretty good shape."

"So why do I need a criminal lawyer?" Diana demanded.

"It's always best to be prepared," Valerie said in a very lawyerlike manner.

But when Diana heard Calahane's retainer for a homicide case was fifty thousand dollars, she shook her head. "It's impossible," she said. "Out of the question."

Valerie hesitated. "It's not really a good idea to go into this alone. And Mitch is worth every penny—he's the best."

"Why can't I just keep paying you at your hourly rate?"

"This isn't my area," Valerie protested. "I know very little about criminal law. The only reason I'm even doing this is because I'm working on your suit against the *Inquirer*. I'm out of my league here. You'd be doing yourself a grave disservice—"

"But you think I *could* get away without him for now?" Diana interrupted. "Given all this lack of physical evidence business?"

"I suppose so—although, as your lawyer, I would be remiss in advising it."

"Well, there's really no choice here," Diana said with more confidence than she felt. "Let's leave things the way they are and see how they play themselves out."

~ 18 ~

$\mathcal{D}$IANA REACHED UNDER HER DESK AND RIPPED THE socks from her feet. Then she unfastened another button on her blouse. Although Indian summer was not an uncommon phenomenon in Boston, it usually hit in late October—often the day after Diana had dragged her shorts and bathing suits to the basement. It didn't usually waft through the week before Thanksgiving. And it was never this warm. Diana lifted the window, and balmy air flowed into the office. This was nuts even for New England. It had to be seventy degrees.

She had just returned from school, having taught her first class since her reinstatement. The class had gone fine, although no one showed up for her office hours. Leaving the department a bit early, she had come home and run some data through her computer in an attempt to make up for the time she had lost on her research project.

Anxious to see the results, Diana read each chart, her head twisted sideways, as the paper chugged out of the printer. Amazing, she thought as she burst the pages. These numbers were even stronger than the earlier ones had been. The new cases she had just added to her database increased the support for her theory beyond her wildest expectations.

She dropped into the chair. According to the data in front of her, borderline personality disorders did not arise from disturbed mothering before age two, as Adrian Arnold and company maintained. Her research showed that a major traumatic event—usually abuse, often sexual, and involving a trusted family member—at a much later age was correlated with borderline symptomology. The data also indicated that the condition itself was much more similar to posttraumatic stress disorder than to the other severe personality disorders.

Her heart racing, Diana tapped her pen on the printouts. This was major league stuff. She checked through the numbers one more time and smiled. Her methodology was tight, her sample size more than adequate, and the numbers were indeed very strong. There was more than enough here for publication. She would try *Abnormal Psychology* first. Wouldn't Adrian just die?

She looked back down at her data. This wasn't just about getting published in a prestigious journal or besting Adrian Arnold—although she had to admit it *was* about those things too. The real importance of these data was their implication for treatment. For, as long as borderline personality disorders were seen as being caused by ambivalent mothers or some kind of interference in the infant-mother bonding process, then those suffering from them were, for all intents and purposes, incurable. On the other hand, if it was a variation of posttraumatic stress, then many types of therapy, including short-term behavioral techniques—could effect a cure.

Diana once again saw James's lifeless body on the stretcher in his living room. She heard the policeman's words: *His head's pretty much gone.* If only she had been smarter. Better. If only she could have held on to him, and to herself, just a little bit longer. She could taste the metallic tang of her failure. And of her guilt.

She remembered the afternoon she had discovered her briefcase missing from her office. "I don't know who might have taken it," she had told James over the phone. "I just wanted to let you know it was missing—and that if it happened to show up anytime soon, no questions would be asked." One hour later James had knocked on the door and handed her the briefcase, furious with her for thinking him capable of such deception and thievery. He was so confused, so conflicted: One part of him tried to do the right thing, while the other part of him just couldn't pull it off.

"No," she said out loud as she pushed away the images and breathed in the preposterous, but delicious, spring-scented air. It was over. No purpose could be served by obsessing. Nothing could be changed. Think of the data, she directed herself. Think of the weather. They were harbingers of her new fate, omens that all of this awfulness was really behind her.

Still, it was difficult for her to dispel James's ghost. He wouldn't go away as easily, or as quickly, as she would have liked. But finally her optimism won, and Diana started to allow herself to think that the worst just might be behind her. That she really might be free of James Hutchins at last.

The phone rang at her elbow and, in a response reflecting her new state of mind, Diana picked up the receiver without screening the call through her answering machine.

"Just wanted to fill you in on the libel suit," Valerie's voice boomed through the receiver. "This could be lucrative as hell. I've done a little research and there's no doubt: We've got a clear case of invasion of privacy, defamation of character, and libel. We might even go for libel directly causing others to slander, although that one's a long shot." Valerie paused. "But with or without the slander, I'd go for a million. Maybe one and a half."

"One and a half million dollars?" Diana was incredulous.

"The *Inquirer*'s got the money. And you deserve compensation. You went through severe emotional trauma. And incontestable damage was done to your professional reputation and earning power."

"One and a half million dollars?" Diana asked again, simultaneously exhilarated and disgusted by the greed and vindictiveness that jolted through her.

"Gotcha!"

Diana didn't say anything as visions of a new car—maybe even two—a security system, and a college education for the baby flew across her mind. Not to mention a tasteful office in the Prudential Tower with "Frey and Associates" on a brass nameplate next to the door.

"It's a strong case," Valerie was saying. "But I've got to be honest with you: It could be years before any award is made—and what we ask for may not be what we get. The thing you've got to remember is that it's not the actual dollar amount that's important—it's getting the *Inquirer* that counts."

Diana shook her head, wondering how a lawyer could possibly make that statement with a straight face. She also wondered if they would really "get" anybody. Would their efforts—and her public humiliation—produce retaliation against any of the people who were actually responsible for her trauma? the *Inquirer* would most likely just shrug it off, chalking the whole thing up to the cost of doing business, letting their insurance company write out a fat check. "What do you think would be the actual amount?" she finally asked.

"Impossible to say."

"Half?" Diana pressed.

"Look," Valerie said. "I got into trouble promising you things I couldn't deliver before, so I'm not going to fall into that trap again. But I repeat, it's a strong case."

"And what about you? How do you get paid?"

"One-third of the award," Valerie answered quickly.

Diana now saw a much smaller car, a less sophisticated security system, and only a couple of years of college tuition in the bank. "If this really is over," she said slowly, "all I want to do is forget about the whole thing and get on with my life."

"After a couple of days, the publicity from this new suit would die down," Valerie continued. "It wouldn't be like the others. You're suing a newspaper—not being tried for murder."

Murder. The word reverberated through Diana's brain. She could have been tried for murder. She could be wearing one of those coarse, scratchy red uniforms and sleeping with a bunch of angry women in a claustrophobic cell. No, she thought, there was a lesson here. She shouldn't tempt the fates. She had just won big. Now was the time to cash in her chips and go home.

As if reading Diana's mind, Valerie made a last stab. "Don't you think you should discuss this with Craig before making a final decision? You told me the other day he was pretty hot on the idea of suing the *Inquirer*. Better check and make sure—he might think it's well worth whatever minor intrusion it might create in your lives."

Diana knew Craig was more than angry enough with the *Inquirer* to put up with a "minor intrusion." But she also knew he would back her decision one hundred percent. "No," she said with conviction. "I just don't have the stomach for it."

"How about letting me continue for a little while longer?" Valerie asked. "See what I can come up with that might change your mind? Can't do any harm—and it won't cost you a thing," she added.

Unable to withstand Valerie's persistence, Diana said, "All right, all right. But I'm not making any promises."

"None expected," Valerie agreed. "I have something else to tell you."

"What's up?" Diana's heart did a nosedive and her body stiffened.

"Mitch's got some more courthouse gab for you."

"What?" Diana demanded, sitting ramrod straight.

"He said that according to his sources on the police department, the Hutchins case is starting to look like a shitcan."

"A shitcan?"

"Police slang for 'homicide not likely to be solved.' "

"Really?" Diana's heart pounded in relief. She slumped into the chair.

"Apparently," Valerie continued, "they haven't been able to confirm Jill Hutchins's alibi either. And the other guy—your patient?"

"Ethan Kruse."

"Yeah. Well, they still can't seem to find him—so he's got no alibi whatsoever."

"So we're all equal?" Diana asked.

"You're all nothing—three suspects with no alibis in a case with no evidence doesn't add up to much. Although they apparently did discover that your Mr. Kruse has got quite a long rap sheet."

"That's no surprise." Diana knew of a few of Ethan's encounters with the police, but knowing what Ethan was capable of, she assumed she only had a small piece of the picture.

"Mitch didn't give me any details, but the important thing is that it looks like you really are in the clear on this one."

"I think I'm finally starting to believe that."

"Good," Valerie said. "It's about time things began to turn around for you."

"Thanks." Diana was caught off-guard by the warmth in Valerie's voice. "Thanks for everything."

"All in a day's work," Valerie said gruffly. "I'll be in touch." Then she hung up.

Diana smiled as she replaced the phone in the cradle.

Less than an hour later, after Diana had only begun to digest her statistics, she heard Craig's key twist in the lock. She jumped from her chair and ran up the stairs. Something was wrong. Craig never came home from work in the middle of the day. But there he was, smiling and holding out a bouquet of carnations.

Slightly breathless, she asked, "What's going on?"

"Smelling the coffee, or the roses, or the carnations—
or whatever," he said, coming over and putting his arms
around her. "Don't you think we deserve it?" He kissed her
before she could answer his question.

"Is this spring fever in November?" she finally asked,
pulling away and smiling up at him. "Are you playing
hooky?"

He nodded, and then his expression sobered. "Sort of. I
just wanted to be with you. To enjoy this day. To celebrate
a little for how everything has turned out."

And so they did. Most of Diana's patients hadn't yet
returned, so her afternoon was open. She didn't even go
back down to her office, she just grabbed her jacket, and
they headed outside.

Craig loved walking through the city as much as she did,
and they meandered along the Christian Science mall while
Diana chattered about her astonishing research results, the
libel suit Valerie wouldn't let go of, and Valerie's report of
Mitch Calahane's shitcan. They had lunch at the delicious-
ly expensive Cafe Budapest—the same restaurant where
they had gone, stunned and starry-eyed, the night they had
become engaged—and toasted their turn of fortune.

Then, hand in hand, they walked along the brick side-
walks of Marlborough Street talking about Craig's latest
plan for the fantasy mural in the nursery. "It's going to go
across all four walls," he explained. "A complete circle of
fairy tale and Disney characters—we'll forget the hobbits.
I've even thrown in a few inventions of my own." They discussed cribs and the toy box Craig was going to build, and
whether, now that Diana's practice was picking up again,
they might be able to afford to have someone come in and
take care of the baby, rather than putting her in day care.

The soft air flowed around them like a mother's caress,
all the sweeter for its unexpectedness and the knowledge
that it would soon be gone. Other couples strolled as they
did, and they smiled at each other, happy co-conspirators,

stealing a May afternoon to be relished in late November.

Dusk came too early, as it does on the edge of winter, and Diana and Craig headed toward home, full of themselves and bittersweet nostalgia for the day not yet gone. But when they turned the corner onto St. Stephen Street, they came to a simultaneous stop.

A police cruiser was parked in front of their house.

~ 19 ~

IANA WATCHED IN HORROR AS A FAMILIAR BEAN-pole of a man, sweating slightly from the warmth of his wool sport jacket, climbed from the black-and-white police car. He unfolded himself to well over six feet and stepped to the bottom of their front stoop. Pressing a handkerchief to his forehead, Herb Levine turned and looked at them expectantly.

Diana swayed for a moment, and Craig grabbed her arm. She closed her eyes, feeling as if a steel door had slammed shut behind her, separating her from the world as it had existed just a moment before and thrusting her into a new, and unwelcome, reality. "Valerie said not to say anything without her," she whispered to Craig.

"Don't panic," he ordered. "Maybe it's nothing. Lift up your head and look him right in the eye." He gripped her elbow more tightly, and they walked toward the house. "Don't make it seem like you have anything to hide," he said out of the corner of his mouth.

"Nice to see you again, Dr. Marcus," Levine said, his smile pleasant. He nodded to Craig. "Mr. Marcus."

"Frey," Craig said. "My name is Craig Frey."

"I'm Detective Levine. Herb Levine." He shook Craig's

hand and then pulled a badge from his pocket. "Homicide." He turned back to Diana, his smile even wider. "Sorry I wasn't more help with your journal."

Rooted to the sidewalk, Diana swallowed hard and stared at the detective. She didn't seem to be able to get her brain to work. Her synapses refused to fire, and she felt incapable of either speaking or moving.

"What can we do for you, Detective?" Craig asked.

"I came for your wife's help," he said, then turned to Diana. He glanced down at her stomach and smiled. "Please don't be upset, Dr. Marcus—I just need some psychological advice. Can you spare a few minutes for me to pick your brain, or should I come back some other time?"

Craig smiled at Diana and nodded. "Please," he said, raising his keys and motioning the policeman up the stairs. Craig gave Diana's arm a gentle tug and propelled her forward.

After Levine refused Craig's offer of coffee, but gratefully handed over his jacket, the two men climbed up toward the great room. Diana hung behind to call Valerie, but Craig shook his head at her. She hesitated, then slowly followed, knowing that Craig was right about not looking guilty, but nonetheless feeling vulnerable without the knowledge Valerie was on her way.

Herb Levine ducked as he walked through the doorway, then settled himself comfortably into the leather chair. Diana and Craig perched on the edge of the couch. Levine didn't say a word. He just crossed his long legs and looked around as if he were a dinner guest waiting to be served cocktails and hors d'oeuvres. Diana and Craig shifted in their seats. Diana leaned forward and rearranged the magazines that littered the coffee table. Still the policeman said nothing.

Craig cleared his throat. "So how can we help you, Detective?" he asked again.

"Well, as I said, it's really your wife's help I need. On the Hutchins case." He leaned toward Diana. "It's about

Ethan Kruse. I understand he's also a patient of yours?"

Diana hesitated. Although his words were reassuring, she still wished that Valerie was coming.

"We were under the impression that this case was going to be closed," Craig said before Diana could answer the policeman's question.

"The Hutchins case?" Levine asked, his gray eyebrows pulling upward. "Unsolved homicides are never closed. There's no statute of limitations on murder," he added, smiling pleasantly at Diana.

Diana knew she should hold Levine's eye, that to look down would imply guilt. But she was afraid he would see the reflection of the terror his words had sparked in her. She leaned over and pulled up her sock.

"We heard it was a—a 'shitcan,' " Craig said, then barked a false-sounding chuckle.

Levine didn't seem to notice that Craig's chuckle wasn't real, and he began to laugh also, a huge belly laugh that lit up his face. He was obviously amused by some private joke that Diana and Craig were not privy to. A joke Diana worried was at their expense.

She looked over at Craig; he shrugged his shoulders and laughed along with Levine. As Diana tried to smile, she had the fleeting and irrelevant thought that Herb Levine must be a fun guy at a party.

"A shitcan!" Levine finally gasped, blotting his eyes with the sleeve of his shirt. "A shitcan!"

"But it isn't?" Craig asked.

"I sure as hell hope not," Levine answered, still chortling. "Gregg. Who I think you met?" He looked at Diana questioningly.

She returned his gaze, confused.

"Detective Gregg," he repeated patiently, still smiling slightly. 'Didn't he stop by to talk to you the other day?"

Diana nodded slowly, a muddled memory emerging that one of the detectives she had spoken with had a name that started with "G."

Levine smiled sympathetically. "When my wife was pregnant, she forgot everything. 'Prego-amnesia,' she called it."

Diana's answering smile was weak.

"Anyway," Levine continued conversationally, "Gregg moved over to Special Investigations, and Hutchins got added to my caseload." He paused and glanced from Diana to Craig and then slowly back to Diana. Suddenly he didn't look like such a fun party guest after all. "I don't believe in shitcans."

Diana placed both palms protectively over her stomach. "Of course not," she finally managed to say. "Of course not."

Levine's eyes followed Diana's movements, and when he looked back at her, his expression was gentler. "So do you have any idea where Ethan Kruse might be, Dr. Marcus?"

She shook her head and explained to him about Ethan's frequent disappearances and apologized for not being able to give him more information due to doctor-patient confidentiality.

He nodded and wrote the few things she said in his notebook. When she had told him all that she legally could—which wasn't much—he stood. "Just one more thing," he said. "What kind of printer do you own, Dr. Marcus?"

"Printer?" Diana asked, standing also.

"Don't you use a computer in your work?" Levine's voice was patient. "I thought I remembered seeing one the last time I was here."

"Oh, my printer," Diana exclaimed. "Yes, of course I have a printer."

"And exactly what kind of printer is it?"

"It's a—a—" She turned and looked to Craig for help, her brain locking up.

"An NEC Pinwriter," Craig said quickly, throwing an arm around her shoulders. "Either a P6 or P7—it's right downstairs. Why?"

"Is it one of those lasers?" Levine asked, ignoring Craig's

question. "Or . . ." He paused and flipped a couple of pages in his notebook. "Is it a dot matrix?"

"Dot matrix," Diana said. "But it has a very good letter-quality setting," she added foolishly.

Levine nodded. "Hutchins had a laser."

"What does that mean?" Craig demanded, shoving Levine's jacket at him.

The detective took his jacket and shrugged nonchalantly. "Probably nothing. It's just that Hutchins's sister received a suicide note that was printed on a dot matrix printer and, according to her, he had one of those newfangled lasers—" He checked his notes again. "Hewlett Packard. She showed it to me."

"She didn't save her brother's body or the gun that killed him," Craig said, his tone thick with disgust, "but she saved his printer." He looked piercingly at Levine. "Seems kind of suspicious, don't you think?"

The detective nodded. "Yes, it does." Then he turned to Diana. "You wouldn't mind going downstairs and printing a page or two off your printer for me, would you?"

"I'm—I'm sorry," she said slowly. "But my lawyer told me to check everything with her first."

Levine nodded and smiled. "That's fine. Fine. I didn't come here for that anyway." He held his hands up. "No problem. I can get a warrant if it turns out to be important."

Diana nodded and led him out of the room.

"Did James Hutchins ever mention his landlady—a Mrs. Manfredi?" Levine asked as he ducked through the great room doorway.

Diana stopped on the landing. "Just that he helped her out sometimes—shoveling snow, taking in the garbage cans, that kind of thing."

"Seems that she thinks she remembers hearing footsteps right after the shooting," Levine said. "Running down the stairs. She says she's sure they were a woman's footsteps. Says she knows they weren't a man's. But . . ." He paused and looked at Diana. "Frankly, Doctor, she just doesn't seem all there, if you know what I mean. So I was just wondering if you knew anything about her. Like if you think I should take her seriously?"

"But the murder was over a month ago," Craig said, stepping between Diana and Levine. "How come she's just reporting this now?"

Herb Levine looked a bit sheepish and smiled. "Because we never asked her before."

"If she really had heard something, don't you think she would have told you without anyone having to ask?" Craig persisted. "And isn't almost five weeks an awfully long time for a memory to remain credible?"

Levine nodded seriously, as if Craig's suppositions were actually causing him to consider the facts in a new light. Then he turned back to Diana. "You told Gregg and Kimberle you were working in your home office at the time of the murder?"

"Yes," she croaked, then cleared her throat and tried again. "Yes," she said more clearly. "We went through this whole thing with my lawyer."

"But no one can verify that claim?"

"My wife works alone a lot of the time," Craig answered for Diana. "It's the nature of her job."

"I appreciate that, Mr. Marcus—"

"Frey."

"Mr. Frey," Levine corrected. "It's just rather unfortunate in this particular situation."

"But we understand that neither Jill Hutchins nor Ethan Kruse have alibis for that afternoon either," Craig said.

Levine's eyebrows shot up again and he looked closely at both of them. "That was true a few days ago," he said slowly.

Diana gripped the banister, unable to ask the question that she needed to have answered.

"But it's not true today?" Craig asked for her.

Levine shrugged and began to walk down the stairs. "And

what about that phone call you told Gregg and Kimberle about?" he asked, turning to look eyeball-to-eyeball with Diana, who was a couple of stairs above him. "The call you claim told you that James had killed himself? The anonymous voice that ordered you to go to his apartment?"

Diana gripped the railing more tightly and said nothing. She too had wondered about that phone call: Who had known to call her, and why? Diana followed Levine down the stairs, placing each foot carefully on the tread in front of her, afraid if she didn't concentrate on every movement, her addled brain would fail her and she would lose her balance and topple right into the detective. "I'm sorry," she finally said as they stepped into the foyer. "I really feel that I shouldn't answer any more questions without my attorney present."

Again, Levine held up his hands. "No problem." But when Craig opened the door, Levine pulled out his awful notebook again. "Two years ago this coming February," he said to Diana, "Hutchins took you to the hospital. Why was that?"

As Diana began to recite her not-without-my-attorney-present line, Craig walked over to where she stood and threw his arm across her shoulders again. He told Levine the entire ectopic pregnancy story, adding that he was indebted to James for his clearheadedness during the incident.

Levine nodded to Craig, appearing truly thankful for the information. Then he turned to Diana again. "Isn't it unusual for a therapist and her patient to eat lunch together—as you and James Hutchins are reported to have done in the Public Gardens during the summer of that year?"

"What?" Craig demanded, dropping his arm from Diana's shoulder.

"Lunch at the Public Gardens," Levine repeated, although neither Diana nor Craig seemed to hear him. For they were carrying on a silent conversation: Diana begging Craig to understand and Craig challenging her to come up with an explanation he could accept.

"We just ran into each other," Diana stammered in answer to both Levine and Craig. "It—it was pure coincidence." When the men just stared at her, obviously doubtful, she launched into a long-winded, bumbling explanation of how she and James had just happened to be at the Boston Public Library the same morning—she to research a new grant application, and he to get information on competing mutual funds for his boss. How stuffy and airless it had been inside the library. How the sun had flickered through the fair weather clouds and the breeze had been coming in off the ocean. How they had grabbed a couple of sandwiches from a kiosk in Copley Square and wandered over to the Public Gardens to eat their lunch in the shade of a huge oak tree. "It was harmless," she finished lamely, her face hot with shame at being caught in a breach of professionalism. "Completely harmless . . ."

"I'm sure that it was," Levine said, snapping his notebook shut and putting it in his pocket. He smiled pleasantly as he headed down the steps. When he reached the sidewalk he turned and waved. "And I'm sure I'll be in touch soon."

As Diana closed the door behind the detective, sweat ran down between her breasts, and she knew if she didn't sit down fast, she was going to faint. She closed her eyes for a moment and pressed her hot cheek to the cool plaster wall. When she opened them again, Craig was staring at her. "It—it really wasn't any big deal," she stammered, reaching her hand out to him.

"Probably not," he said, stepping away from her and pulling the door open. "I'm going for a walk."

It was almost midnight when Craig finally returned. He walked into the bedroom and sat on the edge of the bed. "Diana?"

"I want to explain—" Diana began, sitting up and pulling the blanket around her.

"I think we need to hire that criminal lawyer," he said as if she hadn't spoken. "Valerie's partner."

Diana touched his hand. "He needs fifty thousand dollars up front—we don't have that kind of money."

"We'll borrow against the five hundred grand you're going to get from James's estate."

"The bank won't—"

"Why not?" he interrupted, moving his hand away from hers. "Valerie said we should get the money within a few months—that seems like pretty sound collateral to me."

Diana fingered the edge of the sheet, letting her hair obscure her face.

"We'll invest what's left in your charity trust, if that's what you're so worried about—fifty thousand more or less isn't going to make that big a difference," he said. "This is an emergency."

"You don't understand," Diana whispered, still keeping her eyes lowered.

"I understand plenty."

"No, you don't," she said, finally looking at him. "You can't inherit money from someone you're accused of murdering."

Craig stood abruptly. "Then we'll work out some kind of a deal. Call Valerie. They're lawyers—they'll come up with something." Towering over her, fists clenched by his side, Craig threw a long, menacing shadow across the bed. "We have the baby to think of," he said calmly, his composure more terrifying to Diana than the most ferocious anger. "I won't allow her to be hurt by all this." Suddenly he slammed a fist into his palm. The sound cracked like a whip through the nighttime stillness; Diana's body involuntary jerked. "I won't allow it," Craig repeated, his voice still soft and even.

Diana placed her hands on her stomach and took a deep breath. "I didn't kill him," she said quietly, straining to match Craig's calm, although her heart was pounding and her stomach felt as if it were being squeezed by iron fists.

"Of course you didn't," he snapped. "I might not be sure of much anymore, but I'm still pretty damn sure you couldn't blow a man's brains out with a shotgun."

She looked up at Craig in relief, but his gaze was focused on the wall over her head. "I'll call Valerie first thing in the morning," she promised, reaching over to touch his arm.

"And find out what you have to do to get that fucking detective off our backs," Craig ordered, shaking off her hand. Then he turned and walked from the bedroom.

~ 20 ~

DIANA SPENT A FITFUL NIGHT, TOSSING BETWEEN
wakefulness and flickering dreams. She raced down a long
hall to an arched doorway behind which she knew lay safety. But when she reached it, she found herself facing a
towering blank wall—the door had shrunk into a miniature
of itself, barely big enough to slide her fist through. In the
midst of a loud and crowded party, she offered her brother
Scott and Detective Levine cocktails off a round silver tray,
but they were laughing so hard, they were unable to grasp
the drinks that kept slipping through their fingers. And then
right after dawn, Diana dreamed she was a little girl, standing at the water's edge on a late summer afternoon. Her
mother was singing and wrapping her in an oversized tow-
el, hugging her and nuzzling her neck as she rubbed the
water and sand from Diana's small body.

When Diana woke, there were tears in her eyes. To be
that little girl again. To start over. To have the chance not
to make mistakes. An impossible, unattainable, and foolish
wish, she chastised herself, reaching out to touch the cool
sheet where Craig should have been sleeping. But he wasn't
there, and the stillness of the house told her he had already
left for the day.

Slowly she pulled herself into a sitting position. She paused for a moment at the edge of the bed and pressed her palms to her stomach, hoping to feel the butterfly movement of a tiny foot. But there was nothing.

Valerie was very annoyed. "You better come up with the cash to retain Mitch Calahane," she snapped after Diana described Levine's visit. "Either that, or come up with enough sense not to answer any questions—or at least, to call me before you do. The cop's got no case," she added. "He's fishing, and you're biting at his bait like some pea-brained salmon."

Diana murmured apologies as Valerie ranted on. Finally, when Valerie calmed down, Diana said, "Look, we don't have fifty thousand dollars, you know that. We can't hire Calahane straight out, but I can't just sit here either. I won't," Diana declared. "There's got to be something else we can do. Some way that I can exonerate myself without spending all that money."

"I understand your position," Valerie said. "But I still think Mitch's your best bet."

Diana hesitated, not knowing what to say. She was no good at this; she always paid too much for cars and had been at a complete loss bargaining in Mexico. "Is, ah, is there any other way we could possibly pay for his services? On some kind of piecemeal basis?"

Valerie hesitated. "You know," she finally said, a sly tone to her voice, "there just might be a way to finagle this for you."

Diana pressed the phone tighter to her ear. "Oh?"

Valerie was silent for a few moments, then she said, "Perhaps something involving the *Inquirer* suit . . . Some kind of swap for straight hourly rates . . ."

Diana could almost hear Valerie weighing the firm's one-third of the *Inquirer* award versus what they might lose by not making Diana pay Calahane's retainer. Obviously, Valerie thought the *Inquirer* was a good bet.

"The reason for the large retainer on a murder case is that the legal fees can run well over six figures. Sometimes even seven," Valerie was saying slowly, obviously thinking out loud. "And often defendants don't have that kind of cash."

"And if they're convicted," Diana said dryly, "you might never get paid."

"But, as it's highly unlikely this case will ever go to trial," Valerie continued, ignoring Diana's remark, "the firm might be willing to take the risk. And the truth is, Mitch's a pretty good detective. He's got quite a knack for getting people to talk—I swear he could get a Mafia hit man to sing on his charm alone." The clicking of computer keys came over the line. "I'd have to check it out with a few of my partners—and with Mitch, of course," Valerie finally said. "But I think that maybe we can put something together for you."

"As long as I agree to going ahead with the *Inquirer* suit?"

"Of course," Valerie said sweetly.

At four o'clock that afternoon Diana found herself seated in the mahogany wainscoted reception room of Bogdanow, Federgreen, Starr, and Calahane, antique brass sconces fighting off the encroaching dusk with their soft rose-hued light. The reception area had been carved out of the same ballroom as the conference room where she had gone through James's Mass General records, the room where she had turned her life in a new direction—although it was far from clear whether the new direction was an improvement over the old. Today, as she stared through the mullioned panes at the Public Gardens, at the paper cups and used napkins caught between the naked branches of the scraggly bushes, Diana avoided looking at the oak tree.

"Here she is," Valerie's voice boomed as she strode across the plush carpet. Mitch Calahane, who resembled a good-natured bear with his thick mane of white hair and his rumpled suit, ambled in behind her. "Diana Marcus," Valerie said, waving at them as they shook hands. "Mitch Calahane."

Mitch's handshake was as substantial as he was, and his smile lit up his face in a way that made Diana understand how he got all the "courtroom gab." It wasn't that he was handsome—although he wasn't bad-looking—it was just that he was irresistibly likable in a jolly Santa Claus kind of way. "Nice to meet you, Dr. Marcus," he said as if he really meant it.

"Diana," she corrected.

He rewarded her with an even broader smile and a request for her to call him Mitch. After reminding them to keep their "little swap" under wraps because "Bogdanow would have a shit fit" if he ever found out, Valerie excused herself. Diana followed Mitch into his office. It was much larger and better appointed than Valerie's, he being a senior partner, and its understated elegance made Diana nervous about how high even his hourly rate might be.

She quickly launched into her story. Mitch listened patiently, taking notes and nodding his head as she recounted the details. He stopped her a couple of times to ask questions in a very mild Southern accent. He told her he had worked with Herb Levine, adding that he had always found Levine to be a very good and a very "plain dealing" cop.

Diana wasn't sure whether this was good or bad news. "I didn't kill James Hutchins," she said. "And Detective Levine was acting as if he was . . ." She paused. "Well, as if he was sure that I had."

Mitch chuckled softly. "That's Herb Levine's style, Diana. Don't take it personally."

"But it *is* personal," Diana said. "It doesn't get any more personal than having to prove that you aren't a murderer." She leaned forward in her chair. "Do you think you can help me?"

Mitch was silent for a moment, turning his pencil with his thumbs and forefingers. "What you need to understand is, from the police's point of view, this is one bitch of a case." He smiled sheepishly and tilted his head. "Excuse my French."

"Because of the lack of physical evidence?"

"Combined with reasonable doubt," he added. "Herb Levine's problem is getting hold of enough evidence to build up a case that'll convince a jury that you're guilty *beyond* a reasonable doubt. So, the question is: How is he going to do that?"

"Not easily?" Diana said, her hopes rising.

"Slowly," Mitch corrected and Diana's heart sank. "Piece by piece. Remember that Robin Benedict case a few years back?"

"The one where they never found the body?"

"Never even knew for sure that she was dead," he said. "But they convicted that professor anyway. Weight of evidence." He paused and twirled his pencil once again. When he continued, it was as if he were speaking more to himself than to Diana. "At least Levine's got the fact that there was an actual DB going for him."

"DB?" Diana asked.

"Dead body."

Diana cringed at the image Mitch's words brought to mind. "But Levine's evidence is so circumstantial," she said, pushing the image away.

He nodded. "That's how you build a case like this."

"But it's just a bunch of little bits of nothing . . ."

"Herb Levine's no fool. He obviously thinks it's all going to add up to something." Mitch raised his hand and began ticking off his fingers as he spoke. "Number one: he's got motive—five hundred thousand dollars' worth—with maybe even a few extra motives thrown in to spice up his case."

"Does he need more than one?"

"No," Mitch said. "But a thwarted lover, a difficult patient, perhaps a threat to professional security—these possibilities wouldn't hurt him a bit."

Diana twisted her wedding ring.

"Number two," Mitch solemnly held up a second finger, "there's opportunity. Unfortunately, Diana, you haven't been able to come up with an alibi for the afternoon of the murder."

"How can I come up with an alibi I don't have? I was working at home all afternoon—alone. Before that I wandered around Copley Place—alone." Diana shrugged. "End of story."

"Think about the day for me one more time," Mitch pressed, scribbling on his pad. "Relive it in your mind. Did you talk to anyone on the phone? Buy anything at Copley Place? Charge anything to a credit card?"

Diana did as Mitch asked, then shook her head in frustration. "I've replayed that afternoon over and over again. And the answer to all your questions is still no."

Mitch pushed his legal pad away from him and just looked at Diana.

"So this is worse than I thought?"

"Maybe yes," he said slowly. "Maybe no."

"Maybe no?" Diana asked, hearing the desperation in her own voice.

"We can't forget there are two other suspects with qualifications almost as good as yours."

"Except that Detective Levine seemed to imply that Jill has come up with an alibi," Diana said glumly. "And that Ethan might have one too."

"That's something I can check on for you," Mitch offered.

Diana nodded vigorously. "Please."

"But my guess is," he continued, "unless their alibis are airtight, those two are our answer."

"Our answer?"

"Look, all we have to prove is that someone else *might* have done it. That's the way the law works. You and I figure out a way to show that either one of these other jokers had equal motive and opportunity . . ." Mitch paused and looked Diana straight in the eye. "And you're off the hook."

"It's that simple?"

"And that difficult."

It turned out that Mitch was every bit as good a detective as Valerie had reported. By the following Monday he called Diana with the news that the police still hadn't found Ethan, but that Jill Hutchins's aunt, a Molly Arell of Norwich, Connecticut, had signed an affidavit that she had been visiting with Jill on the afternoon of James's murder.

"She's lying," Diana told Mitch, explaining that James had told her right before his death that neither he nor Jill had seen their aunts for at least five years.

"You really could use a private detective more than a lawyer," Mitch told her. "But as long as Valerie's cooked up this deal—and in case the worst does materialize and we end up in court—here's my suggestion." He outlined a plan in which he, Valerie, and a private detective he often used, worked together. He proposed a three-pronged strategy: researching both Ethan and Jill's backgrounds using his police contacts and access to various national databases; tracking down Ethan; and visiting Jill and James's hometown to investigate Molly Arell's story and just plain snoop around. "I've got a feeling about this last piece," he said. "I'm no detective, but there's something to be found in Norwich. I just know it."

As Diana listened to his reasoned plan, her hopes soared, but when Mitch told her the estimated cost, she was crushed. Although the price was a fifth of his retainer, it was still far too high. "It all sounds wonderful," she said softly, "but we can't afford it." She couldn't tell Craig they had to spend ten thousand dollars to get her out of this debacle of her own making. Ten thousand dollars that they didn't have. Ten thousand dollars that would put him years behind in his plans for Frey and Associates. "We just can't afford it," she repeated.

"What can you afford?" Mitch asked, undeterred.

When Diana told him, he paused, and she could hear the tapping of computer keys. "My hourly rate is higher than Valerie's . . . As long as we don't tell Bogdanow, we could move some of my hours over to her column and save you a few more bucks. And, if I gave you a courtesy discount for a proportion of my time . . ."

"I couldn't ask you—"

"Would you be willing to be the detective?" he interrupted.

"You mean, I would work for you?"

His chuckle was warm. "In a convoluted, incestuous sense."

After she hung up, Diana stared at the phone. The final price she and Mitch had negotiated was still far more than they could afford. But she had almost two thousand dollars in her business account, and they would just have to make up the difference by borrowing from her parents.

She knew her parents would be more than happy to help out; relieved even, that she was finally letting them do something for her. She also knew that Craig wouldn't like it at all—but that he would agree with her decision. Hiring Mitch had been his idea in the first place, and, of course, he would have no qualms about trying to stick it to the *Inquirer*. The truth was, as they were all too aware, there was little choice.

Diana told herself there was no way she was going to be arrested for murdering James—let alone convicted. They were just being cautious; it was better to spend a few dollars to ensure the worst didn't happen. But no matter how hard she tried, the images wouldn't go away. The baby being born in prison. Her daughter growing up with the stigma of an incarcerated mother—a mother she only saw wearing the coarse red uniform of a murderer.

Diana blinked back tears. To lose her family. To be separated from Craig. From their child. To never know her. To never drink in the sweetness of her baby smell, to never feel her chubby arms pressed tightly around her neck. To see them both only on monthly visiting days.

Diana saw the sterile vastness of the visitor's room at Middlesex, the long table running the width of the space, clear plastic rising from its surface to the ceiling, separating the free from the unfree. She remembered the sheriff explaining that although there were bathrooms off the visitor's room, no one was allowed to use them. Visitors had to go back out through the metal detectors to the facilities off the main entrance. This was to keep contraband from being hidden in the toilets for prisoners to retrieve later. "Yes," he had responded in answer to a question. "Even the elderly and small children."

~ 21 ~

$\mathcal{I}$T WAS THE TUESDAY BEFORE THANKSGIVING AND THE roads were busy, but traffic was flowing smoothly. Diana figured that with a little luck, she could make it to Norwich by ten-thirty, thereby giving herself half an hour to get lost before Molly Arell expected her.

When Mitch had advised her to call ahead to arrange to meet with Molly, Diana had balked. But to her surprise, Molly had been very pleasant. Diana hadn't even had to use her half-baked explanations for the trip—her meeting in the area and her need to get a few final bits of information on James to close out her files—for Molly had immediately invited her to stop by anytime.

"People love to talk about themselves," Mitch had said. "Always have, always will." As Diana's class was canceled due to the Thanksgiving recess, she had proposed to Molly that she come down the next day. James's aunt had graciously offered to fit her in between her nine-o'clock tennis game and her noon literature class. Diana had been forced to shuffle her afternoon patients around, but it had all been accomplished with surprising ease, and now she was flying down the Mass Pike toward a meeting she anticipated with both excitement and dread.

Mitch had spent almost an hour on the phone coaching her. "Remember," he had advised, "the one and only purpose of this visit is to see if you can get the aunt to slip up and reveal that Jill's alibi is a lie. So do everything you can to make her feel comfortable. Never be antagonistic. Never threaten or intimidate. Only if she trusts you will her guard drop."

He was a good teacher, and Diana felt much more confident than she would have expected under the circumstances. She also had found his optimism contagious. "I can just feel it in these old bones," he had told her. "You're coming back with something."

Diana's heart beat faster at the idea of actually finding some evidence that would implicate Jill, of coming home exonerated and triumphant. Stop it, she warned herself as she turned off the highway. Raising her expectations for what promised to be a difficult encounter—to say the least—was not a good idea. But she also knew that she needed every possible ounce of confidence she could muster to walk up to the door of 52 Pine Street.

Consulting Molly Arell's directions and the map Mitch had suggested she buy, Diana drove through downtown Norwich—"downtown" being a rather long stretch of the term. The place had that depressed-fifties look that indicated it had never seen better times, Diana thought as she took a left turn around a jewelry store with a huge banner declaring that they had lost their lease, and a right two stores beyond a closed-down moviehouse. She was relieved as she headed away from the drab narrow streets toward the more suburban part of town.

She rode for a couple of miles past unpretentious houses and strip shopping centers—one named Marcus Plaza— and found the corner of Warren and Pine just a little after ten-thirty. She returned to Marcus Plaza and sat in the small parking lot, revving up her confidence and reviewing Mitch's instructions, until just before eleven.

A beaming Molly Arell greeted Diana at her front door.

"Please, please do come in, dear," she said, leading Diana through her unassuming living room into a bright homey kitchen that flashed Diana back to childhood afternoons of Oreos and milk. "I'm so glad you're here," Molly continued. "This whole thing has just been so difficult for all of us—for the family." She touched Diana's arm and her smile faded. "And I'm sure it has been equally difficult for you."

Even though she had come to this woman's house to get proof she was a liar, Diana couldn't help warming to James's aunt. The aunts hadn't technically done anything wrong, after all; they had been only guilty of disinterest and silence. According to both James and Jill, their mother and her three sisters had known when Hank Hutchins first moved to Norwich that he was up to no good, although it wasn't clear exactly what that "no good" was. And although Hank was from James's father's side of the family, he spread his money around James's mother's family—helping pay off Gertie's mortgage, "loaning" Molly what she needed for a new refrigerator, paying a year's college tuition for Hallie's oldest—so it was convenient for everyone to keep their eyes averted. And after Uncle Hank got caught and sent to prison, the sisters were so humiliated they continued to act as if nothing untoward had occurred. On second thought, Diana realized that an act of omission was still a wrong.

Diana accepted the older woman's offer of coffee and sat down at the large and comfortably worn table. She watched Molly, who must have been in her early sixties but moved as if she were half that age, as she poured from a coffee maker standing on the immaculate counter.

"Decaf, I presume?" Molly asked, smiling at Diana's stomach. "My daughter just had her second, so I know all the rules."

"Thank you," Diana said again, pressing her damp palms to the skirt of her jumper. She felt as she did on the first day of class: nervous and hyped-up, full of both excited anticipation and an almost uncontrollable desire to bolt from the room.

Mitch had instructed Diana to take her lead from Molly, to sit quietly and politely and just let the woman jabber. And Molly was doing exactly as he had predicted. "I felt just terrible when Jilly was so hard on you at James's funeral," she was saying. "But you have to understand that the poor girl was beside herself. James meant the world to her. Everything, perhaps." She stared into the depths of her coffee mug and sighed. "I don't think she ever really accepted how truly disturbed that boy was." She shook her head and looked up at Diana. "You're not by any chance related to any of the Norwich Marcus girls, are you? I went to school with Beatrice, but there was Bertha and Rose and Doris and Sandra—and a son too, I think. One of their husbands—Sandra or Doris's, I can't remember which—built a shopping center just around the corner from here." She nodded as if she didn't expect Diana to believe her words. "Named it after them."

"No," Diana said politely, although she was worried that the older woman's tangents might whittle away her short hour. "My father was an only child."

"Too bad," Molly said, playing with the handle on her mug. "I understand Jilly was also quite rude to you when you went to visit her at her apartment."

Diana took a sip of coffee in an attempt to cover her surprise.

"Oh, yes," the aunt said, nodding sagely. "Jilly and I are very close now. And I know she felt quite badly about the incident."

"She did?" Diana asked, not bothering to conceal her incredulity.

"And that's why you're here, right?" Molly tilted her head and smiled at Diana. "You want my help getting back that journal or whatever it is."

Speechless, Diana resisted the urge to shake her head. Mitch had cautioned her to watch her body language, to modulate her voice, to play to Molly's lead. So Diana tried to control her movements. She swallowed her words and nodded encouragingly.

Diana's reaction must have been acceptable, because Molly continued, "You have to forgive Jilly's rudeness. You must," she pleaded. "We—the whole family, that is—knew right from the start, when we thought it was suicide, that you couldn't be held responsible for what James had done." She raised her eyebrows. "Let's just say that no one was overly shocked. And now, well . . ." She looked meaningfully at Diana's stomach. "Well, it's obvious that you had nothing to do with this either."

Diana nodded and sipped her coffee, trying to figure out how to take control of the conversation. According to Mitch, she shouldn't interrupt Molly's prattle, but her time was running out, and she had to get the woman to the subject of Jill's alibi. "Bite your tongue if you have to," Mitch had advised. "But keep yourself quiet." So, against her better judgment, she did. And once again Mitch's recommendation was right on the mark.

"I was so happy that Jilly and I reconciled before all this happened—it would have been just too horrible for everyone involved had the family not been back together. Ironic, isn't it? To think that I was actually up in Boston visiting with Jilly on that very day . . ." She stared off into space. "Frankly, I don't know if Jilly could have survived it all without us."

"Families can be a tremendous source of strength in difficult times," Diana murmured, hoping to encourage Molly to let down her guard and say something that would reveal what Diana believed was her charade.

"Yes," Molly said, nodding her agreement. "And even though our family has had its rocky moments, we've always stuck together when times got difficult."

Diana tried to smile at Molly, but it wasn't easy. She knew too much of the history, had felt too much of James's pain, to believe a word of Molly's close-knit-supportive-family rubbish. According to James, it had been Jill who had raised him, Jill who had made him do his homework, Jill who had bailed him out when he got caught shoplifting, and Jill who had helped him write his college application essays. Their mother had slipped into a deep depression after the Uncle Hank episode—a depression from which she never recovered, a depression, it seemed to Diana, that she had been in all her life. And although all three of her sisters lived in Norwich, they went out of their way to maintain their distance from James. James had laughed and said he was just the family black sheep, claiming that every family needed one. But Diana had seen the hurt in his eyes when he told her his aunts had stopped inviting him to Thanksgiving dinner after Jill moved to Des Moines.

"Like when my poor sister Gertie—Jilly's mother—was having all those troubles with James," Molly was saying. "The drinking. The drugs. The police." She stared out the front window and sighed with labored sincerity. "It was a burden we all shared together. It was so hard for Gertie to understand, James being so smart and handsome and all. She just couldn't see—kind of like Jilly—couldn't see that the boy was plain bad." Molly turned and looked at Diana. "It was his own fault, I always said. Someone that smart could have helped himself, if he had really wanted to. With his looks and his brains . . ." She shook her head and clucked her tongue. "Don't you agree?"

Diana looked at the older woman, amazed at the capacity of the human mind to deny what it didn't want to see, to truly forget what it didn't want to remember. "These things can be very difficult to understand," she said slowly, straining to follow Mitch's advice, but unable to help herself. "More complex than one might think."

Molly pursed her lips. "If you had known him as a child, I'm sure you *would* agree. He had the devil in his eyes from day one." She stood and looked out the window as a car pulled up in front of the house. "Day one," she repeated, then frowned. "My son, Adam."

A tall blond man in his mid-twenties sauntered through the kitchen door. "You're James's doctor," he said when he saw Diana. "Adam Arell." He held out his hand and smiled warmly. "I know that you were a good friend to James."

Diana took his hand, vaguely remembering him from the funeral. "And I know that you were too." James had spoken often of Adam: of how they had fended off Jill and the older cousins together; of how Adam had stood up to the high school principal for him; of Adam's problems in Baltimore. Diana looked into Adam's pale eyes and smiled. Although his coloring was completely different, there was something of James about him.

Molly pursed her lips again. "Why aren't you at work?" she demanded.

Adam dropped Diana's hand and winked at her. He turned to his mother. "I've got early lunch today. I'm due back at the store at noon." He walked across the room and began pulling sandwich-makings from the refrigerator. "My mother mentioned that you were coming down this morning," he said to Diana. "Would you like something to eat?"

Diana shook her head and, out of the corner of her eye, caught Molly glaring at Adam. Molly quickly rearranged her face for her guest. "Used to be that children grew up and moved away," she said, sighing heavily. "Now they grow up and stay."

"Aw, you love it, Ma," Adam said, winking again at Diana. "You're going to be crying in your coffee when my commissions get big enough for me to get a place of my own."

"I doubt it," Molly said.

Diana smiled slightly at this pseudo-friendly repartee. She didn't need a Ph.D. in psychology to sense the undercurrent of tension. She watched and listened in silence for a while, her eyes moving between mother and son like a spectator at a tennis tournament. Mitch might not approve of her aggressiveness, but it struck Diana that in this family animosity lay an opportunity that would be lost if she continued to remain passive. "So," Diana said into a moment of silence, "your mother has been telling me how close your family is."

"Ha!" Adam snorted as he spread mayo on a couple of pieces of bread.

"And," Diana continued, as if unaware of Adam's cynical response, "how pleased she is that she and your cousin Jill have reconciled their differences."

"Not the we're-all-so-happy-sweet-Jilly-has-returned-to-the-fold bullshit again?" he said, pulling a thick wad of turkey from a plastic bag.

"Adam!" Molly stood abruptly and carried her cup to the sink.

He sidestepped neatly around her and grabbed a glass from the cabinet. "Along with the James-was-plain-bad-from-day-one story, I suppose?"

"You know that James was in trouble all of the time." Molly slammed her cup into the sink and turned to her son. "You know that just as well as I do, Adam Francis! You can do all the pretending that you want, but he—"

"And the rest of us were all perfect?" Adam asked.

Now Diana took Mitch's advice. She sat back in her chair and said nothing, letting Adam and Molly take their argument wherever it might go, hoping it would give her what she needed.

"Far from it," Molly said with venom in her voice. "Especially when you were around *him*. But that doesn't change the fact that—"

"Did I ever tell you what really happened the time Elizabeth broke her arm?" Adam asked his mother.

"We have company, Adam." Molly's voice rang with icy authority.

Adam carried his plate to the table and placed it across from Diana. He sat down and addressed Diana as if his mother hadn't spoken. "When we were kids, all the cousins were afraid of Jill. She might not have been 'bad from day one.' And she might not have been 'in trouble all of the time'"—he flashed his mother a roguish grin—"but she was a real hothead. No way to figure what she was going to do next. Even James was afraid of her—and he thought she could walk on water. One minute she was protecting you from Mike Carlson, the bully of Hilldale Road, and the next she was pushing you off the jungle gym."

"That's quite enough, Adam," Molly ordered. "I won't have this kind of talk in my house."

"You and all the aunts thought Elizabeth fell and broke her arm, didn't you?" He shook his head sadly. "Wasn't so. 'Twas your precious Jilly who pushed her."

"I won't listen to your nasty lies," Molly said. "And I must apologize to you, Dr. Marcus. Adam has been so surly and hateful of late." She glanced down at Diana's stomach. "You do everything for them when they're young. They're the light of your life. Your beautiful children. And then—"

"Cut the crap, Ma," Adam said. "It's important for Dr. Marcus to hear both sides of the story. Did you bother to tell her anything good about James? Anything about how close he and Jill were? How he supported her for the last decade or so? What about how he helped her when she got into that mess in Des Moines? Or how about when he dropped everything and came down to Baltimore to bail me out?" Adam waved his sandwich in the air. "Did you tell her any of that, Ma? Did you?"

Diana shifted in her seat, trying to look as if she were terribly uncomfortable, although actually she was thrilled by the family feud she had so easily instigated. She was also enthralled. This discord was the soil in which James had been nurtured, in which he had grown. Jill too.

"No," Molly said. "Nor did I tell her that since James cut Jilly off, the poor thing's been in terrible financial straits."

"Not that sad car repossession story again," Adam said,

his voice dripping with sarcasm. "Seems to me Jill is old enough to be responsible for herself."

"Oh?" his mother asked, raising her eyebrows. "People who live in glass houses . . ."

"Touché!" Adam said, grinning, then took a bite of his sandwich. "So who do you think killed James?" Adam asked Diana conversationally.

"I have my literature class at noon," Molly said before Diana could answer Adam. "I'm on my way out the door." She picked up Diana's mug and placed it in the sink. "And so is she."

Diana didn't move.

"I don't have your book—and neither does Jilly." Molly handed Diana her purse. "I know that for a fact." She grabbed Diana's coat from where she had placed it over a chair. "I'm sorry if I got you here under false pretenses. Perhaps it was terribly selfish of me, but I just wanted to apologize to you. I had been feeling badly about the whole thing ever since the funeral. Although"—she scowled at Adam—"I suppose you have no better picture of our family after today." She held Diana's coat open, politely—and pointedly.

Diana's own politeness overcame her desire to stay. She stood and slipped into the offered coat. "Thank you for the coffee," she said.

"So do you think Jill could have done it?" Adam asked, then took another bite of his sandwich.

"You have gone quite far enough, young man," Molly said, glaring at Adam as she put on her own coat. "You know that I was up in Boston that day—"

Adam raised his eyebrows. "Jill was always good at covering her ass."

"Don't be ridiculous!" Molly cried. Her son's implication that she might be lying caused her voice to quiver with anger. "You yourself said how close Jill and James were—you know how much she loved him. She didn't kill him anymore than I did!" Molly ripped her purse from a kitchen chair with such force that the chair toppled to the floor. She grabbed it and thrust it back into its original position.

"Then how come she flipped when she found out that Dr. Marcus here got all of James's money? Why is she planning to contest the will?" Adam asked, his demeanor growing increasingly calm as his mother's became more agitated. "How come Zach had to give her those tranquilizers?"

"You should be ashamed of yourself for even thinking such nonsense," Molly growled. "The poor thing had just lost her only brother. She was a complete wreck that afternoon. A complete wreck," she repeated, twisting the strap of her purse around her fingers.

"But my question is why?" He tilted his head and looked up at his mother. "Which brings me back to my original question: Who killed James?"

"Don't you see that neither of those questions matter anymore?" Molly snapped. "What matters is picking up the pieces and going on. What matters is for a family to stick together." She pulled the door toward her and then turned and glared at her son. "Something you could learn a bit more about."

Diana caught Adam's wink over Molly's shoulder as she was ushered out of the house.

~ 22 ~

DIANA'S MIND WAS REELING AS SHE HEADED TOWARD Boston. With only one wrong turn, she found the two-lane highway that would take her north to the Mass Pike. The road was clear, and the sun hung above the bare treetops. Mitch had been wrong. She wasn't coming back with anything. All she had gained was a conviction she couldn't prove: Molly Arell was lying.

Even her son knew it. And Molly's agitated response to Adam was further testimony to her guilt. But the fact that Molly was lying didn't prove Jill had killed James. It didn't prove anything. And as long as Molly stuck to her story, Jill had an alibi that would eliminate her as one of the police's suspects.

Diana cranked up the heat as a thick bank of clouds streamed across the sun. *Show that either one of these other jokers had equal motive and opportunity,* Mitch had said. *And you're off the hook.* While the fact that Jill had gotten upset after discovering she wasn't the beneficiary of the will, and that her car had been repossessed, indicated a possible motive, the operative part of Mitch's sentence was the word "and." Without opportunity, all the motive in the world was useless to Diana.

About half a mile ahead, Diana could see an overloaded truck dragging its way up a steep incline, slowing all the traffic behind it to a crawl. The double yellow line to her left forbade passing, but in any case, it was obvious that there was nowhere to go.

Diana smiled ruefully to herself. She should have been clever, like Jill. She should have gotten someone to cover for her too. Maybe she could have talked Gail into claiming that they had had a late lunch that afternoon, or perhaps Sandy could have been confused into thinking she had been at Diana's office for an appointment. Diana shook her head in frustration; she would never involve a friend or a patient—or anyone—in a lie. Adam would say that Jill was far better at "covering her ass" than Diana was. And Adam would be right.

Diana was exhausted, her back ached, and she really needed to get to a bathroom. If only she were home. Here she had rearranged her entire day—and would have to make up the work over the rest of the week—and placed herself in an awkward and difficult situation, just to come home empty. Worse than empty. For now she knew there was no salvation for her in Jill.

Diana finally pulled onto the Mass Pike and around the slow truck, only to find the six-lane highway moving at a skulk that matched the road she had just left. What was the use of all the nudging and maneuvering? What was the point of her becoming Mitch's detective? Did any of it really matter? Yes, she reminded herself: It mattered a lot. It mattered because she needed an alternative plausible suspect in order to clear herself. In order to keep the police from arresting her for murder. Diana saw all too clearly how the scenario would appear to Levine: She had both motive and opportunity, Jill had only motive.

The traffic thinned, and Diana pulled into the passing lane. She wouldn't allow herself to succumb to depression and self-pity. She had too much to lose, too much to fight for. If Molly's statements destroyed Jill as a plausible suspect, then she would just have to switch to Ethan. She would call Mitch as soon as she got home and start focusing on the elusive Ethan Kruse.

Diana tuned the radio to an oldies station and tried to cheer herself by singing out loud to the Beatles. The clouds thickened, and the sun dropped behind the Worcester hills. Although it was early afternoon, she turned on her headlights.

A shiver ran down her spine and silenced her singing. She jacked up the heat, but it didn't help. It was that feeling again. The eyes. She glanced nervously in the rearview mirror. She turned to her right, and then to her left. But no one was looking at her.

No one had any interest in her at all.

When Diana got home she wasn't able to call Mitch, for Sandy Pierson was huddled in the alley waiting for her, hollow-eyed and scared. "I'm sorry, Dr. Marcus," Sandy sobbed from her seat wedged against the cold brick of the house. "But I—I couldn't help it. I did it again," she wailed. "Even though I promised I wouldn't, I did it again."

"Come on in," Diana said, reaching her hands out to help the younger woman up. Even in her misery, Sandy rose gracefully. Diana waved Sandy into her office, hung up her coat, and went to the bathroom. When she returned, Sandy was still crying.

"I wanted to be like you," Sandy said. "For you to be a part of me . . ."

Diana walked around the perimeter of the room, her hand pressed to her lower back, watching Sandy. It was almost impossible to believe that the stringy-haired, white-faced woman sitting before her was the same person who had smiled so alluringly out of a Filene's "Night on the Town" ad in the *Globe* last week. Diana dropped heavily into her chair and swiveled so that she faced Sandy. "Why don't you start from the beginning?" she suggested.

Sandy hung her head, twisting a thick clump of hair

around her finger. "I made a chocolate-chip cookie," she whispered.

Diana nodded.

"I know chocolate-chip are your favorite," Sandy said to her feet. "Your very favorite food in the whole world, you told us once. Full of wonderful memories that you could relive again and again. Every time you ate them. Smelled them even, you said."

When had she ever told Sandy that? Diana wondered. And why? Then she remembered a group session early on, when James had been so promising, before Ethan arrived on the scene. Everyone was telling a story about a positive childhood experience. When James asked Diana to tell them one from her own childhood, she had agreed. "Psychotherapy cannot proceed without empathy on both sides," Adrian had pounded into her during her postdoc. "You must offer yourself as a positive, supportive figure. As a real person— with your own foibles and fantasies—for identification to take place." So much for Adrian's great advice, Diana thought. "You made chocolate-chip cookies . . ." she coaxed, glancing at the clock and wondering how late Mitch stayed in his office.

"I only did it because I love you so much," Sandy said sharply, as if somehow tuning in to Diana's distraction. "If it weren't for you"—she raised her head and stared at Diana, defying her to disagree—"I never would have done it at all!"

"Is what you did really so bad?" Diana asked softly.

Sandy crossed her arms over her chest. "I made a huge chocolate-chip cookie and I shaped it to look just like you!" she said, glaring at Diana's stomach.

"And?" Diana kept her voice soft and her emotions from her eyes.

There was silence as the two women looked at each other. Sandy's expression slowly shifted from defiant to confused, then settled into a sulk. "I ate the whole thing," she finally said.

Diana nodded.

"But it didn't fill me with wonderful memories—and it didn't fill me with you," Sandy said sullenly. "So I stuck my finger down my throat and threw it all up."

Diana closed her eyes for a moment, and when she opened them, Sandy was standing, facing the back wall. Diana watched Sandy square her shoulders and turn with the fluid motions of an experienced model during a photo shoot. The woman from the Filene's ad stood facing her.

"I guess you're right," Sandy said, as if she had not just told Diana she had vomited her into a toilet. "Now that I've actually said it, it doesn't sound all that bad after all."

Diana watched warily as the self-confident model approached and sat gracefully in the chair, throwing one of her long legs across the other. "You feel better now?" Diana asked.

Sandy leaned back in an overly nonchalant manner. "Yes," she said as if she wasn't all that sure. "Yes," she repeated more loudly, but with no more certainty.

Diana looked at the beautiful but terribly damaged woman before her. How could people do these things to their own children? she wondered, not for the first time. How could Sandy's father have locked her up in a dark closet every day after school? How had Uncle Hank brought himself to photograph his nephew being sodomized? Resting her hand protectively over her stomach, Diana thought of her new research data: If it actually *was* these horrendous—but isolated—events that caused the disease, then there really might be hope for a therapeutic cure. And then maybe Sandy wouldn't have to relive—and relive and relive—her fear of abandonment; maybe she could be freed to put her trust in another human being. "Does this remind you of anything that's happened before?" Diana asked softly.

Sandy shook her head. "No, not that I can—" Then she stopped and her eyes widened. "The time I called everyone and canceled group?" she asked. "To have you all to myself?"

Diana nodded.

"James and Ethan said I was selfish and spiteful. Terri and Bruce too." Sandy stared over Diana's shoulder, through the window beyond, but Diana knew from the pain in Sandy's eyes that she was not seeing the alley. "They didn't want me in the group anymore."

"And do you remember what I told you at the time?"

"You—you mean," Sandy began, her eyes welling with tears, "you mean after my binge?"

Diana nodded.

"You told me a good expression of love might make me feel better," she whispered.

"And did it?" Diana asked, handing Sandy a tissue.

Sandy nodded, wiping her cheeks. "Remember?" She smiled through the tears. "I did something nice for everyone. I cleaned James's apartment and loaned Bruce my car."

Diana returned Sandy's smile, remembering very clearly how good she, Diana, had felt when the group reconnected, how proud of herself she had been. Until Ethan had caused it all to fall apart by fighting with James. Her smile disappeared.

Sandy sniffed and raised her chin. "I did it even though I was really pissed off at them."

"You did giving things," Diana said. "Loving things." She flashed to James's sweetness during her ectopic pregnancy; she could almost feel his hand covering hers as he sped toward the hospital, almost hear his soft, crooning voice. Even Ethan had helped her once when her jeep broke down—shrugging off the fact that it made him late for a date. How much could be salvaged? she wondered. How deep did the damage have to go before the true person was irretrievable?

"And they decided that I could stay." Sandy played with the wet tissues. She shredded them and then molded them into a ball. She clenched the ball tightly in her fist. "So I should do something for you?" she asked without raising her eyes.

"That's not necessary, Sandy," Diana said. "Just remember that things can be undone. That people who care about you are willing to accept you—even if you're not perfect." Diana rested her arms on her desk and leaned closer to Sandy. "None of us is perfect."

Sandy glanced up, then quickly looked out the window. She twisted her hair around her finger and inspected her nails. Then she clutched her hands together and looked straight at Diana. "I want to give you something because I love you."

Diana nodded.

"But I don't have anything to give," Sandy wailed.

"It's really not—"

"There were a lot of things about the group that you never knew," Sandy blurted. "That we kept from you. Especially James and Ethan. James's sister too."

"Oh?" Diana gripped the edge of her desk, her surprise at the mention of Jill catching her off-guard. She carefully folded her hands and forced herself to relax in the chair.

"We all knew it was against the rules." Sandy's words came out in a rush. "We knew it was dishonest and not fair to you. But Ethan made it into such a fun game. You know, like when you were a kid and there was a substitute teacher?" Sandy's eyes begged Diana's forgiveness. "He—he made it exciting—like, to see how far we could go." She hung her head, shielding her face with her hair and kneading her wet wad of tissues.

"How far you could go?" Diana prompted. The rules of the group were that anything that transpired between members outside group hours would be discussed at the next session. Diana knew that this was virtually impossible, as James and Ethan had been friends prior to Ethan's entering the group—and that had been one of her many reservations about Ethan joining—but Sandy's words made it sound much more sinister than the few undisclosed pranks Diana had suspected.

Fright crossed Sandy's face and she shrugged and looked

down at her feet. "I promised never to tell," she mumbled. "Ethan said he'd find out if I ever did."

Diana bit her lip and stared at the fearful woman in front of her, caught between her own needs and those of her patient. Maybe Sandy knew something that could help her—but maybe she, Diana, knew something that could help Sandy more. "Thank you," Diana finally said. "It means a lot to me that you shared this."

Sandy jumped up and looked around the room as if she thought it might be bugged. "I can't," she said, grabbing her coat. Then she leaned toward Diana and tilted her head, her voice dropping to a whisper. "We used to go to Ken's Pub in Cambridge. All together. All the time."

"Sandy—" Diana began, standing also.

"It doesn't matter anyway," Sandy said, shaking her head. "Nothing matters anymore." She began to cry softly. "They've both left me. Everyone's gone." She shrugged into her coat and, shoulders drooping, walked out the door.

Diana sat back down, knowing that Sandy had said all she was going to say, that it was best for Sandy to work this through by herself for a while. Diana swiveled her chair and watched as the lonely, beautiful woman climbed gracefully into her car.

Sandy had offered her a gift: a "good expression" of her love. Ken's Pub. But before Diana could fully take in the information, before she could figure out if Sandy really wanted to help her or hurt her, before she could consider how—and if—Sandy's information could be of any use, she felt a gush of warm dampness. She jumped from the chair and a bolt of terror highlighted every nerve in her body. She was bleeding.

As she lunged for the phone, nauseated with fear, Diana imagined herself lying within a softly billowing curtained enclosure, lost and empty and crying, her dead baby leaking from her body. James was holding her hand.

~ 23 ~

CRAIG SAT ON THE EDGE OF THE BED AND BRUSHED the hair from Diana's forehead. "How are you doing?" he asked. It had been a long, stressful afternoon and evening in the emergency room, and they both looked it: pale and drawn and droopy. But the news had been good, and the doctors had sent Diana home to rest for a few days, optimistic that she could resume her regular schedule on Monday with the expectation of a normal delivery—and a healthy child.

"Now that I'm home, I feel much better," she said, although what she felt was exhausted. Completely and totally drained. All she wanted was sleep. But Craig looked so much like a little boy who had been lost and finally found, the fear and relief equally mixed in his tired eyes, that she didn't have the heart to ask him to leave.

He picked up her hand and kissed her palm and then pressed it between his two. "We'll get through this, Diana," he whispered, his voice cracking slightly. "All of it. Whatever it takes. Even if there's only the two of us, we're still a family." He squeezed her fingers so hard that they hurt.

She gently extricated her hand. "They said everything's going to be fine." According to the doctors, she had had a "minor bleeding episode," a not-uncommon event. They had quickly determined that she wasn't miscarrying, that she didn't have placenta previa, and, in answer to her repeated questioning, that this pregnancy was not ectopic.

An ultrasound had been performed, and she and Craig had watched the screen, breathless and grinning, as the technician focused first on the baby's face, then on her legs, pressed tightly to her belly. At one point, the baby had turned and popped her thumb into her mouth. They even had a photograph: an eerie but beautiful grainy black-and-white reverse image of a perfect nose, a perfect mouth, and two perfect eyes, widely spaced and wide open. Their daughter appeared to be smiling at them.

"This whole thing today scared the shit out of me," Craig said. "Made me think about things—about what's really important." He stood and began to pace their small bedroom. He ran his hand along the edge of the bureau and the brass railing at the foot of the bed. Through half-closed eyes, Diana watched him as he walked to the closet, then abruptly turned and walked to the door. Finally he stopped at the window. His back toward her, he crossed his arms and stared silently into the dark alley.

A shiver ran down Diana's spine and she tucked the comforter up around her chin. "Please close the drapes," she asked. He immediately jerked the cord, and the heavy fabric closed over itself. The room was brighter and warmer, and, Diana thought, somehow safer.

"I know I haven't been completely supportive," Craig said, still facing the window. "That I've been thinking of myself and worrying about stupid things that happened in the past."

"That's ridiculous," Diana said, pushing herself up in the bed. "You've been fabulous—wonderful. Much more understanding and tolerant than I would've been if our roles were reversed."

"No." He turned and looked her straight in the eye "You would have had more trust in me." Coming over and kneeling by the side of the bed, he reached for her hand under the comforter. "It's you and me against that detective."

"Craig—" Diana began.

"No more questions," he said, holding a finger to her lips. "No more recriminations. Just trust."

Diana closed her eyes, both from exhaustion and the need not to look at Craig. She was grateful for both his love and his willingness to forgive, but it was all too emotionally overwhelming. And it made her feel guilty, not worthy of him. All she wanted was to go to sleep. She pulled herself into a fetal position and pressed a pillow to her belly.

"Sleep. You need sleep." Craig stood and kissed her forehead. "Is there anything I can get for you?"

She shook her head, keeping her eyes closed.

"I'll leave the door open and be right downstairs," he said. "Just call. I'm not going anywhere." He kissed her again, and to Diana's great relief, finally left the room.

By Friday Diana was feeling much better, but she was worn out from Craig's hovering. Laughing, she handed him his briefcase and ordered him to the office. "If you don't get out of here and leave me alone for a while, I'm packing my bags and moving in with my mother until this baby is born," she warned him. He agreed to go into work only after she arranged for Gail to come by and keep her company.

"Rumor has it that you did this on purpose," Gail said from her chair across from Diana, who was ensconced on the couch. "To get out of going to your mother-in-law's for Thanksgiving."

"Well, you've heard all those overcooked turkey stories." Diana kept her expression serious as she rearranged the pillows under her knees. "I just couldn't face it another year."

"You look damn healthy to me." Gail narrowed her eyes. "One might even say you have 'that glow.'"

"Not 'that glow,'" Diana said, holding her hands up in front of her face as if to ward off a vampire. "Please, please, tell me anything but that I'm glowing."

"Okay, you may not be glowing, but you do look damn good, sweetie." Gail leaned over and touched Diana's foot. "So everything really is okay?"

"The doctor said I can get back to real life on Monday. The ultrasound was normal and the bleeding stopped by the time I got to the hospital." She shrugged. "Apparently this isn't all that rare—it just really scared me."

"Did they say anything about the baby being small? You look more like you're four months pregnant than six."

"They said she is on the small side—but not unusually so." Diana patted her stomach affectionately. "When I insisted, the technician guessed a birth weight somewhere just under seven pounds."

Gail looked at Diana with envy. "When I was six months pregnant, I was the size of a house. People thought I was ready to drop the babies any minute."

"Twins don't count," Diana said, swinging her legs from the couch to the floor. "Can I get you something? Tea? Diet soda? How about a glass of wine?"

Gail jumped from her chair and grabbed Diana before she could rise. "Don't you dare move!" she ordered. "I don't want a thing!"

"You're as bad as Craig," Diana muttered, shaking Gail's hands from her shoulders and pointing to the chair. "I'm not an invalid—let go of me and sit down." When Gail returned to her chair, Diana said, "So, you promised me some good gossip . . ."

"This really *is* good. You're gonna just love it . . ." Gail rubbed her hands together and wiggled around in her seat. "Guess who's in major league trouble?"

Diana groaned and looked at the ceiling. "You mean out of every person in the world?"

"Nope," Gail answered. "Just out of every person we know." She paused and then added, "Professionally."

"Every person we know professionally," Diana repeated. "Got to be someone we don't like . . . Especially me." She looked thoughtfully at Gail and then her face lit up. "Pumphrey?" she asked.

Gail shook her head. "Not quite *that* good."

"What kind of trouble?" Diana demanded like an overeager child playing Twenty Questions.

"Financial. Personal. Maybe even legal."

"The only person I can think of is Adrian." Diana shook her head. "But there's no way he could be in financial trouble."

"Don't be so sure . . ."

"Adrian Arnold's in financial trouble? That's impossible. Not with a thousand courses around the country using his textbook every semester."

"True enough, Counselor," Gail acknowledged. "But remember how he was always complaining about Rebecca the Princess driving him nuts with her demands for more alimony and child support?"

"I thought that was just because she was jealous of . . ." Diana paused. "What did she call them? Oh, yeah, his 'young tarts.'"

"Apparently it wasn't only the tarts—although I heard his latest is *less* than half his age and quite a hot ticket." Gail's eyes sparkled as she leaned toward Diana. "Because Rebecca just won!"

"Won what?" Diana asked, completely baffled.

"A huge settlement for back payment!" Gail cried triumphantly and sat back in the chair. She swung her leg nonchalantly. "Seems our little friend Adrian got caught hiding almost ten years' worth of royalties."

"Ten years?" Diana whistled. "On all those books?"

Gail raised her eyebrows. "I don't know the specifics, but I heard the number was well over six figures."

They gossiped some more about Adrian, then the conversation jumped and skipped, as it does between close friends. They discussed how Gail's two-year-old sons had mashed sweet potatoes into her mother's new carpet, then switched to the effect of national health care on psychotherapists, the latest Barbara Kingsolver novel they were both reading, and the cover story in the *Atlantic* exploring the significance of divorce on children. Then Diana told Gail the Sandy chocolate-chip cookie story—omitting Sandy's name, of course. Gail laughed uproariously, making only one passing comment about Diana's obsession with borderlines. But when Gail's chortling died down, her face sobered, and she began watching her swinging boot, uncharacteristically silent.

"What?" Diana demanded. "You think this woman's dangerous?"

"It's possible—but I doubt it," Gail said, continuing to watch her foot. Then, with false casualness, she asked, "So how's everything else?"

"Everything else?" Diana repeated, fear gripping her stomach, although she wasn't sure why.

"You know." Gail looked up for a second and then concentrated once again on her boot. She shrugged.

"Fine," Diana lied. "The police seem to be at an impasse because there's so little physical evidence." She had told no one but "her lawyers"—as she now thought of Valerie and Mitch—about Levine's visit, figuring the fewer people who were aware she was still an active suspect, the better. The lack of an immediate arrest, combined with the Thanksgiving holiday and numerous catastrophes both local and international, had pushed her case from the public eye—and she was going to do everything she could to ensure that it stayed that way. Diana felt a little guilty not confiding in Gail, but knew it was for the best. Swallowing hard, she attempted a laugh. "The police say it's a shitcan."

Gail glanced up, her eyes dark with sympathy.

"That means a homicide not likely to be solved." Diana's voice was upbeat when she started the sentence, but the expression on Gail's face caused her words to dwindle off toward the end. Her hands trembled slightly, and she clasped them together. "What?" she demanded. "What is it?"

Gail bit at her thumbnail, and then began to speak. "I might as well just come out and say it . . ."

Diana swung her legs from the couch and planted them on the floor as if to better brace herself against the impact. She waited silently.

"A policeman came to see me on Monday," Gail said, speaking quickly. "Asking questions about you and James. He—"

"Tall and skinny with gray curly hair?" Diana interrupted, her voice remarkably calm considering the turmoil that raged within her. "Seems like a real nice guy?"

Gail nodded, her eyes so filled with compassion that Diana felt tears pricking behind her own. "He talked to everyone else in the group too," Gail continued. She leaned across the table and grabbed Diana's hands. "But no one told him anything—even Adrian. I know. I grilled them all."

Diana stood and walked into the front bay. She looked out on the narrow street, watching the college students and tourists and neighborhood people jostling each other for sidewalk space. The Friday after Thanksgiving, she thought somewhat irrationally, was the busiest shopping day of the year. But the creatures outside her window might have been from another planet for all she had in common with them, worrying about what to buy for whom, and which of their charge cards still had a viable credit line. She hated them. Every last one of them.

She hated every person who walked on the earth, who ate dinner with a fork, and who called his mother on Sunday. Every person whose life was still normal. Every person whose concerns were the mundane. Her anger and frustration grew as she watched the preoccupied crowds until she feared her turmoil would burst from her as a living, breathing, hating demon. "Did he ask you if I was a money-hungry bitch who would kill to get her hands on half a million dollars?" She whirled around to face Gail.

"Come and sit down," Gail said, striding over to Diana and trying to help her to the couch.

Diana threw off Gail's hands and remained rooted in the bay. She hated Gail too. Crossing her arms, Diana glared at her friend. "Did he ask you if I had sex with James?"

Gail stepped back and said nothing. Then she walked to the chair and sat down. "He wanted to know if you ever discussed having a sexual attraction to James," she said quietly. "And he did ask if you were aware that James was planning to change his will." She pointed to the couch. "That's all he asked anyone."

As she listened to Gail's calm words and watched her friend's quiet movements, Diana went suddenly numb. She felt no more anger, no more hatred. All she felt was a deep, searing emptiness. Perhaps, she thought with some removed, still-rational part of her brain, this was shock. She grabbed the window molding for support, almost as if her anger had been holding her upright, and now that it was gone, she had nothing to support her. Pushing off the wall, she moved from the bay and slumped into the couch. "Sorry," she said.

Gail nodded her understanding and then continued. "No one told him anything. Everyone quoted him the 'privileged information' line, and, to his credit, he accepted my refusal very graciously. Marc said the same thing."

"Oh, Levine's gracious all right." Diana's voice was without affect. "Gracious as a cobra."

"I checked with my friend Stacey—she does litigation— after he left," Gail continued. "Stacey said that the only way we can be forced to break confidentiality is if this cop gets someone in the DA's office to convene a grand jury." She paused and took a deep breath. "She said we could be sub- poenaed to appear . . ."

Diana looked up at her friend. "Can they do that before someone's been arrested?"

Gail shrugged. "Stacey called it pre-litigation deposition,

or discovery, or some such thing." She touched Diana's knee. "But she said if it happened, we'd have to talk. That we'd be under oath."

Diana closed her eyes, remembering all the things she had said in peer review. Every concern she had ever voiced, every confidence she had ever shared. About her sexual attraction for James. About her erotic fantasies. About her feelings for him. She remembered the day she had told Gail what James had said about his will, never believing for a moment that he meant a word of it. "Can you believe that one?" she had asked Gail, laughing. "A new way to get rich: knock off a grateful patient." Diana's eyes flew open and she stared into Gail's, fear nibbling at her numbness. "You'd have to tell that I knew about the will?" she said.

Gail nodded miserably. "And what you said when you told me about it."

Diana closed her eyes again.

"You look tired, sweetie," Gail said softly. "Would you like me to stay—or would you rather I left?"

Diana was tired. Exhausted. Bereft of energy. She leaned back against the couch and imagined friendly ol' Detective Levine shmoozing with some assistant district attorney, getting him or her to convene a grand jury. She closed her eyes again. If her peer supervisory group talked, she was a dead woman.

"I'll let myself out," Gail said softly. "I'll call you tomorrow." Gail's boots scraped against the floor as she stood. She left a light kiss on Diana's brow.

Diana sat silent and still, listening to Gail's footsteps descending the stairs, a dreamlike kaleidoscope of unrelated images shifting across her mind's eye: Adrian Arnold's malicious critique of her sampling procedures when she presented her preliminary research results at peer review; Jill stabbing a poker into her living room carpet; Sandy's stunning face smiling out of the Filene's ad; Ethan's hollow, vacant eyes; Craig, pale and scared, standing next to her in the hospital; James, his chiseled face lightly covered with sweat, his shoulders exposed by a blue cotton tank top, shiny and achingly erotic.

She saw Detective Levine laughing uproariously in the great room, and a picture that had run in the *Globe* of an imprisoned mother nursing her baby, separated from the photographer by a seemingly endless row of vertical bars.

~ 24 ~

ON MONDAY MORNING DIANA RESUMED HER FULL schedule. The first thing she did was call both of her lawyers. Valerie was ecstatic about their progress on the *Inquirer* suit, but Mitch was not so upbeat. "As far as the police are concerned, Molly Arell is an upstanding citizen," he told Diana. "So, regardless of Jill Hutchins's actual guilt or innocence, if the aunt can maintain her alibi, they'll probably look to another suspect."

They both knew without needing to specify just who that other suspect might be.

He was also concerned about Levine's aggressiveness. After some deliberation over the cost, Diana authorized Mitch to have his detective, Norman Seymour, spend three hours on the case. Mitch agreed with Diana's assessment that they needed to focus on Ethan, and he suggested that Norman do just that. Norman would start with Ethan's rap sheet, following up all the arrests to determine if there were any outstanding warrants or parole violations—or anything the least bit suspicious that might be used to convince the police Ethan was a better suspect than Diana. "And maybe Norman'll be able to get a lead on Kruse's whereabouts,"

Mitch said, although the tone of his voice suggested that he believed otherwise.

When she told Mitch about Jill's repossessed car and Adam Arell's reference to a problem Jill had had in Des Moines, he suggested that Norman devote one of his hours to Jill. "Just because the police eliminate her as a suspect," Mitch said, "doesn't mean that we have to." Norman could check into the seriousness of Jill's financial problems through some national credit databases and run her name through some criminal databases to which he had access. Diana was skeptical about the possibility of Jill having a criminal background. But she agreed with Mitch: They might as well check it out.

They also decided Diana should go to Ken's Pub.

By two o'clock Diana had completed her work commitments for the day. Her borderline group had just finished and she had no more appointments. If she left the house immediately, she could be at Ken's by two-thirty—the perfect time, according to Mitch, to get information from someone working in a restaurant. "They're tired and bored in the mid-afternoon," he told her. "Most apt to speak to a stranger. Most apt to let down their guard."

Diana wanted desperately to find Ethan. She *had* to find him, for she and Mitch had agreed that Ethan could very well be her only chance. But Diana didn't want to go to Ken's. She didn't want to find him. The truth was, she was a little afraid of Ethan—maybe more than a little. And she always had been.

Pulling open a file drawer, Diana ran her finger along the tabs until she came to the one she was searching for: "Borderline Group Session Notes." She pulled the file from the cabinet and brought it to her desk. Without sitting, she quickly sifted through the contents, searching for a photograph that had been taken almost exactly a year ago.

Sandy had brought a camera to group—a gift from her new boyfriend, a photographer—and had been so excited and anxious to show off its features, that in an attempt to calm Sandy's mania, Diana had asked the group if Sandy could take a few pictures. It was right after Ethan had joined, during those short weeks when openness and affability had reigned and everyone was still optimistic, so no one objected. When Sandy suggested a group shot using the automatic timer, even Diana had agreed to be photographed.

The picture was facedown at the back of the file. Gingerly, Diana lifted it without turning it over and held it away from her for a moment. She remembered the afternoon clearly: Ethan clowning as they waited for the timer to release; the serious case of the giggles they had all caught; how warm James's arm had felt across her shoulder.

She took a deep breath and slowly turned the photo over. Looking down at it—at them as they had once been—she felt such a bittersweet stab of nostalgia that she almost winced. They looked so happy. So carefree. So hopeful. How could only a year have passed?

Now James was dead. Ethan had disappeared. Sandy was more lost than ever, Bruce was still fainting, and Terri couldn't bring herself to go anywhere near the subway. And she? Diana narrowed her eyes and studied the laughing woman in the picture. She had aged a decade in the past year.

Diana forced herself to look at James, at the perfect line of his cheekbone, at the deep happiness in his eyes as he rested his arm on her shoulder and his chin on top of her head. Ethan stood next to James, almost the same height and of comparable build—even their hair was a similar chocolate-brown color—but the look that glinted from Ethan's eyes could not have been more different from James's. Ethan's eyes were hard and cold, almost colorless. A shiver ran down Diana's back. Ethan's eyes were empty.

"Sometimes I think there's nothing inside Ethan," James had once confided to her. "Like he's hollow. Just a shell pretending to be a human being." He had stared silently at her for a moment, then added, "Sometimes he scares the shit out of me."

Diana dropped the picture into her purse, reminded once again of James's uncanny perceptiveness. One of the most common characteristics of Ethan's illness—antisocial personality disorder—was the inability to experience emotion, particularly guilt or empathy: Ethan was a truly hollow man.

Diana took her coat from the rack and buttoned it, but it did little to ward off the cold that emanated from the marrow of her bones. She was afraid. Afraid she wouldn't find Ethan. And afraid that she would.

For although it wasn't unusual for people with Ethan's disorder to die young, she wasn't worried that Ethan was dead—he was far too cunning and street-smart for that, and he had left a message on her machine just last week. What Diana feared was that he had caused another to die. And that if backed into a corner, he would have no qualms about doing it again.

She began to unbutton her coat. She couldn't put herself in this kind of jeopardy. She couldn't take this kind of chance with her baby's life. Then, once again, she heard the grim bleating of the Middlesex horn prodding the sluggish prisoners into their tiny cells.

And Diana knew that she had no choice.

Diana was disappointed when she found a parking spot in front of a small Cambodian restaurant just a couple of blocks down from Ken's Pub. She had been hoping there would be no spaces on Mass Ave. Then she would have to go home. Craig would never let her park on a side street in Central Square when it might be dark by the time she got back. Too risky, he would say. Much too risky. She smiled wryly at herself. In this instance she would have been more than happy to comply with Craig's cautiousness.

Slowly she climbed from the jeep, wishing she were

back at Molly Arell's. Talking with James's congenial aunt now seemed a picnic compared with looking for someone who might be a psychopathic killer. Stop it, Diana reprimanded herself. Aside from Ethan's lengthy rap sheet—which she knew would include a number of DWI and petty-theft arrests, as well as one for "hurricane drag racing," a variation on chicken in which both drivers must be loaded to the gills—there was no indication he was a killer. None whatsoever. She swung her purse over her shoulder and marched down the crowded sidewalk toward Ken's.

Actually Ethan had always been particularly gracious to her. Congenial, polite, always calling when he disappeared to let her know where he was. Never threatening or mean, never the least bit dangerous. The only thing she could really accuse him of was oversolicitousness.

She smiled as she opened the heavy oak door of the restaurant, remembering a session when Ethan had reprimanded Sandy for interrupting Diana. "Eddie Haskell clone", she had scribbled in her notes, a reference to an obsequious character from "Leave It to Beaver." "Figure out what he wants." Her smile disappeared when she realized that she never had.

Diana blinked into the dimness of the pub, the dark wood and glazed windows giving the place a clandestine, cavelike ambience. A small woman approached her from the dusky shadows, and Diana indicated her preference for a table near the bar, as Mitch had suggested. "Talk to the bartender," he had instructed her. "They're the ones who know everything that's going on." They had discussed the fact that she could't sit at the bar—a lone pregnant woman on a bar stool sipping club soda was a bit too peculiar—so they decided on a nearby table from which she could easily rise and request some change.

Diana self-consciously settled herself in the chair, removing her coat and smoothing her jumper in a manner that emphasized her slightly protruding stomach. "Too bad you aren't further along," Mitch had said. "Nothing like a pregnant woman to elicit sympathy and loosen a tongue." Disgusted as she was by the idea, Diana could appreciate the wisdom of his words.

Although she wasn't hungry, she ordered a sandwich and picked at it as she watched the bartender enclosed in his large oval-shaped bar, her unease growing along with her scrutiny. He was a gruff and reticent black man named Marcel. He waited on his two customers with unemotional efficiency, running tabs, making drinks, even getting a pack of cigarettes from the machine, without moving a muscle in his expressionless face. One of the waitresses appeared truly afraid of him, and the other, a long-legged student type, joked with him, although Marcel's response was invariably a scowl.

Diana knew this man wasn't going to give her any information. How could he? she wondered, taking a tiny bite of her sandwich: She was never going to get up the guts to talk to him. Then she remembered the tightness around Detective Levine's jaw when he said he didn't believe in shitcans. She stood up.

"Could I please have change for a five?" she asked, holding out a bill toward Marcel while pressing a hand to the small of her back.

He glanced at her stomach as he took the proffered money and grunted in a somewhat friendly way.

"A dollar in change, please," Diana added, not knowing what else to say. Mitch had told her to be pleasant and tentative. To try to elicit sympathy. When Marcel reached over the bar to give her the change, Diana dropped her hand from her back and sank onto a stool. She ran her fingers through her hair and sighed.

"You okay?" he asked, his voice rich and low with concern. "Can I get you something?"

Diana felt heat rise to her face and the sweat of embarrassment prickle under her arms. "No, no," she stuttered, horrified at what she was doing—and how good she was at it. "I'm fine. Really I am."

Marcel looked at her closely. "My wife just had her second," he said.

Diana nodded. "Maybe a little water?" she asked tentatively.

He quickly produced a glass of water. She took a few sips, and he watched her impassively until she emptied the glass.

"Thanks," she said. "I guess I just stood up too fast." He nodded and began to turn away. Diana knew if she didn't speak up now, she never would. "Excuse me," she called, her voice a little breathless with trepidation.

Marcel turned back to her. He said nothing, just waited, pokerfaced.

"I—I was wondering if you could please help me?" Diana asked. When Marcel took a step closer, the flicker of concern registering on his stolid face, Diana shook her head. "I'm fine," she said, pulling the photo from her purse. "It's something else."

Warily, Marcel stepped back as she pushed the picture across the bar.

"I'm looking for someone," she said, her nervousness adding just the right amount of shakiness to her voice. "I really need to find him."

Marcel glanced down at the picture, then up at Diana. His face was expressionless. He didn't move. "Never seen any of them."

Diana pointed to Ethan. "Please," she said plaintively, trying to make her eyes moist and sincere. "It's really important." She blinked rapidly and then looked down at the photograph, placing her hand lightly on her stomach. "I don't know where he is," she added softly, hating herself for what she was suggesting, while hoping that it worked. "I just need to talk to him."

Marcel reached for the picture. He studied it for a while, then placed it back down on the bar.

"Ethan Kruse is his name," Diana said, pointing again. "Do you know him?"

Marcel squinted at Diana. "You're that psychologist," he said, his voice deadpan, but his eyes reflecting his all-too-complete awareness of her situation.

Diana's face flushed as she nodded. She felt naked and ashamed, unmasked for the liar she was. "Has he been in here lately?" she asked quickly to hide her embarrassment.

"Not since before that Hutchins guy died," Marcel said, pointing a splayed finger at James.

Disappointed, Diana slumped on the stool. She twirled the empty glass on the bar.

Marcel's eyes flickered over her face, and a flash of empathy passed through them. "That one's been here since then," he said, pointing at Sandy. "With the other woman and her boyfriend, the professor."

"The other woman—was she tall with red curly hair?" Diana asked, figuring he must be talking about Jill.

Marcel nodded.

"But not Ethan?"

Marcel turned and picked up a rag, studiously wiping the counter along the other side of the bar. Then he pivoted back toward Diana and added, "Been a lot quieter since those two guys stopped coming by."

"What do you mean?" Diana asked, leaning her elbows on the brass railing.

Marcel said nothing for a moment. He studied Diana, then seemed to come to some kind of decision about her. "Especially Kruse. He's been a regular here for years. I've had to cut him off lots of times. Got into fights." He poked the picture again. "Was yelling at Hutchins one of the last times I saw him."

"Ethan and James had a fight in here?" Diana demanded. "Right before James was killed?"

"Don't know about right before," Marcel said, picking up the rag again. "And it wasn't a fight. Just yelling." He turned and walked down to the far end of the bar.

Disappointed, Diana watched his retreating back. Like so much of what she had learned about Jill, she already knew just about everything Marcel had told her about Ethan. His penchant for fights. His aggressiveness toward James. His disappearance. She was coming up empty again.

Slowly Diana climbed off the stool and gathered her things. She left money on the table with her check and headed toward the door. As she passed Marcel, who was engrossed in his scrubbing with his back to her, she called out her thanks. Even she could hear the frustration and tiredness in her voice.

"Try his landlady," Marcel grunted without turning around. "He lives just down the street."

When Diana stepped out of the restaurant, the winter sun was still above the buildings. There was enough time and light left to go to Ethan's apartment—she had even brought the address with her, knowing it to be the logical next step. But, as before, she didn't want to go. For the more she thought about Ethan—about what he was capable of, about what he might have done—the more frightened she became. She might be stalking a killer. Or, if the eyes were more than her overactive paranoia, he might be stalking her.

She glanced down at the piece of paper on which she had copied the address and phone number from Ethan's chart. She had already called the number many times, listening to its hollow ring over and over again. And she knew the street. It was narrow and dingy and lined with seedy double- and triple-deckers. It was in one of those "low-rent" districts in which poor people paid high rents to avoid security deposits and credit checks. The kind of neighborhood where everyone studiously minded his own business.

Diana stood in front of the restaurant and eyed the traffic inching its way along the congested street, listening to the horns honking, the people yelling. She tried to convince herself that the trip would be pointless, that the landlady was sure to be oblivious of the rovings of her transient tenants. But, according to what Ethan had told her, Diana figured he must have lived at Sunderland Court for at least three or four years. So most likely the landlady knew something about him. If she was willing to talk.

A truck was triple-parked in front of the karate studio next door to Ken's, trapping a man who had double-parked. "Son of a bitch!" he was yelling, waving his arms indignantly, as if he were completely guiltless in his current bind. "Stupid, selfish son of a bitch!" Diana watched his futile flailing and then swung her purse over her shoulder, once again marching toward a destination she did not want to reach.

Two blocks in from Mass Ave., Diana felt as if she were in a different world. She pulled her coat more tightly around her, although the afternoon was not cold. She stepped into the middle of the street, although the sidewalk was empty. The bustle and diversity of Central Square had silenced into a grimy sameness of streets littered with garbage and rusty cars. The houses she passed were tired structures whose sagging porches supported families of three-legged furniture. No one was about. If not for the haunting vision of the nursing mother behind bars, Diana would have quickly turned back.

She rounded the corner onto the deadend Sunderland Court, finding more of the same kinds of houses as she tried to avoid the muddy potholes while searching for the correct address. She was surprised to discover that number 17 appeared to be a large, rather respectable house surrounded by a huge porch. But as she drew closer, she realized her original assumptions had been correct: the paint was peeling badly; the railing was broken in places and missing in others; and the floorboards of the porch were so rotted that she had to step carefully to make sure she didn't fall through.

The front door was slightly ajar and lopsided, swinging inward on only two of its three hinges. Diana glanced over her shoulder and then looked into the vestibule—if the dingy space filled with cartons and an amazing number of old television sets could be called a vestibule. She decided not to go in.

Stepping back, she searched the row of buttons to the left of the door. A sign above the top button, scrawled in barely legible Magic Marker, read: "R. M. Masdea, D.D.S. No Appointment Necessary." Next to the other half-dozen buttons were slots either empty or stuffed with ill-fitting pieces of paper. "E. K." was scribbled along the side of the one that must belong to Ethan.

As she pushed the buzzer next to the designation number one, guessing that might belong to the landlady, Diana looked through the murky window into Dr. Masdea's mean little office. Despite her own fear and discomfort, she felt a rush of sympathy for those who had to let someone touch their teeth in such an awful room.

"What?" demanded an annoyed voice from inside the house.

Diana stepped gingerly around the television sets and looked up the large staircase that still retained some of its original grace, despite its missing balustrades and pitted wood.

"What?" asked the young woman who approached the landing. Aside from her hair, which was wild and huge and unkempt, she seemed normal enough, as did the two toddlers peeking out from behind her legs.

"I'm, ah . . ." Diana paused, although she was calmed by the sight of the children and the relatively ordinary-looking woman. "I'm looking for the landlady."

The woman squinted down at Diana and ran her fingers through her hair. "I'm her," she finally said.

Diana unbuttoned her coat and pressed her hand to her lower back. "Could I possibly speak with you for a few minutes?" She smiled and waved her fingers at the children and then added, "I promise I won't be long."

The woman took in Diana's stomach and walked closer to the edge of the stairs, dragging the children along with her. "What do you want?" she asked, not unpleasantly.

"I'm looking for Ethan Kruse," Diana said, deciding on the direct approach, although she wasn't sure why.

"Comes and goes," the woman said, crossing her arms. "Same as I told that cop."

Diana climbed a few steps and stood on a landing about a quarter of the way up so that she was directly facing Ethan's landlady. "Have you seen him lately?"

"You ain't no cop, are you?" the woman demanded. The children were big-eyed and strangely silent, watching Diana.

"I'm a friend of his," Diana said, keeping her eyes locked onto the woman's, trying to look as sincere as she could.

The woman snorted. "Always had a lot of them," she said, eyeing Diana's stomach again. "You're older than most."

"It's really important that I find him," Diana said, letting the woman think what she would.

"You're better off without him, honey," the landlady said. "That guy's no good. Never has been. Never will be. Best you take your baby and go."

"I plan to," Diana said, nodding. "When was the last time you saw him?"

"Slipped his rent under my door first of the month. Full amount in cash. Same as always." She shrugged. "Last time I seen him."

Diana calculated quickly. The first of the month was well after James had been killed. This woman had seen Ethan more recently than anyone else. "So he was here within the last few weeks?" she asked. "He's been home?"

"Guess so." She shrugged again. "Rent got paid. Like I told you, he comes and goes." She leaned down and deftly lifted both children, mounting each on a hip. "Probably shouldn't have let him stay after what happened before," she said as she turned toward her door. "But he pays the rent—and that's more than most of these losers do."

Diana charged up the stairs, sidestepping the toys that

littered the landing. "What do you mean," she demanded. "After what happened before?"

The woman surveyed Diana, then she smiled slyly. "After his last girlfriend got herself a shotgun and blew off her head," she said, her voice filled with equal measures of pity and disgust. "Made a hell of a mess in the apartment." She shook her wild mane of hair. "Hell of a mess," she repeated.

Then she kicked the door closed with her foot, leaving Diana standing alone in the silent, toy-strewn hallway.

Dusk was falling quickly, filling the murky alleys and doorways with ominous shadows. Diana clutched her purse tightly and hurried down the stairs. Ethan's girlfriend had killed herself with a shotgun blast to the head. It probably meant nothing. But it could also mean everything. It could save her neck legally. Or it could get her killed.

Right now, she didn't care much about legal. She was edgy and scared, her nerves like frayed rope, her every sense heightened and painfully alert. All she cared about was getting home.

And then, as she stepped into the street, she caught a movement along the side of one of the houses. She froze for a moment, like a deer caught in headlights, then whirled around. Nothing. Buttoning her coat, Diana focused on the cross street in front of her. Get off Sunderland Court. Turn left and head west for two blocks. Another left and in two blocks she would be on Mass Ave.

She rushed down the street, oblivious of the muddy potholes, stepping wherever her long-legged stride placed her boot. Then she saw it again. There was someone near the doorway of the decaying house on her right. Someone hiding in the gloom of the listing porch. A man. A large man in a bomber jacket. Watching her. He slipped back into the shadows, but Diana knew that this time the eyes were for real.

She began to run and didn't look back. Hearing the footfalls pounding behind her, she ran even faster. She turned the corner of Sunderland Court and raced to the lights of Prospect Street, her body flying on the adrenaline of pure fear. She felt the darkness of his shadow fall onto her back. She felt the weight of it. The terror. She dashed around the corner on to Prospect, toward the bustle of Central Square.

~ 25 ~

DIANA JUMPED INTO HER JEEP AND PUNCHED THE locks on both doors. She rammed the key into the ignition, gunned the engine, and pulled away from the curb. A horn blared in anger, but she didn't care. All that mattered was that she lost whoever was following her. All that mattered was that she got away.

Ethan. She knew it was Ethan. She had seen enough before he ducked inside that doorway. Enough of him, and enough of the jacket. James's leather jacket. The jacket he and Ethan had fought over. The jacket Ethan had never returned.

Diana slammed on her brakes at a red light, her eyes darting feverishly to the left and then to the right. She looked in her rearview mirror, straining to differentiate among the headlights that followed her, struggling to discern if he was still there. She stared at the light, willing it to turn green. She had to get away. Now. This instant.

Ethan was capable of anything.

He was stalking her as she was stalking him. But what did he want? What might he do? The array of possibilities was endless. Frighteningly infinite.

She darted across the Mass Ave. bridge into Boston, weaving carefully between the lanes of traffic. She managed to twist around a truck making a left turn onto Marlborough Street, but was halted by the light at Boylston. When the light finally changed, she stepped on the gas and glanced behind her. As before, a pair of headlights clung to her tail-lights as if leashed by a powerful magnet. But it didn't seem possible that a single car could have stuck with her at every intersection. Or did it?

She moved past the Christian Science Center at a maddeningly slow pace and then turned the jeep sharply onto St. Stephen Street. Checking her rearview mirror again, she saw a line of headlights, paired and strung behind her. But there was no way of knowing whether a set belonged to Ethan.

Diana didn't turn into the alley. Instead she stayed on the street, pulling into a spot a few doors down from the house. She kept the engine idling as she scrutinized the cars attached to the headlights she had feared. They streamed benignly by her. She took a deep breath and dropped her head to the steering wheel. She rubbed a muscle in her neck.

She had either lost him or he had never existed. He had never existed, she told herself. She was running from shadows. Just like last week at the library when she had been so sure Jill was on the other side of the stacks, slinking along the aisle, peering between the volumes. Diana had felt the danger like a physical presence; she smelled it. But when she had marched out to confront Jill, Diana found a redheaded student, at least ten years Jill's junior, sitting cross-legged on the floor. The girl glanced absently up from her book, then returned to her reading.

All Diana had smelled was her own fear.

There was a message from Ethan waiting for her when she went into her office. Diana's hands trembled as she listened. "I'm in Charlotte," he said. "North Carolina. At my brother's. I probably won't be north for a while—but don't worry, I'll keep in touch." Diana shook her head. She knew exactly where Ethan was—and it wasn't North Carolina. Ethan was here. Watching her. Following her.

She snapped the blinds shut and checked the lock on the back door, thinking of the small handgun Craig had ordered. Double-action, he told her when he came home from the store last week, showing her a picture in a catalogue. Some kind of revolver, she remembered, tiny and mean-looking. "Consider it a temporary alarm system," he said in response to her horror at the idea of having a weapon in the house. "I'll get rid of it as soon we fix the real system—well before the baby's old enough to walk." For the first time since the Brady Bill passed, Diana was sorry there was a waiting period to buy guns.

Stop it, she told herself as she removed the message tape and dropped it into her desk drawer. She didn't need a gun. Last week, Detective Levine had asked her to save all of Ethan's messages for him, so she called the police station and told the dispatcher that she had another tape for Levine to pick up. She was being ridiculous. The episode with Ethan's landlady had just freaked her, as had her illusionary pursuit. Most likely Ethan *was* in North Carolina. His taped message did have that long-distance crackle to it, and she thought she remembered a brother somewhere in the South. Most likely it was just the same as the incidents at the library and in the alley: She had imagined the whole thing. There had been no man in a bomber jacket, no footfalls chasing her, no headlights following her. The eyes were not real. She had to stop running from shadows. She had to stop scaring herself with outrageous fantasies. Reality was more than scary enough.

Diana fiddled with the tape in the open drawer before her, trying to catch an elusive memory that danced away every time she got close to it. She thought she remembered something that might impress Detective Levine. Something Ethan had once said about shotguns. And girlfriends.

She went over to the file cabinet containing her group session records, trying to recall exactly when Ethan had started. She pulled two files from the drawer and carried them back to her desk, then flipped open the first one. It had been Halloween—just over one year ago—and by Thanksgiving she had known she had made a terrible mistake.

For months James had been begging her to let Ethan into the group, convinced that she was the only one who could help his friend. "He's a good guy underneath all the cocaine and bravado," James had told her. "I know you could really help him."

After a couple of phone conversations, she had invited Ethan for a preliminary interview. He came in late one afternoon, a sly I've-been-a-bit-naughty aura about him. He was forthcoming about his drinking and drug use, and even admitted to a few petty crimes. "I don't want to be like this anymore," he said, his eyes wide and locked onto hers. "I want to change."

He told the classic borderline tale of constant abandonment by those closest to him. And he had the major single trauma—cringing in the corner of the kitchen as his mother's boyfriend slit her throat—that Diana was finding so common among her research sample. Although a small voice in the back of her mind told her not to do it—a voice she now wished she had heeded—Diana had agreed to let Ethan in the group for a three-month trial period.

Diana didn't need to read her notes to remember that he had shown up for that first session wearing a wide orange tie with skeletons dancing all over it—and flying high on cocaine. Ethan had squirmed in his seat, played with the ring on his finger, and sniffled and swallowed a lot. His pupils were dilated, and he excused himself twice to use the bathroom—presumably to take a few snorts. Had she known him better she might have challenged him or brought it up to the group, asking them what it felt like to have their cohesion upset; but she hadn't been sure he didn't suffer from allergies—and she had known the group wasn't ready.

Her notes did remind her that, despite the cocaine, he had been "attentive and sweet," listening to Sandy's struggles with her father and even offering a few, quite sensible, solutions.

But within a month Ethan's flimsy veneer of charm had worn through. He was edgy and irritable, snapping at Sandy to grow up and for Bruce to get a life. By Christmas he was swaggering around the room, taunting James and Terri for being "wimpy-assed teetotalers" and bragging that he could drink an entire bottle of Jack Daniels and not feel a thing. And then there had been the fistfight over James's bomber jacket. She had asked him to leave and he had—for almost two months.

When he returned, all contrite and apologetic, full of resolve to change and willingness to meet all her demands for his reentry into the group, she had allowed him back in. It had been a mistake, but terminating a patient was a ticklish and formidable task, one that Diana had always found extremely difficult. Gail claimed it was because Diana's heart was too soft—that her patients had survived before they had started seeing her, and that they would survive long after her as well. Diana grimaced, thinking of how long James had survived after she had terminated with him: less than three months.

With James there had just been no choice. He had gotten completely out of hand. Although he had been on a downward slide the entire last year of his life, this past summer had been a disaster—a disaster for which Diana held herself responsible. "I need you to think of me as much as I think of you," James had begged one July morning after Diana caught him following her to the library. "Otherwise there's no purpose to my life." When she told him that his purpose for living had to come from within himself, he had blamed her for his inability to get his life together, declaring that if she were a better doctor he would be better too. Diana had known his words held more than a grain of truth.

So she had tried to be a better doctor: talking to her peer supervisory group, consulting an expert on borderline disorders at Harvard, working out her feelings in her journal. But the damage had been done, and James only got worse. "I'm going to kill myself and it's up to you to see that I don't," he warned, trying to use her feelings for him against her. Where before he had pretended to accidentally bump into her at the store or the library, he now blatantly followed her to class, to the parking lot, to the dry cleaner's. He hid in her car and harassed Craig's secretary with phony appointments. He also began stealing her things: the hairbrush she left on a shelf in the office, the coral paperweight her parents had brought her from Greece. When she confronted him about his inappropriate behavior, he crossed his arms and said, "If I'm going nowhere, you've only yourself to blame."

Gail and Craig and her entire peer group argued for termination. "You're not doing either one of you any good," Gail told her. "If you really care about him, refer him elsewhere." Craig was even more adamant—especially after they discovered Diana was pregnant. "I don't want him around you," he said. "We don't know what he's capable of."

With much ambivalence and trepidation, Diana told James she couldn't be his therapist anymore. Rather than the anger she had expected, James's face crumpled and tears streamed down his cheeks.

"Please," he had begged. "Don't turn me away. I've nowhere to go without you."

Although she wanted to take him in her arms and tell him he could stay, Diana remained resolute, explaining what a good doctor Alan Martinson was and how much better off James would be with him. She set up a series of termination sessions, but James never returned. Within the week, he was at Mass General having Seconal pumped from his stomach. Less than three months later, he was dead.

Diana closed her eyes against the pain and forced herself to return to her search for Ethan's shotgun reference. After about an hour of fruitless reading, she finally found the reference in the notes from a group the following spring: Ethan had talked about how his mother's boyfriend had taken him duck hunting and taught him to shoot—before the boyfriend killed the mother, that was. Diana shook her head. Nothing that would impress Levine. Anyone could have been taught to use a shotgun. And the truth was, a person didn't need lessons to know how to blow someone's head off.

Disappointed, Diana put the file back in the cabinet. She called Mitch and briefly summarized her afternoon; he was very interested in Ethan's girlfriend's death, and they made an appointment for the next day. She called Craig and asked him to pick up Chinese food on his way home. Then she pulled out her notes and began reviewing for the next day's lecture.

When Craig got home they ate in front of the evening news, pressed close together on the couch, open boxes of moo shu chicken and Hunan-spiced shrimp spread on the coffee table in front of them. Diana told him about her visits with Marcel and Ethan's landlady—omitting her fears of being followed. Craig told her his client in Nashville was concerned about a slip in the construction schedule and that he had to go down there on Wednesday.

"I worry about you here by yourself for three days," he said, putting down his chopsticks and looking at her seriously.

"I'll be fine." Diana loaded more moo shu chicken into the empty pancake on her plate and carefully rolled it into the shape of a fat cigar. "Gail stays home alone all the time when Shep travels." Diana wasn't nearly as confident as she sounded, but Craig was having enough trouble at work because of her; if he refused to go to Tennessee—which she knew he would if she seemed the least bit afraid—it could make things extremely difficult for him. "It's not a big deal," she added, smiling and taking a bite of the sloppy pancake.

"I'll be right back," Craig said, standing up and walking into the hallway. He returned with a large white bag. Slowly he removed the contents: a box of bullets, a Ziploc bag containing some oddly shaped tools, and a black rectangular box that Diana knew contained the gun. "I know you don't want this in the house," he said before she could speak, "but it'll make me feel a lot better if you just let me leave it in my night table drawer."

Diana put down her moo shu chicken and pressed herself into the couch. "I don't like this."

"And you think I do?" Craig asked as he snapped open the box and showed her the gun lying on ridges of foam rubber: It was shiny and small and looked more like a toy than a deadly weapon.

Despite her aversion, Diana reached out and touched it. "I thought it would be a bluish color," she said.

"I got a license so it's all legal and official. I signed up for lessons at a firing range somewhere out in Weston. You should take a few too. This thing doesn't have a safety— once it's loaded it's ready to go."

Diana pulled her hand back as if it had been burned. "I'm not learning how to shoot a gun."

"Okay, okay," Craig said, snapping the case shut. "I'll load it later and put it away—you can forget it's even here."

But Diana knew she wouldn't forget.

The next day Diana decided to walk to her appointment with Mitch. Although it would be dark by the time the meeting was over, her path home from his office crossed some of the brightest and busiest segments of Boston—especially now, as the city was festooned with millions of Christmas lights and what seemed to be almost as many shoppers. She hoped the gaiety would be contagious.

The late afternoon sky was an unforgiving steel-gray as Diana stood in front of Symphony Hall waiting for the light to change. A cold wind was kicking up off the water, and she wrapped her scarf an extra time around her neck. Across the street, the Christian Science Plaza was blazing with lights and bustling with people, as if defying both the weather and the calendar. But neither the lights nor the people could fool Diana. It was cold, it was bleak, and today was the first day of December.

As she walked across the plaza, ignoring the Salvation Army Santas and the street merchants hawking Christmas baubles beneath the columns, she reviewed all she had to tell Mitch, and worried about all he had to tell her. She had detected both an edge of excitement and a tinge of despair in his voice when she had called to set up their meeting. "We'll go over everything tomorrow," he had promised. "Tomorrow we'll sort the germane from the irrelevant." For some reason, Diana found the idea of sorting the germane from the irrelevant quite ominous.

She was so distracted that she almost tripped over a child turning circles along the side of the reflecting pool. A little boy in a bright purple parka bumped into her, lost his balance, and sat down hard on the concrete. Surprised, he leaned his head backward until his eyes met hers, then began to giggle. His mother ran over to them and scooped the child up in her arms. "Sorry," she said to Diana, smiling as she nuzzled his neck. "He never watches where he's going. Do you? Do you?" she demanded in mock seriousness. The little boy continued to giggle. As his mother turned around, he raised a red mittened hand to Diana and waved good-bye.

Diana stopped and watched the small red mitten disappear into the crowd. She continued to wave, somehow uplifted by the encounter, although the child was no longer aware of her. She strode more purposefully toward Mitch's, focusing on the encouraging things she had to tell him: that Ethan and James had been heard arguing at Ken's right before James's murder; that Ethan had most likely been to his apartment within the last couple of weeks; that she had the feeling the bartender knew more than he was telling. And she already knew Mitch considered her discovery about Ethan's girlfriend's "suicide" germane.

Not bad for an amateur, she thought, riding the escalator down toward Boylston Street. And as she walked past the towering Prudential Center Christmas tree, she was reminded that the coming of December also brought her that much closer to the birth of her child.

By the time she stepped into Mitch's office, she was feeling much better, almost optimistic. "So, let's sort the germane from the irrelevant," she said cheerfully as she sank into the chair he pulled out for her.

Mitch raised his eyebrows in mild surprise and went around to the other side of his desk. He nodded and pulled a folder from the drawer. "You first." As before, he took notes and listened carefully, stopping to ask her a question now and then. She told him everything she had discovered and everything she thought about each piece of information. When she finished, he seemed very pleased and declared all of her information germane.

"Kruse never said anything to you about the girlfriend's suicide?" Mitch asked.

She shook her head. "Patients only tell you what they want—and there's no way for a therapist to find anything out unless you're told."

"But wouldn't the police call you?" Mitch asked, obviously surprised.

"About what?"

"I don't know—like if something strange happened involving one of your patients? Or if a patient got arrested?"

Diana smiled; the outlandish assumptions people had about therapists always amused her. "How would the police know that he was one of my patients?"

Mitch nodded. "I'll have Norman run a check on the girlfriend's suicide—we just might have something here. And," he added, pulling a small packet of computer printouts from the file, "I've got a few interesting tidbits for you too. Many of them based on the information you got in Norwich." He smiled at her. "Maybe you're in the wrong occupation?"

Flushed with optimism and Mitch's compliments, Diana grinned. "It's nice to know I have a fall-back career if this one blows up in my face." Her grin disappeared as she listened to her own words.

"Here's my good news," he said quickly. "Jill Hutchins may have an alibi, but she's looking more and more suspicious with every additional piece of information we discover about her."

"She is?"

He flipped through the printouts. "According to this preliminary credit check, the woman is deeply in debt, and her credit rating is abysmal." He tapped the desk with his pen. "But there's something else here . . ."

"Something else?"

He locked his fingers behind his head and looked at the ceiling. "It's subtle, but her pattern of debt seems to indicate a kind of desperation," he said. "At various times, on a single day, she's pulled cash from every credit card. All the cash she could get." He turned and looked at Diana. "That and her criminal record."

"Jill has a criminal record?" Diana leaned closer to Mitch. "Something we can use?"

He held up his hands. "Don't get too excited. We don't know if it's germane or irrelevant yet." He smiled at her, then continued, "But it appears that Ms. Hutchins was arrested for assault with a deadly weapon out in Des Moines a few years back. And she also had a run-in with the police in Omaha, Nebraska, in the early eighties. Grand theft auto."

"Molly Arell's perfect little angel . . ."

"The aunt probably never knew anything about it. The Nebraska thing happened a long time ago—and a long way from home." He checked his pages once more. "And the Des Moines charge was dropped rather abruptly."

"Whom did she assault?" Diana asked, beginning to enjoy herself. "With what deadly weapon?"

"Her husband, with a knife, in the kitchen," he said, his voice serious, but his eyes laughing.

Diana flashed on Jill holding a poker to her stomach the afternoon she had gone in search of her journal. She saw herself on her knees, looking into Jill's feverish eyes. Perhaps this wasn't so much fun after all.

"This isn't a parlor game," Mitch said, as if reading her mind. "We've got to watch this woman. I think we should follow up on why the Des Moines charges got dropped."

Diana nodded. "What about Ethan?"

Mitch pulled out another folder, flipped it open, and glanced into it. "Nice company you're keeping," he said.

"That bad?" Diana asked.

"He starts off with everything from disorderly conduct to burglary to DWI . . ."

Diana nodded.

"Spends some time in Leavenworth—but he's released early for his good behavior, and, I quote, 'impressing the authorities with his attitude, remorse, and plans for the future.'"

"I believe that," Diana said, shaking her head and smiling slightly. At least she wasn't the only one Ethan had bamboozled. He had told stories Diana believed to be true because no one could make up anything so detailed and complicated—but she'd discovered later they were pure fabrication.

"Kruse's list ends with compounding a felony, arson, and rape," Mitch was saying.

"Rape?"

"It wasn't just Ethan involved in that rape," he said slowly.

Diana's heart sank, and she knew before she heard the words what Mitch was going to tell her.

"He and James Hutchins were arrested last November—November 15, to be exact—for rape. A young woman claimed they gave her a ride home from a party and then wouldn't leave her apartment until she had sex with them both."

"That's impossible," Diana cried. "Something like that couldn't have happened to James last year—he would have told me about it . . ." Her voice dropped off at the end of the sentence; as she said the words, she knew they weren't true.

Mitch raised his eyebrows, and Diana looked at her hands. "If it makes you feel any better," he said, "these charges were also dropped rather abruptly."

"You think there's a connection between this and Jill's thing?" she asked. "Because the charges for both were dropped?"

He shrugged. "Given the size of James Hutchins's bank account, I think it's a distinct possibility." They looked at each other in silence for a moment. Then Mitch said, "So now are you ready for the bad news?"

Diana smiled weakly. "I'm finding the good news hard enough to take."

"The police seem to be buying Molly Arell's story," he said quickly. "And they haven't had any more luck than we have finding Kruse."

Diana nodded.

"But it's Herb Levine I'm worried about . . ."

Diana rubbed her palms on her jumper and said nothing, feeling as if her neck were in a guillotine.

"Word on the street is that Levine's convinced some ADA to convene a grand jury—"

"ADA?" Diana asked, more to slow Mitch down than because she really needed, or cared, to know.

"Assistant district attorney. Your colleagues will be served subpoenas to appear—"

"But how can they do this before anyone's been arrested?" Diana interrupted again.

"It's a discovery suit," he explained patiently. "The grand jury will use the testimony to determine if there's probable cause to issue an arrest warrant."

Arrest warrant. The words reverberated through Diana's brain and her fingers began to shake. She pressed her hands under her arms to still them. *Arrest warrant.*

Mitch leaned toward her and asked gently, "Will it be really bad for you if they talk?"

Diana thought of the dream she had described to her group in which she and James had been living naked and happy on a desert island populated by blue trees that grew upside down. She thought of how she had told them of Craig's anger at James's stalking—and of his fury and threats to confront James after the car accident. She thought of the conversation she had had with Gail about James's will. It was all she could do to nod her head.

~ 26 ~

*T*HE NIGHT WAS CLEAR AND BRITTLE AS DIANA WALKED past the Ritz Carlton on her way home from Mitch's office. She glanced upward in confusion, thinking she remembered the afternoon being gray, her walk overedged by clouds. But even through the city lights, she could see that the sky was now black and empty, a vacant backdrop. Was she mistaken? Had she come so unglued that she couldn't tell this day from another? Or had the wind just blown the clouds away while she had been in with Mitch?

She remembered a comment Mark Twain had once made about New England's climate: that he had counted one hundred and thirty-six kinds of weather inside of twenty-four hours. But Twain's thoughts didn't cheer her. Helplessness and despair surrounded her like a shroud. Despite Mitch's guarded optimism and the open expanse of the Commonwealth Avenue mall in front of her, Diana felt crowded and claustrophobic. And a little unsteady.

For after Mitch had told her about the grand jury and the possibility of an arrest warrant being issued, she had separated from herself. Completely detached. Suddenly, instead of sitting in the chair across from his desk, she was off to the side, hovering somewhere above the small couch, watching herself as if she were an actress on the stage.

Diana stopped at the corner of Fairfield and Comm Ave. and grabbed a streetlamp. Although she hadn't been frightened at the time—it had actually been a strangely pleasurable experience—she was very frightened now. And although it had never happened to her before, except perhaps for a few moments in the shower or walking on a treadmill, she knew what it was: She had dissociated.

Releasing her grip on the streetlamp and pushing herself toward Boylston Street, Diana reminded herself that dissociating could be a perfectly normal, even desirable, phenomenon. That people aspired toward it during meditation, that artists and writers found it to be the highest plane of creativity. She knew it could be brought on by simple fatigue or stress. But she also knew it could be a sign of a serious mental problem.

She had actually dissociated, she thought as she stepped onto the escalator that would take her to the Prudential Center mall. It had actually happened. As a detached, almost disinterested observer, she had watched herself nod agreement to Mitch's confident declaration that they would find a way to break Molly Arell's alibi and use both Ethan and Jill's criminal backgrounds against them. She had also nodded her acceptance of his recommendation that they wait until they had amassed more information before going to the police with their discoveries—even the news about Ethan's girlfriend, he had said, would be more powerful if it was presented along with all the incriminating facts. Then she had watched herself authorize him to have Norman do more intensive investigations of Ethan, Jill, and Molly. But she had felt as if it weren't she, Diana Marcus, doing these things. Although she knew that it was.

Then the Diana who was simultaneously herself and not herself, had agreed to go back and talk with the bartender at Ken's—this time focusing on Jill while trying to gain Marcel's confidence so that he would tell her whatever it was he had withheld before. And she had offered to search her records once again for clues to Ethan's possible whereabouts.

As she had left the office, Mitch squeezed her arm and she was tremendously relieved to find herself fused with herself once again. "Chin up," he told her. "I've seen bleaker cases turn around."

But Diana didn't believe him. Molly wasn't going to crack. Ethan wasn't going to be found. And she, Diana, was going to be punished for her mistakes in a way she never could have envisioned: She was going to prison. Levine already had her on opportunity, and once the grand jury convened and her colleagues testified—especially Gail— there would be more than enough motive. In her distraction, Diana tripped getting off the escalator on the back side of the Prudential Center. Flailing her arms wildly, she was overwhelmed by her own powerlessness. In that fleeting second of vertigo and terror, she saw herself hunched on the sidewalk clutching her stomach, blood running between her legs. She cried out and a teenage girl grabbed her arm. Diana righted herself and smiled weakly at the girl.

Oblivious to the cold and the crowds, Diana dropped to a concrete bench not far from the escalator and stared at the towering buildings and glass walkways of Copley Place, at the flickering Christmas lights adorning the Colonnade Hotel, at the water rolling over the edge of the reflecting pool. The world she thought she knew, the city she loved, the people she had cared for, were all alien and frightening. She pressed closer to the couple sharing the bench with her. Everyone and everything was so much more dangerous than she had ever imaged.

But Levine was her biggest threat. He and the assistant district attorney and the grand jury. None of them were psychologists; they would never understand why she had needed to discuss her attraction to James with her peers, why it had been necessary for her to confess the depths of her passion, the fire he had ignited within her—any more than anyone had understood why she had needed to write about it in her journal. And no one was going to believe that she hadn't followed through on such powerful feelings.

Everyone was going to think that she had had sex with James—and that she had killed him.

Diana rubbed her arms briskly, but her external actions could do nothing to ward off the cold that emanated from deep within the marrow of her bones. The grand jury would not only hear of her sexual feelings for James, but once her peer group explained the basis for countertransference, they would also hear of his passion for her. They would learn she had been forced to end his therapy because her husband was worried James might harm her; and they would most likely wonder if Craig hadn't also been a little bit jealous. But most damning, the grand jury would learn from Gail that James had indeed told her that he was going to change his will—and that she had actually joked about killing him for the money.

Diana stared upward, straining to glimpse the heavens through all the earth light; but from where she sat, she could not. The couple on her left rose and wandered off toward Copley Place. The bench felt empty and cold, exposing her unprotected flank.

Diana stood and headed home, taking the path of least resistance between the swarms of hurrying shoppers. She allowed an ample woman gripping two matching shopping bags to elbow around her. She slowed behind an elderly couple holding hands. She skirted two boys playing tag. But she knew that the path of least resistance was not going to be the road she could take for long.

Diana forced herself to go to the Stop and Shop and pick up some chicken for dinner. She also bought some grapefruit and salad and wild rice. She headed home with the rest of the working hungry, balancing her parcel and straining to occupy her mind with the pros and cons of various recipes. But the words *arrest warrant* kept pushing against her mind's debate between barbecue versus honey-mustard chicken.

As she chopped tomatoes and cucumbers and whipped up a honey-mustard sauce, she focused on the things she could do to keep Levine at bay. Absently she boiled water for the rice and set the table. Tomorrow was Wednesday; her last patient was at noon. After she dropped Craig at the airport, she would be free. She tossed the salad and cut the grapefruit. She would go to Ken's and talk to Marcel. Then she would come home and go through Ethan's records to search for hints of his whereabouts.

Her reverie was broken by the chime of the doorbell. When she saw Levine standing on the stoop, she froze.

"Got the message that you had another Kruse tape for me," he said. "I know it's dinnertime, but I was in the neighborhood." He smiled sheepishly and shrugged. "Do you mind?"

"No, no, of course not," Diana said, ushering him into the house.

He glanced around. "Your husband isn't home yet?" he asked.

Diana shook her head. "The tape's just downstairs in my office. I'll get it for you. Do you want to come down with me? Or would you rather wait?" She gestured awkwardly in the general direction of the kitchen. "I was just making dinner. Can I get you something to eat or drink?" she blurted before thinking.

To Diana's chagrin, Levine happily took her up on the offer, declaring he would just love a cup of coffee. Furious with herself for her stupidity, she told him to go sit in the kitchen while she ran and got the tape.

When she came back upstairs, she handed him the plastic box and smiled in what she hoped was a perky—and innocent—manner. "Regular, I presume?" she asked, waving him into a chair and walking to the refrigerator for the coffee.

The detective eyed the two place settings on the table and sat down in the extra chair. "You bet," he said. "I'm on till eleven." He crossed his long legs casually, resting one ankle on the other. As he watched her setting up the coffee maker, Levine turned the rectangular tape box from side to side, hitting it on the kitchen table, saying nothing.

His silence and the dull clunk of plastic against wood got on Diana's nerves. She bit her lip and kept her back to him. But when she finished putting the filter in place, scooping the coffee, pouring the water, and pushing the appropriate buttons, she had to turn around. "It'll be a few minutes," she said lamely.

He nodded, still clunking the tape. "As long as I'm here," he said, "and as long as we have to wait for the coffee, perhaps you won't mind if I take advantage of your professional expertise again? I really could use some help understanding the more complicated psychological stuff." He flashed her a winsome smile. "To be perfectly honest, I'm pretty damn confused."

Diana sat down in the chair across from him. She had to be cautious here, she had to remember not to be disarmed by his charm: Levine was sharper than he let on. He probably hadn't come just for the tape, he had most likely chosen the opportunity—and even this particular hour—for his own ulterior motives. "I'll be happy to try," she said, her voice guarded.

"I've been going through James Hutchins's medical reports and talking to doctors and psychologists—sometimes I think I've talked to every shrink in town." His eyes sparkled mischievously. "I've even tried reading some of those deadly psychology textbooks . . ."

Diana nodded, hoping she was keeping the fear his words elicited from showing in her eyes.

"And, frankly, Dr. Marcus, I'm very confused about this whole diagnosis thing." He lifted his hands and turned his palms up. "I just don't understand how one expert can say a man's so sick that he's a danger to himself and others—

and another expert thinks there's nothing much wrong with him at all."

"You're talking about John Pumphrey?"

Levine pulled the ubiquitous notebook from his pocket and flipped a few pages. "And Benjamin J. Talcott, M.D."

"Borderline personality disorder expert," Diana muttered.

"He's not?" Levine asked.

Diana stood and took a coffee mug from a doorless cabinet. She filled the cup and placed it before the detective. "Dr. Pumphrey spent three days with James Hutchins," she said. "I spent three years."

He nodded his thanks. "So you're saying you knew Hutchins better?"

"I'm saying that James Hutchins lied." Diana put cream and sugar on the table and handed Levine a spoon. "It's part of the disease. People suffering from borderline personality disorder are often quite inventive—and quite believable—liars. 'Lucid and forthcoming' is how I think I remember Pumphrey describing James in his report. Pumphrey didn't know James, so he couldn't tell." She had known James, Diana reminded herself, and she hadn't always been able to tell either. He had obviously failed to mention the rape incident with Ethan, Jill's reconciliation with Molly—who knew what else. "It can be very tricky," she added, whether in her own defense or Pumphrey's, she wasn't sure. "His diagnosis was probably reasonable, given the information he had."

"But even your friend . . ." Levine glanced down at his notes. "Alan Martinson. Even Dr. Martinson said Hutchins might not have borderline personality disorder, that he might only be suffering from posttraumatic stress syndrome."

Diana turned abruptly and picked up the wooden spoon resting on the stove. Despite his claims of ignorance, Detective Levine sounded as if he knew exactly what he was talking about. She stirred the rice, then checked the chicken. She turned and leaned back against the counter. She looked directly at Levine. "You haven't actually talked to Alan Martinson, have you?"

The detective looked a little sheepish and had the grace to blush slightly. Then he grinned at her. "I just read what he said in the *Inquirer*."

"Go talk to Alan," Diana told him, her confidence growing. "He'll explain the part of the story that the *Inquirer* chose not to print. The part about how some of us are starting to think that the label of borderline personality disorder or posttraumatic stress makes no difference. The part about how sick James was either way." She crossed her arms over her chest. "I had terminated with James. He was very angry with me."

Levine stirred some sugar into his coffee and looked at her thoughtfully. "So Hutchins did the whole thing just to get you in trouble? The Scotch-and-Seconal suicide attempt? The lies to Pumphrey, Martinson—and that other guy, Talcott?"

"Benjamin J. Talcott, M.D.," Diana said, "never met James Hutchins in his life."

"But Dr. Pumphrey said—"

"Look," Diana interrupted. "Pumphrey's a first-year resident—and James was an extremely smart and manipulative man. It was no contest. James could be very charming when he chose to be. He could present himself as very normal."

"But he wasn't?"

"Let me put it this way, Detective. Dr. Pumphrey did a suicidality risk assessment on James and, based on his analysis, determined that there was very little danger that James would kill himself." Diana raised her eyebrows. "And then look what he went out and did." She tilted her head and smiled at Levine.

"Except, Dr. Marcus," the detective said, his eyes locked onto hers, "as it turned out, Mr. Hutchins didn't kill himself at all—somebody else did."

Diana felt Levine's words like a blow. She knew the impact registered in her eyes and she quickly turned to stir the rice. How could she have been so stupid? she berated herself as she removed the chicken from the oven and placed it on the stove. How had she gotten so damn cocky and self-confident that she had forgotten James had been murdered? She had fallen right in Levine's trap, that was how. And she had shown him how close to the edge she actually was.

Diana jabbed a couple of pieces of chicken with a fork to test them for doneness; the inside was just pink and the juices were slightly opaque. She slipped the pan back into the oven and switched off the heat. "Of course," she said, turning and trying to arrange her face in as innocent an expression as she could. "What a stupid thing for me to say."

Levine took a sip of his coffee. "This case is confusing everybody." He glanced at the clock and leaned back in his chair, as if he were planning to stay for dinner. "You should see poor Mrs. Manfredi." He shook his head. "She sure is one for your books."

"James's landlady?" Diana asked, relieved with Levine's change of subject. "The one you think might not be 'all there'?"

Levine sipped his coffee and recrossed his legs. "She suddenly remembers everything—and recognizes everybody. I think if I showed her a picture of Sigmund Freud, she'd tell me that he had been to visit Hutchins right before he was killed—and that he had been fighting with him." The detective chuckled. "Is there a name for someone who thinks everybody's a suspect, Dr. Marcus? You guys got one for that?"

Diana dropped back into the chair, suddenly not happy with the turn of their conversation, worried that this wasn't really about Mrs. Manfredi at all. That this was really about her. Paranoia, she thought in answer to Levine's question, although she didn't speak it aloud. Paranoid, just like me.

"Do you know," Levine continued, leaning toward her, "that Mrs. Manfredi claims that sometime right before the

murder, she saw an entire cast of characters fighting with
James: the sister, Kruse, the sister's boyfriend, you . . ."
He paused and put his mug on the table, watching her
closely.

Diana nodded for him to go on, as if unconcerned that a
policeman had just told her she had been seen arguing with
a man "sometime right before" he was murdered. Levine
seemed unperturbed; therefore, so would she. Diana swallowed the bile that rose to her throat, wishing she hadn't
promised Mitch not to discuss what they had discovered
about Jill and Ethan.

When Diana didn't say anything, Levine continued,
"According to her, a whole bunch of people—including
the mailman—were all at Hutchins's apartment fighting
with the him in the weeks prior to his murder." He
shook his head. "She even says your husband was
there!"

"My husband," Diana gasped, glad that she was sitting
down. "That's impossible. Craig doesn't even know where
James lived."

"That's why I figure this woman's going round the bend,"
the detective said, glancing at the clock again. "Do you think
he'll be home soon?"

"Craig?" Diana asked, knowing that, of course, Levine
was referring to Craig. "You want to know when my husband will be home?"

Levine nodded as if her questions weren't stupid.

"He's—" she stammered. "He's already late. He should
have been home about fifteen minutes ago." Could Craig
have gone to James's? It didn't seem possible. But the truth
was, he could have gotten the address from her files. And
he had definitely been angry enough after James had popped up in the back seat of the jeep, causing her to hit that
parked car. "If anything had happened to you or the baby,"
Craig had said, "I would've killed that guy." Then another
thought struck Diana. "How did this Mrs. Manfredi identi-
fy my husband?" she demanded.

Levine shrugged. "Oh, you know, I was just showing her a bunch of pictures, and she was pointing out who she had seen at Hutchins's and who she hadn't. Your husband was one of many she claimed to have seen—too many for my taste, I might add."

"But I don't understand why you were showing her pictures of Craig in the first place," Diana said, her blood running ice-cold. "Or where you got them."

The detective grinned and slowly lifted the coffee mug to his lips. "Just thorough, I guess."

⌒ 27 ⌒

$\mathcal{D}$IANA FELL INTO COMPLETE SILENCE. SHE KNEW SHE should chat, discuss the weather or politics or the environmental crisis, but she didn't. She just sat at the table and stared mutely into the doorless cabinets, trying to keep herself from fixating on the clock that refused to move, on the doorknob that didn't turn, on how long she would remain a prisoner in her own kitchen. Levine casually sipped his coffee, seemingly unperturbed by the quiet. They waited for Craig.

After the longest fifteen minutes Diana had ever lived, he finally showed up. "Detective," Craig said, walking into the kitchen. He draped his jacket over a chair as nonchalantly as if it were an everyday occurrence to find a homicide detective seated at his dinner table. Looking at the small box Levine held in his hand, he asked, "Here for the latest Kruse tape?"

"And a few cups of coffee," Levine said, lifting his mug and smiling. "Along with some of your wife's psychological expertise."

Craig stood behind Levine and raised his eyebrows at Diana; she pretended not to notice. "I think I'll join you,"

Craig said smoothly, walking over to the coffee maker. "Can I pour you some more?"

"I've had enough, thanks," Levine answered. "But I did have a couple of questions for you."

"For me?" Craig put his coffee cup down on the counter and went to stand behind Diana. He placed his hands lightly on her shoulders. "I'd be happy to answer anything that will help solve this case."

The detective leaned back in his chair. Diana wanted to warn Craig, to prepare him, but she knew there was nothing she could do. "Did you ever go to James Hutchins's apartment?" Levine asked.

Craig's fingers clutched Diana's shoulders for a brief second, then relaxed. "Of course not," he said, coming out from behind her, his hands held lightly behind his back. "Why would I go there?"

"Someone said they saw you arguing with Hutchins in front of his house." Levine didn't move a muscle; his eyes remained glued to Craig's. "Not long before he was murdered."

"Then someone is wrong." Craig was as self-possessed as if he were explaining a design to one of his architectural clients. "I don't even know where James Hutchins lived."

"That's what your wife said." Levine nodded and stood. "Frankly, I'm starting to think this so-called witness is a little bit suspect."

Craig offered his hand to Levine. "I've heard there are a lot of crackpots out there always wanting to confess or give evidence in big cases." He smiled winningly. "It must be hard to sort the real ones from the cranks."

Levine pumped Craig's hand and chuckled. "And to sort the truth from the lies," he added. Then he turned to Diana and pulled a notebook from his coat. "Remember you told me how you and Hutchins met accidentally for lunch one day?"

Diana couldn't move; fear gripped her in the chair. The policeman had been sitting here for almost an hour, but he had waited until this particular moment to bring up this particular subject; whatever was coming wasn't good. "We met accidentally at the library," she corrected him.

"Right, right." Levine flipped through his notebook. "Did you also meet accidentally at the Capitol Theater in Arlington one afternoon this past winter? On January 10, to be exact."

"You went to the movies with him?" Craig demanded, oblivious of the close scrutiny the detective paid him. "Diana?"

"It—it was a documentary," she stuttered. "About a woman overcoming childhood abuse." Diana clasped her hands tightly under the table and looked at Craig for support; but there was none to be found. "It—it was a therapeutic outing," she tried to explain. "Purely therapeutic . . ."

Craig stood completely still, staring at her, his face pale and his fists clenched. He said nothing.

Herb Levine nodded. Then he told her he would be stopping by with a warrant to take custody of her printer, wished them bon appetit, and left.

Craig brought the salad and rice to the table. He poured them each a glass of water and sat down, placing his napkin on his lap. "Chicken smells good."

"I'm so sorry—"

Craig waved Diana's apologies aside. "It feels weird," he said calmly. "I've never been a murder suspect before."

"I don't think you are now." Diana forked a piece of chicken onto each of their places. "I think this is just Levine's way of freaking us out."

"Well, it worked," he said, then started eating the dried-out chicken and limp salad as if nothing unusual had occurred.

Diana poked at her chicken, then cut a tiny piece and tried to chew it, but it was no use; nothing would go down, and she discreetly spit it into her napkin. Craig was too composed. And too distant. She wanted him to yell, to scream, to cry—to do anything but just sit there, calmly eating his dinner; she needed him to connect with her. "What time's your plane tomorrow?' she finally asked, although she already knew the answer.

"I need to be at Logan by one-thirty. But I decided I'll just take my suitcase into work in the morning and take a taxi from there. There's no need for you to come get me and drag all the way out to the airport. No point in messing with your schedule," Craig answered, although she had told him yesterday that her afternoon was free.

"My last patient's at noon," she assured him. "It won't be a problem. I'd like to drive you." Diana could see from the set of Craig's face that he wanted to argue, but instead he slumped back in his chair and said nothing. "Nashville's supposed to be a nice town," she added. "Weather should be warmer than here."

Craig agreed, and they talked politely of the clients he would see, the hotel he would stay in, the building he was designing. But it was as if neither of them were really there. As if they were automatons Diana and Craig, playing their parts, saying their lines, while the real Diana and Craig were elsewhere.

They fell into silence, and Diana played with her rice, concentrating on sorting the dark grains from the lighter ones. But the rice was mushy from too much stirring and the kernels wouldn't separate. She raised her eyes and looked at Craig, at his clenched jaw, at his eyes staring unseeing into the dark alley. She thought of the empty whitewashed room upstairs, of the fantasy mural he was going to paint. Of how happy she had been standing in that room right before she got the call that James had died. She began to cry softly.

Craig turned his eyes from the window, but they remained empty and vacant—just like the nursery. He watched her tears, but didn't rise to comfort her. He just continued to eat his chicken, saying nothing at all.

Diana swiped at her face with her napkin and stood, dumping her uneaten food into the sink. Slowly, deliberately, she pushed it into the garbage disposal. Turning on the switch, she watched, mesmerized, as the swirling water washed her dinner down the drain. She imagined it spilling into the sewers and traveling under the city until it merged with the sea.

Craig brought his plate over and they cleaned up in strained silence. "If you don't need me anymore," he said, "I think I'll go pack."

Diana nodded. Pushing a sponge across the already clean counters, she listened to him muttering and slamming drawers and closet doors. When there were no more surfaces to wipe, she went down to her office and turned on her computer. She had to focus. She had to think about something besides the emptiness.

She pulled out her notes and flipped through the introductory section of her article. Finding her place in the document, she ordered herself to write. But she couldn't concentrate. Her mind wandered to an article she had read in the *Globe*. It had described a new "humane" program in a women's prison in New York in which incarcerated women who gave birth were allowed to keep their babies for a year. The program was run much like a kibbutz, the article had explained, allowing visits for nursing and special play hours, but separating the babies from their mothers at night. The women took parenting courses that continued even after their children were placed in foster care. This "humane" program taught mothers how to care for their babies—and then it took their babies away.

Diana pressed her hands to her stomach, searching for the butterfly kick. "Don't you worry," she whispered to her child, her voice cracking. "I won't let them take you away from me." But she felt nothing under her palm, and despair surrounded her like a shroud.

Although she tried to force her mind back to her research, her heart ached and images of her childhood filled her vision: herself as a four-year-old, skipping along the beach, her tiny hand encircled by her mother's large, warm one;

standing in a boat gliding under Niagara Falls, her head tipped back to catch the spray as Scott and her parents laughed; eating Thanksgiving dinner with the whole noisy extended family clustered around her mother's not-quite-large-enough dining room table.

Then, in a strange mental juxtaposition, she flashed to sharing a turkey sandwich with James that day at the Public Gardens. She had known it wasn't quite right, and her every sense had been heightened by the faint aura of wrongdoing. When James's arm had accidentally brushed hers, Diana had felt the heat of the contact long after it had ended. She imagined she could still smell his cologne.

Craig stopped down around nine and told her he had forgotten something at his office. Diana waited up for him to return, wanting to reconnect with him, to make sure he was still her ally, to convince herself that their marriage wasn't dead. When he didn't come home by midnight, she dragged herself up the three flights of stairs and flopped onto the bed. She lay there, waiting. But still he didn't come. He didn't return until well after she had fallen into a fitful sleep.

The next day, despite Craig's protests, Diana took him to the airport. As they drove through the exhaust-filled tunnel, Craig was the perfect robot of a concerned husband and she of the dutiful wife. He reminded her to take her vitamins and lock the door, and promised he would phone every evening. She agreed to all he suggested, only requesting that he call early so she could get a good night's sleep.

But she was too smooth. And his eyes were too hard. He was so distracted that he misstated his airline, first telling her to go to Delta, then changing to American. She made a wrong turn leaving the airport and found herself stuck on a highway with few exits, driving away from Boston, headed north toward Saugus.

As she had planned, Diana went straight to Ken's after dropping Craig off. She knew Marcel had seen her when she walked into the restaurant, that he was just pretending he hadn't. She noticed his eyes flicker toward the door as her own were adjusting to the dimness. Then he turned his back and put a drink before his lone customer.

The hostess seated Diana at a tiny corner table at the far end of the service bar. Whenever the waiter came up with a drink order, Marcel would place the filled glass diagonally on the counter so that he could avoid looking over the waiter's shoulder and right into Diana's face.

While Marcel ignored her, Diana tried to eat. She ordered a chef's salad and a glass of milk, but found she could do little more than move the meat and vegetables around in the bowl. She knew that worrying about Craig wasn't going to help, but she couldn't stop herself. His anger terrified her, her complicity in his anguish tormented her, but the thought of her life without him was something she couldn't even begin to contemplate.

She chewed on a piece of turkey for what seemed an inordinately long time, finally forcing it down with a large gulp of milk. She had to get rid of Levine and his allegations; she had to get him out of her house and out of her life before he tore apart everything she had. If she cleared herself, Craig would be able to forgive her. If she cleared herself, they could still be a family.

Diana stood up. While Marcel was at the cash register making change for a waiter, she positioned herself behind the man so Marcel would have no choice but to look in her direction when the waiter stepped away. "Hi," she said as soon as she caught his eye.

Marcel grunted.

"I never did find Ethan," she continued, as if he had actually greeted her. "I went to talk to his landlady, like you suggested." She flashed Marcel what she hoped was a sympathy-eliciting smile and shrugged. "But she hadn't seen him either."

"Must've split town," Marcel mumbled, picking up his rag.

Encouraged by the fact that he had spoken, Diana leaned against the bar. "Now I'm looking for James Hutchins's sister—the tall one with the curly red hair?"

"Maybe you should stop looking for so many folks." He turned and headed toward the other end of the bar.

Without conscious awareness of what she was doing, Diana thrust out her hand and grabbed Marcel's upper arm. Caught completely off-guard, he grew rigid. He turned his head slightly and stared at her. "I can't stop." Diana's voice was soft but firm. "If I don't find these people, I'm going to be arrested." She dropped her hand and felt her eyes filling. In that split second, she decided to let Marcel see the tears. "I don't want my baby to be born in prison," she added.

He looked at her coldly for a long moment, and Diana was sure she had lost him, that she had overplayed her part. But then his shoulders dropped and his eyes visibly softened. "They're a fucked-up bunch," he said. "Every last one of them."

"I know," Diana said, smiling slightly. "I'm their therapist."

Marcel snorted. "Guess I'm not telling you anything new." Noticing the waving hand of his customer, he nodded and poured a Scotch on the rocks. After he had delivered the drink, he returned to Diana. "That professor one of your patients?" he asked.

"Professor?"

"Boyfriend of the one you're looking for—what's her name, Jane?"

"Jill," Diana corrected. "Jill Hutchins."

"The professor's the one acting like he's headed for the loony bin."

"Has Jill been acting strange too?" Diana pressed, not the least bit interested in Jill's professor. "Has she been in lately?"

"Don't think so." Marcel shrugged. "But the professor's been in a lot. Crying in his beer, so to speak. Romance is on the skids. And someone told me he's having money troubles."

"Who isn't these days?" Diana said in an attempt to change the subject. "But what about Jill? Has she been upset also?"

. "Like I told you, she hasn't been in much." He shook his head and picked up his rag again. "Way I figure it, you should be more concerned about the guy."

"Why do you say that?" Diana demanded as Marcel turned away. "Why should I be more concerned about him than about Jill or Ethan?"

"Don't really know," he answered. "But I'm telling you he's on the edge. Looks to me like he's the kind likely to do just about anything." He picked up his rag and walked to the other end of the bar. Clearly the conversation was over.

Deflated, Diana returned to her table and sat down. She watched Marcel from her shadowy corner as he signaled the hostess to replace him and slipped out from under the bar. He walked into the kitchen without even a nod in her direction. So Jill had a crazy boyfriend. If Jill had a boyfriend who *wasn't* crazy, Diana would have been surprised.

She took a last sip of milk and pushed the salad bowl toward the middle of the table. She and Mitch were just going to have to go to Levine with what they had on Jill: a strong motive and a criminal background. If it weren't for the damn alibi, Jill would be a far better suspect than Diana. Molly was the connection that needed to be broken. Molly was Diana's only hope. It was time to get in touch with Adam Arell. Time to go back to Norwich. She would call Mitch and regroup. Diana signaled for her check.

As she waited for her change, Diana stared at the leaded panes of the heavy wooden entrance door. She watched the door swing open and admit two men in wrinkled business suits. Absently she followed their progress as they walked to the far end of the bar and sat down. When one offered the other a cigarette, she turned her eyes back toward the entrance. The door swung open a second time and a couple emerged from the shadows: a tall woman with wild curly hair, followed by a much older man about the same height. It was Jill. And behind her was Adrian Arnold.

Jill and Adrian didn't see Diana in her dimly lit corner. They waved to the hostess and seated themselves at what was apparently their usual spot, a small table kitty-corner to the front door. They began talking immediately, gesturing and touching each other.

Diana stared at them, unable to believe what she was seeing. Jill and Adrian couldn't possibly know each other, let alone be lovers. She was their only connection, and she had certainly never introduced them. They were so different: in age, in education, in temperament. It wasn't possible. But there it was.

She nodded her thanks to the waiter, but didn't move from her seat. Could this have anything to do with James's death? Were they plotting against her? She closed her eyes and reminded herself that everything didn't have to do with her. Her paranoia was just running amok. There was some logical explanation. Some explanation that had nothing to do with either James or herself.

Then she remembered. When Jill had come north to find James a therapist, she had interviewed a number of people in the Boston area—and Adrian had been one of them. Could Jill and Adrian have been having an affair all these years? It didn't seem possible, but that would explain why Adrian had been at James's funeral. And how Jill had known the baby was a girl. In its own bizarre way, the whole thing made sense.

As Diana stared, another thought crossed her mind. Between the two of them, there was plenty of motive, and with another person in the picture, Levine might be convinced that there *was* opportunity, that Jill and Adrian had killed James together. Diana's palms began to sweat.

The scenario would have to have been premeditated murder: Jill and Adrian killed James and set up the fake suicide so that Jill would inherit the money. Then, when it turned out that Diana was the beneficiary, they decided to ruin Diana so that the money would revert to Jill—and as an added bonus, save Adrian's career by keeping Diana's research from being published. But would Levine buy that? It had possibilities, but also seemed rather farfetched. Then Diana remembered what Mitch had told her. All she had to do was convince the police that it was possible. Reasonable doubt was on her side.

Marcel's words echoed through her brain: *Looks to me like he's the kind likely to do just about anything.* Gail would attest to Adrian's financial difficulties, Marcel to his instability, someone else in their peer group would explain how discrediting Diana would save Adrian's future book royalties. Combined with Jill's own money problems, her ambivalent and sometimes violent relationship with James, her criminal record . . .

Watching them from her corner, Diana realized that Jill and Adrian were having some kind of disagreement. Jill was sitting back in her chair with her arms crossed, a petulant look on her face. Adrian leaned toward her, talking and gesturing rather frantically. Jill remained impassive.

It just might work, Diana thought. She had heard of much weaker motives for murder. Jill and Adrian might be the alternative plausible suspects she had been searching for. They did it together to get out from under, to start a new life. James and Jill had had a huge row right before his death. And hadn't Levine just told her that Mrs. Manfredi claimed to have seen Jill's boyfriend at James's apartment?

The waiter stopped by and asked if she wanted anything else, blocking her view of Adrian and Jill. Diana shook her head, and, as he stepped from her line of vision, she peered once again at the small table by the door. But now Jill and Adrian were not looking at each other. They were both looking straight at her.

~ 28 ~

TRANSFIXED, DIANA STARED ACROSS THE DIMLY LIT RESTAURANT. It seemed to her that the tables and the chairs and the few other scattered patrons didn't exist; there were only she and Adrian and Jill, locked together by the intensity of their fixed gazes. Then Adrian blinked, his expression of abashed surprise taking on even stronger shades of guilt. Jill's gaze remained unwavering. At the first moment of recognition, a gleam of hatred, almost a physical aversion, seemed to flash from her eyes, supplanted swiftly by a look Diana could only describe as cordial. Jill smiled slightly and nodded. She waved and motioned for Diana to come over to their table.

Diana hesitated, her brain function returning slowly after the shock of eye contact. She remembered Jill's rages in her office, at the funeral, at Jill's apartment. She remembered James's stories of slashed tires and dead tropical fish—and the police report of assault with a deadly weapon. *We've got to watch this woman*, Mitch had said. *She was a real hothead*, Adam Arell had told her. *No way to figure what she was going to do next*. Diana knew a friendly little chat was hardly what Jill had in mind.

Diana's stomach squeezed as she placed her change in

her wallet. What were her options? Either she pretended
she hadn't seen them, and stayed in her corner until they
decided to leave, or she went over for a moment to say a
quick hello. She supposed she could leave without speaking
to them, but, given their proximity to the door, this seemed
a rather difficult feat to pull off. She rummaged through her
purse for her car keys. The last thing she wanted right now
was to have a friendly chitchat with Adrian and Jill.

A sharp knock on her table jolted her from her reverie.
Startled, she dropped her purse on the floor. Her wallet
skidded across the tiles; her lipstick and a small prescrip-
tion bottle rolled under the next table. The remainder of the
contents of her purse lay in a messy pile at her feet.

"You lucked out," Marcel said, knocking on the table
again. He pointed across the restaurant at Jill, who was
still smiling and waving. "Your friend and the professor
are here."

Diana crouched on the floor, grabbing for her way-
ward possessions. "Thanks," she managed to mutter. "I
sure lucked out."

"Yoo-hoo, Diana!" Jill called.

Marcel grunted and slipped back under the bar. Diana
stood and gathered her things. She walked resolutely toward
their table.

"Adrian," Diana said, slipping on her coat and throwing
her purse over her shoulder so as to leave no doubt as to
the imminence of her departure. "Jill."

"It's so great to see you," Jill said, as if she really meant
it. She reached out and grasped Diana's hands, as if they
were old chums. "You must sit down with us for at least
a few minutes. You must!"

Before Diana could answer, Adrian said, "I don't mean
to be rude, but maybe some other time would be better."
Although ostensibly speaking to Diana, he was looking at
Jill.

"I can't right now, thanks," Diana said, detaching her
hands from Jill's. "I really have—"

"Nonsense," Jill interrupted, smiling warmly up at Diana. "We won't take no for an answer." She removed her jacket from the extra chair and hung it on the back of her own.

Diana looked to Adrian for help. Jill wasn't a bad actress, although the clipped preciseness of her words told Diana that this facade of friendly cordiality was all too thin. Adrian met Diana's eyes for a moment, but his expression was inscrutable. He shrugged in defeat. Jill pointed to the empty chair and tugged on Diana's sleeve. Diana sat.

For a few moments, the silence was thick and uncomfortable, the tension between them almost palatable. Jill smiled brightly, clinking her ice with a stirrer, while Adrian stared into his drink and Diana fidgeted with the strap of her purse.

Diana took a deep breath and looked right at Adrian. "So how long have you two known each other?" she asked, tipping her head and trying to smile. Although she and Adrian had had their problems of late, they had been close at one time; the two of them had spent many a lunch discussing Adrian's marital difficulties.

Adrian had the grace to blush slightly and shrugged again. Before he could speak, Jill answered Diana's question for him. "We've *known* each other since I first moved to Boston." She smiled wickedly. "But if you're speaking of the biblical sense, it's been just over a year."

"We ran into each other again at Quincy Market last summer," Adrian added.

"And as they say"—Jill pinched his cheek—"the rest is history."

Adrain twisted his face away from Jill's hand and shot her a look that clearly told her he was not happy with the conversation.

Jill tossed her head and turned to Diana. "So," she said with the overly festive voice of a hostess attempting to liven up a dull dinner party. "It seems to me that the last time we met, we were talking about drinking and bartender liability." She chuckled. "And here you find me in a bar with a drink," she raised her glass as if in toast to Diana, "in the middle of a Wednesday afternoon."

Diana looked at her in confusion, then, just as Jill had desired, she went cold at the memory. Once again she was in Jill's apartment watching Jill's charm disintegrate into fury. Once again she was on her knees, a poker being held to her stomach.

"Diana stopped by for a little chat," Jill was explaining to Adrian. "We had coffee and a bit of girl talk." She flashed Diana a playful smile, as if intimate secrets had been shared between the two women that no man could ever be expected to understand. Then she turned back to Adrian. "It seems to me, we were discussing responsibility . . ."

"Don't do this," Adrian hissed at Jill, slamming his drink down on the table. "How's your research going?" he asked Diana. "Still having those sampling problems?"

Although she would have loved to rub her latest data in his face, Diana controlled herself. Now was not the time to antagonize him, not when she needed him as an ally against Jill, not when she wanted to get information out of him on his own possible alibi—or, she hoped, lack thereof. "Oh," she sighed, figuring two could play the actress game, "you know how difficult it is to achieve statistical significance with such small samples." She shook her head and frowned. "Sometimes I wonder if it's ever going to happen."

Adrian's grin contradicted his words. "Too bad," he said. "I know how tough that can be. How disappointing."

"That's enough shop talk about your silly statistics," Jill declared, patting Adrian's hand and shaking her head. "I'd much rather just gossip." She took a sip of her drink and leaned closer to Diana. "Let's talk about our mutual friends."

"I didn't know we had any," Diana said, wondering what Jill was getting at.

"Why, but of course we do." Jill's voice was perky and cheerful. "There's Adrian, here." She tilted her head and looked at him with the amused smile of an overindulgent mother. "And then there's Ethan and Sandy—and of course there was James." As she pronounced her brother's name, Jill's voice wavered and her face lost its polite veneer, but she recovered quickly. "Poor Sandy seems to be having quite a difficult time these days," she said with great sincerity. "I do worry about her."

It struck Diana that Jill's smile was taking on a touch of shrewdness, that her eyes were slightly glazed. Diana wished she too had a drink. "I'm hopeful that Sandy's going to be just fine," she said carefully.

"It's this whole alibi thing that she's doing for you." Jill sighed and put her drink down on the table with a resounding clank.

"What are you talking about?" Diana was completely confused by this turn of conversation. "I don't have an alibi."

"Yeah, right," Jill said, looking directly at Diana. "As if you didn't know Sandy was planning on going to the police to tell them she had an appointment with you that afternoon."

"That's ridiculous," Diana said. "And it isn't true."

"Then how come you convinced her that she was with you?"

"I never convinced her of any such thing," Diana sputtered. She looked at Adrian. "You know full well I'd never do anything like that."

"Oh, right," Jill said, waving her hand dismissively. "You had nothing to do with creating your own alibi." She leaned even closer to Diana, pushing her face so near that the gin on her breath made Diana recoil. "Do you want to hear the really interesting part?"

"Stop it, Jill!" Adrian ordered.

"The really interesting part is that when I went through Sandy's appointment book, I couldn't find any entry for that particular day—and you and I know, Dr. Marcus" — Jill's smile was wide, smug, and full of hatred—"that Sandy would never miss an appointment with you, her idol."

"Of course there was no appointment in her book," Diana snapped. "She didn't have an appointment—"

Jill continued as if Diana hadn't spoken, all pretense of cordiality gone. "No one ever forgets an appointment with the perfect therapist," she spat at Diana. "Not the most perfect one!"

Adrian touched Diana's arm. "Go," he said, his voice low and insistent. "Now."

But Diana didn't move. "Why are you doing this?" she asked Jill.

"You don't know the half of it." Jill's laughter was tinged with hysteria. Her eyes gleamed with hatred. "You don't know the half of what I've done to you."

"Diana," Adrian pleaded.

"What?" Diana demanded, beyond caring about anything but the danger Jill's madness posed to her. "What other half?"

"Your journal. Detective Levine." Jill's voice began to rise and Adrian put his hand on her arm. She shook it off with disgust. "I've had a lot more to do with your troubles than you'll ever—"

"Jill," Adrian said sharply.

"Why, I even knew you'd be in here spying on us." Jill continued as if Adrian hadn't spoken. "Sandy told me you'd come."

Diana gripped the edge of the table, her knuckles white. "I don't understand," she said, her voice shaking slightly. "What have you done?"

"You killed my brother," Jill said, her voice suddenly soft, but somehow even more ominous. "You killed James, and I've been doing everything I can to make you pay." She placed her fingers on the table and leaned toward Diana again. Her breath was foul, but this time Diana didn't move. When Jill began to speak, her voice was barely a whisper. "Who do you think got her dear, sweet friend Ida Manfredi to babble to the cops?" she asked, beginning to chuckle softly. "Who do you think stole your precious

journal and sent copies to the *Inquirer*? Or told Mr. Fake
Friendly Detective to look at the end where you implicate
yourself in spades?"

"What at the end? What are—"

"And don't think I'm going to stop," Jill continued,
speaking between hysterical cackles. "I won't stop until
your life has been ruined just like you ruined James's!"
Her laughter broke into tears, and she began to sob quietly. "Just like you ruined mine . . ."

Adrian rose from his chair and knelt by Jill's side. He
gently wrapped his arms around her. "It's okay, baby," he
murmured, rubbing her back. "It's going to be okay."

"It'll never be okay," Jill wailed. "It'll never stop hurt-
ing," she sobbed into Adrian's shoulder. "It'll never go
away."

Adrian held Jill more tightly and kissed her brow. He
looked up at Diana. "Do you think you could go now?" he
asked.

Diana stumbled out the door. She stood, stunned, on
the sidewalk, unable to remember where she had parked
the jeep, unable to comprehend the full impact of all she
had just heard. Confused, she looked around her, trying to
ground herself in some reality she could grasp. A Salvation
Army Santa swung his bell on the corner, indifferent to the
fact that no one was putting money in his bucket. A large
woman, overdressed and smelling of far too much perfume,
elbowed her way between a group of teenage boys wearing
dark leather jackets. The gang strutted toward Diana, but
still she didn't move. For a moment she was encased in
shoulders and darkness and marijuana-tinged body odor;
then she was in the open again, staring into the street. A
screech of tires jolted her, and she watched in dazed surprise as a car and a truck came to a simultaneous stop—
about two inches from each other and about a foot from
her.

Stepping backward until her coat touched the cold

facade of the building, Diana pressed herself into the brick, relishing the iciness as it seeped through to her skin. Harder and harder, she twisted her shoulders and head until her shoulder blades hurt and her hair felt as if it were being ripped from her scalp. But it was okay. It was just physical pain, and nothing on a purely physical plane could possibly match the despair within her. A despair that threatened to engulf her, obliterate her. Jill would never make a plausible suspect. For Jill was far too grief-stricken and crazed over James's death for anyone ever to believe that she had killed her brother. And moreover, Diana knew that Jill had not; she had seen it in her eyes.

Diana felt as if she had been turned inside out, as if the innermost part of her being was raw and exposed, just waiting for execution. She stepped from the building, and the physical pain disappeared. She pushed backward again.

A chill wind ruffled her hair, carrying the scent of winter. She glanced upward and recognized the low white-gray sky. The first snow of the year was inside those clouds. Her gaze returned to the street, and as she watched the world going about its business she wondered how soon it would be before she had no business to go about at all.

~ 29 ~

T WASN'T UNTIL DIANA REACHED THE CORNER OF MASS
Ave. and St. Stephen Street that the world began to return
and she realized she had no recollection of her drive from
Central Square. Slowly, as if emerging from under water,
she became aware of the low rumble of the car stopped next
to her, of a horn honking on the other side of the street, of
two women chatting as they stepped into the crosswalk in
front of her idling jeep. Diana blinked. Dusk was beginning
to fall, and she was freezing.

It was over. She had come to the end of the line. Jill was
not a plausible suspect. Craig was furious with her. And
Herb Levine was soon going to knock on her door with an
arrest warrant in his hand.

Still, despite the gathering gloom, Diana found herself
fighting against the inevitable. Jill might be a lost cause,
she thought as she pulled the heat lever to high, but what
about Ethan? There had to be something that would impress
Levine with Ethan's viability as a suspect. Staring out the
window, she was hit with an ugly, tempting thought. She
could plant something incriminating in her notes. She could
write that Ethan had stayed late one afternoon, after everyone else had left, and broken down and confessed to killing

his girlfriend. She would tell Levine that she had been horrified at the time, of course, but doctor-patient privilege had
kept her from going to the police.

An insistent horn from behind brought Diana back to
reality, and she threw the jeep into gear. No, she thought,
it was a completely contemptible idea. She couldn't blame
a man for a murder he possibly didn't commit. It was disgusting of her to have even considered it. Plus it wouldn't
work anyway. The same laws of confidentiality that had
held then would still hold now.

As she walked into the house and hung up her coat,
Diana's thoughts turned to Sandy; she wondered why Sandy
had suddenly decided she had had an appointment with
her on the afternoon of James's murder—and why now.
Although Sandy had had a few minor delusional episodes in
the past, if she insisted that she had been at Diana's despite
the fact that it wasn't recorded in her day-timer, if her delusion could stand up against such irrefutable evidence, then
Sandy was in worse shape than Diana had thought.

She went into her office and dialed Sandy's apartment,
letting the phone ring for what seemed an interminable time.
Finally Sandy picked it up, breathlessly explaining she was
in the middle of her exercise routine, but would be able to
take a break when she finished her abdominals. Diana asked
her if she could stop by her office; Sandy readily agreed to
come over as soon as possible.

Relieved, Diana went to the file cabinet and got Sandy's
records, hoping for clues on how best to handle the situation. Sandy loved attention and acted as though she was
entitled to it, based on her beauty. But Diana knew that this
facade of self-confidence hid a frightened and lonely little
girl who really thought of herself as ugly and stupid—and
unlovable. Sitting in her chair, she tapped the back of her
pen on the open folder and waited for Sandy to arrive, trying
to remain focused on Sandy's troubles, not on her own.

But despite her earlier dismissal, the thoughts about Ethan
that she had had in the car wouldn't stay away; the idea was

just too persistent—or perhaps her desperation just too great. Diana strained to remember her ethics course. If someone's life was endangered, the need to inform took priority over doctor-patient privilege. Protection of the victim overrode confidentiality.

Her mind whirled with possibilities, and she could hear the blood pounding through her ears. Perhaps she could say that Ethan had left a message threatening to kill her with a shotgun? No, that wouldn't work because she, the victim, would already be informed. But if Ethan left a message threatening Sandy, then Diana would be forced to tell Levine and show him Ethan's previous murder confession in her notes. That, combined with the incriminating girlfriend-shotgun story, would rekindle the police's search for him—as well as incriminate Ethan in James's murder. She twirled in her chair and stared into the alley; darkness was already embedded in its corners, although the time was barely five. It might just work.

No, she told herself, snapping the blinds shut, it was out of the question. She was *not* going to falsify records, she was not going to lie about phone messages, and she definitely was not going to malign a possibly innocent man.

Sandy showed up in a sweatsuit that had obviously been hastily thrown over her workout clothes. "I came as fast as I could. Just had to finish up a couple more repetitions," she said as soon as she entered the office. Then she hesitated, standing uncertainly behind her usual chair. "You did say that *you* needed *me*, didn't you?" she asked, twisting a slightly damp piece of hair.

"Yes, I did." Diana nodded solemnly. "I need your help."

Sandy's chest puffed out with pride, and a radiant smile illuminated her beautiful face. She sat down and looked expectantly at Diana.

Diana steepled her fingers and pressed them to her upper lip. "I saw Jill Hutchins today," she said, looking directly at Sandy. "And something she said confused me."

"You talked to Jill?" Sandy was obviously surprised.

"And she claimed you told her you were with me the afternoon of James's murder."

"Yeah." Sandy inspected her fingernails. "She's been talking a lot about it lately. Grilling me. Sort of obsessive like, I guess."

"Why do you think that is?"

Sandy frowned. "Because she hates you." She looked up at Diana apologetically.

"It's okay—no one's liked by everybody," Diana said. "Why else do you think she's doing this?"

"She thinks you killed James and doesn't want me to give you an alibi. She doesn't want me to go to the police because she wants you to be punished." Sandy grabbed her purse from the back of her chair. "But I know it's not true. I know you'd never do anything like that—and I can prove it."

"You can?" Diana asked, hope rushing through her in a way she wouldn't have thought possible just a few minutes ago.

"It's in my appointment book." Sandy pulled her daytimer from her purse and began flipping through the pages. "I have it right here. I always write down when I'm going to see you. Look," she said proudly, pointing to October 15. "Dr. Marcus," it said. "Two o'clock."

Diana stared at the notation, her heart pounding in her ears. She knew Sandy had not been in her office on the afternoon of October 15. She knew Sandy had added the entry just recently—obviously after Jill had pointed out its absence. But there it was in front of her: her alibi, her salvation.

"Jill's wrong," Sandy said, pulling her face into a pout. "She never wanted James to like anyone but her."

Diana nodded, impressed with Sandy's perceptiveness. "Don't you think it's possible that you might have made a mistake?" she asked gently, trying to assess the strength of Sandy's delusion. "Just this one time?"

"Can't be a mistake." Sandy's voice was emphatic. "I know that for a fact."

"How can you be so positive?"

Sandy clicked the latch on her day-timer a few times, then looked up at Diana, her expression sheepish and childishly appealing. "I count them."

"Count them?" Diana repeated, not sure she had heard Sandy correctly. "Count what?"

"I know you're going to think I'm stupid and immature . . ."

"I'd never think that," Diana said, a flood of warmth for Sandy pouring through her. Underneath all that damage, Sandy was just a little girl trying desperately to make people like her, trying to keep them from leaving her.

"I always write down the times I see you because I count them," Sandy mumbled. "I keep track of them so that I'll know when you start to get tired of me—or are trying to get rid of me. I even sort of have a chart." She lifted her head and stuck out her chin. "And that's how I know that the appointment really happened," she added, crossing her arms defiantly over her chest.

Diana watched Sandy carefully. It was obvious Sandy was completely convinced of the truth of her words—and that, because of her conviction, she would make a compelling witness. That was the thing about a true delusion. The person suffering from it wasn't lying; he or she was certain of the veracity of their memory. But Diana also knew that a person who believed in this kind of delusion was also quite ill: sick and fearful and confused. Sandy was her patient; Sandy trusted that Diana would do what was best to help her, the patient—not herself, the doctor.

Sandy fiddled with her clothes and her hair for a few moments, not raising her eyes. "I'd never make a mistake about an appointment with you." She played with the clasp on her day-timer. "I'm always very careful. Always."

"Sandy," Diana began and then stopped. The battle raging within her caused nausea to twist her stomach. She paused to let the wave of sickness pass, knowing there was no way she could ever consciously hurt this woman. "Sandy, it's okay to make a mistake."

"I know for a fact that I was here that afternoon," Sandy answered quickly, but with less certainty. The telephone began to ring, and Sandy looked at Diana questioningly.

"The machine will get it," Diana said. "What else do you remember about that afternoon?"

"We talked about my father."

Diana hesitated for a long moment. "Not that day," she finally said, her sense of both relief and disappointment at her victory over self-interest so powerful it caused her voice to break. "Don't you remember? We met *after* James's funeral," she said gently. "We talked about your memory of your dad and that Red Sox game." Diana reached into her drawer and pulled out her appointment book. "Look," she said, flipping to October 15. "The afternoon's empty."

Sandy let her hair cover her face. "I thought we talked about it that day," she whispered.

"I only wish we had." Diana sat back in her chair, exhausted from her internal battle, unsure whether she was the victor or the vanquished.

"But—but it's just that it's not like me," Sandy said, wringing her hands. "You know how I can get a little obsessive about things . . ." She glanced furtively at Diana, then her eyes began darting around the room. Suddenly she jumped from her chair and stood behind it. She gripped the back cushion tightly, as if using it for protection.

"Sandy," Diana said, standing and starting to walk toward the frightened woman. "What—"

"Don't come any closer!" Sandy cried, holding the chair even more tightly, her knuckles turning white. "You—you made me lie."

Diana stopped walking. She stood completely still, her hand resting on the edge of her desk in a casual gesture. "Okay," she said softly. "I'm not going to touch you. If you don't want me to come any closer, then I won't."

Sandy backed slowly toward the door, horror contorting her beautiful face. "You were the best person in the world. The one I admired the most," she said, her voice registering both fear and disappointment. "I—I wanted to be like you. To be you. And now . . . And now . . ." She leaned over, pressing her day-timer to her stomach. "I feel sick," she moaned.

"Sandy, honey," Diana began.

Sandy shook her head and started to cry. "How could you?" she asked plaintively. Then her eyes became wild, full of terror at the horrible truth she thought she saw before her. "How could you kill James?" she screamed, and ran out the door.

Diana was stunned into immobility. She just stood there, motionless, her hand clutching the edge of the desk. The pain she had experienced on the street in front of Ken's was nothing compared to the dark despair that flooded her now. She had failed everyone.

Then her paralysis loosened, and she followed Sandy down the hallway. "Stop!" she called when she reached the open door. "You're wrong. You don't understand!"

But Sandy ignored her, running from her in terror, flying across the alley. Sandy stumbled, fell, then righted herself as she lunged for her car. She grasped the door handle and pulled it, then frantically pawed through her purse and thrust her keys into the lock. Suddenly she stopped and stood statue-still, her tear-streaked face haunted and pale.

Diana didn't move. She didn't call out, afraid to startle the terrified woman, afraid of what Sandy might do. But all Sandy did was turn and vomit violently into the trash barrel.

After Sandy's car careened out of the alley, Diana walked back into her office. She stood in the center of the room, looking at it as if she had never seen it before, wondering how the next owners of the house might choose to use the space. Perhaps as an au pair's room. Or maybe a teenager's hideaway, a gentleman's library, a sewing room, or an art studio. So many possibilities. She walked to the window and opened the blinds, looking into their "back city." The back city that would now never hold a swing set. She snapped the blinds shut. If Sandy—who knew her, and loved her, and understood how much she had cared for James—concluded that she had killed James, what might Herb Levine's conclusion be?

Numbly she pressed the button on her answering machine. When Levine's voice boomed out at her, she jumped. "Got that warrant I was telling you about the other day," he said. "I'll be by later this evening—around eight. Please be home." Warrant, she thought, her hands beginning to tremble. Herb Levine had a warrant. Was it for her printer, or was it for her? Diana knew it had to be for the printer; Levine's voice had sounded too casual for it to be an arrest warrant. Nevertheless, Diana paced her small office in fear.

She walked over to the file cabinet in the corner and stood in front of it. Then she pulled Ethan's records from the top drawer and sat down at her desk. Without conscious awareness that she had come to a decision, Diana took a few pens from her drawer and scribbled on a pad of lined paper with each. Selecting the one with the most faded ink, she calmly and deliberately began to jot short notes on various sheets of paper in his file. "Threatened Sandy and Bruce," she wrote on one sheet. "Told James he would kill him," she wrote on another.

Then she switched to a different pen and wrote a much longer paragraph, in a much neater hand. "E confessed to murdering glfrd in apt. No details 'cept it was messy," Diana began, using the cryptic notations she always employed in her personal files. She ended the paragraph with the words, "No remorse. Laughed. Said: 'She deserved it for lying.' I feel terrible. Scared. Can do nothing. D-P privilege." It was as if some outside force had control of her actions, a force more concerned with her survival than she was. But whether it was a benevolent or malevolent force, she wasn't sure.

When she completed her work, Diana took the pens she had used and carried them upstairs. She put the pens underneath a few inches of garbage in the trash compactor and turned the knob. Then she went back downstairs and called Gail.

"I'm having some trouble with my answering machine," Diana said. "Could you do me a favor and call me right back? Just say something like, 'Hi, this is Gail,' so I can test it?"

"Sure," Gail said. "But, sweetie, I need to talk to you. It's really important."

"We'll talk when you call back," Diana promised and hung up.

But when Gail called back, leaving a message on the machine that would erase any earlier ones, Diana told her that she had to run, she had a patient arriving in a few minutes and a lecture to prepare for the next day. Not easily brushed off, Gail refused to hang up until Diana had promised she would call her as soon as she got home from class in the morning.

Then Diana took a deep breath and held it in. Just when she thought she would explode from lack of air, she dialed the police station and asked for Detective Levine. While she waited for him to come to the phone, she held her breath again.

"You," she gasped when she heard his voice, letting her breath out with a rush. "You've got to come over here now—this can't wait till later. There's a message and I'm scared. I think that . . . I don't know what to think, but you need to hear this. And—"

"Whoa," Levine said. "Slow down and start again."

So Diana told him that Ethan had just called and left a message threatening both her and another one of her patients. That she needed Levine to come right away because she had some new evidence for him. Evidence she hadn't been able to reveal before. Evidence she was sure he would be very interested in seeing.

After she hung up, she sat at her desk, dead-calm and waiting. Waiting for what she knew would be her last chance.

~ 30 ~

WHEN THE DOORBELL RANG, DIANA STARTLED IN HER chair. It didn't seem possible that more than a minute had passed since she had hung up with Levine, but then again, her senses had been so distorted lately, it could have been three hours. Wiping her palms on her jumper, she started slowly out of the office, trying to calm her pounding heart and silence her ragged breathing, trying to hide her nervousness from the suspicious policeman who stood on the other side of her door. From the man who stood between herself and prison.

But as she reached the hallway, Diana realized that it was reasonable for her to be nervous. That even a completely innocent person would be unnerved by the circumstances in which she found herself. She pulled open the door and offered him a damp palm. "Thanks for coming so fast," she said softly. "I'm glad you're here."

He grasped her hand in both of his and held it for a moment. His hands were cold and tiny flakes melted on the shoulders of his ski parka. She had just been staring out the window but hadn't even noticed that it had started to snow. "Let's see what you've got," he said.

Diana brought Levine into her office and told him about

300

the message Ethan had left threatening Sandy. "He said she was 'going the way of James,'" she stuttered, feeling both guilty about her lies and exhilarated with how well she was lying. "He said, 'The bitch better watch her back.' But he didn't sound like he did on the other tapes," she added breathlessly, "He—he sounded clearer, closer." A shiver ran down her back, a shiver she didn't have to fake. She rubbed the goose bumps that rose on her arms. "Should I call her, or will you?"

Levine took Sandy's phone number and promised he would take care of it.

Then Diana showed him the notations in her records. She explained how Ethan had confessed to murdering his girl-friend and how he had made violent threats against Sandy and other group members in the past. She added, although she knew Levine understood, that doctor-patient privilege had not allowed her to disclose this information before now—even though she had known it would probably have helped her own case.

He was very encouraging, asking her to repeat things and clarify a detail here or there. He took copious notes and appeared honestly relieved, almost happy, to have an alternative suspect to Diana. He even seemed to believe the part about how she had been in the bathroom when Gail had called just a few minutes ago, how she had raced out as soon as she heard a voice coming through the answer-ing machine, but how, unfortunately, she had not been fast enough to keep Gail's voice from erasing Ethan's message.

"I should have taken the tape out of the machine as soon as I listened to it," Diana berated herself. "I've done it every other time—I don't know why I didn't today. It was stupid. Just plain stupid," she repeated, almost believing her own lies.

"Don't blame yourself too much," the detective said, lifting the tape from the machine and dropping it into his pocket. He skimmed one of the files she had given him and

added absently, "You were obviously shocked. Scared. You
can't expect yourself to act as you might under more normal
circumstances."

"Thanks." Diana ran her fingers through her hair and let
her breath out in a rush. She took the rest of the files and
placed them in a neat pile in the middle of her desk, trying
not to think too much about what she had just done. She
fiddled with the edges of the manila folders, then turned and
opened the blinds so she could watch the first snowflakes of
the year. They were coating the alley with a pristine layer
of white.

She glanced at Levine, his head bent over a file resting
on his crossed leg. He was reading her lies, believing a possibly innocent man was a murderer because she wanted to
save her own skin. She was scum, despicable and disgusting. But it was too late to change anything now. Levine
scratched his stubbly chin and flipped a page.

Turning back to the window, Diana watched the snow
growing on the slats of the fire escape across the alley,
transforming the pile of garbage some animal had scourged
from the Dumpster into an unsullied, and quite striking,
abstract sculpture. Maybe it wasn't a lie, Diana thought.
Maybe Ethan *had* killed the girlfriend. And if not the girlfriend, then someone else—in the past or possibly in the
future. Perhaps she was actually *saving* a life. Lives, even.
For she knew Ethan had no conscience, that he was without guilt or remorse. That Ethan Kruse was a violent and
dangerous man.

"Nice guy," Levine grunted, snapping the file shut and
breaking into her reverie.

Diana turned from the window and faced the detective.
"Do you want to make copies or should I?" she asked, pushing the rest of the folders across the desk to him. He told
her he would and reached over and took the pile. She held
out her hand, relieved that it had all gone so well, relieved
that it was over. "Call me if you have any questions."

But instead of standing and shaking her hand, he pulled

a slip of paper from his pocket and placed that in her palm. "The warrant."

Diana felt heat rising to her face and staining it red. It wasn't over. She stared down at the flimsy yellow document in her hand. The warrant. How could she have forgotten?

"It's for your printer." He nodded toward the NEC sitting on the small cart off to the side of her desk. "Even with this new stuff on Kruse, I've got to keep moving on all fronts."

"Printer," she repeated stupidly, trying to subdue the relief—and fear—that spiraled through her. "Of course." She walked over to the printer and knelt behind it, hiding her red, sweat-beaded face from Levine as she fiddled with the wires. She realized she was going to need a screwdriver to separate the printer from the cable. Rising, she asked him to excuse her for a moment.

Diana headed toward the kitchen, but when she got halfway up, to the point where the stairway twisted and she knew she was not visible from below, she stopped and pressed her hot cheek to the cool wall. It wasn't over. It would never be over. She had lied. She had falsified medical records. She had given the police false evidence. And it still wasn't over.

"Diana?" Detective Levine stuck his head around the corner of the stairwell and called up to her.

Diana jumped, almost losing her balance. She pressed her palms to the wall, steadying herself. "Y-yes," she stuttered, trying to get a grip, to appear calm and innocent, but knowing that her terror must be glowing like a spotlight from within her. "Yes?" she asked again.

"You were gone so long," he said, as if she were acting completely normally. "I was just checking to see that you were okay."

"Fine," she said, smiling weakly. "Just a little shaky, I guess."

"To be expected," he assured her and disappeared back down the stairs.

When Diana reached into the junk drawer to get the Phillips-head screwdriver, her right hand was shaking so badly that she had to grab it with her left. She couldn't lose it now, she warned herself. She had to hold it together for just a few more minutes. She rummaged through the drawer and finally found the small tool for which she had been searching. Levine didn't know she was lying. He had no reason to suspect.

Coming back into the office, Diana raised the tiny screwdriver. "I'll have it unhooked for you in a second," she said, trying to keep her voice light, but knowing that she was failing abysmally.

"No rush," Levine answered, glancing up at her from writing in his notebook. "I've got a couple more things I want to talk to you about anyway."

It took her a long time to unhook the printer. The silence in the room hung heavy and portentous as Diana struggled with her fears and the trembling screwdriver. *A couple more things.*

Finally Diana succeed in separating the machine from its cable. Unable to completely control her shaking hands, she gripped the printer tightly and carried it to her desk. She placed it in front of the detective, and, unwilling to trust her voice, stood silently, hands clasped behind her back. *A couple more things.*

After a few minutes Levine looked up from the file he was thumbing through and smiled at her as if they were casual acquaintances meeting on a streetcorner. He placed the file on top of the printer. "Interesting stuff," he said conversationally.

Diana nodded.

Almost as an afterthought he reached into a deep pocket on the outside of his parka and pulled out the aqua-and-purple book she knew so well: her journal.

Instinctively Diana reached for the journal, her fingers longing for the comfort of just holding it. Then she yanked her hand back. "Where did you get that?" she barked, although as soon as she spoke the words, she knew the answer: Jill had given it to him.

"I thought you knew we had it," he said, casually flipping through the pages. "Got it from Hutchins's sister."

The familiarity with which the detective held her book, the purposeful manner in which he touched the water-marked paper that held her most private thoughts, caused Diana's fear to burn toward rage. Don't, she ordered herself, forcing her clenched fists to loosen. It's his job. It isn't personal. But no matter how much she reminded herself of the deadly folly of anger, she was unable to will away the boiling sea that seethed within her.

"There's something in here I wanted to ask you about," Levine said as he searched through the pages. "Ah, here." He handed the journal to her, pointing to the entry she had written right after James's funeral. "What exactly did you mean by this?"

James is dead and Jill says I killed him. She shouted it in the middle of the funeral—although I'm sure no one there believed her. Most likely everyone just assumed she was addled by grief.

Her words echoed off the hard marble walls, and they will always echo in my heart. They will be with me forever. As will be my guilt.

It hurts. It hurts so much. It hurts because James is gone. And it hurts because Jill spoke the truth.

Diana could see exactly what her words would say to a detective investigating James Hutchins's murder. "It's not what you think," she said lamely.

He nodded, waiting for her to correct his misapprehension.

She sank into her chair and heaved a large sigh, Jill's words reverberating through her brain: *Who do you think . . . told Mr. Fake Friendly Detective to look at the end where you implicate yourself in spades?* Jill was obviously pulling every string she could find in her marionette game of "Let's Hang Diana."

Diana swiveled her chair slightly so that she could watch the falling snow softening the harsh angles of the alley. She sat silently, wondering whether it was even worth the effort to try to explain. Finally, she said "I was speaking metaphorically."

"You mean you just *felt* like you had killed him—not that you really *had* killed him?"

Surprised, Diana swiveled back and looked at Herb Levine's face. He actually appeared to understand. "Exactly," she said hopefully. "I just felt responsible because he was my patient. I wasn't really responsible." But the eyes that met hers were ice-cold. Disappointed, Diana slowly turned back to the window. She heard Levine pick up the journal and heard the flutter of pages. *A couple more things.*

"Unfortunately, Dr. Marcus . . ." The detective paused, and Diana whipped her head around, alarmed by the tone of his voice: He hadn't called her "Dr. Marcus" since they'd first met. "I've got some more bad news for you. Did Hutchins ever mention a Harold Berger?"

"No," Diana said slowly, wondering what disaster Harold Berger had in store for her.

"It seems that this Mr. Berger lived downstairs from James—"

"Mr. Berger, the parapalegic?" she interrupted.

"Yup, he's in a wheelchair. Seems real fond of Hutchins too. It doesn't seem to fit"—Levine shook his head—"but Mr. Berger told me Hutchins once painted his apartment for him—as a favor."

"It's true," Diana said. "And it fits."

"Anyway, it seems that Mr. Berger was in California visiting his daughter when the murder investigation started. Called the station this morning when he got home. He was

very upset by the news." Levine raised his eyebrows at
Diana; when she didn't respond, he folded his hands over
the closed journal on his lap. "He claims," the detective said
slowly, "that he heard you and James Hutchins yelling at
each other on the morning of October 15. At the apartment
on Anderson Street."

Diana's heart seemed to stop beating in her chest. "The
morning of October 15?" she whispered.

"It appears that you've now been placed at the scene on
the day of the murder," Levine said, not taking his eyes off
Diana's face.

"I, ah, I . . ." she stammered, remembering. It was about
a week after James had hidden in her jeep, causing her to
hit the parked car; it was a few days after he had shrieked
at her in the alley, causing her to call the police; it was the
morning after she had a nightmare in which James was a
vampire, sucking blood from her baby's neck.

It was early, before her class, and she had gone to James's
apartment to beg him to leave her alone. To plead with him
to get on with his life—and to let her get on with hers. Craig
had given her an ultimatum: Either she talk to James or he
would.

"This is the way it has to be," she told James. "This is
the way it is."

But James had refused to listen. "You can't throw me
away like a sack of yesterday's garbage," he screamed at
her. "I'll never let you go—never!"

Closing her eyes against the memory of James's enraged
face, Diana swallowed and tried to speak again. But no
words could get past the huge lump of terror in her throat.

Levine stood and held up his hands. "You don't need to
say anything just yet. Just think on it for a bit." He put her
files on top of the printer and lifted it easily. But it was
bulky and difficult to maneuver. "Can you help me with
the door?" he asked.

Diana jumped up and led him up the stairs. When they
reached the foyer, she pulled the door open and pressed her-

self to the wall so he could pass. "I'm real sorry to have to tell you this," he said, raising the printer over his head and swinging wide of her stomach, "but we'll find you wherever you go. So do me a favor: Please don't leave town."

~ 31 ~

DIANA STOOD IN THE DOORWAY LONG AFTER DETECtive Levine's taillights disappeared down St. Stephen Street. Then she ran downstairs, grabbed her coat, and climbed into the jeep. She didn't know where she was going, but she figured it didn't much matter. All that mattered was that she was moving, that she was acting. Even if her motions were pointless.

Although the snow was tapering off and the flakes were melting as soon as they hit the macadam, because it was the first snow of the season the traffic inched along as if in the middle of a raging gale. But for once, Diana didn't care. She sat patiently, her mind blank and her hands resting lightly on the steering wheel, staring at the snow waltzing in the beams of her headlights.

It wasn't until she found herself headed west on Route 2 that she realized where she was going: to Gail's house in Lexington. It was just past five, so Gail and her husband Shep were sure to be home, tending to dinner and the twins. Diana turned off the highway and drove past the historic Battle Green and the stately old homes of Lexington Center, then she crossed to the other side of town and wound her way to Gail's contemporary home, set amid a cluster of similar houses on large wooded lots.

Gail was a lot less surprised to see her than Diana had expected. She ran to the kitchen and held a hurried, whispered conversation with Shep, then came back and led Diana into the family room. She closed the door behind them.

Diana stood in the middle of the room, the bright havoc of the primary-colored toys in such contrast to her mood that she was momentarily disoriented. She tried to smile at Gail, but her facial muscles refused to cooperate, pulling instead into what felt like a grimace.

With a sweeping motion of her arm, Gail dumped a pile of Legos onto the coffee table, clearing two seats on the couch. "Sit," she ordered.

Diana sat. She sat and stared at the jumble of picture books on the shelves across from her. She sat and stared at the miniature plastic kitchen in the far corner of the room, at its red seats and orange countertop, at its sink full of stuffed animals. She played with the Legos, flattening them all out on the table, then carefully picking them up one by one. Slowly, methodically, she built a series of small towers. "I'm lost," she finally said, knocking down the towers and leveling the Legos.

Gail reached over and touched Diana's knee. "It's going to be okay, sweetie."

"I'm not myself," Diana whispered. "I don't know who I am anymore. I've become deceitful, manipulative. A liar. I feel empty. Hollow." She barked a laugh without humor. "I sound like a symptom checklist for borderline disorder."

"Sometimes I think the line between 'us' and 'them' is a lot thinner than we'd like to believe . . ."

Diana stared at her friend in silence for a moment. Then, not wanting to linger too long on the frightening truth in Gail's words, she launched into a detailed description of every blunder she had made: of how she had failed everyone, from James to Sandy to Jill to Ethan, and, finally, to

Craig and the baby. Then she told Gail how she had duped her into helping her lie to Levine—and how she had falsified Ethan's records. It was a long and exhausting speech, and when she was finally finished, she looked over at Gail, not knowing whether she wanted absolution or censure.

She received neither. Instead, Gail looked at her *symptom* fully and said without judgment, "You forgot a symptom on the checklist."

Diana could feel the blood drain from her face as she scrambled to imagine what Gail could possibly know. "I did?"

"Obsession."

"Obsession?" Diana repeated. "That's probably the only borderline symptom I don't have."

Gail gripped one of Diana's hands tightly between her two. "It's your obsession with borderlines," she said gently. "With your patients, your research. With curing them. It's no good for you," she added. "Or them."

Diana played with the Legos, saying nothing. She had heard all of this from Gail before—many, many times. She hadn't believed it then, and she didn't believe it now. Diana knew that it was only through this kind of dedication—the kind of dedication Gail labeled obsession—that real breakthroughs were made.

"Hutchins was just another sick puppy," Gail continued, lecturing her willful pupil. "Probably too sick for you—or anyone else—to do anything for."

"I could have helped him," Diana said, raising her chin. "My research is showing—"

"Forget your research," Gail snapped, dropping Diana's hand in disgust. "This isn't about ANOVAs and regression analyses. This is about you and Craig and the baby—about your life. This is about how you have to let go of your patients—of your obsession with curing them. About how you have to let go of your neediness."

"You mean *their* neediness," Diana corrected.

"Listen to me, Diana. This murder thing is going to blow

over. It may be ugly and it's bound to be awful, but you
 ́dn't kill James Hutchins, and somehow that'll come out.
 ̇ real mess, though—the mess that's making you so cra-
 ̇ on't be over until you free yourself of *your* need to
need mighty fixer. Your need for them to love you. Your
"What eir idolatry."
cess " Di u perceive to be *my* need is all part of the pro-
 ̇ ̇, Diana said stiffly. "To quote Adrian: 'Psychotherapy
cannot proceed without empathy.' "

"You've got to admit your obsession with Hutchins goes
a bit beyond empathy—"

"Of course I'm obsessed," Diana interrupted. "I'm going
to be charged with his murder, for Christ's sake."

"—and that it always has," Gail continued as if Diana
hadn't spoken. "This hasn't been just a professional relationship since the first day he walked into your office. He's
feeding something in you. Some empty place you're trying
to fill. Maybe you've been using James as a way to atone
for what happened to your little sister."

"Don't give me that psychologist crap," Diana said.
"James *was* special. He was a remarkable man. Talented,
brilliant . . ."

"All that was remarkable about James Hutchins was his
face." Gail stood abruptly and began pacing the room.
"Can't you see it? The guy looked like a fucking movie
star, and he thought you were the most desirable woman in
the world!" She whirled around and grabbed Diana's hands.
"Sweetie, anyone would fall for that—I'm not faulting you.
The guy had more charisma than Jesus Christ! But you
were blinded by it. You let his charm fool you into thinking
that he—and you—could be something neither one of you
ever could be." She sat down and added more softly, "He's
dead. And once this murder thing is worked out, you've got
to let go of him—and of your need to cure everyone—or
you'll never be free."

"That's ridiculous," Diana sputtered, throwing off Gail's
hands. "I don't think I can cure everyone. I just think I

may have found a way to help borderlines. It's this traumatic stress thing—"

"Don't you see?" Gail interrupted. "Can't you hear what
you're saying? Diana, your fascination with them is almost
as sick as theirs is with you." She shook her head. "Maybe
you're right. Maybe you *are* checking off a lot of symptoms on that list."

"Oh, so now I'm a borderline?" Diana demanded. "Is
that your professional opinion, Dr. Galdetto? Or are you
just armchair psychologizing?"

"I didn't mean—"

"You want to know what I'm really wishing in this
heart of all terrible borderline hearts? Want to hear my
truly depraved fantasies, Doctor? I'll tell you: My fantasy is that James is alive. That he and I are together. Just
gorgeous James and me, alone on some deserted island."

"Diana, please—"

"The beach is long and white and empty," Diana continued, her voice low, rumbling with barely suppressed
anger. "And do you know what I dream? Do you know
what I fantasize about my sexy dead man come alive?"
she demanded. "I dream that I'm sitting next to him on a
large blanket, sitting next to that magnificent hunk who's
stretched out in the sun, all shiny and glistening. I run my
fingers along his perfect cheekbone. I lightly touch the deep
cleft in his chin . . ."

Gail watched Diana silently, her eyes dark with sadness.

"Then I reach into my beach bag and pull out a shotgun,"
Diana said softly. "I press it to his temple, and before he
even opens his eyes, I blow his brains out all over again!"
She chortled at the relief on Gail's face. "Murder is better
than sex, huh?"

"I suppose that's what I'd prefer for you in this situation."

"Then don't be too pleased," Diana flung back at Gail.
"Because I did that too."

"Did what too?" Gail asked, alarm replacing the relief in her eyes.

"Had sex with James Hutchins," Diana said. "Right on the floor of my office."

Diana fled. Ignoring Gail, who stood on the stoop imploring her to come back inside, Diana grabbed her coat and raced to her car. The snow was coming down more heavily and beginning to stick, but the jeep held its own as she screeched out of Gail's driveway.

The ride home was a blur of swirling white flakes and shifting realities. One moment she was driving along Alewife Brook Parkway on a snowy December night, and the next she was back in her office on that sweltering summer day, James's arms hard and hot around her, her body turned inside out with pure desire.

It had happened just as she had described it in her journal. She had wanted James for years, longed for him; but she had fought it. She had written about it, and talked about it, and tried to work it through; but nothing had made it go away. That hot July afternoon when her tenuous control had finally snapped had been the most glorious and the most horrible moment of her life. James was so gorgeous, so tender, and so full of passion. When she finally touched him, finally allowed herself to press her body against his, she had laughed out loud; the relief alone had been almost orgasmic.

She began trembling so hard that James had to undress them both. When they were naked, they stood motionless for a long moment, staring into each other's eyes. "Just let me look at you," James had said. "Just let me look." But the ache of the wanting was too great for Diana, and she reached out and pulled him to her.

They slid to the floor. James kissed her forehead, her eyelids, her earlobe. Arching her back, Diana pressed her breasts to his chest, her stomach and thighs to his. Desire rose from deep within her and spread outward, a desire so painful it was as if her every nerve were exposed, bared to an excruciating—and wonderful—agony. She wrapped her arms around him even more tightly, wanting only to merge her body with his.

"We fit perfectly," James whispered as he trailed kisses down her throat. Then he gently pulled away and stared deep into her eyes. "As if we were made only for each other." Diana raised her hands to pull him to her again, but his fingers gently encircled her wrists. "Slowly," he said, releasing her hand and running his fingers down the length of her body. "I've dreamed of doing this slowly." Diana moaned as he bent down and kissed her breast. They made love as if they had been lovers for centuries.

But when it was over, as they lay wrapped in each others' arms, the old air conditioner creaking above them in the window, the reality of what she had done cascaded over Diana, and she began to cry. "Don't," James said, stroking her cheek. "This was unstoppable. It was meant to be." And despite all that had happened since then, Diana knew that James had spoken the truth.

But still, Diana thought as she peered into the oncoming snow trying to find the edge of the road, she was being punished. Punished for the worst transgression a therapist could make against a patient. Diana saw herself reflected on the milky surface, seated behind an endless row of tall iron bars, nursing her baby. Her mind, her whole being, was slipping and sliding along with the jeep. She was losing control—of the jeep, of her life, of herself. She slammed on her brakes and skidded to a stop, her fender brushing up against a rusted metal guardrail.

Somehow she managed to back up and make her way home. But when she pulled into the alley, instead of relief, all she could feel were the eyes. They were everywhere. In the flat faces of the dark windows next door. Flickering on the snow-edged brick of the restaurant's backside. On the fire escape. In the trash cans. She scurried into the house and bolted the locks. Leaning against the closed door, her heart pounding wildly, Diana felt herself separate from herself once again. And she was grateful.

She watched herself slowly climb the three flights of stairs to her bedroom. She hovered somewhere above the stoop-shouldered, listless woman who, if not for her slightly protruding abdomen, would have appeared from her movements to be quite elderly. She contemplated the situation with a cool detachment.

She was a dead woman. A deceitful, hollow, manipulative dead woman. There was nothing she could do about it. No one to blame. No one to call. She was a dead woman. She was bone weary. She might as well get some sleep.

Diana watched herself lie down in the middle of the bed and turn on her side. She pulled a pillow to her belly and curled herself around it. There were no tears, no screams of rage, no prostrations of grief; there was only overwhelming exhaustion. As her lids dropped shut, Diana saw deep smudges of darkness circling her eye sockets, standing out in stark contrast to her chalky complexion. I'm already dead, she thought as she swooped down to meet her body in sleep. I'm already dead.

Diana dreamed she was walking through a thick forest in a raging gale. The wind tore at her hair, and the rain beat on her face. But the noise was the most potent and terrifying force. It was so loud and all-encompassing that it seemed that sound alone held the power to tear the towering, ancient trees from their roots.

And it did. Trees plummeted all around her, dropping in front of her, halting her in her place, cutting off her path. Frantic, she turned as a falling tree trunk darkened the gloomy sky. She leaped high over already felled branches as more and more trees toppled around her. Then the wind picked her up and whisked her away. All was quiet and still.

Until she realized she was in a murky, brooding castle, a castle whose ceiling was so pointed and tall that she could not see its apex. Until she realized she was on a towering metal rack, its rusted beams soaring so high that they too were lost in the shadowy heights of darkness. Until the noise began again.

This time the sound was mechanical and human-made, but no less frightening than the organic noise of the forest. She tried to run from the racket, but she could not move. She was in something's grip. Twisting and turning her neck, stretching her muscles until they screamed from the punishment, she was finally able to see that her arms and her wrists were bound to the metal bed with thick leather thongs.

Then the bed began to move. As the noise grew, the bed slowly pulled apart, pulling her apart with it. She was being torn in all directions, severed from the outside in—and from the inside out. The sound of scraping metal and splintering bone screamed in her ears, louder and more horrible than any sound she had ever heard. Pain wracked her body, and agony filled her being. "No!" she cried, finally pulling herself awake.

Diana was disoriented, but relieved, to find herself fully dressed in the familiar bedroom. The city light reflecting on the newly fallen snow threw an eerie, artificial brightness through her undraped window. But before she could calm her ragged breathing, before she could slow her pounding heart, Diana heard the noise once again.

For a moment she thought she was still asleep, that this was just a new setting within the horrible noise dream. Then a powerful bang reverberated throughout the house, and Diana knew that someone had just broken in. Ethan. It had to be Ethan. He had been watching her, and now he was coming to kill her.

Suddenly time became stuck. It took her forever to sit up. And when she finally did, she had to swim through molasses just to raise her arm. She caught Craig's night table in the corner of her eye and painstakingly pushed her head toward it. The brass handle, which splayed into small bunches of roses on the face of the night table drawer, seemed to grow until all Diana could see was the tarnish outlining the flower petals. Behind that handle was the gun. She froze, knowing it was a physical impossibility, yet knowing she heard, and felt, the soft tread of footsteps climbing thunderously toward her from three floors below.

She looked at her own night table. The telephone sitting on top of it seemed to swell and expand, as if she were zooming in on it with a telephoto lens. Phone before gun, her numb mind finally processed. Phone the police. On all fours, she crawled across the suddenly enormous bed toward the telephone, her knees buckling under her on the spread, the impossibly loud thump of approaching footsteps reverberating through her body.

Finally she grasped the receiver in one hand; the fingers of her other hand hovered over the keypad. The number. Her brain strained for the number. Emergency. The police. Three digits. A three-digit number. But her brain gave back nothing. There was only a blank empty wall were the number should have been. She couldn't find it. She couldn't reach it. All she could see was her own number, glowing up at her from the face of the phone.

The footsteps grew louder, closer. The room became brighter, hotter. Suddenly released from their amnesia, her fingers punched three numbers. Relief flooded through her as she clutched the phone.

"Directory assistance. What city, please?" whined a nasal, bored voice in her ear. Too stunned to speak, Diana gripped the receiver more tightly in her hand. "For what city?" the voice demanded.

Diana slammed the phone down and lunged for Craig's night table. As she scrambled to reach the drawer, she felt the footsteps leave the second floor landing and begin their slow climb toward the third.

And once again, time became stuck. She froze like a frightened and trapped animal. Although she was unable to move, unable to breathe, her other senses were unbearably alive. She saw every detail of the night table's wood carving, highlighted by the reflected snow-light. Every honking horn and every squeak of the stair reverberated through her brain like an air raid siren. She heard the soft, measured footsteps pounding inexorably toward her. She smelled her own sweat and fear. She was going to die.

A surge of adrenaline hit her frozen limbs like a blast furnace, and she was able to move once again. With awkward, jerky motions, she clawed at the handle and yanked the drawer open. She grabbed the gun but couldn't keep hold of it. It slid from her damp, trembling fingers and bounced on the bed. Frantic, she dove after it, seizing it with both hands. She held the unfamiliar weapon out in front of her, but she was shaking so badly she was sure she would be unable to shoot. The footsteps reached the third-floor landing, and Diana turned to face the door.

As she curled her finger around the trigger, she remembered Craig telling her it didn't need to be cocked. "Just press," he had said. "Point at his midsection and press."

A long shadow fell across the hallway floor. Diana raised the gun a little higher, gripping it more tightly, steadying it, telling herself she could shoot it if she had to. That any fool could fire a gun.

But Diana was too startled by the sight that filled her doorway to do anything but stare. For the intruder, highlighted by the brightness streaming through her bedroom window, was James.

James Hutchins, supposedly dead for almost two months, was standing there, grinning and holding his arms open wide.

~ 32 ~

DIANA WONDERED IF PERHAPS SHE WAS STILL DREAM-
ing, if the terror of the dripping forest and the towering rack
had metamorphosed into a ghoulish nightmare of the walking dead. She blinked and the gun in her hands trembled,
but still she held on to it, still she kept it pointed at the man
in the doorway. The man who was, yet could not be, James
Hutchins.

James dropped his arms, and his grin slipped into a
sheepish smile, his eyes bright with the delight of one
who has pulled off a successful surprise. "I'm alive," he
said softly, handing her his gift. "It's really me." He leaned
against the doorjamb and casually crossed his arms, looking
as brash and appealing as he had the first time she had seen
him.

Diana felt as if she had been punched in the stomach.
"Don't move," she ordered, gripping the gun as tightly as
she could.

"You look wonderful," he said, his eyes soft and mag-
netic, pulling her to him, drawing her in.

She shuddered and lowered the gun. "James," she whispered.

He smiled at her, and a piece of hair fell to his forehead

with a motion so achingly familiar that Diana longed to push the hair back with her fingers, longed to touch his brow. "I knew you'd be pleased," he said.

Pleased? she wondered. Was she pleased? Staring at James, at the sweep of his cheekbone, at the cleft in his chin, at the excitement and delight that radiated from his eyes, Diana realized she was far more than pleased, she was ecstatic. Her James was alive. He was standing there, breathing and living. Her mistakes hadn't killed him. She was being given the greatest gift of all: another chance.

As swells of glorious relief rolled through her, Diana suddenly saw the full impact of his return: If James was alive, then she was free. There would be no arrest warrants or barbed wire or coarse red uniforms—and the long shadow of Herb Levine would disappear from her life. Unconsciously Diana touched her stomach. Her family was free too. The nursery would be filled with laughter, and there would be a crib and a bureau and a changing table, bright-colored bumpers and quilts and a rocking chair where she would sing lullabies to soothe the baby into sleep in the dark silent hours of night. Craig would build a toy box and paint his fantasy mural on the walls.

Waves of pure joy engulfed every part of her being, inundating her, flooding her chest, almost choking her with their power. She was as light as air, weightless, almost floating. Her fingers and toes tingled with elation. It was over. Diana's hands trembled as she began to raise her arms toward James, to touch him, to hear his heart beat beneath her ear, to bury her nose in the smell of his cologne. To feel, to really feel, to know with every part of her, with her every sense, that he was indeed alive. That she was indeed free.

But something in his eyes made her hesitate. Something in the way he was looking at her stopped her cold. Something that began to suck the joy from her. "I did it for you," he said, taking a step toward her. "For us."

Diana scrambled backward on the bed and raised the

gun. "Don't move," she ordered again, a sudden slew of agonizing questions flooding in to douse her happiness.

"You're not going to shoot me," he said with perfect logic. "You need me to love you." Stepping up to the footboard, James calmly rested his hand on the curved brass, secure in his insight. "And I do."

She let the gun drop to the bed. Diana looked at him standing there, so hopeful and so much in love. Who could resist the power of being so adored? she wondered. Who could resist the power of almost unbearable charisma? *He's feeding something in you,* Gail's voice filled her ears. *Some empty place you're trying to fill.*

"I love you more than anything," James said softly, his velvety voice drawing her to him. "That's why I did it."

"It's . . ." she stuttered, simultaneously wanting to hold him close and push him away. "It's just so incredible . . ." James's words finally got through to her, cutting off her own. She stared at him, unable to speak. Someone was dead because James was alive. *Too sick for you—or anyone else—to do anything for,* Gail had warned her. Diana's stomach squeezed in panic as she groped toward the answer she didn't want to find.

Images of Anderson Street flashed through her mind. The steep roadway clogged with emergency vehicles and yellow tape and gawking crowds. The cracked sidewalk under her feet. The scraggly geraniums flopping in the window box next door. The covered stretcher. The paint-splattered sneaker and the naked foot. *It's a real gory mess in there. Bone . . . on the walls.* Then, suddenly, Diana knew. Suddenly she saw the whole thing—and understood it all too well. "Ethan," she whispered, her voice hoarse with disbelief. "It's Ethan who's dead."

"I thought of it the first time I met him," James said, his eyes sparkling with pride. "Same hair color, same size—from behind, we could have been mistaken for each other."

"Ethan's dead," Diana repeated stupidly. So this was what James had gotten out of his relationship with Ethan. This was the elusive payoff she could never figure out. "But what about—"

"You want to know about the messages," James interrupted. "That's the best part: Ethan thought it was a big joke—I got him to tape them all before I killed him. There's still a few left I never used," he bragged.

Dazed, Diana nodded, her stomach churning at the careless way he spoke of killing Ethan. Her James was a murderer. Cold-blooded and unremorseful. *You let his charm fool you* . . .

"And then I would have Ethan leave a message whenever you went out," James was explaining, oblivious to her growing horror. He waved at the window. "I sat there on the fire escape and watched you. Right across the alley. I could even tell when you were taking a shower."

A furry shiver of revulsion ran up Diana's back. She hadn't been paranoid. She hadn't been imagining it. The eyes had been real. Someone *had* been out there. Watching her. Someone more dangerous than she had ever dreamed. Someone she never thought it could have been.

"How did you miss it?" he asked. "I was even afraid that you'd guess right away—I was sure you'd recognize my voice that first day when I called to tell you I was dead." James shook his head as a mother would at a naughty but well-loved child. "I planted the whole toe business so that you'd figure out I was alive. I didn't expect you to think I was murdered."

Diana just stared at him in stunned silence, trying to grasp the meaning of his words, trying to comprehend the deranged complexity of his scheme.

"I actually was going to kill myself," he continued conversationally. "To show you how much you loved me. But then I realized it would be a waste." He grinned, and for the first time Diana saw the depravity lurking below his gleaming smile, a depravity she had been blind to before. "I realized that if I were dead, we'd never get to be together.

"So I decided to fake it." James's face glowed with excitement. "Got the idea about the shotgun from Ethan's girlfriend blowing her head off."

"Ethan's girlfriend," Diana repeated.

"I figured that after grieving for me, when I showed up alive, you'd be forced to admit to yourself how much you loved me—and then you'd come away with me." James threw his arms upward, almost touching the ceiling, a look of wild ecstasy on his face. "And now," he cried, "now it's all happened. Now you can leave here. You've no husband, no career to hold you anymore. I made sure I got rid of them all—everything keeping you from me. I destroyed them so that *we* could be the family." James glanced lovingly at her stomach. "Once our baby is born."

Diana was filled with an icy dread as the jagged edges of James's horrible puzzle began to come together. "There is no 'our baby,'" she said, moving her hand slowly, casually, toward the gun at her knee. "The baby is Craig's. Mine and my husband's."

"Craig's left you. I saw him leave with his suitcases this morning." James took another step toward her, stretching out his hands. "And you know the baby's mine. You know—"

"Don't come any closer!" Diana warned him. "Don't touch me."

His face crumpled. "I thought you'd be so happy . . ."

She looked at James, her James, the light in his eyes clouded by disappointment that, once again, she had caused. Despite all that had happened, despite her fear and revulsion, Diana was suffused with compassion for the young boy who had been so violated that he could not be helped. No treatment, no therapy, no rehabilitation could undo the catastrophic harm that had been done to him. Uncle Hank had taken James's promise and made him into this horror. Hank Hutchins had stolen James's life from him. And Diana could not give it back. She couldn't be the great rescuer. No one could. James, her handsome, brilliant James, was far too damaged.

He must have seen the compassion in her eyes, for he dropped to his knees by the side of the bed. "I felt it that day in your office when we made love—I felt your love." His voice was deep with passion, and, despite everything, was so powerfully evocative of that afternoon that Diana began to tremble. "I know you want us to be together again," he said, grabbing her hand and pressing it to his lips. "And so do I. Come away with me," he begged, kissing her open palm. "I love you so much."

"James," Diana began, gently pulling her hand from his, filled with such conflicted emotions that she wasn't sure she could speak. For despite her clear understanding of who—and what—he really was, she still felt such tenderness, such empathy, for him. Diana brushed the hair back from his forehead and sighed. "That day in my office was a terrible mistake. Probably the worst mistake I've ever made in my life. It's—"

"You can't deny us that day," he said. "I won't let you. We're not children, Diana. You and I both know magnetism like ours happens once in a lifetime—if you're lucky."

"It's over," Diana said, choosing her words carefully. What he was saying was true. All too true. She had never felt anything like the powerful magic of that afternoon. She had been bewitched by him, drawn and pulled beyond her power, or her desire, to resist. She had never been so encompassed by passion. Never felt so masterful. So alive. "It will never happen again," she said, her voice low with sadness for everything that couldn't be. "Never."

"Come with me now," he begged. "It *can* happen again. Now is our chance."

"It's impossible, James. I'm not going anywhere."

"But the baby. I figured it out. The timing—"

She shook her head. "I found out the next week that I was already pregnant."

"I planned how this would happen," he said calmly. "I worked it all out in my mind. Over and over. I've been controlled all my life and now I'm in control. I'm not going to let my plan fail." His eyes burned into Diana's, and again his depravity showed through.

"James," she said softly, trying to distract him so she could grab the gun at her knee.

But he saw her eyes flicker downward and seized the gun before she could. He jumped up and backed toward the door, pointing it directly at her. "You're coming with me," he ordered, his quiet voice much more terrifying than if he had been screaming. "Right now."

"James," Diana said, trying to sound calm, "it's no use. It's over."

"Not if I kill us both, it's not," he said, his eyes glazed. "If I kill us both, we'll be together always."

Unable to speak, unable to move, Diana felt time once again stall. James loomed enormous and hulking, growing thicker and wider, grotesque and terrifying. The ambient light glinted off the shiny gun barrel. James could very well do what he threatened. He had killed before, and she knew that to his deranged mind, his solution was all too plausible. She stared at the gun in horror, scrambling frantically for the response that would save her life and the life of her child. But she found only blankness. "The baby," she finally sputtered. "You can't kill our child."

His eyes narrowed, and his handsome face became shrewd, the planes of his cheekbones shading to evil. "You said it was Craig's."

"I lied," Diana lied. "You figured out the dates. You know the truth."

He stood with the gun pointed at her belly for a long moment. "I don't believe you," he finally said.

"But what if you're wrong?"

They remained that way for what felt like an eternity: James with the gun to her stomach, Diana still. To lose all she had just regained was more than Diana could bear.

To lose it all once again because of her weakness that one afternoon—because of her obsession with James Hutchins. She knew she deserved punishment for her wrongdoing. But her baby didn't. And neither did Craig. Diana didn't move a muscle. She held her breath and kept her eyes locked on James's, pleading sincerity, pleading for a chance to live.

Then James broke the eye contact and stared over Diana's head at someplace far away. After another eternity he slowly lifted the gun with robotlike jerks of his hand. He placed the muzzle to his temple. "One word and I won't pull the trigger."

Diana gasped, her eyes glued to his. She clearly felt his sincerity, his need, his love—no less real for its debauched nature. And she also saw the hopeless depths of his insanity. *You've got to let go of him—and of your need to cure everyone . . .*

"One word," he begged. "Just tell me that you want me to live."

And Diana knew in that moment that she could not take responsibility for his life. That she could not save him. She closed her eyes, tears running down her cheeks. She wanted to open them. She wanted to scream out for him to stop. For him to save himself. That she would try to help him again. But she did not.

"Diana, please . . ."

She kept her eyes closed, kept her silence, until a powerful explosion shattered the stillness. Then Diana began to scream. And it seemed to her that she would scream forever.